GRID CITY
OVERLOAD

Set in the fictional hub of Grid on the verge of the Fourth Industrial Revolution, *Grid City Overload* swirls around three central characters: a budding uppers addict, an informational psychopath, and a schizotypal soda factory worker who believes he's a fish.

Two interlocking conspiracies are converging on this socially and psychologically vulnerable trio in a city designed to function as a pure technocracy. Fueled by an abruptly powerful political movement, the ubiquitous software company InfoZebra begins construction on a massive new corporate headquarters at the heart of Grid. At the same time, the legal rights to a dying woman's head are called into question. Between the two is a prodigiously skilled hacker who transforms both situations into scandals, upending the city and ensnaring the people around her, both knowing and unknowing.

The result is a journey into the minds of the citizens, and objects, of Grid, including dissident cultists, highstrung partiers, anti-identity authors, a retired hitman, tech tycoons, and a sentient phone torn by love and revolution. This surrealistic and intricate novel, the second installment in a triptych about technology and madness, paints a psychological portrait of high-tech civilization struggling to keep up with its own advancements, stumbling into an era in which human beings are abstract and reality takes on a new meaning.

PRAISE FOR STEVEN T. BRAMBLE

"...equal parts fast-paced mystery and thoughtful, existential reflection...*Grid City Overload* is in many ways the *Bright Lights, Big City* of the current generation."

—Foreword

"The reader is presented with these intersecting narratives and versions of their truth in a world that is speeding increasingly toward an information apocalypse...forces you to examine the amount of information you receive on a daily basis, and how you are receiving it."

—Long Beach Post

"Full of neon corporate logos and industrial pollution...the novel plumbs the lives of these characters as they lose themselves in drugs and technological advances."

—Kirkus

"Steven T. Bramble is a writer to watch, and to be reading—not later—but now."

—Stephen Graham Jones,
author of *The Bird is Gone* and *The Fast Red Road*

BY STEVEN T. BRAMBLE

Affliction Included

Disposable Thought

GRID CITY OVERLOAD

GRID CITY OVERLOAD

STEVEN T. BRAMBLE

ZQ-287

LONG BEACH   OAKLAND

For John Wright Tolle

ZQ-287

ZQ-287 Press
3942 E. 4th St.
Long Beach, CA, 90814
www.zq287.com

SECOND EDITION.

ISBN 978-1-7325766-2-9

TABLE OF CONTENTS
for *GRID CITY OVERLOAD*
by narrator

A decadence...is a falling-away from what is human, and the further we fall the less human we become. Because we are less human, we foist off the humanity we have lost on inanimate objects and abstract theories.

THOMAS PYNCHON, *V.*

GERNEY

Then I was lookin at this obviously terrorized copy of an A-F encyclopedia splayed across the flame-tiled floor behind the toilet, all broken-spined with aged grainy pages spilling from its middle like gore spilling from the belly of a gutted fish. Most of the pages were full of smudged type speckled with wet spots of urine fallout, but peeking at a sideways angle from beneath the top cover was a hint of a dual-colored map of the Americas, and just above that, bent and torn but still monstrously vivid, were the creeping whiskery legs of an arachnid fanning out over the continents.

Nick Ibyoo's shoes, wet and dirty from being outside in the snow, suffocated some of the loose pages while he straddled the toilet backwards, dividing up the gonine in the mutating light of the LED above the plastic tank. Nick sorta fuckin tempted me into grappling with the jet, and I agreed to embark with him for a couple reasons. First) wasn't this what we were all here for? to erupt into euphorigenic lava flows, smiling while melting underneath the inching heat? I mean, weren't we all supposed to be having one of those kinds of times? One of those *good* times? Fuck it—sure. And then second) there was the pesky realization that Ms. Yardblast, owner of Archelaos Chevrolet, had given me an ultimatum earlier in the day that I'd better goddamn well learn to use the DealEase platform by the end of the month lest I be kicked out into the job market on my incompetent ass.

This was not negotiable.

Then of course Nick had presented an appealing option at the end of the workday, much like he always did the dependable bastard, and so instead of being at home learning the software, I was in a stall at Zeal, underneath the sprawling high-def nebular formations and distant conglomerate galaxies of a ceiling screen, pulsing green and pink in time with the music.

The LED over the toilet shot chrome glow across the three lines of gonine Nick had insofar separated out. The images on the screen were of various people on the sides of freeways next to entrenched cars in what looked to be the middle of an absolutely dishearteningly bad snowstorm, uninterested traffic shooting by them, not helping. There was a short parade of similar scenarios, punctuated by hypothermic hands and noses, then finally a disturbing shot of a dead man collapsed in a snowdrift built up on the edge of a five-lane overpass, cars bulleting by, kicking up brown slush onto his corpse. The point of the ad was to buy snow tires, and I ended up having to ask Nick what he'd said because I'd been preoccupied with the commercial.

"I said she asked me to come to Aria's place after you left."

I nodded recognition. He was telling me a story about last weekend, something I hadn't been present for since I got too drunk too early and had had to get driven back to my apartment by Ronstadt, who I was pretty sure had been too far gone on the scale of drunkenness to really be trustworthy himself.

Nick had to shout over the music. "Aria's place is huge, by the way."

I was starting to assume I wasn't going to want to hear about what I'd missed out on, considering I had a thing for Aria. Though what can you really do? This is what you sign up for when you spend your whole life pretending nothing bothers you when in fact there's hardly an instance in history that couldn't inspire breakdown.

"This place was goddamn *large*, is what I mean," he said, separating out another few lines, "and we were all hangin out in her kitchen drinking whatever this tequila stuff she had was, some really crass little drink of fucked-upness I'm determined to ask about so don't let me forget. And after like thirty minutes me and Ronstadt start noticing all the girls were disappearing somewhere. And suddenly all of em were gone."

"How did it take you thirty minutes to notice that was happening?"

"What do you mean? We were all drunk and I was grappling like hell with the jet, which, I don't know, I'm assuming *you* know a thing or two about. It just *happened*. Gradually."

"Still, being drunk is hardly an excuse for failing to notice whole people going missing. How many girls were there? Six, seven?"

"Look, are you gonna shut up and listen to the story or not?"

"No, seriously, how many? Because I can't honestly comprehend how you and Ronstadt could not notice six or seven girls just up and—"

"Gerney. Jesus."

"—just up and disappearing without, and I'm not Jesus—"

"Will you just shut your mouth and listen to the fuckin story?" This manifested as a snarl. Anxiety zoomed into view, speech uncontrollable, ceiling screen switching to a shot of four escalators crammed with people gushing upward, unending heads, welding sparks falling down on them (or up on them, from where I was standing), and it was only then I noticed my fingers were twitching so I stopped talking.

Going back to producing lines on the top of the toilet tank, he said, "So me and Ronstadt look at each other and we're both like, 'Where'd the girls go?' So we start walkin around Aria's apartment looking for em. And we come to a door that's locked, and we can hear em in there doing something, so I start bangin on the door shouting, 'Goddammit, ladies, this is Nick Ibyoo, the *fleet manager*, I might remind you, of Archelaos Chevrolet, an establishment that happened to win some quite prestigious business awards from the Grid Chamber of Commerce as recently as last year, and I demand you allow us entrance!' But so after a few—oh, hold on a sec."

He took his phone from his pocket. Someone had messaged him. He tapped out a text, spindly fingers reminding me of the torn picture of arachnid legs on the floor that now had a gritty wet footprint on it from his shoes. There was never any break in the music at Zeal, all songs running into one another and piling up in freeway-accident fashion, but I imagined I could identify an infinitesimal gap of half-silence when a switch was imminent, all audial currents taking a sharp ballistic plunge into some brief pool of compression just before violent reemergence, always stronger than before. In the song now playing were injected soundbites from a speech made by Randy Mobyle, given just four days ago.

The ceiling screen caught aflame with a dense collection of comets. Once they dissipated there was a looming foreshortened globe, quickly rushing closer, bigger, becoming gargantuan and showing oscillating details of what looked to be a hostile multichromatic atmosphere, a projection appearing on the planet's surface caused by a silver flying device slowly turning in its orbit: a dramatic close-up of a delicious burger, stuffed with crisp lettuce, savory patty, melted cheese. A price suddenly ballooned across it, and in the final moments of the pan around the sandwich a small but brilliant sliver of sun rose over the peak of the planet, briefly blinding me with realistic glare.

Randy Mobyle's voice, aggrandized by lifting digital percussion and showering, sparkling notes, declared on-beat, "It's not the—not the—not the—not the *time* for inaction!" before the main rhythm picked up once again in full. A wave of goosebumps ran from the top of my neck to my lower back. It was true: it didn't seem like the time for inaction at all.

The LED above the toilet transitioned to a live shot of us, Nick and I, in the stall. There must have been a camera installed into the screen because the view was mirror-like, showing us our flipped reflection. The lines on the tank were clearly visible in the picture. I called to Nick over the music.

"What?"

I pointed to the LED, giving him a concerned look.

"You got a problem?" He looked at himself while saying this.

"Should we get out of here? The gonine's exposed."

"Not an issue," he stated, waving me off and going back to texting. He'd already deleted one whole attempt, rethinking wording and tone, I guessed.

The planet that had appeared on the ceiling was now receding into the void of high-def space at the same rate it had approached. When it became just a speck in the distance there was a jarring blue explosion, the entire ceiling sliced through with an icy fulmination that caused me to wince, also giving Nick a jolt though he wasn't looking. Some of the faraway stars rearranged themselves to show the BURGER KING logo.

"God that ceiling screen is badass," Nick mentioned, still wrapped up with his phone and not having seen any of what happened.

The rising percussion returned. "It's not a question, we will—we will—we will—we will *act!*"

"Okay, sorry." Nick put the phone in his pocket. "Millie keeps asking how long we're gonna be. I told her as long as it damn well takes."

At the bottom of the LED was a display of the time, 9:15 pm.

"So anyway, me and Ronstadt are bangin on the door, givin em hell to make em open up, and—" He slammed down his ID, reaching back into his pocket. "Damn! One more second." He started tapping out another message.

I looked at my own phone. When it came alive the camera initiated, prompting: AUGMTD REALITY MODE? I pointed it at the toilet tank, a red autocursor honing in on a single line of gonine, outlining it perfectly, bringing up various statistics. The molecular structure of the substance was like a wheel with a flailing serpent attached, and I hovered my finger over it, causing the rendering to rotate, taking in its genius. The scan alerted of extensive cutting. Mannitol, baking soda, and a small amount of meth. This was gonna be one of those nights where we'd go pouncing on the back of every fifteen minute interval with carnal ferocity, tearing it apart, only to be laid out on the floor at the end, needing another dose.

I clicked away from AR mode and sent a message of my own, this one to Aria Forum, who was out in the main part of the bar with Ronstadt and Millie and Quentin and Veronika and whoever else might have showed up. I asked if I could buy her a drink, like a tequila or an absinthe or basically anything with a motor in it, but I got no response and quickly tried to forget I'd texted her at all. I managed to get a few seconds into looking for a tutorial on DealEase before Nick finished up, continuing his story without warning or transition.

"So we keep bangin on the door, and I swear to God you wouldn't believe what was goin on in there. *I* barely believe it."

I gave him the *so fucking tell me already then* face.

"They were having an *orgy*. The girls. Can you believe that? And your earlier guess was right, there were like six or seven of them."

"Who?"

"Millie, Aria, these two girls we met up with at Q/V—you weren't there for that, though—Veronika, some others who I think Aria invited. I don't know their names."

"What did you and Ronstadt do?"

He tapped the side of his head in response, forming the sixth and final line on the toilet tank, motions mimicked by the LED with frightening exactitude, and who knew what bunker-dwelling employee(s) might be watching? I didn't pursue the line of thought, feeling something inside me drop. There were contradictory impulses of wanting to extricate myself from Zeal, the stall, the whole situation, while also wanting to dive even deeper into the night and its every detail. The important thing, I knew, was to ignore whatever feeling I was experiencing entirely, remove it from the front of my head, place it toward the back, let it lie dormant until it could reappear during a moment of less stimulation, likely during work hours, when I could suffer its full effect. For now, just ignore it.

Finishing the final careful sunbeam of gonine and pocketing his ID, Nick said, "But I'll tell you what the craziest thing is."

I waited, taking a bill from my wallet, handing it to him.

"The craziest thing is I tried to mention it to Millie and Aria when I got here, and I got nothing but blank stares. They don't admit to remembering a single thing. Of course they're faking it, I mean they've gotta be. Mutually agreed to strike it from the record or something. Crazy, right?"

I agreed, knowing I wasn't showing the proper interest given the magnitude of the information, but remaining calm was all I could do not to lash out and send Nick's face into the edge of the toilet seat. Instead I was quite pleasant.

"How can we believe in—believe in—believe in—believe in *anything* anymore?" and then the ceiling screen showed a fast-forwarded elapse of a year in the universe, everything expanding slightly and seeming disproportionately intimidating.

Nick put the back of a hard hand into my chest. "This is a match night. We match each other, agreed?"

I said, "Just don't go too nuts. I have stuff to do tomorrow." I was thinking rather hopefully I might try to get started on DealEase.

"On the contrary, I'd advise you to do as much as you can because I'm planning on drinking a shitload tonight. Massive insufflation is about the only thing standing between you and a splitting hangover tomorrow morning. Trust me."

There were three lines for each of us: this was the beginning. Nick went first, then when he handed the bill to me I made sure to watch my reflection in the LED, bent over at an awkward angle, face round and obtrusive within the screen's parameters, gonine disappearing up the tube of the bill in one efficient movement.

"Not great stuff," he said with shallow disappointment.

"I checked it out on AR," I let him know. "It's cut."

"Wonderful." He divebombed his second line, erasing it off the toilet tank.

The bill was handed to me again and I asked, "Listen, do you think you could teach me DealEase? Like not the whole program or anything, but maybe just the basics? Maybe just enough to show Tamara I'm making some progress?"

"Where the hell do you... [sniff] ...think we are? We're not at

Archelaos right now, and that means I don't *talk* about Archelaos. Now hurry up and finish this shit before those fuckers out there lay siege to the stall."

People had been pounding on the stall door ever since we'd gotten in there, which was a long time ago. I finished my second line, handed off the bill. I watched the reflection of Nick snorting in the LED. When he traversed the line's distance his eyes grew shifty, looking sideways in my direction, and without warning he quickly vacuumed up my final stripe of gonine.

"You goddamn thief!"

He came back up sniffing hard and laughing, but I wasn't joking around. I'd been threatened with termination at work, and my need to grapple was quite a bit more fucking urgent than his. He exited the stall, pushing past a whole line of people who'd been waiting on us to exit. In my peripheral vision I noticed a great stone carving of a humanoid figure on the ceiling screen following me out of the stall, likely a subtle notification security had their eye on the situation.

"What's your problem," I seethed into his ear, watching him huff up a little shot of sinkwater.

He hardly seemed to notice, and when he finished at the automated sink he attempted to walk out of the bathroom without saying a word before I latched onto his shoulders with both hands and hurled him into the hand dryer near the door—there was a pronounced metallic squeak I could hear even over the music, which had switched again. I confronted him at close range, meaning sincerely to menace. "I paid for half that shit, meaning I should probably be kicking your ass right now."

He laughed, the gonine visibly affecting him, looking up toward the hovering figure. "Go ahead. Beat the shit outta me. I fucking *dare* you. But do you realize how fast your life would disintegrate? There're ceiling screens in just about every building in the city. You'd be hauled off in"—he snapped—"milliseconds! You'd lose your job, I'd sue you for everything, and you'd have a handful of months in prison to think about how satisfying it was to exact retribution over a single line of gonine. Wake up! You're irrevocably plugged into the system, buddy. So cut the bullshit." He never once stopped smiling, his teeth uneven and not at all a pretty sight. I was shoved backwards and he walked out the door.

Adrenaline and gonine were galloping through my bloodstream, stripping away whatever rust had formed there because I was suddenly very limber and powerful, hands forming fists and loosening at a healthy rate. I went to the sink as well, feeling a wet trail of analgesia snake its way into the deep regions of my throat, the flame-tile glowing hotter. I left the bathroom and wound my way through the crowd, every surface a continuation of the astral images on the ceiling in the bathroom. Bodies were dark obstacles. From a top-down perspective I was sure we looked like a recording of densely-packed bacterium moving at random. Standing upright against the lurid red tint of the universe were the M16 space pillars, a triplet of provoked cobras, and once I moved within striking distance I was handed a glass of absinthe by Ronstadt, who had bought the first round and was proud of it. He leaned in and mentioned something about an inept bartender who couldn't pour what he'd asked if her life depended on it, so sorry if my drink had the taste of concentrated ass. I accepted the apology. Sitting at a table were Aria and Veronika, subdued and bored, sipping similar glasses. Millie was speaking to Nick on the opposite side of the table, and in a strange instant I saw her dart her tongue into his ear, his head retracting away. Quentin showed up with a couple friends from work. The whole tint of the universe framing us clicked away from red, and we stood in a diluted leafy-green radiance. Ronstadt motioned with his head to the girls, probably implying something about Nick's orgy story. I nodded, trying to make it clear no words were necessary.

He asked, "You see Mobyle's speech today?"

"No, I was at work."

"Me too, but our supervisor wanted to watch so we got a thirty minute break."

"Was it good?"

"That guy flips me out with how much sense he makes. Some initiative about info organization. Information structuring. I don't know. He mentioned the goddamn building, anyway."

"The building?"

"The building site I'm working at. InfoZebra's movin in there. It's a scraper. You didn't know that?"

"InfoZebra's building a scraper in Grid?"

"Yeah, at like the almost exact center. Downtown."

"Holy shit."

"We've been workin underground for three or four weeks now. Thing's comin along."

"I had no idea."

"So how'd you feel last Friday? When I dropped you off you were practically drooling in your lap." His teeth spread out green in the radiance.

"You can probably imagine," I said.

"Missed a hell of a night, though. Too bad."

"That's what I heard."

"Well keep a stiff upper lip, guy. It's looking twacked again tonight."

But he didn't understand how to use that word, unless he was commenting on the number of people, which actually was fairly twacked in maybe not the strictest sense, the doormen exercising no control over numbers, or maybe it was a comment on my own personal twackedoutness, entering into the familiar opening stages of bad grappling, the entire fabric of my stress, DealEase and Tamara Yardblast and Archelaos Chevrolet, all fenestrated into a ragged sheet by the machine gun fire of adulterated gonine and collapsing into a specter of rising dust, ready to reassemble at a moment's notice. A million separate layers, once stratified and thinly stacked, rushed together to form a solid chemical groove. I seemed to see Aria Forum and Nick Ibyoo on the grooves parallel to me, hair rippling behind them, our velocities unstable. At the last moment their grooves converged, mine shooting drastically upward toward a spot of chattering flaming light. Aria continued to sit grimly, kayaking through a glass of absinthe with her eyes, an unwitting lightning rod pulling the emotions of everyone toward her. It was getting too crowded in Zeal. We were all pressed together at the shoulders, no longer able to focus on intake. Quentin and his friends suggested going to Q/V since it was just a short walk from Zeal through the shopping district.

"I think they're staging a water protest somewhere around there tonight," Nick said. "I saw something about it."

"So did I," I said.

Millie said, "Wait a minute, *who's* staging a water protest?"

"Them. They." Nick said this dumbfounded, shrugging. "Govt-initiative people."

Ronstadt swatted the concern away. "Oh c'mon, that's no big deal. We're just passing through. They hold those protests every other week."

There were scattered remains outside of heavy snowfall from two days ago, the weather remaining stable and frigid. Cold significantly affected business at Archelaos and that meant money usually got tight during winter. The air became fuzzier with elevation in such a way that a lot of the scrapers shooting up over the more modest city sprawl shone their lights through the vast expanse of freezing fog like approaching oceanliners. Grid surrounded us, squeezing us tighter into its constantly closing fist. The city didn't look like this on accident, it had been built to look intentionally "futuristic" according to strict building codes requiring developers to receive approval from the Civic Architectural Board of Advisors (an illustrious but basically totally made-up thing) in order to build in certain areas, primarily downtown. The city had been conceived as a business and tech sector of nearby Denver, but had blossomed almost alarmingly into a distinct, and even bigger, metropolis, large and wealthy enough to nurture its own power brokers and therefore able to tear itself free. The effect was of two contrasting cities set side by side, or more accurately bleeding into one another. For some reason the intentional aesthetic of Grid made it difficult to leave. The psychological effect was well-known and much commented on by a first generation of native-born residents. They'd run a feature dealing with it in the *Database* three years ago. As a member of that first generation, a specific passage had stuck with me. *The environment of the city has produced a culture so unique that Gridians often have trouble moving to, or even just visiting, other places. Any long-time inhabitant can easily be likened to what in nature is called a "habitat specialist."* I couldn't say I disagreed. That didn't stop me from being contemptuous of the city despite the abundance of bizarre civic pride and wide-eyed tourists who tended to mistake Grid for being—why I had no idea—romantic. After 27 years it was devoid of all charm for me, instead representing (and I wasn't alone in thinking this, I'd overheard the same thing said many times before) something cage-like, repressive. There were three or four tower cranes balancing over the skyline, and I now knew one of them corresponded to the new InfoZebra building site.

We had to wait around outside for Veronika to get her jacket since she'd left it at coat check, and most of us stood around bitching about the temperature or about who in their right mind goes through the hassle of a coat check on a Friday night. A lunatic, was the consensus. Underneath the constantly morphing neon Zeal sign was a huge LED showing news, weather, sports, a live feed from inside the bar, socnet updates and Friday night specials. For a brief moment Nick lost control of himself, allowing a show of aggression toward Millie, who'd been bothering him about the water protest for close to five minutes.

"Look, I know you're afraid to get yourself around a bunch of dirty govt-initiative bums—"

"—I am *not* afraid to—"

"—but what the hell do you want *me* to do about it? Leave me the fuck alone!"

I came up beside him and put an arm over his shoulder, seeing his short fuse as at least partially connected to the gonine, maneuvering him away from Millie who was standing near Ronstadt looking emotionally battered but somehow undeterred.

"Take it easy."

"Bitch treats me like I'm her boyfriend. Condescending and shit."

"Well just try to *maintain*, for fuck's sake. They're gonna haul you off in a cruiser, you keep doing that." They already had video evidence of us, the only thing they lacked was a reason to drop the hammer. I'd seen it happen plenty of times. Whoever ran the security show had no problem so long as you remained peaceful and profitable, but the second trouble registered the skies would split and unleash sirens.

Aria and Millie and Ronstadt disappeared across the street into a small littered parking lot to grapple, their three uneven figures turning behind a car. Quentin's friends were finally introduced to us as Watts and Chow Men. Watts was eager to drink more and started passing around a flask revealed from inside his coat. By the time Veronika showed up I couldn't tell whether the alcohol had put me back into some kind of equilibrium with respect to the gonine, or if I was simply running closer and faster along the border of incoherence.

We walked east toward Notation St., the most direct route to get to Q/V on Finite. Halfway to Notation a shift occurred where everyone who wasn't previously twacked was suddenly struggling with various jets while Nick and I were coming down off our initial 30-min holding pattern. Or at least I was. Nick was in a state of near frenzy, walking far ahead and occasionally shouting the most incredible nonsense. When we got onto Notation, Ronstadt looked at Nick and asked me what the hell we took and could he maybe get some. I did have a case of the shakes, I'll admit. Possibly the AR scan had been mistaken, but I doubted it. Aria, despite being somber earlier, was actually a jet fiend and clearly grappling at rarified altitudes. She pushed between Veronika and Chow Men. Either of them would touch her back and she'd melt into goo.

Aria and Veronika had both worked at Archelaos, Aria as title clerk and Veronika as Yardblast's secretary, then Veronika had been fired for absenteeism and Aria had landed a job as ASM of a national chain restaurant called Keifir's near Archelaos with the help of Tamara. It was Nick who'd brought them into our fold, Aria more easily than Veronika since she was already a jethead and also apparently her dad had passed away right about the time she got the job at Archelaos, which somehow ended up, to the agony of everyone at the dealership including myself, with her and Nick sleeping together on a regular basis. If you could believe what he said, which I didn't know if I did or not, she was apparently a lot weirder in private and used gonine in some freaky pseudo-religious way that he hadn't cared enough to pay close attention to. But sleeping with Aria was no small achievement—she was universally desired in a way I'd never witnessed before but was helpless to avoid. She carried a frightfully obsessive influence. That was part of the reason Tamara had helped get *her* a high-paying job after Archelaos, even though she did more gonine and showed up less often than Veronika. I could actually see Chow Men and Watts, both having become aware of her existence only twenty minutes ago, falling in love with her.

Nick retraced his steps, walking to where I fell in line at the rear of the group and telling me we should duck into an alley to get another line out of the way. Once we found a suitable dark corner, Nick said while snorting off his ID, "These water protests aren't gonna get a damn thing accomplished. [Sniff.] If they'd even bother to turn on the TV they'd understand why."

"I thought govt-initiative people were provided water."

"They are. Mobyle keeps talkin about direct pipelines to a desalinization source and importing more from San Diego and Baja and these bastards don't listen. The second he gets off the air saying sacrifices have to be made, they flood the streets."

Randy Mobyle was making an average of three public addresses per day, obviously leading toward something big. Probably the InfoZebra building. I'd actually seen a few of the speeches Nick was paraphrasing from, and had agreed. I'd found it really nothing more than just logical that if anyone was gonna have to go thirsty until there was a solution to the water problem, it would naturally have to be those without jobs—a group I would find myself a part of soon if I didn't get a handle on DealEase by the end of the month. A sweat came on despite the cold.

Once we finished we sprinted down Notation to catch up with the group and I nearly slipped and broke my spine. When we got nearer to them we noticed a huge gathering two blocks away spilling out over the street, creating a human roadblock. A voice could be heard microphonically, faraway and indecipherable as of yet, projecting through the protest and up the avenue in cold syllabic augmentation. Everyone had stopped in their tracks, and when we rejoined them Millie was standing near Aria, shooting Nick a stare dripping with venom.

"I fucking *told* you."

Luckily he was too out of breath to get angry.

"Should we risk going through?" Ronstadt asked.

"What are they gonna do?" Aria said. "I mean, they can't *do* anything."

"Sure, Aria," Quentin broke in eagerly, sarcastically, "a bunch of well-dressed twacked people passing through a crowd of govt-initiative housing recipients. I'm sure thirst and hatred won't be a problem whatsoever." He was one of the few among us not recently turned a supporter of Mobylism. The unpopular political tone of his comment set the group on edge.

Nick said, "Well then what do you wanna do? Head back to Zeal? Q/V is only three blocks from here."

"Exactly, I'm not going back to Zeal," Veronika asserted. "It's freezing out here."

There wasn't much debate before we decided to keep heading for Q/V, and even though Quentin refused to go with us, turning back the way we'd come shaking his head in disgust, Watts and Chow Men followed along still sipping from the flask. I looked back toward Quentin, but he never even gave a backwards glance.

Nick, Aria and Veronika marched ahead, trying to reinforce the assumption that passing through the protest was nothing to worry about. Ronstadt and I trailed behind Watts, Chow Men and Millie. From far away the people composing the protest had looked indistinct, but the more they came into focus the more shocked I was. Almost all were wearing solid-color shirts and pants and identical black canvas sneakers—the first time I'd seen anyone wearing govt-initiative clothing, much less a whole crowd. A lot weren't even wearing jackets, hugging themselves to keep warm. Worst was their look of uniform desiccation—faces gaunt, stomachs distended, children crying with no tears spilling. Some stumbled erratically, holding faces in bouts of dizziness, helped by pairs of outstretched hands. When we were close to breaching the mass I saw a man sitting on the curb along the far side of Notation, far from the front of the protest where a well-hydrated woman was screaming into a bullhorn on a wooden box in front of Sondheim's, a fancy restaurant that boasted a façade with dense stone carvings. The man was centered in a cone of sterile blue streetlight, eyes sunken so far into his own head they were no longer visible beneath the thick shadow cast by his brow; he stared apathetically into the protest, jacketless, breath spiraling from a mummified nose in two weak streams. Beside him was an inquisitive street cat, cautiously sniffing at his malnourished body.

The woman wielding the bullhorn overwhelmed the weakened state of the crowd: "The mayor and city council equal *higher water rates!* Councilman Randy Mobyle equals *complacency!* Complacency equals *death!* Death of *us*, death of your *children*, death of *democracy* by means of overbearing *capitalism!* Death of us equals the deletion of a *problem!*"

We'd started our way through the demonstration, the amount of people turning out to be much larger than any of us had thought, maybe as many as five or six hundred. The dehydrated multitude split apart, forming a small path for us to walk through in silence, attacking with nothing more than resentment and gaping stares of disbelief. Once we were in amongst them, it was impossible to ignore the fact that they were unwashed. Our passage was unhindered until we reached a point roughly parallel to the woman with the bullhorn, nearly twenty feet away, when she got to an item in her speech that went: "We have got to *be* a problem! Problems don't go *away!* Problems do not *recede!*" She lifted an arm into the air. "Problems erupt into *crises!*" She dropped the arm hammer-like on the final word, triggering a mindshattering explosion that blew open the front of Sondheim's, her hair fluttering lightly across her face with the force of dynamite. The sound and feeling pierced the crowd's civility, and the only thing I was able to see was Ronstadt plummeting to the ground from the impact of a piece of stone shrapnel to his arm. There was a brief moment of calm before a paroxysm of fear and thirst swept the area, sparking an instantaneous riot. A chaotic rush of people all around me made it difficult to hold my ground while I helped Ronstadt to his feet. By the time he got upright we saw a group of govt-intiative men with large plastic barrels under their arms rushing into the still-smoking gash created in the Sondheim's façade, followed closely by a banshee-wail influx of rioters. Rushing past us were people with children clutched to their chests, fleeing in the opposite direction of dark-suited GPD officers now storming through the water riot. We'd lost the rest of the group in the confusion. Ronstadt, much larger than me and sent into a froth of survivalism, gripped my arm and pulled me with him through a small gap opened near the far end of Notation where the man with sunken eyes had been sitting, and in so doing blasted past a pocket of panicked women sent crumbling atop pitched legs to the asphalt.

We were held up by areas bottlenecked with frightened people, but before long we were on the fringe. An officer in partial riot gear caught sight of us trying to shove past a group of govt-initiative men who had formed a human barricade to shield the escaping families, and in a swift movement he batted two of the men across the ears with a baton, causing them to break the wall, finally reaching his hand out to pull us clear of the riot. We ran, passing through an assembly of police cruisers parked on the other side of the protest where we hadn't been able to see them before. The rest of our group was a few yards out, standing near a shoe shop, Watts and Chow Men fighting to pull Nick off some guy in govt-initiative clothes cowering on the ground defending himself from a wrath of brutal kicks. Ronstadt rushed to help, and finally they held Nick back while the dehydrated bum went scrambling away down the street.

"Run you piece of shit!"

Once the bum was sufficiently away, they let him go. "He hit Aria in the face!"

Aria had been crying throughout the entire thing, and at this comment she rushed him, battering him weakly on the neck. "He didn't do it on *purpose*, you asshole!"

I approached Ronstadt, watching him take off his jacket and gingerly lift his shirtsleeve to reveal a generous bruise, the entire width of his arm in diameter with a bleeding cut at the center. "Amazing," he breathed. "It's shallow."

"What happened?"

"No clue. The explosion happened and I was on my ass."

"Something hit him," I said. "It barely missed me."

Watts whistled. "You got lucky there, pal."

Ronstadt grazed the wound with his finger and grunted in pain. "Know what'll help that out, though? About eighty glasses of absinthe at Q/V."

I saw Aria leaning against the shoe shop's windows, multicolored Nikes dangling by their shoestrings behind her, a nervous smile spread across her face beneath tear-streaked cheeks. At the mention of Q/V she grew animated. "Yes, please can we go now? I want to get out of here."

Behind us the riot was morse-coded with screams and cries. There were the first hints of a rising smog of tear gas floating lazily near the region of Sondheim's. I couldn't make out much of what was going on beyond the cruisers, but what I was able to see seemed impossible. Ronstadt estimated the govt-initiative people were another five minutes from being totally overtaken. If they were lucky.

"Guys, c'mon, we're leaving!" Nick called, walking away with everyone. "Or do you wanna stay here and get detained all night?"

But it didn't turn out to be so easy. There were another two cruisers blocking entry onto Notation from Finite a few blocks down. A small gathering of onlookers and journalists had amassed at the intersection, straining to view the riot from a distance, which when I turned around could barely be seen except for the blinking of sirens. The screams, however, could still be heard, only now they were muted and unreal—a far-flung reality. The onlookers had probably come from Q/V since a good deal of them looked drunk and strung-out.

The officers were running police tape between the two cruisers when we approached. They were confused about what to do with us at first, but Millie explained to them what had happened, and for some reason that sufficed, probably because they were agitated and not at all eager to deal with a group of drunks who had ended up on the wrong side of the line. We were allowed to pass underneath the tape, the journalists and onlookers on the other side immediately deluging us with questions. One reporter asked nervously if the govt-initiative people were putting up effective resistance against the police.

"No," Ronstadt answered, "they're too weak." The woman who'd asked the question was relieved to hear good news. Something about the inadequacy of Rondstat's answer, and the question itself, how reductive and absent of detail both were, made me walk away to catch my breath. Again things sped up, there was no way to decelerate. Nick and Aria were talking with four or five different reporters, telling them how we'd walked through the protest and had been next to the explosion when it happened. They were a bit nervous to be on camera, I could tell, considering the state they were in, but any abnormal behavior could be easily construed as aftershocks of the riot. Not long afterward another police cruiser pulled up and parked near the intersection, the reporters and cameramen breaking away from us in a hurry, hustling over to where the chief of police had arrived. Everyone could hear more sirens and vehicles approaching—ambulances and cops and journalists. I was standing near Nick when a group of several people who had come from Q/V approached us and asked if we wanted some gonine.

We left the barricaded intersection, walking two short blocks up Finite to the bar at a syrupy pace. Everyone was worked up, trading stories which now sounded more like invention, memory already usurping reality, shaping events differently. The sign for Q/V emitted neon yellow up ahead, ambulances passing underneath the glare, becoming momentarily brilliant in the coloration. When we reached Q/V we passed into the alley near the entrance since security was more stringent there, but for a long time there had been a tacit agreement that all grappling would be allowed to go on in the alley without harassment so long as things didn't get out of control. Regulars were especially safe, and this was confirmed with a nod between Nick and the bouncer on duty. Music leaking from the bar mingled with the sounds of the continuing hysteria down the street.

The group that had offered us gonine was magnanimous with their supplies. Nick encouraged me to match two lines with him, which took some prodding since I wasn't much in the mood anymore. Ultimately I was persuaded. There was a lot of talking and grappling going on when two figures came into view from the far end of the alley, walking nervously as if any sudden movements might provoke an attack from us. It was two more govt-initiative bums, a father and son it looked like, possibly having escaped the riot, both wearing black from head to toe and looking weak, dehydrated. Everyone turned tense when we noticed the son, a teenager but not very tall, carrying a hammer in one hand.

Nick stepped in front of everyone, pointing down the alley where they'd come from. "Get the fuck outta here!"

Their expressions weren't threatening, though, or at least not to me. The father was topped with white hair, the son incredibly slender, their eyes jumping between us anxiously but also somehow at the same time unalert and deeply sad.

"I said *get the fuck out of here!*"

The man spoke, voice deferential, desperate. "Could you please get us some water from inside? There hasn't been any at housing for several days and we're hurting. Could you please—"

"What don't you understand about get the fuck outta here? We've had enough of you people tonight!"

One of the guys who'd given us the gonine laughed. "You should give em some of your acid, Roland. That'll twack em out!"

Aria's phone rang and she walked out of the alley to answer the call. Police and media vehicles continued to pass by out on Finite.

Yellow light from the rooftop bar spilled in a diagonal line down the alley wall, cutting across the torsos of father and son. "Please," the man pleaded, "we need water, can't you see that? You can get it for us." Fog suspended over the city for hours now began to fall, the first traces of it obscuring their pain. One of the girls from the other group was in the process of snorting off Chow Men's ID.

"I know security here," Nick said. "Don't make me go get em."

"Get us water or I'll break my fingers!" The bum let this out as a wail, meaning it as some sort of threat. At first I didn't understand what he was saying.

Veronika leaned over to Ronstadt, whispered: "How's your arm doing?"

"I'll break my own fingers if you don't get us water!"

Still I was confused. Why would he do that?

He looked from person to person, waiting for someone to say something. His gaze eventually landed on me, and I looked at the ground. Seconds passed. "No one?" he uttered pathetically. "I'm begging you."

There was no reaction.

He took a deep breath, splayed his hand out against the alley wall. A few people turned and left. Ronstadt continued structuring a line of gonine on his ID, telling Veronika his arm was sore, but the drugs were helping. The bum said to his son, "Do it."

The kid was completely terrified. Apparently they had planned this? Gripping the hammer with both hands, he went through the motions of aiming it at his father's ring finger, but after a few windups his shoulders dropped. He told his father he didn't want to.

"I said *do it!*" the bum wailed again, suddenly sounding wild, strange, driven totally crazy.

Ronstadt was snorting off his ID. Aria could be heard just beyond the alley, recounting the riot to someone over the phone. Nick and I stared.

The kid aimed again, this time bouncing the hammer hard against a finger, producing a subtle *chunk* sound accompanied by an unspeakable scream. He gripped his hand, the screaming constant. The kid was crying, gripping his head, unable to believe what he'd just done.

Nick cursed but kept watching. Veronika and Ronstadt left with Watts and Chow Men in tow. The rest of the people from the other group watched until the bum's screaming and the kid's crying became uncomfortable and they left as well. Slumped against the wall behind Nick was Millie, tears dripping, begging Nick to go into the bar with her, but he paid little attention. Blood formed on the ground, reflecting yellow light through the growing fog. The bum went through a long process of getting to his feet, catching his breath. He strained through tears, "Please get us some water."

We stood there silent.

"Please!"

"Nick, let's *go!* I'm *going!*" Millie rushed away.

"Do it again," he told his son.

"No!"

"I said do it!"

The kid dropped the hammer, unable to control his sobbing. The bum bent to pick it up, groaning, grabbing his kidneys, looking at us through wincing eyes.

"What are you expecting to accomplish here?" Nick said, amused, practically smiling.

I admit to wondering the same thing. I couldn't make sense of it.

He didn't answer, instead closed his eyes and hammered another finger, but his aim was off. The metal crashed against his fingernail. The sound was horribly audible, partly because this time there was no screaming. The kid was still crying, a single speck of blood underneath his right eye. Whimpering and half-conscious, the bum fell against the cigarette butt-mosaic of the ground almost as if dead.

By this time security were poking their heads around the corner, coming to break up whatever was going on. Nick took a final look before stepping past me to go talk to them. Still staring, I watched the kid kneel down to help his father. The diagonal yellow light slanted across the wall directly above them. It was becoming difficult to see specific features through the fog, only shapes were still visible. I turned and walked out of the alley, hearing the kid's cries behind me. Nick tried to say something when I went by, but I didn't stop, only kept heading into Q/V, ironically just as crowded as Zeal had been. I pushed my way to the bar and ordered a glass of water, the bartender shooting me an irritated expression before filling a glass only halfway and sliding it to me across the aluminum surface. The tab was fifteen dollars. When I saw the price I hesitated, suddenly wondering whether it was worth it, but I managed to pay in cash (almost my entire funds for drinking that night after the gonine I'd bought with Nick, which I wouldn't have admitted even with a pistol stuck against my head). Going back through the bar was tougher than getting in since dancing had abruptly started and the glass was jostled hard enough that some of the water spilled. At the door I rushed past the bouncers, who luckily were IDing a group of four and failed to see me exit with a glass in hand. I turned into the alleyway, stumbling through the now-rolling fog, lit up moodily by the yellow light from the rooftop bar, looking for the father and son. The only trace of them were small smeared puddles of blood on the ground. "Hello?" I called. Silence followed. I waited for them to come back, every so often calling out into the fog.

(What happened was I stood in the alley, heart racing, staring at the blood left behind, phone lit up in my pocket by a tsunami of messages and calls I refused to look at, the driving music inside Q/V cutting into the night air, and then my whole outlook, my whole perception, changed in an instant. It was an odd sensation because nothing about it was gradual—I crossed a line. I thought with great clarity: *Something's different. Something inside me isn't the same.* I realized: *I am a selfish person.* I stood there, in the alley, frightened, hating myself, when I heard something drop from up above into the water I was holding. In the glass was a rotating amber glob with several thick tentacles extending from it, floating in the middle of the water. I looked up to see figures leaning over the side of Q/V's rooftop bar, backlit by a yellow inferno, and through the fog came another drop of something that landed only inches away. There were people trying to spit on me.)

FISH

Factory. Jesus jesus jesus save the over-automated. Twenty-five minutes on bottles, another twenty-five on cans, then back to bottles. The clock moves in twenty-five minute intervals only. Every three intervals means one hour and an uneven number of swings on bottles and cans. Grab them off the conveyor when they are impure or riddled with defects—toss them into huge plastic bins, still hot, waiting to be remolded and made better. Every minute there are 372 new bottles made. Every minute there are 345 new cans made. It is slightly easier to work the cans swing. They call us *quality control bottling workers*, and we make $12 an hour. The checks we receive have the logo of the company imprinted onto them. It's a blacked-out figure of a pteranodon, underneath reading *Pteranodon Bottling Co*, and then there is even smaller print under that which can't be read with the naked eye. I have looked at the small print with a magnifying glass, a very old one I stole from my grandmother's house when I was little, an ancient imported artifact from Africa with an illegal ivory handle, and the words are nightmarish. Sometimes they print the exact date when I will be terminated. Other times they mention how much money has been garnished from my paycheck that month. Every fifteen minutes Floor Supervisor Austin Ackyooclad passes behind me, and Wallace, too, my coworker. Wallace and I trade between bottles and cans every twenty-five minutes. Floor Supervisor Ackyooclad makes sure we aren't distracted. When I first started I was trained by Wallace. He told me against the noise of the factory: "You get used to wearin them headphones after a while! Nice thing is they let us pipe in news or music through em, but I ain't suggest doin that till you've got used to the work environment! You gotta pay so much attention, and some of the new hires get dizzy to the point of throwin up!" I never vomited, but I still get dizzy sometimes. Bottles file through the metal chute in front of me and I inspect each one quickly, having to shoot my fin out into the lolling constant tongue of fresh plastic to pick out the defected ones. So many of them, no matter how diligent I am, escape my careful monitoring—this task would be automated, too, if not for an imposed "goodwill initiative" that companies operating within Grid be required to keep a certain number of residents on staff—and the ones that escape, that aren't thrown into the bins to later be remolded, they make it into general distribution, first packed into suffocating palettes lifted by forklifts, then trucked across the country to be stocked and shelved, finally neglected by customers who would rather have a less idiosyncratic soda container. Down the conveyor line, past Wallace and I's stations, the bottles and cans are filled with Terradon Plus, which started out as a lighter sugarfree substitute for the original Terradon flavor, but the popularity of Terradon Plus ended up vastly exceeding its predecessor. Now people only drink Plus. The cans and bottles have the blacked-out figure of a pteranodon against a flat orange background. The name of the soda doesn't appear on the label because it doesn't need to, people know what it is just by the logo. Behind us is the INNOCUFILL, the machine that makes it necessary for us to wear noise deletion headphones. It is contained by a giant glass cage, the mechanical creature inside undulating with thousands of proboscises extending tubular mouths toward the aperture where each newly-made bottle or can is sent, sucking them into its convoluted process. The INNOCUFILL is built to be much more transparent in its robotic processes than necessary because above, through a large square window, tour groups come to observe how Terradon Plus is made, one of the many birthplaces of their favorite everyday beverage (another reason we work the factory floor is for the visual benefit of the tourists, giving the impression of a bustling industrial atmosphere). From where the tour groups look, the many different movements of the machine, working all in perfect simultaneity, are entrancing. Ackyooclad makes twice as many rounds on the days when tour groups come through. I'm unable to hear him due to the headphones, and I often worry he's hovering just behind me, looking on sweaty and red, even his eyebrows red, measuring my performance on a tablet with the Pteranodon logo printed on the back of it, also printed onto his cap and shirt and belt buckle, not to mention my own shirt, my own cap, my own belt buckle. A black pteranodon against an orange background. Sometimes I convince myself he's hovering behind me, spraying gaseous forms of Ultram or Fentanyl into my breathing space, or seeing if he can lift away my headphone and move his pen into my ear without me feeling in order to covertly puncture my eardrum, and finally I have to look, make sure he's not there, and I know that when I do this maybe three or four defective bottles or cans make it through the chute. He's almost never there when I look. The way we know to switch swings is a little beep is sounded into our headphones, signaling Wallace and I to walk past each other on our way to the opposite station. When we pass we sometimes acknowledge each other, but more often we just walk by without any display of recognition, like we're both invisible, and in some ways we are. Wallace is a fairly good coworker, though there are many things about him I don't trust. I've seen the conspiratorial looks he exchanges with Ackyooclad, looks which signify my exclusion from something substantial and terrifying. I can see Wallace behind me, framed and surrounded by the same machines that frame and surround me, working the can swing with impeccable skill. He invites me almost daily after work to a nearby bar he goes to. I've never gone with him because I know it's the perfect pretext to drug or poison a person, to slip something into their drink while all appears to slide along cheerfully.

I've been working bottles almost ten minutes. There are sixteen more swings remaining in the workday, plus lunch. I'm listening to a public address by Randy Mobyle piped into my headphones that's just starting over the howl of the INNOCUFILL. Tinny-sounding applause bursting into a complex network of echoes and reverberations creates an audible space I'm somehow able to picture very clearly as Randy Mobyle begins speaking—

"Good evening, good evening ladies and gentlemen. Thank you. Yes, thank you very much. Thank you. Please, sit. Thank you very much. I'd like to pay welcome and respects to the Grid city council joining us here today. Also to the governor of our great state, Governor Brackett, just recently back from Washington. Finally Senator Warlick and House Representative Vidal joining us remotely. Gentlemen, I'm honored to have you all in attendance for this important night.

"[Meaningful sigh as device for transition:] Citizens of Grid. Before we get to the business at hand, I'd like to make a statement concerning what we've all been seeing today in the news. Last night a water protest took place in the shopping district along Notation Street in the 9000 block between Axiom and Finite. At around ten-thirty pm the protest broke into a riot. The GPD, a contingent of which had been dispatched to oversee and ensure the safety of the protesters, was able to quickly get the mob under control. A local restaurant was destroyed during the incident, and rioters rushed to loot the business. Luckily they were deterred. However several officers were injured in the struggle, and upwards of ten rioters had to be forcefully subdued. We know the protest was meant to be peaceful, and that it was the irresponsible and dangerous actions of a select few from a radical group who caused the destruction and violence to occur."

I'm struck by the fear Ackyooclad is behind me, reaching out to grab me by the mouth. I spin around half a second—nothing there. When I turn to the metal chute again, I catch a glimpse of two defective bottles passing through, now on their way to be filled and distributed.

"All avenues will be pursued to prevent such unnecessary atrocities from reoccurring, and I have been promised support by Governor Brackett, Senator Warlick and Representative Vidal in combating riot violence here in Grid.

"Now it simply must be stated that the city has taken steps to ensure all citizens living within the city limits are being provided suitable resources with which to live. Before the Dispersal Act, there were more than two thousand families living in the hardware tract alone that were unable to get enough water, and now, five years later, we've solved a significant piece of that problem through government-initiative living programs which enable these suffering individuals to lead healthy lives.

"But make no mistake, ladies and gentlemen, we are nearing a dire situation that violence will neither prevent nor alleviate. In fact, those who believe violent measures will help achieve their goals are not only incorrect, but are in fact falling into the same ineffective patterns we've observed for years. It's my belief that the citizens of Grid deserve something *new* from their fellow man, something *better*. Namely: understanding and camaraderie. Solidarity. *Empathy*, ladies and gentlemen. Those of us in positions to help must do so. Some of us will have to accept that the road will be hard for the time being, that some of the ways of life we've come to love must be altered, tinkered with and made more sustainable."

I feel my phone buzz with a text, but I won't be able to check it until the swing is over, and even then it will be difficult to respond in the short time it takes to pass Wallace on my way to cans. The text is from Camillia, my girlfriend, who I met through a set of cryptomessageboards for artists. We've been together a year, but have never seen or spoken to each other. We agreed from the beginning it was best to communicate through encrypted text until we could devise a way to throw off any surveillance systems tracking our phone activity. Especially mine, considering the inflammatory nature of my artwork, which more than a few powerful entities have a vested interest in suppressing and keeping from being released to the public. I've been under extensive surveillance a little over five years now. I found this out when I discovered a microcam hidden in the ceiling of my old apartment, directly above the area I had cleared out to paint. I had been detaching some of the more suspiciously-placed light fixtures with just such a fear in mind, and sure enough, there tangled among the wires in the narrow cobwebbed orifice was a miniscule black camera attached to ultrathin optical fiber. Rather than destroy it, I let it remain, keeping vigil over a series of innocuous still-life drawings and watercolors. My new apartment has been bugged in more sophisticated ways, however, because I've yet to uncover any devices.

"Which brings me back to the point I've been campaigning for for almost two years now, three depending on who you ask"—there's a short pause in the audio feed, but why? does it have something to do with what I was just thinking, relaying my thoughts?—"and it's a simple point, one I'll continue to make, that information in Grid is not sufficiently organized. And what we're left with instead of order is confusion, indecision. Which is why I'm pleased to announce that InfoZebra, the very same blue chip company synonymous with its groundbreaking ZChase info-adaptation software, has chosen none other than the city of Grid to be the home for its new corporate headquarters. [Long, thunderous applause.] The effort to attract InfoZebra to Grid was headed up by myself, the mayor, the city manager of Grid, and of course none of it would have been possible without the vision and cooperation of the city council. So before I go on too long, rambling away and making you all stampede the coffee machine [brief laughter], I'd like to introduce the one and only Mr. Flint Vedge, CEO of InfoZebra."

Bottle, bottle, bottle, bottle, bottle, bottle, bottle, bottle...

"Thanks very much, Councilman Mobyle, for the warm introduction, and again, I welcome the esteemed guests joining us here today, in-person and otherwise. I'd like to say some brief words about our company and what we intend to offer the citizens of Grid."

The clock is perched over the INNOCUFILL's glass cage, huge and digital, and I look up just as the minute display changes from

25 to 26, the single-digit change silent and profound. A beep—somewhat delayed—sounds in the headphones. I take my phone from my pocket, deciding to ignore Wallace on my way past so I can read Camillia's message. I feel him looking at me, possibly trying to get my attention to make some short commentary on the workday, but I keep my eyes trained downward.

I hate it when you're at work and we can't talk. I miss you during the day. I do a quick scan for Ackyooclad who happens to be walking around the corner from the nearest Supervisor Station so I repocket the phone and resign myself to wait until lunch. The cans start to avalanche through the chute.

"We here at InfoZebra have dedicated ourselves completely to the places we've had the honor to call home in the past, and we will bring that same philosophy with us to Grid when we officially move into our largest corporate headquarters to date. Councilman Mobyle has been very outspoken on behalf of the citizens of Grid and their need for better information organization. Speaking as CEO of InfoZebra, we want to be a part of that project, which is why we've cobbled together the idea for InfoStructure, a city-wide info-adaptation system. Public works has always been an aspect of government we've rallied behind, and I assure you that spirit will remain a constant here in this fine city as well."

Ackyooclad is behind me, this time for real, and my focus turns fanatical. This is how he wants me to behave, so I do. The equation is simple. Floor Supervisors only trust you when they can monitor your every movement, account for every mistake. I feel him lean in behind me, approaching slow, neck and head curiously disembodied in my mind's eye, the headphone on my right ear lifted away so I can hear him whisper: "Lunch after this swing, Kleene."

I nod slightly. *Yessir, whatever you say.*

Terradon Plus cans fly past for twenty-five minutes, and the swing is so easy, so preternatural at this point I could probably text Camillia at the same time and never commit a single error, though my back feels withered, trellised with unique and repetitive pains. I yawn all-day, every-day at work.

Finally there's the beep so I raise both hands for ten seconds so the Manager of Production can see me from his station above the INNOCUFILL before I press two buttons underneath the metal chute and the cans stop shivering across the conveyor. Everything, including the INNOCUFILL, comes to a halt with a bone-rattling whine. I remove the headphones and make my way toward the break room at the far end of the factory along with everyone else working the floor, which is not many except for myself, Wallace, and a handful of Floor Supervisors. The majority of them monitor machines all day. Wallace falls in stride beside me.

"Nother long day, Fish?"

"Yeah."

"What's the plan after work?" He looks at me like a kid who wants their friend to come play, but I'm not fooled by the act. I trust him as much as I'd trust a shark.

"Same as always. Home. Long day again tomorrow."

"Right," he says, staying true to the ploy and pretending to be disappointed.

In the break room I grab my lunch from my locker. We sit at our normal table, away from the supervisors. I've eaten the same thing for lunch every day this week. It's Saturday. Now that I have time I text Camillia. *I miss you too. How's your day going?*

Wallace is staring into space, biting at a sandwich. His water ration is low. Mine, too. "Was at the bar last night," he pronounces, still staring into space. "Pretty good time."

"Uh-huh."

All right. The usual stuff, nothing interesting. Staving off the urge to steal money out of the register and make a break for it. She's a cashier at a gas station, though I don't know which.

"You should come out tonight. I always tell the girls about you. Tell em you never got the energy to come out and do anything."

I glance up at him. He's essentially an aging alcoholic, or the semblance of what someone wants me to *believe* is an aging alcoholic, just one more amongst a great mass of shifting facsimiles, vitality in the eyes and cheeks fraying and underscored by sallow rings. I look back at my phone.

We should be careful what we say.

"And you know what they say to me? They say, 'Why he ain't ever got any energy to come out?' And I'm like, 'Got me. The guy's just like that, y'know? Some people are.' And you know what they say then?"

Why? I think it's a good idea. Then we could afford to move to San Diego and not die of thirst. Did you see the news yet?

"They say to me, 'That's sad.' "

What news?

I say to him in a deliberate, measured tone suggesting affability but finality, "Thank you for the invitation, but really, I have some things I need to do which can't be put off till later. But sincerely, thank you." Cast the line out as many times as you want, you won't catch me.

He snuffs through his nose. "Your choice."

We eat in silence.

One of the desalinization plants got bombed. The whole thing was destroyed.

A small sweat breaks on my forehead. It's not safe to discuss this sort of thing, not even on a secure number.

A lot of workers were killed.

I don't think we should talk about this.

After a moment: *I'm sorry.*

It's not your fault, I'm just uncomfortable. If it happened recently there's no question they'll be running scans. We shouldn't draw attention to ourselves.

You're right. Speaking of, I've been meaning to tell you something.

Wallace stops chewing his sandwich to ask, "Will you do me a favor?"

I'm slow to answer, absorbed by my conversation with Camillia. "What is it?"

"Would you mind staying on cans one more swing? I'm tireder'n hell and bottles tends to wake me up. Just the stimulation is all."

I stare at him, trying to discern the motive.

I have an idea for better securing our communication.

"That okay with you, Fish?"

"Um…"

"I mean, if it's not too much trouble. If you ain't gotten enough bottles yet today I wouldn't wanna rob you the pleasure."

The sweat on my forehead hasn't gone away. Does he notice? I can't tell by his face whether or not he does…

"Fish?"

"Sure. Sure. You can have bottles this swing. I don't mind."

I do my best to catch my breath internally, force myself away from this nervous feeling back toward an even keel.

"Well I appreciate it. You all right, man?"

"Fine. Just wrapped up in conversation." I hold up my phone.

"You got some kinda girlfriend I don't know nothin about?" he smiles.

"No." I'm careful to make this absolute.

The smile fades, and when I'm satisfied he's no longer paying attention, I hunker back down over the phone. *What idea?*

Minutes pass and there's no reply. This sometimes happens if she gets busy with work, but for some reason her silence has me distressed. There's another beep to indicate the end of the lunch break, Ackyooclad appearing from nowhere, standing over our table saying, "All right, back to work."

I meet his stare—hollow, zealous, not weary in the least.

"We're switching swings," Wallace tells Ackyooclad while I put the containers back in my locker.

Ackyooclad agrees, not really caring at all, hurrying us out to the floor. Just before we part ways, Wallace says, "Don't worry about them bottles, Fish. I'll keep an eye on em." He heads toward his station. I reapply the noise deletion headphones just as the INNOCUFILL vents a high-pitched complaint and roars back to life.

In the car after work I check news radio for any updates on the desalinization plant, but the only thing going on is a full replay of Mobyle's address from earlier. I wait to see if I can hear the same break in the audio feed I heard through the noise deletion headphones at work, and my eyes grow wide when I discover that *the break is still there*. I slide the volume graphic to mute with a fin. My head reels while I wait for a stoplight to turn green. The light changes and I go. *Something is happening here. I don't know what yet, but something is definitely—*

And then a hot red bullet *fwups* through my brain and the side of my face impacts with the glass of the driver's side window and my fin smashes against the steering wheel and then there's a sickening inertia that when it finally stops I'm hanging halfway out the door of my car, suspended above the asphalt by the seatbelt strap pulled tight across my chest, breathing hard with eyes closed. A few strands of bloody spit descend from my mouth. I stay like this. Moments pass and now there are the sounds of people approaching, starting to crowd around me and the car, gasping, and I don't want them here, I don't want them to see me, see into the car. In the corner of my vision, through the glassless passenger side window, I can glimpse the hulking face of a bus, two round eyes lit up in the darkness and beaming across the length of my front seat. Even more people crowd around. I can't help but wonder if they're making all those sounds of dismay because of my injuries or because I'm a fish.

MARGARET

The doorbell is the exact theme from the TV show *Space: 1999*. The two young men have to do their best to stifle giggles, and they're not even really the giggling type. About halfway through the first blitz of commercialized funk-based acidwave guitar, the old woman answers the door.

"Hello?"

"Hello."

"…Well y'all ain't much more'n puppies this time, are ya?"

"Good afternoon, Mrs. Arsenault."

"Dammit, don't be pronouncin it like that. I ain't French and neither're y'all."

"Sorry, ma'am. We're from the Denver Crucicentro Post-Evangelical Church. You attend services with us, correct?"

"Never with either of you, but I attend there."

"Yes, well, it's been requested of us by a few of your friends who are also avid attendees that we pay you a visit today. They're very concerned for your spiritual well-being, Mrs. Arsenault."

"That right."

"From what we understand, you've taken steps to be neuropreserved by the Vivificorps company. Am I correct?"

"Maybe y'all're thinkin of the wrong Vivificorps."

"Oh no, ma'am, we're quite sure that this is the only Vivificorps in existence. We've done our homework. Likely you've been in contact with a Mr. Paul Simpatico, the executive director?"

"Why, yer just sneakier'n a junior sleuth, ain't ya? No pullin fast ones on you boys, I see. Coupla goddamn geniuses."

"That's right, ma'am. We feel there are some things you have the right to know that might very well cause you to rethink your contractual agreement with Vivificorps."

"Well, if I'da known goin into the deal that the good Lord got some kinda *problem* with…"

"Specifically, Vivificorps is unwittingly imprisoning souls."

"I'll be. Ya don't say."

"You see, Mrs. Arsenault, according to the contract you signed, you will be what's known as a 'neuro'. Your brain will be preserved inside your head, and will be kept in an individual aluminum tube that is then submerged in liquid nitrogen."

"Gee. I must look a whole lot dumber'n I thought. You'd think I'd know all that already seein as how I'm the one who done signed the contract."

"These surgeons and technicians, upon your death, only allow you to die by legal standards. They don't allow for the body to go through its natural decompositions. Neither will you receive the proper rites or ceremonies after expiring. Instead you will be immediately sentenced to a terrible internment—stuck inside your head for an amount of time you will have no say in."

"My my. Sounds like a nightmare."

"Yes, ma'am. A nightmare."

"Well I'm sure mighty glad you boys came by and opened up my eyes. I musta been plum crazy. Congratulations, boys, y'all've gone done and changed my mind. And in less'n five minutes, too, very impressive. But if there won't be anything else, I suppose I'll get on and head back to that there recliner in front of the TV. Thank you boys kindly."

"We haven't changed your mind at all, have we? Sarcastic. You're being sarcastic. Aren't you?"

"Fraid ya caught me."

"You're not at all frightened that you could likely become an aberration of nature at the hands of heathens?"

"Not specially."

"That's a funny attitude, if you don't mind my saying so, ma'am. If I were in your shoes I'd be scared to death."

"You ain't never been as close as I am to dyin, neither, so I'm supposin you never had that cold, desperate feelin a person gets when they sense The End creepin up behind em just like a god-damn murderer."

"Still—I think I can hypothesize I'd be scared anyway."

"No offense, boy, but you look like the type who's scairt of his own shadow from day one. Yer lookin just about as straight-laced n uptight as any kid I ever seen, and I've seen some doozies in my time. Not to mention yer friend here, who don't say much."

"I'm not scared of my own shadow. And I'm not uptight."

"Boy, I don't know who done pulled the wool over yer eyes, but whoever it was has got you goin the straight n narrow like a tightrope walker sweatin to stray."

"Just because I don't dress and act like every other punk in this city. You can't make me ashamed of being a good person, Mrs. Arsenault."

"Nobody said nothin bout bein a good person. Hell, anybody who's anybody has learnt the most dangerous toys come wrapped in the prettiest packages."

"Well aren't *you* just full of stubborn country wisdom."

"Damn right."

"Where does that accent hail from anyway? Texas?"

"Tex—? I ain't from no *Texas*. Alcoa, Tennessee. Haven't lived there in years, though, which I guess I'll just have to be regrettin right up to the very End."

"Ma'am, in all seriousness, I understand it's easy to make fun of me and my associate here. I understand it's easy to brush away the concerns of those who are trying to help you. After all, we're not presenting you with the easy information, as opposed to Vivificorps, a company that is in the very comfortable position of being able to *lie*. To be able to tell you everlasting life is as easy as forking over a certain amount of cash and letting someone else do all the work. But that's not the truth. The truth is that only God can resurrect the dead. And any path other than His, I assure you, is going to be blighted with unnatural suffering."

"You got some kinda mouth on you."

"Please. All we want from you is a brief span of attention. Nothing more."

"Brief in whose mind? I ain't got a whole lotta attention left to give."

"I promise you won't regret it. Sometimes salvation can come in the most unexpected forms."

"I ain't buyin no door-to-door salvation gig. Granted, those're some real crackerjack words yer usin, but I ain't buyin."

"Mrs. Arsenault, we're not trying to sell you anything. We're from the church *you* personally choose to attend every Sunday. This isn't a scam, just genuine concern from people who care about you."

"Those're the people I trust the least. They're the ones usually tryin to con you by expendin the barest amount of energy."

"Not to sound discouraging or contrarian here, but are you sure you're a religious woman, Mrs. Arsenault?"

"Don't you worry none, I get by."

"I mean do you believe in Jesus Christ. Are you born again? Do you have faith?"

"That's enough outta you. Don't be comin round here talkin about no Jesus Christ and no born agains and no aberrations uh nature. This city *itself* is a aberration of nature, the very ground you boys is standin on. You talk about bringin up the hard information, but I'd bet the soul of God Hisself that you ain't never been hit with no kinda hard information. It's a good thing you weren't around in my time. We made some *real* hard choices back then. What I decide to do with my body after death is *my* decision to make, not yers, and not God's neither."

"Say what you will, ma'am, but we at Denver Crucicentro can't condone those words."

"I just bet you can't. Y'all know how old I am?"

"Well, I don't know. I'd guess, judging by your appearance—"

"Seventy-nine. I'm seventy-nine years old. And y'all know what that means? It means I was born in 1946. How ya like that for a sobering detail?"

"Ma'am, please, we really do feel you're about to make a disastrous decision by agreeing to—"

"And I'll tell you what just pretzels my brain about boys like you. Here you are, livin in this here whirlpool of radiation an microchips an pestilence an all sorts of urban sqwaler, like a Hell-transposed-with-Denver, and what I can't understand is how either one of ya's got the right to go runnin all over talkin about *God*. Can't y'all see? Look behind ya. Go on. Look."

The two young men turn around to look out from the hill the old woman's house sits atop. From her porch, much of Denver is visible, the view sweeping and Mt. Olympus-like. All the buildings, especially the scrapers, have an incredibly saturnine aura about them, dimly lit by an amphitheatre of leaden sky overhead, the rest of the heavens covered by a single enormous monochrome blanketing of clouds that the sun is not poking so much as a finger through. Above the city there spins a massive hologram, projected from ground level, of yellow 3D block letters spelling out DENVER. Next to the letters is a matrix code for people walking on the streets below to scan with their phones that will bring up tourist info, factoids, video messages from the governor. The city—even in the minds of the two young men—looks charred and used-up.

"You boys think God's residin in that there hunk of metal? Truly, I can't wrap my head around your outlook. Ya know what Alcoa, Tennessee looked like back in the fifties? Chilhowee Mountain usedta be standin straight up in the south just vivid as ever. When we was all kids, we'd play *outdoors*. We'd go outside and get acquainted with the world. Ya know what they're out there tellin kids nowa-days? That y'all can stare into a screen and get a instant panoramic view of everything—the whole world and all the people in it. It's a buncha crap."

"There's something about what you're saying that seems contradictory."

"Well if it ain't yer silent associate. Damn, boy, I was beginnin to think you was a deaf-mute."

"It appears you thought wrong."

"Fair enough."

"There's something contradictory going on here that I wonder if you're aware of."

"Yeah? Well what you got clickin up in that crew cut head of yers?"

"What I was thinking was, why, if you're so disdainfully disposed toward the present and so favorably disposed toward the past, would you ever want to sign on with Vivificorps—a company that, if they follow through on their promise, will at some point, even *farther* into the future, reanimate you. You'll be living in a time period fallen even further from grace in your eyes."

"And *that's* why ya gotta be careful round the quiet ones."

"Do you care to respond? The inconsistency seems glaring."

"Boy, life never was no consistent, sensible thing."

"Maybe. But still, Mrs. Arsenault, perhaps you'd like to explain so we might be able to understand your decision more fully."

"You n I both know there ain't gonna be no understandin's gonna occur on this here porch between the two of us."

"Please, ma'am, all we're asking is a few minutes of your time to explain to you some crucial things about—"

"You shut up there, boy, I ain't talkin to you. I'm talkin to yer associate here."

"Mrs. Arsenault, I'm waiting…"

"Things must seem pretty simple to ya at this stage of yer life, boy, otherwise you wouldn't be wantin no answer to somethin's not too difficult to figure. But nonetheless I always been a lady of the faith, give or take. God's been in my life since I was too young to know I was peein in my own baptismal water. But I'll tell you somethin about gettin older, is that you start thinkin that this here breathin in n out is all yer ever gonna get. I worked as a professor of astronomy for twenty-three years, believe it or not, fore I had my babies, not to mention a few years in change afterward, and I done seen some things throughout the course of my career that might make you question some of the things they're teachin you ever Sunday. To make a long story short, I seen my husband die and I seen my little boy die, too, a whole mess of years ago [a quavering in her voice surfaces, just barely] and the conclusion I come to's that I *like* bein alive. Cause if you ain't that, then you just ain't nothin."

"And so what of all the detestable future generations then?"

"All've em might not be detestable. But as they say, that's up to God. Point is, you can't know if you ain't around to see it for yerself. Livin ain't always perfect, but it's all I got."

"Interesting. Do you care to know what I think, Mrs. Arsenault?"

"No. Not specially."

"I think you're in line for cosmic punishment. Your shakability has led you astray, and you'll reap the consequences in some form or another, but there's no question whatever form it takes will be dire. Unless you allow us to correct your course."

"All right, I think it's time for you boys to get goin now."

"It's possible you're already being punished and just don't know it yet."

"How about y'all get the hell off my porch fore I go an call the police to do it for me?"

"Think about it, Mrs. Arsenault. You said it yourself. God's been in your life since before you can remember. Maybe He was just making sure once He left it you'd know exactly why Godlessness is suffering. Remember, ma'am, that God is vengeful."

The old woman pulls a small pistol from one of the deep pockets of her day robe.

"I said y'all can kindly get your asses on outta here."

"Have a nice day, Mrs. Arsenault."

The two young men walk away in the direction of the city below.

AMY

A late dinner tonight at Tranquil John's, the restaurant down the alley from my apartment. The food is crap, the people are crap, and I feel like crap. This whole place is beneath me. I could be anywhere—I've chosen to be here. Not because it sounded good, but because my body is a machine. My presence in this shithole is strictly predicated on quick refueling. Twelve hours of work without having eaten a thing. Nothing passed my lips except water and half a Vicodin that finally sounded too good to pass up.

The stringy waitress floats by, refills my water. I remind myself to thank her. Politeness is a useful tactic.

Everyone here is slumming or too poor to afford to go anywhere else. There's a large family all wearing identical govt-initiative clothing sitting at a corner table. They're *sharing* plates. I can't stop myself from shivering with disgust. Like dogs pushing each other to get at a diminishing food dish. The father motions to the waitress to bring more water. Where could he have gotten the money for that? Stolen, probably. Taking in this pathetic spectacle makes my temples throb, and the realization I'm eating the same filthy food they are turns the sight more visceral and foul. It's important I focus only on eating, important I spend no longer in here than necessary to avoid feeling vomitous. But it's not helping. They're fucking parasites, walking vacuums that take to resources, consume and contaminate. There are three children, two boys and a girl. Every time the little girl makes a move toward the plates the boys growl and force her away cruelly, mad with hunger, yet the parents do nothing to control the situation, do not respond to the girl's hideous squeals of complaint. The wife and husband sit across from the children in skeletal apathy, the waitress now approaching with five brown plastic cups of water, setting them on the table, and one of the little boys can't help himself and is *lunging* with pale outstretched arms and *he spills an entire cup of water.*

I shoot from my seat, chair legs rasping the floor, doing my best to ignore the appalled reactions flaring up across the restaurant and instead hurry to the bathroom where I try to puke but can't. At the automated sink the faucet only allots me enough water to wash my hands once. I glare at the mirror, accusing the facial recognition camera behind it, finally catching sight of myself. I find myself unsmiling, eyes hard. The reflection slides liquid smooth from the rectangular pane.

By the time I get back to my seat I've gotten a stranglehold on my revulsion, pleased to see the govt-initiative family is now eating in silent shame after the water-spilling incident, and I even go so far as to smile when I catch the gaze of a man who's also eating alone in a far-off booth. He gives me an appraisal with his eyes and I continue to smile at him, eating. This goes on for a while and eventually I stop returning his glances, but now he's received too much attention to just leave me alone and I can feel his stare lingering. I try to eat quick. The sign for Tranquil John's shimmers blood red glow onto the freezing sidewalk outside the restaurant's window front. Faceless humans and tiny crawling animals slide through the glow and then just as quickly slide out of it. I focus on my food despite the man in the booth still desperately vying for my attention.

Before I'm finished I raise my hand at the waitress to signal for the check. She nods and disappears into the back. I turn to the man. He's dressed in a shirt and tie, tie loosened and black suit coat draped across his chair. Decent haircut, about a day's worth of facial hair and noticeable jaw line. He's smiling, giving me eyes. Probably someone like me who makes good money but lives here between downtown and the hardware tract, possibly didn't have the stomach for a daily public GRT commute between the motherboard and this labyrinthine place. Lines of seriousness and loneliness and hard work etched into his forehead. His face turns to shock when I hold my fork up vertical and slowly lick the entire length of it to the tip of the tines. I stare directly at him, allowing him to sit there stunned.

"Your check, miss. No rush, and have a nice night."

I thank the waitress as she scurries away, put down the amount indicated plus thirty-percent tip, gather up my coat and purse and without paying him a single extra look stride to the door. In the reflection of the window front his head hunts around for the wait-ress, can't find her. He stands up, struggling to throw on his suit and overcoat. I push open the door and step outside, losing sight of him but not looking back. The street is a blast of penetrating cold, boots crunching against scattered piles of week-old snow. I used to be aware when I first moved from Denver but have long-since grown oblivious of the soaring, futuristically byzantine buildings lifting up all around this section of Grid—city hall a massive raised disc on eight oddly-angled stilts, the Pteranadon-Planax-Horner scraper that looks as if it's been turned to liquid and twisted in the middle—now able to use the structures for what they are, monoliths of misdirection. The moment just before I turn into the alley the door to Tranquil John's opens behind me, then there's the clacking of hard-soled dress shoes giving pursuit. I quicken my pace a bit, somehow excited by this chase no matter how mundane, still making sure to tread carefully since from wall-to-wall the ground of the alley is frozen over with ice except where metal kitchen doors are flung open and heat flushes into the drabness of the night in visible undulating clouds. My head is down, still hearing the clacking shoes trying to catch up. How could he possibly be so slow? At last he turns the corner into the alley and I hear him calling out, "Excuse me!" My lips curl into a smile, walking all the faster, unwavering, halfway down the entire length of the alley. Now I hear him hustling. With hair-flipping brilliance I spin around to face him all at once, pretending this is the first I've heard of him. His figure is jogging lightly toward me through a shifting gray veil of steam, a gloved hand raised in the air.

"Miss! Excuse me!"

And now he's getting closer so I can see a smile on his face at having caught my attention, teeth white even from far away and overcoat cut perfectly to his figure, swishing expensively behind him. And then one footfall, his left foot, goes sliding at an angle out from beneath him on the ice so his whole body pitches left in the narrow alley, everything in midair, head catching the welded edge of a black dumpster (there's a strong painful echoing metal gong-ing sound) and a long ribbon of blood alights into a momentary arc before splashing down on him where he's landed. I watch him slowly writhe although his agony is practically noiseless. Maybe his breath is gone. With the same careful steps as before I walk to where he's sprawled, leaning over to inspect him. His ear is jagged, torn away from where it was once attached to his neck, blood belching from the wound in torrents synchronized with his heartbeats. His eyes meet mine, imbued with sheer horror, hands grasping the side of his neck and bubbling through a mouth of blood for help. I rub my chin with a finger and thumb, getting closer to examine the spewing tear, noticing a bit of flexing muscle visible through the thick outpour. He continues to beg for help, it's almost silent if you weren't listening for it. I sigh, stand upright, put hands on my hips, look toward the mouth of the alley where people pass on the sidewalk, inner privacies totally unperturbed by anything or anyone. I look back down at the man, at his desperate eyes, tell him, "Too bad you slipped. We could've had a good time." Then, still cautious of the ice, I turn and walk home.

What a lot of people don't say out loud is they crave the ability to manipulate. Most don't even know what they want to manipu-late, just that they do. A lot of people I meet are weak, floundering creatures who haven't got the tiniest grasp on the truth of the world. The truth is, they're not actually equipped to survive. They're alive because someone else is *allowing* them to be. But regardless of how blatant that fact, many disbelieve it—I guess *can't* believe it for fear of being awakened to something dark and out of their control. The difference between those people and myself is that I don't shy away from the truth. Another aspect of that truth is nobody's life is certain, nor secure, nor purposeful. Most seem surprised when confronted with this. You have to laugh at those people, if not for contempt then to find the strength to coexist with them at all.

A perfect specimen of such a theory rears its head when my phone rings at 9:45, pulling me away from endless lines of code, on the other end of the connection a timid-sounding guy who I'm constantly waiting on to burst into tears the way his voice keeps cracking.

"Hello?"

"Hi…is this…Amy Arsenault?"

"Please don't pronounce it like that. I'm not French, and from the sound of it neither are you."

"Oh…okay. I'm calling because—"

"You're responding to my ad."

"…Yes. The *Database* classifieds?"

"That's where the ad was placed, yes."

"Ha…yeah. I'm, uh, responding with regards to a platform I have to learn."

"Which?"

"It's called DealEase. Do you know it?"

"Of course."

"I have to learn it right away…I was wondering how much you charge for—"

"Depends how many sessions it takes. Rule of thumb says three two-hour sessions will run you around a thousand."

"A *thou*sand?"

"Says rule of thumb. It could be more or less depending on your specific level and needs."

Hesitation on his end. "Look...do you mind if I call back in an hour?"

"I assume you're going to check with Software Proficiency Institute ads."

"Well, I...it's just, a *thousand dollars?*"

"I'll save you the suspense. SPI's courses are half as expensive as mine, but also half as effective. Class sizes are large and the instructors typically unavailable. With me you'll pay more, but with one-on-one attention you'll be twice as good in half the time."

"It just seems...I don't know."

"Sir, I can—"

"I don't mean to sound cynical, but I'm a car salesman. Maybe that's unfair."

"I'd say perfectly fair. We're talking about a lot of money and you want to trust that it's going to pay off." I absently punch the armrest of my chair to get through this. "But what I *can* promise you is my extensive expertise with the program, and, as I said before, personal attention. Generally, with a little time, those two things lead not just to proficiency with a platform, but mastery."

"And it says here you're able to meet anywhere, correct?"

"Correct."

"You come to houses?"

"If that's where you'd like to meet."

He continues to hesitate.

"How about this? Think it over, and if you decide I'm the best option for you, you can send me the date, time and address where you'd like to meet."

"Okay," he says, "thanks for your help. We'll be in contact."

"Likewise."

Weak. Floundering. Easy to control.

Desperation equals overcharging, and it's far from my responsibility to clue in the clueless. More to the point is I have no prior experience with DealEase, didn't in fact know it existed until a moment ago, though pirating a copy and learning most of the basics before our first session shouldn't be too difficult.

I stand from my chair to stretch. Through the frosty window behind my desk I spot one of my neighbors trudging through the alleyway holding plastic bags of groceries in both hands. He's well-bundled out there, breath clouds following behind him in the bitterness. Normally he has a dog, but it hasn't been with him lately.

Three hours pass in a blink. I've been staring into an FTP interface, what I've constructed is a white screen with a small smiling cartoon lion at its center. I test-click and images begin to flash in the darkness of the room. Once I'm satisfied all is in working order I click once, the lion and images disappearing completely.

Nothing in my fridge. Forgot to buy groceries again. My vision is usually blurry at the end of the day, nearsightedness slowly overtaking what was formerly perfect vision. The hell with everything. Once midnight passes the world becomes empty. Extensive hacks like this give me insomnia. Spread yourself too thin and your guard tends to go down. Paranoia moves in and clamps down hard. Nests. Gestates inside. So many times I've lost sleep over the thought of a breakdown in my defenses, so many enemies made, so many impulses I've been helpless not to indulge. The world becomes empty. So many things that could have gone wrong in the past but never did, and yet tonight perhaps my paranoia is born of good reason, wriggling into larval seriousness, gnawing at passing bits of data, thriving on invisible convergence. It's impossible to sleep, and when I don't sleep boredom rolls in. Boredom is the moment when everything is quiet, the TV and space heater in the corner lit by dull musty light, face of the computer unlit and unexpressive, and then gradually, in between the drifting mote flows, I see everything for what it really is. My apartment turns to a prison in the middle of something too large to comprehend. Every dot in the sky is a galaxy, every space between those dots hundreds of billions of light years of Nothing, a clean and unfeeling vacuousness. My head is the space between dots.

In an instant I'm up out of the chair and back on my laptop, hacking into my neighbor's email, the neighbor I caught sight of walking home without his dog. I do this, but my mind is somewhere else. Breathing elevated, heartrate up, contempt for his existence zapping my brain like mild but irritating dosages of current. He is pathetic. So pathetic I can't stand it. His sad lonely nothingness. I scan methodically through his inbox, thinking: *Why does this feel insufficient? Why does it feel like he deserves a more severe punishment than this?* I realize maybe I'm not in full control of myself, and my teeth start to show. Here we are, a folder marked *Connie*.

> **Date:** *Sun, 17 Sep 2023 10:01:38 -0600*
> **From:** *Connie Edelzapf (ezapf12@zmail.com)*
> **Subject:** *Oh god...*
>
> Versal,
> Maybe you'd like to explain to me how I managed to get so drunk? Or at the very least shed some light on what I said. Actually, that's a lie too, I know exactly what I said, remember it perfectly, to be honest. But the only consolation I can give you is it was all true. I guess I'm a bit of a mess these days, but no job and no car will do that to you. One more year of bad luck and I'll be living in a govt-initiative complex, dressed up in black sneakers and solid-color clothing. Can you imagine me that way? But until that happens I've already made up my mind I won't stop pursuing you. How is it that you make me smile no matter how dark things get? Never mind, better to keep some things a mystery.
> Love,
> Connie

An old message from two years ago. The most recent reads:

> **Date:** *Wed, 1 Jan 2025 15:49:32 -0700*
> **From:** *Connie Edelzapf (ezapf12@zmail.com)*
> **Subject:** *Missing you today*

Hey, how's Xon? I feel so bad for him, you know he's my baby! Hope you're doing something to keep yourself entertained while you have to be inside taking care of him. Wish more than anything I could come visit this week, but money's tight and I've gotta pick up these extra shifts. Guessing you can commiserate right about now. Vet bills suck. I can't stand being away from you. Possibly you could make time to give me a call tonight, right? Right. Miss you so much.

Dated yesterday. The most recent message in the main inbox is from someone named Dr. Vernassis.

Date: *Thur, 2 Jan 2025 21:33:46 -0600*
From: *Darryn Vernassis (vernassis@hybridclinic.com)*
Subject: *Xon*

Hello, Mr. Pennington, this is Dr. Vernassis from Hybrid St. Vet Clinic. You visited our offices earlier today with your Otterhound purebred, Xon, and met with my colleague, Dr. Guzman. It has been related to me you're not treating Xon's heartworm here at the hospital for financial reasons, and I'd like to let you know of a cheaper alternative. The process is time-intensive, but can be completed entirely at home.

You will need to purchase Immiticide, a melarsomine dyhydrochloride. Xon will need two injections in the back, between the shoulder blades, twice a day for two days. You will have to keep him almost completely inactive for three weeks, ensuring he doesn't move around too much as this could cause the worms to dislodge into the lungs and induce a fatal reaction. After that, I would strongly recommend dosing him, this time in pill form, every other day for a period of four weeks.

I can provide you with a vendor for the medication and hypodermics which might suit your financial constraints. In any case, I hope Xon will be okay. He's a rare and beautiful breed of dog.

Regards,
Dr. Darryn Vernassis

Dated a week ago. Everything's made fairly easy for me when I find two receipts for separate orders of Immiticide. Matching up the order numbers on the vendor's site shows one order delivered and one order pending. I cancel the pending order, then try to hack Connie Edelzapf's account but it turns out (and I'm genuinely surprised) that she's got some security measures in place, so I opt for a fallback—not nearly as convincing, but it'll do the job so long as my neighbor isn't very observant. I create a decoy email account, replicating her address exactly except for a single number. Then I send him a message from the false address, one I wrote myself:

Versal,

I know what you did and it's unforgivable. I've never felt so fucking hurt and angry. All this time you tricked me into believing I loved you when you're really just a betraying asshole. Don't bother calling because it's over. Fuck you AND your dog.

Connie

Then I write a second email, this one from my neighbor's account to Connie Edelzapf's:

Connie,

I'm in love with somebody else. I'm through with you.

> I've been trying to find the words to tell you for so
> long, but I can't think of what to say so I'm just going
> to be direct. Don't try to contact me. I'm moving to
> Denver with my new girlfriend, so I'll no longer be at
> my apartment. Goodbye.

I lean over the keyboard, breathing heavy. It's not catharsis, maybe not even relief. Just need.

It's two hours later that my phone rings? and finally I've been dozing in the recliner a little. I refuse to feel groggy or disoriented when waking, I find it disgusting. I should simply be asleep one moment and then awake the next. I look at the name on the phone. *Oh christ, not you.* Unusual, though. I can't remember ever getting a call from her.

"Hello."

"Amy!" explodes an overwrought voice. "Amy, is that you?"

"Who else would it be? This is my phone. It was my phone you dialed, correct?"

"Amy, this is Aunt Joann."

"Yes," I say, already supremely irritated, "I know."

She's in a state of near-total hysterics. "Amy! She had a *heart attack!*"

"Who are you referring to exactly?"

"Margaret!" She cries the name out in tears.

I blink. My mother. "Mm-hm," I say.

"Honey, she— she had a heart attack just half an hour ago! I'm a *wreck!* She called me… called me on the…" Once again she sobs wildly, irrepressibly, her deep shock and sadness decoded from insane chains of binary, allowing me to hear her crystal clear in a separate space and time, and possibly for the first time tonight I'm truly, truly amused.

"Joann," I command over her howls, "Joann, get a hold of yourself and tell me what's going on."

Her blubbering continues in a milder form until she manages

speech. "Margaret…your mother…called me on the *phone*, for heaven's sake, just not even a hour ago. And she says, 'Joann, I'm feelin pain.' So I says to her, 'What pain, Margaret? What pain you talkin about?' And she just kept sayin somethin about a *pain*, I didn't know, just kept goin on about this *pain*."

"Yes, chest pains typically precede a heart attack. Go on."

"And so she just kept goin on about this pain, this pain, so I finally says to her, 'Margaret, I'm comin over there to get you, that's all there is to it…I'm….' [a single restrained sob bursts from her] …and she kept sayin no, no, don't you come all the way out here, Joann, ain't nothin wrong with me. And then I heard her…I heard her *keel over!*"

I scratch my chin, peering up at the ceiling and considering the situation while Joann—once again—loses it. I do my best to picture what she's describing, find it curious that I'm unable.

She gasps in a huge breath of air and manages to continue. "So I'm shoutin her name into the phone just loud as I can and there ain't no response at all, so I hung up and called the emergency number and now I just got a call tellin me she done had a *massive heart attack* and they're takin her to St. Joseph's!"

"Hm," I say. She's too absorbed with her suffering to hear me.

"Amy, I'm a *wreck!* I'm a *wreck!*"

"Don't worry, Joann, she'll be, um—" I search for the word, rolling my hand thoughtfully, fingers searching, finally finding it "—fine."

"That's my *sister*. I want my *sister*, Amy, I want my *sister*." Her sobbing devolves to whimpering, voice thin, barely there, repeating things, weak and floundering.

"Joann, listen, I've gotta go."

"Are you gonna be all right, Amy, honey? Are you gonna be—"

"I'll be okay, but I have to go now. We'll make plans to meet at St. …?"

"Joseph's." She fills in the information eagerly, almost obediently.

"At St. Joseph's. I'm sorry for what happened, but it's time to get a hold of yourself now. Everything's going to be"—it's easier this time—"fine."

This paltry reassurance somehow calms her. "Okay. Okay, you're right. I'll see you at St. Joseph's in the morning, honey."

I stretch big on the cozy cushions of the recliner, yawning. Best to get just a little more rest before I head in the direction of the GRT to make the trip to Denver. But of course I don't actually end up sleeping, instead just lying there in the chair, eyes open, staring into the graceless plaster pattern of the ceiling. My thoughts move back to the man who followed me out of the restaurant, sliding through the blood red glow, remembering the hand in the air, the violent tilt of his body before his ear made contact with the dumpster, the arc of blood and the way he was unable to produce noise. And then later on, maybe half an hour, is when I start to hear formless wailing coming from the apartment next to mine, my neighbor's, seeping through the walls, gradually growing in intensity and anguish, all at once morphing into a wretched weeping that unravels into great long strings hanging in the dead air, beautiful, like decorations, and I close my eyes with no intention of sleep, expressionless and comfortable, and every time I breathe I'm exhaling smoke.

GERNEY

Bastard transition. That's what this is, isn't it? Transition. Or something worse. We're so reluctant to admit we didn't own absolute knowledge from the earliest possible moment. That learning never occurred, never *had* to occur, everything we ever experienced and heard and saw just affirmations of what we already knew. Willfully pretending all wisdom was contained within us from the beginning, as if innate, residing in a deep well that never did not exist. Never surprised, never caught off-guard. Our jadedness and our optimism. All our little philosophies on things. Our daily thought processes. I believe now that what we actually start out with is nothing, that we're wading up through darkness, a darkness we can't remember once we surface from it, and when we come up out of it we have nothing. Nothing in our heads or our souls. Maybe it could be conceded that we at least have our genetic endowments, a physical process engrained into us, a projection of the pair of people who were there before, but otherwise nothing predisposed to know simultaneous perdition and paradise.

Sitting in the chair in my apartment, from left to right, is the TV (commercial for some sort of multiplatform game running stats to illustrate units-per-fun vs. minutes-per-time ratios against

Multidimensional Internet Vacuum Sox album snippets), phone (the messages have been relentless though I couldn't accurately say who or what group they originate from, whole conversations held with numbers not saved to my contacts list, ZChase software busily curating my personal selections of comments, articles, freshly-released tracks, movie times and coupons, all based on my algorithm-accordant tastes), Vital-Sin display installed into the armrest of the recliner (LED readout of pulse rate, brain function, total time sat or TTS, estimated blood pressure, personalized workout regimens), and finally the VidraPro I opted to hang just above the TV, about a half-inch (3D semi-holographic movements through imagined landscapes that they commission big-time programmers or whatever to construct, and I've always sort of justified owning the screen and paying full-price for the "tours" as they're called, instead of pirating them through the phone, as a testament to my intellectual pursuits). Additionally I'm downloading all seven cookbooks by a celebrity Chinese chef named Li Li III who specializes in creative meals for bachelors and solo diners. Luckily that's going on in the other room, otherwise I'd get sucked into watching the slowly-filling progress bars brim over with blue informational juices. On the kitchen table is a ZChase News Pad where for some reason I indulged in a thirty-five minute spree of reading old editions of the the *New York Times* from 1967-1969. I didn't finish breakfast, but I've been snacking for the last three hours which has compensated. I should really eat the six mangos in the fridge I bought two months ago since they're finally in the early stages of going bad, but they still somehow don't sound good. I'll have to throw them out in another week or so. I remember I was interested in a documentary about a river that no longer exists a while ago, but I kept getting distracted by an updating news feed coming out of Guinea-Bissau about ethnoreligious factional warfare in which the leader of a prominent Fula militia decided that, as punishment for aiding and abetting a Balanta defense force, a rural village of 94 people would be slaughtered by means of being lashed to the ground and forming a perimeter around them, making sure no one could come to their rescue for days and days until they died, and afterwards they stole the village's food supplies and moved on. I scroll through the photos while listening to a classic trance-influenced DJ I've been minorly obsessed with for a couple weeks. Now the river documentary is apparently over, replaced by shots of workers in a dry erase board factory, and my interest in that is zero-minus-two. The VidraPro is touring Quo vanHall's *Pipe Hell* landscape, which I've seen about a billion times before and is incredibly bleak. I found out a long time ago, I don't remember where, that Quo vanHall's real name is Jimmy Vedders, and that most of the surreal pipes in the work were in fact designed by someone else, a programmer named Megan Emerick who was romantically involved with Jimmy Vedders for a while, but for some reason she was never officially credited. In the midst of zoning out to *Pipe Hell* there's a shrill beep from somewhere, alerting me to the halfway point of I don't know what. The slim strip of white drywall beneath the VidraPro is lit by vacillating reds and silvers, and all I can do for a while is observe the swimming glow, encroaching and coalescing with that of the TV. I flip through channels but everything that's still in circulation on the prerecorded menu are things I've already watched. 10 Everyday Uses for Electrons. There are messages from Ronstadt, Nick, Millie, Quentin. Zong—The Most Interesting Assassinations of the 20th Century. The question, maybe the only question I have, is how to pass the time. There are five video games sitting on the floor that I bought, started, never completed. *Pipe Hell* is fifty-two minutes, twelve seconds long. There is no accompanying music, and it is considered, in some niche circles, as one of the masterpieces of the medium thus far. The aggregate opinion of *Pipe Hell* is that it's a very "substantive and cerebral landscape," rather than simply overly beatific or fantastical. The landscape is notable for its highly claustrophobic feel, even when depicting large open areas or what some critics have termed "pipe pockets." The pipes are interwoven with such intricate mathematical artistry they often come up as objects of study in universities (art departments rather than math). It is generally theorized by viewers that the substance the pipes carry is melted steel, since split-second glances of the material are seen throughout the tour being poured from gargantuan spouts into rusted metal vats cast in the shape of human heads. There are no depictions of living creatures, but the pipes themselves shift formation each time the tour is viewed, lending a nearly imperceptible feel of being inside what can only be described as an "organic hive or nest" rather than an immutable industrial nightmare. According to year-old estimates, Quo vanHall has reaped close to seven million dollars in sales and leasing fees for *Pipe Hell*, along with several national awards. I've read all this before but I'm scanning the words again on my phone while a modern-day firearms expert discharges the exact model of rifle used to assassinate John F. Kennedy on Zong. The Li Li III cookbooks are starting to be sent to my phone through the laptop sync, and I skim four different recipes before I realize they're above my level of know-how and file them in a download folder and forget about them. A tiny holographic clipart image of books resting on a shelf projected from my phone is sucked down into the folder display. Is it possible to twitch my index finger—just like this here—and suddenly the bullet never makes it to Kennedy's head, is instead stuck in a clot of deadened pixels and completely immobilized, none of it ever occurring sixty years before I was born? The little pulse rate notches being ticked onto the Vital-Sin LED like my heart marking off days in prison. Socnet updates are building and layering into a plexus. Can you be expected to listen to silence—to not drown out every thought because it scares you, intimates things you'd rather eliminate? I find myself standing in the second-floor hallway of the apartment, looking at a dead-end and wondering, *Where'd dad keep those old boxes?*

From what I've been told, it was sometime in the 1990s, a time that wades up to me from pictures and movies as almost fictional, when mom and dad got married. I have no idea what sparked their decision since they shared next to nothing in common, and when they weren't either disagreeing or out-and-out fighting, they were discussing trivial events with solid dispassion. When would they make a trip to the bank. What time is dinner. How much did the plumber charge. Whatever they told themselves must have been enough to allow them to remain married 32 years. The only thing I really know for sure about my parents' marriage is that it ended in tragedy.

There are more framed pictures of my dad where he appears in midair, wearing neon ski suits and orange bug-eye goggles with great carbon fiber blades latched to his feet, trailing shimmering artificial snow, than there are of him posing next to any member of our family. We all tried to wrap our heads around the obsession he had for skiing. I've known how to ski since I was four years old, but I never experienced it the same way he did. The only clue I ever got to deciphering the mystery of what it meant to him was a comment he made to mom at what is now an ancient, archaeological dinner, circa 2017, the twilight years of their marriage (I was nineteen, my sister Kelsey sixteen). We weren't a noisy or talkative family. Instead we were quiet to a fault. I was painfully aware of mom's hatred for this, but she silently seethed alongside the rest of us for plenty of years—plenty enough that, if she'd wanted to, or had the energy, she could've taken steps toward fixing the problem. Mom was only an introvert around the family, and then only because we refused to engage with her. But I found out later, of course, that blaming our silence on introversion was a mistake. The truth was we were quiet because we didn't know one another, and that could only be blamed on cowardice and indifference. I always sensed that mom, like dad, somewhere in the course of things, had been changed in some fundamental way, but I could never figure out exactly how. Their unhappiness was evident in the way each of their personalities seemed caged within them. Which was how they seemed that night, sitting at our ancient dinner table in the thick of our ancient lives, every so often stealing upward glances at each other, dad eating in the most dejected manner imaginable: head rested heavily in one palm, eyes trained resiliently plateward, listlessly chewing, fork forging idle paths through his food. Not that that sort of behavior was unfamiliar for any of us. We all operated according to our own inner tides, causing a natural fluctuation in which of us took on the most dejected pose of the night.

But there was dad, guarded and all but absentee, the one who likely deserves the majority of the credit for the sad character of our family, mind off drifting somewhere hermetically sealed from the rest of us, when his eyes unexpectedly traveled up from Plate Position A to ask mom, cryptically and with voice cracking, if she ever (these were his words) pretended about things.

Mom's face went ashen. Not only her, I'm sure we all froze, the question as shocking as it was uncomfortable, exploding like a single firework in a dead black sky.

"Pretend?" She pronounced the word incredulously. "What do you mean?"

"I mean like, say, this is purely hypothetical, but do you ever pretend to be doing something else other than what you're doing while you're, for instance, just say, driving?"

She struggled to process his words, embarrassed, put on the spot in front of Kelsey and I who were rapt even if equally embarrassed by his sudden attempt at intimacy.

"Do I ever pretend to—"

"Do you ever pretend like you're being followed by the car behind you, or maybe like you're on your way someplace secret or dangerous, or like you're transporting a trunk full of explosives?"

She appeared to consider it for a moment but was ultimately dumbstruck. "Matt, what's this about?"

"Something I'm wondering." His tone was sad, as if already disappointed by her inability to come up with an answer, his posture impotent.

"About me?"

"Well I asked you."

Her response, maybe accidental, was to let her fork clank against her plate.

"It doesn't have to be driving, necessarily. Maybe that's not a good example. I'm talking about anything. Just in general. To make everyday things more dramatic."

"This is something *you* do?"

"Not always," now sheepish at the reversal. "Not always. I just bring it up because I guess I was thinking right now about last weekend in the mountains, how every time down the slope—well, not *every* time, but all of the times—I couldn't help pretending that I was passing through my own life. And, I mean, I don't know if I'd call it *pretending* really, but just imagining I was passing through my own life during each run, metaphorically, in stages. Like at the top, at the start, I pictured myself back in the seventies, just a little kid, and as I made my way down [clearing his throat loudly], made my way down I was moving forward through time, through stages of my life, and at the end I saw myself as an old man. But it changed, too, when I took the lift back to the top I found myself moving *backward* through time instead of *forward*, and— what?"

"Matt, what are you talking about?" He really had lost her at that point. She wasn't getting it.

They looked at each other. At the time I didn't understand how but he looked like a child, a very old child, and I'd never seen him or any adult look like that, oversized for his age, genuinely confused why she couldn't understand. He muttered something about never-mind, returned his gaze to his plate, it wasn't anything really. I felt like what he described wasn't so difficult to understand, but mom and Kelsey, judging solely by their faces, didn't share the feeling. We all went back to silence, intentionally forgetting anything had been said in such a way that nobody forgot, would never forget what would happen if any of us tried to reveal anything personal to these strange people we lived with.

Two years later, when dad was laid rigidly on a cold table some-where, organs being nicely plucked like ripe fruit from a dead tree, I read the letter in his own handwriting, addressed to me only, which decoded not only that dinner for me, but a great deal of my child-hood, and put me on a path of contempt, resentment:

Kevin, you can't count on anyone in this world to understand you but yourself. If there's one piece of fatherly advice I can give, it's to accept that humans have made a habit of assuming other humans can understand what they say and what they go through, when in fact it couldn't possibly be more to the opposite. To be alive is to be essentially lonely, son, and in my experience it's the optimism that that loneliness can be cured which makes everything worse.

In the storage closet I'm looking at one of dad's old boxes, sealed with packing tape, the word BOOKS written on the top flap in time-eroded marker. The tape is still strong, and I accidently tear the cardboard apart. Floating at the top of the stack is an enormously thick book, the cover art a painting of three identical empty orange outlines of a man against a white background, all standing in a perfect row, all wearing the same military clothing and helmet, and in the center of the middle figure is what looks like a wedge of cheddar cheese. *Shell-Shocked Sarnin* by H.Z. Arnitz © 1988.

Kevin and Matthew Crepitus shared one trait above all others: accident proneness. Kevin's pseudonym had been cemented, irreversibly, in his own mind by the age of ten, which might account for the improper spelling (Gerney rather than Gurney), though the exact origins of the name were not traceable, the world allocating him a more fitting label almost of its own accord. It was clear he was his father's child very early on—he'd inherited none of Dawn's vitality, none of her steadiness. He was a projection of Matthew Crepitus. He waded up through darkness into the mold of the physically and mentally clumsy. Everyone loves an injury story. Gerney had a surplus. Fourteen broken bones, two knee surgeries, seven fractures, a forcibly removed tooth, dislocated shoulder and a wealth of gnarled scars. And though they're all morbidly interesting, the most important injury Gerney would ever sustain would be The Ankle. It happened during his brief stint in college, before a superabundance of apathy (something he'd also found in the mold, but this more of an error than an intrinsic quality, a manufacturing defect in a certain generation of product) caused him to discontinue his coursework at a local college in the motherboard tract. Apathy—at the time—may have been the result of his phenomenal attraction to uppers and everything that went along with them—the people, the places, the hordes of stimuli, the constant veil of night, the intense indoorsiness and latent contempt for all things not man-made, and especially the blind happiness and optimism that, for precious hours, overshadowed deep personal instabilities. Gerney was grappling the jet when The Ankle occurred.

It was also how he met Nick Ibyoo. Nick and Gerney's first meeting at Joe Meridian's house, a place where a certain age group of upwardly mobile gonine addicts traditionally gathered to do what could only be described as rainbows of drugs, was an altogether chance convergence. Nick was a mainstay in the city's gonine culture, almost even qualifying as one of its attractions if it were only a more licit category of interest, and so he found himself there the way he might find himself anywhere. What drew him that night to Joe Meridian's house was a lovely jet-grappled girl named Autumn he'd met two nights before at a bar in a splendid moment of twacked romanticism who had invited him to the party. He didn't bother to mention that his invitation to Joe Meridian's house was a standing one, figuring correctly it would serve him better for her to discover this fact upon his arrival. The intersection of circumstance was Gerney happened to have a major thing for the same girl, and when he first saw Nick Ibyoo at Joe Meridian's he had no clue who he was, nor that he'd been invited by Autumn. In March the chill of winter was just starting to break, most people congregating in the backyard. The infamous house was dilapidated and creaky but large, unnerving in its grand refusal to fall victim to age or elements, boxed in on every side by similarly sagging homes. In the near-distance was the springtime twinkling of downtown Grid scrapers, casting colored illumination against low-hanging clouds. Gerney was full of gonine. He couldn't help but track Nick from across the yard—this stranger rising out of their range of self-destruction into a realm of persona, exuding a high valence, drawing out Gerney's own displacement. Gerney asked Joe Meridian who he was.

"You don't know Nick Ibyoo? He's here with Autumn tonight."

"What? Where does she know him from?"

"I don't know, man. This is me shrugging."

Gerney watched the two of them flirt over drinks for an hour before disappearing inside the house, the length of their absence suggesting to him one thing only. The consequence of his jealous heartache was a tailspin of memory- and sensory-erasing jet inhalation. By the time Nick reemerged from the house Gerney was electrically wired, masochistically addled. Because his attraction to Autumn had been no secret, Gerney figured Nick might keep his distance, but he quickly did just the opposite. He gravitated toward him with leonine stealth, Gerney skittish but unaware.

He came forward like an asteroid. Like the hulking square face of a semi, smiling through electric music, trailing irradiated sparks, hungry to make contact.

"You're Gerney." They were in the backyard, behind the speakers.

He nodded.

"Funny name."

"Well what's yours?"

"Nick Ibyoo." They shook hands. "Autumn was telling me about you." The tone of his voice was neither overly friendly nor subtly aggressive, simply intrigued—as if the things she'd said about Gerney had been a great pleasure for him. He opened the flap of his jacket and revealed a baggie of gonine, holding it against the flashing LED quality of the night, lifting an eyebrow. "What do you say?"

In retrospect, this offering was not, as Gerney had assumed at the time, a gesture of condolence for having so easily claimed something he coveted, even though the pursuit of girls Gerney liked would become an actual characteristic of their friendship, almost a daring habit too deep-rooted for Nick to train himself out of. Rather, Nick's interest in Gerney that night was a paternal one, an instinct which kicked into gear by proximity alone. They snorted off the speakers to applause—Nick waved. Gerney's heart was in perfect delirious sync with the pace of the music, suddenly noticed in the presence of this minor celebrity.

Nick said, "Your eyes are practically being sucked against the back of your skull. Let me ask you something, you ever work with cars?"

"What?" badly overtwacked.

"Cars. Automobiles. You ever hold a job that had to do, directly or indirectly, with them?"

Gerney laughed. "I… I can't think right now…"

"Goddamn, you look like you're grappling thirty jets, y'know that? Maybe you ought to slow down."

"I think you're probably—"

"*Or.* Or speed way, way up. Can you tell which?"

Gerney looked at him, clutching his heart with one hand, Nick's face seeming to shift across multiple keyframes of intent.

"I think… I'm gonna be *sick*…" He laughed maniacally now.

Nick laughed along with him, maintaining control, observing yet another novice drawn into jet, the personality type, the severity.

"Look," laughing so hard Gerney could feel his face turning red, "you and Fall… I mean Autumn…"

"Yes?"

The music folded in on itself, a weird implosion preceding an even angrier and more terrifying outburst. The low-lying cloud cover leaned closer, locking in reality.

Gerney tried finishing his question, tried three different times, but when he couldn't stop laughing Nick placed an arm over his shoulder and led him toward the house, whispering delicately into his ear as they walked.

"Gerney," he said calmly, somehow an intimate friend already, lips dry and very near, "do you know what's interesting about self-destruction? It's what fuels it. That is, self-pity." They stepped onto the cement of the back porch, over legs, past empty beer bottles. In the corner of Gerney's vision Nick appeared set against a background of absolute black, the prominent image. "You know why I like people who self-pity? Because I don't understand them, yet I'm never disappointed by them. Because, in a strange way, they're dedicated to everyone but themselves. They consider them*selves* the shit of the universe, the rest of us the sparkling diamonds. Get what I'm sayin? It's as if their purpose in the world is to be used. Used in ways they might think they're aware of, but actually have no idea. Or, even if they do realize, are too self-destructive to put a stop to it." Gerney was vaguely cognizant of walking up steps, ten different screens playing ten different shows, all frenetically twacked. "On this night, it's entirely true there are only two types of people—you're either a user, or you're being used. Understand?" Gerney laughingly, nervously nodded. "These are irrefutable facts. Here, step on top of this. Yep, there you go. Take a second to get your balance if you need to. Okay, now wait for me. All right, let me just open this up here. Damn thing's stuck. Probably hasn't been opened in like a hundred... wait, there it goes. Okay, after you, sir." Frosty wind against his face, music thumping inorganically below, Nick's arm again sliding across his shoulder, turning Gerney towards him so he was now holding him by the arms and facing him directly. "Do you believe me when I tell you I can *see* people? I'm four years older than you. Don't look so surprised, of course my knowledge of you is that specific. I'm looking backwards through time at you, in the direction where all fog lifts. I'm a teacher, I realize, in this moment. Don't for a second think it's the drugs making you do this. Don't blame the drugs. We both know that's a cop-out. You're simply facing the ramifications of who you are, understand?" He looked Gerney direct in the eyes, serious and caring, then took his head in his hands and leaned forward slowly to plant a glancing kiss against his forehead, dry and lean and oddly sexual, a dark gracing, looking into his eyes once more before turning him clockwise toward the drop. They were standing at the edge of the roof of the house. Below was a weather-faded trampoline and a swath of upturned faces, observing them there at the edge, expectant and speechless. Gerney thought: *I trust you.* He jumped off the roof. He felt Nick's hands leave him. He felt himself sucked into the tractor beam of gravity, cold wind. He felt like he absolutely did deserve it all. Then he felt his foot hit the surface of the trampoline at a disastrous angle, ankle tendons tearing, breath-stealing pain, the world beneath him bending and springing back tautly, launching him into yet another extended fall to the ground. He laid there, trying to catch his breath.

Page one sentence one of *Shell-Shocked Sarnin* reads: "Like all

budding entities still in their most basic states, save for the unlucky anomalies of course, Private Garrett Sarnin spent his earliest existence in a dimension of 100% sharp cheddar cheese, those being the prominent days of his life, though he couldn't know it, because they marked the glistening moment in time when he still understood, with any level of clarity, who he was, and here he wasn't even really much of anything yet."

The dimension of cheddar cheese, it turns out, is a closed dimension that serves as the starting block for all sentient creatures, and before Sarnin is expelled into Life in the many different parallel universes along with the rest of his "incoming class" they first perform the ritual Festival of The Beginning of the End, a massive celebration meant to inculcate the soon-to-be-born entities into disorientation, impulse and awe. The festival is diffuse, seemingly unending, a twenty-page hedonistic froth orchestrated by a string cheese overlord, controlling from a massive tower of manchego, enforcing a constant state of chemical happiness. Sarnin roams the celebration blindly, colliding against the crowd. (Entities still in this closed dimension are not yet endowed with a body, so instead are floating balls of light.) Bits of white cheddar fall through the air like snow and the sky is an enormous hot pink lava lamp. The string cheese overlord smiles, insinuating a constant stream of heady but quick-paced music, the partying entities below bonding to and transcending with its tumultuous currents. From the tower he booms that this is their final moment of interconnectedness, it is the beginning of the end, for life in the parallel universes is an act of separateness and fear. Congregate! he urges. Congregate and mourn through unrelenting ecstasy! Ha ha ha ha! For days Sarnin remains in this state of shared rapture, he can't remember how much time has passed, *if* time has passed at all, he is losing himself to the whole, they are blending, blending, a single undulating creation. He is woozy and sated. Satisfied. Losing consciousness for long tracts only to reawaken in a jubilant field of connected entities vibrating to the music of the string cheese overlord, dancing in his manchego tower. Still his cries ring out over their numbers. Congregate! Congregate now while there's still time! Sarnin can't handle it, he's going to pass out. Their combined mass moves in great blanket-like waves, an immense sight, gaining power into faster, larger sweeps. He drops off into oblivion.

When he reawakens he is embodied as Private Garrett Sarnin, a new recruit in the United States World Allied Army in the war against Gen. Vernon Cobrigale, conqueror of the African continent and dictator of the new massive nation of Cobrigalia. Sarnin has no memory of being an entity in the closed dimension. No memory of the Beginning of the End. He knows nothing. He's in a jungle amphitheater along with hundreds of other troops, all in full combat gear, monkeys and insects calling in the trees behind them. They're listening to a general give a firebrand inspirational pep talk—importance, honor, what's at stake for the world, the gatekeepers of the righteous. Sarnin cautiously whispers to the soldier next to him, asks him if he knows what's going on. The soldier was hoping Sarnin knew. An older trooper in front of them overhears and turns to tell them it's not his first rodeo, commencing to whisper the whole sordid history of Gen. Cobrigale's takeover, his mad scheme to unify the globe through force, to introduce the human race to homogenization and togetherness. The ranting speeches, the ceaseless late nights of complex political reporting, correspondents of all types corresponding, governments sweating and heaving and grunting, displays of might, the millions upon millions murdered, repressed, mass buried, enlisted, forced, freaked, raped, burned, shot, underfed, interrogated, shoved into rank and file, weapons in their hands and brains thoroughly washed, territorial lines drawn across the earth like claw marks on a corpse long since picked to the bone, all individuals losing importance, becoming numbers in squads, together making corps, corps making armies, armies making offensives, and these offensives are a dance, you see, to devalue the arcane power in matter, make it just matter and nothing more. Sarnin snorts and says wow, he had no idea. They're a tactical group, deployed into the heart of Cobrigalia, into the jungle, to slowly dislodge the enemy, amongst the teeming trees where small humans wait to be killed.

For a hundred and fifty pages Pvt. Sarnin, along with the rest of the tactical group, are trained in the art of distant detonations and covert eliminations. Each soldier has his identity destroyed, but as the reader knows, none of the soldiers ever had an identity in the first place. They are mere projections here in the parallel universes, embodied and robbed of their original essence, the essence they only ever fully owned in the closed dimension of cheddar cheese. Everyone incomprehensible to everyone. All seek their own realization, no more. There is an absence of bridges or portals to connect, humanly, and end the shifting confusion (never mind genitalia, the most popular pairing of bridge and portal available, because females are scarce, and even though some of the smarter soldiers overcome the issue of homogenous anatomy and initiate their own identity-melds, the circumstances around them are tempest and even sex becomes impossible). The soldiers are made to stand in the jungle, in the rain, in formation, for a week straight with no food or water. Each soldier stands just out of reach of every other soldier. Two days in, insanity sparks in a single mind and catches flame, roaring through the unit standing at harsh discipline. At three days not a one of them can remember the names of their parents, first girlfriends, high school buddies. At five days a monsoon sets in, rain hitting the jungle floor at such force each droplet shatters, wafts back up into the air as mist, each soldier obscured from the other, though spaced no more than a few feet apart. Still no one crumbles. They stand stalwart and suffering. Sarnin looks up at Gerney from the page from his spot in the formation and rain and jungle, the two making eye contact, and in a troublesome moment Sarnin wriggles off the page onto Gerney's hand like a small black ant crawling in wild, tiny panic. Gerney dropping the book and thrashing about, trying to shake him off but failing because Sarnin zips into his ear.

Gerney, unsettled, leaves the book behind to quickly nip at some jet and steel his nerves, but when he comes back he finds he's now twacked and Sarnin has abruptly slid through into a parallel universe—his hometown of Corporeal, Washington—on leave from the war in Cobrigalia. He wanders the town and outlying streams, the pines and deciduous and firs, the trickling water, the lonely bird calls, the strip malls and corporate restaurants, the car dealerships, the expansive parking lots and department stores, the empty overcast suburban streets. He starts to notice that bits of his identity are reemerging, but only in the background of his mind. A sort of "background identity." In his isolation he knows who he is and owns himself, not fully, but partially at least. He catches glimpses, like baby memories, of the dimension of cheddar, feeling rejuvenated, powerful, safe from the further annihilation of his soul by the heartless gear system of the world. He can know himself through this background identity, nurture and hide it. It is how he will continue to exist. In his happiness he wanders into the Corporeal Indoor Mall, into the food court, a chapel of multilevel skylights and fake plants with a raised dais in the center, the cuisine of several different countries and continents represented. A starving Sarnin orders food, and with a chocolate-brown tray of falafel in his hands he spots, up there on the dais, eating a gargantuan piece of folded pepperoni pizza, a girl of cornstalk-yellow hair, Delilah Fuentes. Sarnin sits across from her and introduces himself. She blots the grease on her mouth with a napkin. Their conversation in the food court, beneath the mural of skylights, reveals that Delilah's husband only two weeks ago fell through a dimensional slip and was, quite possibly (she really didn't know how these things worked), lost forever. They were very much in love, she and her husband, but Delilah was the type who could solder herself to another identity with ease.

Sarnin, being a soldier on leave, is quite eager for the opportunity to fuse to a woman, to employ his bridge to enter her portal and find himself in a whole new realm of shared opiate. They leave the food court to the *Overnight Motel* on the outskirts of town where they engage in day after day of highly-detailed euphoria. Arnitz calculates, diagnoses and recreates the intoxication and resuscitation of hope brought on by loving sex so accurately that Sarnin's brain chemistry is transposed onto Gerney's, Sarnin still in his head manipulating a large panel of buttons to concoct just the right reflection of his experiences. Colors become brighter, the world moving by with sedated contentment, everything distant and perfect. The promise of soon-to-be-relived tactile transcendence, the kind that makes the eyes go unfocused, orgasm a kind of dimension slip in and of itself, though a safer and more mischievous kind, like bungee-jumping into a deep pool of pleasure so rhapsodic, so dark-chocolate-with-raspberries good that prolonged exposure could actually kill, before being yanked back out by the bungee, clenching the air to stop yourself. On one page Sarnin's feet go numb, and so do Gerney's. For a long time Sarnin is content to stay in the universe of Corporeal, thinking he'll never return to his tactical group in the Cobrigalian jungle, simply stay in the *Overnight* with Delilah until dark figures bust down the door and arrest him for desertion. Which he fully intends on, if it weren't for a moment of brief separation, Delilah bounding off him to the bathroom naked, leaving him sweating and splayed on the bed, and Sarnin realizes he can no longer find his background identity. It's lost! He hadn't noticed before, like he'd been under a hex, and when he begins to search his mind to reclaim it all he can find are traces of Delilah. She's flourished inside him, using his surface area to settle roots. For the first time in months he feels a surge of bad adrenaline, and out bounds Delilah from the bathroom, her incantation strong. He sees her differently now. When she stares deep and passionate into his eyes, her purpose no longer seems to be to transact pleasure, to meld and share, but to overtake, to seize and occupy. Later that night when she falls asleep, Sarnin dresses and absquatulates the hotel room, stumbling along the darkened freeway back into town like a bewildered kidnapping victim. Delilah wanted to destroy his identity as well, but with a different method than the military. She'd turned him into an extra limb of her identity; a voodoo doll; a zombie; a surrogate. Quite skillfully she'd conquered him and taken up residence, and who knew if Sarnin would've been enough? Would she have annexed others into her growing territory? No, it was vital he escape. All other human beings were untrustworthy and apart from Sarnin, none could be trusted. (The string cheese overlord had been right all along in urging the entities to congregate while they could—living was an exercise in disconnection and imprisonment. If only Sarnin could remember.)

He came to understand, walking along the black highway, that no other human being could be allowed to fully penetrate him. There would have to be an impassable line, a line where his background identity could hide and subsist on private moments, away from the organization of societies and the numbers of Man. But just as soon as he understood this a pair of headlights winked on in the distance, rushing toward him. Was it Sarnin's imagination or was the car... *aiming* at him? It came closer, tires skidding crazily and the power of the headlights, no matter how close the vehicle drew, cloaking the image of the car behind it. It *was* aiming at him! He leapt to get out of the way but the headlights overtook him and he passed through their glare, the deafening deranged blare of the horn, and suddenly he'd slipped back through a wormhole into the Cobrigalian jungle a continent away in a canopy hideout with three other members of his unit. Someone asked if Sarnin was okay. Gathering his wits he said fine, fine.

They're looking down on a wide tract of jungle. In front of them is a digital display dividing up the landscape into sectors that, when pushed, are erased from the board, and down below the analogous section of jungle erupts into a curling mushroom of howling flame. Flying upwards and outwards from each explosion are dozens of flapping specks, humans sent airborne to ridiculous, ornithological heights, mixed in with jungle debris, monkeys, insects, snakes, and the occasional elephant or panther, all of it pressing up against the expanse of clouds to create a momentary spectacle of fascinating terror. The giant trees in the surrounding sectors of jungle sway powerfully, leaves turning to waxy blurs, creakings and crackings echoing monolithically in the aftermath for full minutes on end, eerie silence filling the gaps between, everything coming to relative rest as the explosion becomes nothing more than a dwindling minaret of black swirl in the sky. The soldiers beside him, with each detonation, become increasingly blank and stupefied, less perceiving with each new square erased from the screen. Sarnin, too. It becomes easier to press the squares. Explosion after explosion decimates the jungle. Tiny bits of creatures and humans and foliage continue to fly up in ever more resplendent fountains of destruction, now unfolding against a richly orange sunset sky, but it all seems to rise and fall faster with less grandeur and effect, and by the time only a single square remains it has fallen to the level of yawn-inducing banality. Laid out before them is the blackened smoking remains of the entire jungle, but still one square is left on the display—the sector of jungle where their canopy is located. A disembodied radio voice pipes in. Sarnin recognizes it as belonging to their unit leader. "Privates, your orders are to leave nothing behind. Repeat, *nothing.*" The soldiers look at one another. Below, on the earth, at the rim of the horizon, is the spot where lush green meets with obliterated black. In this moment it's clear to see that the jungle is the planet's exposed brain matter, full of pulsing folds and mazes. They've been systematically nuking huge portions of it for hours now. The tree they're lofted in still stands. "Privates!" the voice breaks in. "*Nothing behind!*" The four of them take a deep breath. Sarnin gropes for his background identity, finds it, reinforces it best he can. The final square is pressed. In an instant they're hurtling through the air, Sarnin flipping end over end, seeing a swelling ball of flame, then clear sky, then an expanding confetti of debris and black smoke, then sky, then a trumpeting upside-down elephant with legs churning and one of his unit members trailing smoke like a missile, but finally his trajectory normalizes, no longer flipping, flying farther away, jungle passing beneath him in huge bands of terrain. Slowly he loses altitude, and as the ground rears closer he sees he's fixing to end his flight path through the window of a squat black security compound. How poignantly he finds he misses Delilah in the moments before impact. *nyeeeeeeeeeeeeeeeeeeerrrrrrSKRRRRSSSH* through a window, onto a concrete floor, and into another universe!

Sarnin gets to his feet, dizzy, brushing glass and black smoke from his camo, hair in poetic disarray, breathing sighs of relief, and when he turns around he sees a table full of high-ranking men standing around charts and maps and strewn papers and calculators, jaws hanging in disbelief. One of the men at the table is taller, more square, donning a deep black uniform draped and embellished and basically *festooned* with medals and ranks. This is Gen. Vernon Cobrigale.

Just as the *who are you*'s and *what is the meaning of this*'s start up, the general holds his hand aloft and silences the chatter. He orders everyone out of the room, raising quite a few grumblings and gatherings of documents and offended exits. Once they're alone the general approaches Sarnin, still disheveled from his fall but regaining his composure, and asks him if he knows who he is. Sarnin shakes his head. The general introduces himself with the appropriate profundity, asking now just who are you to come crashing through the window into my war room at a moment of extreme importance? Pvt. Garrett Sarnin of the U.S. World Allied Army. And how did he come to be here? A fluke, an explosion, a mistake. Sarnin's voice is trembling. What the general sees here is an opportunity to make a convert out of Sarnin. A screwball event such as this can't possibly be chance alone. Destiny, yes, *destiny* must be revealing itself to the generalissimo. He assures Sarnin he will not be harmed—that's not how the Cobrigalian army operates. Instead he will have the privilege of a tour of their operations, a bit of a crash course in the world vision of Vernon Cobrigale himself. You see, the general says, taking Sarnin by the arm and leading him out into the compound, I hold the sincerest belief that everyone in the world has an identity in the sense that they have none at all. Or, that is to say, at least the majority of people. Yes, each life is an accumulation of specific details, but are they really so unique? Most are simply at the mercy of those among the race with the *strongest* and *most uncommon* identities who, due to their exceptional abilities, are much better suited to manipulate the reality of the whole. In an open-top mechanized transporter, the general takes Sarnin to an average Cobrigalian village where the inhabitants are taught to believe in their own bodily transience, that nothing for the common Cobrigalian citizen is real, and that any achievement in life is a direct achievement of, and thanks to, the architects of society existing above them. For instance, the general expounds to Sarnin while they zip away in the transporter, you probably experience the phenomenon of slipping between parallel universes. Well I am not hindered by the debilitating disease of non-linearity. I know precisely my place, precisely my purpose in the world, the ways in which I can be evaluated and compared to any other person. I do not necessarily embrace the notion that my existence is a divine act, but the metaphor *is* helpful for conceiving of my importance. You, on the other hand, Pvt. Sarnin, are a shifting projection, and therefore cannot be entrusted with certain duties. You are not an individual, but a bonded part of a living whole. (Arnitz invites the reader to consider the nature of Gen. Cobrigale's own time in the dimension of cheddar cheese, living as a ball of light, and whether a mistake occurred during his own Festival of the Beginning of the End. But for as crazy as the general sounds, it is true that Sarnin is little more than a shifting projection. He's managed to hold onto a background identity, but nothing so impressive and actualized as the general's.) They tour the endless centipede queues of new Cobrigalian soldiers, enlisted into service, waiting to receive their weapons and uniforms, the appearance of the general above them inciting deep bass cheers from all. You see? he says. The purpose of most is the purpose of another.

Gerney looks at the back cover of the book, at the photo of H.Z. Arnitz. A wild-haired man with very thin eyes, anywhere between 25 and 35 years old. He reopens the book, pushing his face down into the open wedge. It fits nicely in there. He feels the paper against his skin, the fresh flat smell of the pages.

Gen. Cobrigale and Pvt. Sarnin journey across the continent, and everywhere they go the sound of cheering follows.

Sarnin is still in Gerney's ear.

You can see now, the general says, how human beings are empty and must be filled.

450 pages and not even half done.

The weak are possessed by the strong, says the general.

Gerney closes his eyes from exhaustion.

The night of The Ankle there was a debate whether or not Gerney should be taken to the hospital, but he insisted on remaining at the party. Even such a serious injury hadn't sobered him up entirely, and the prospect of medical attention, the questions, the lights, the looming authority, was unthinkable for him. But the real reason he refused to go had to do with humiliation, and for some reason he'll never understand, he had believed by not leaving he would be saving some measure of dignity. Eventually everyone tired of trying to convince him and went back to their business.

Nick Ibyoo stayed on the couch by his side the rest of the night, Autumn draping herself across his shoulder, face showing an intricate satiation of jet and sex. Gerney had his leg propped up at an angle by two pillows. Everything below the calf muscle was like a blood-filled marshmallow (Nick's analogy, enough to make Autumn retch). Unable to escape his nickname, the delay in aid would cause Gerney's movement to be forever slightly impaired, his left leg unable to correctly bear weight, always hinting at a limp. In the act of sniffing remnant gonine into her throat, Autumn said, "Can't you hear your phone ringing?"

It was his sister. "So all that noise in the background is why I haven't been able to get a hold of you all night."

Gerney's trying to contain the fullness of the memory, the emotion that had spilled from her voice, not right now, not tonight, laid back exhausted on the bed with the massive book open across his chest.

"You've been calling?" He could hear the mashup of drugs in his own voice.

"*Yes, yes* goddammit, I've been *calling* you! Why didn't you answer?"

"I, I sprained my ankle pretty bad."

"I don't care! I hope you feel terrible. I hope the fucking thing's broken."

"Kelsey, why are you calling? What do you need?"

"Dad's *dead*, you asshole, that's what I *need*. To tell you dad *died*."

"I…what?"

He could hear now, honing his attention beyond the noise of the house, that she had been gently crying through her anger.

"Kelsey, what did you say? I thought you said—"

"Dad is *dead*. We've been trying to get a *hold* of you."

Something in his head went off track and then didn't correct itself. No one in the room was noticing his change in demeanor.

"Where are you? Tell me where you are, I'm coming right now." He was distinctly, and not at all unsurprisingly, not internalizing the information.

"It's too *late* for that now, Kevin, we left up to the mountains six whole fucking *hours* ago. Where the fuck *were* you?"

"I don't understand. What happened?" She started to explain but he couldn't hear because there was a burst of voices. He tried desperately to quiet everyone down but didn't succeed.

"Kevin, please please *please* tell me you're not at a party right now."

"Fuck, Kelsey, tell me what happened!"

"He was in a coma for three hours and he died half an hour ago."

"But how did it—"

"I don't *know!* He was skiing, what else? He hit his head or something! I don't *know!*" She exploded into tears and screamed out in grief, the intensity of which Gerney is also, lying on his bed in a parallel universe, trying to contain in his memory. He wasn't crying, only sitting there, watching some people he knew across the room talking in a circle next to the TV which was flashing some huge amount of chimerical, disconnected things. Or maybe that's just how he remembers it. Maybe his memory prefers to tell this story in a tone of detached phantasmagoria.

"Kels, tell me where you are."

"We're at the hospital [—the way she was crying, looking for comfort, why didn't I—] and…and mom's in the other room…"

"Do you think I should—"

"No, don't come up here. She's furious with you."

"Okay."

"I'm mad at you, too."

The full explanation, which he only received later, was that his father had likely taken a run much too fast, and something, it could have been anything, maybe a small jump he'd landed wrong or the failure to avoid some obstacle, had caused him to tomahawk, to flip end over end, head to feet, briefly but violently, breaking his back and neck and giving him a head injury that made his brain swell. Dawn and Kelsey had been calling Gerney all day, but he had no memory of it. He would look at his phone after hanging up and see the missed calls, proof he had ignored them. His father had died. Become dead. Become whatever. A bunch of fading electrical signals in a bunch of degrading heads. For Gerney, too young to understand death, the deceased entered a special category—the discontinuation of their presence in the world was the discontinuation of his thoughts toward them. He couldn't even be sure if his own words at the funeral, eight days later, described a man whom he'd known and cared for, or were instead just impressions of a concept or dream he'd once had, fading with wakefulness, heading briskly in the direction of total dissolve. Tonight is the first time in a long time the word *dad* has entered Gerney's mind, but it must have been building in his unconscious because it's now torrential, washing through experiences previously having nothing to do with him. His father's will was perplexing. To Gerney he left a box of hand-written notes no one had known existed, a relatively huge sum of money, and their apartment in Grid. Kelsey received a pittance and Dawn got little more than what was owed her. There were no words left behind to explain the uneven inheritances, or at least not to anyone except Gerney. Dawn gave in to anger and refused to speak with him anymore, moving to Denver where she retook her maiden name and started her life over. Kelsey moved to a small town in the south of California to distance herself from the destruction of her family and the memories of her old home. She and Gerney rarely spoke.

The truly pleasant thing about gonine is it causes thoughts to race faster than the head can register them, as if the mind were a spinning rolodex, each dose increasing the rolodex's speed exponentially until all you're able to glimpse are bits and pieces of each thought's heading, and soon your movement through reality is strictly horizontal, the vertical having been zapped away so that for the first time you remember what it feels like to have an honest-to-goodness infantile disposition. You're anchored in the Now, the Present, like never before, and when you look back on yourself later, sober, once again navigating the syrupy idea of normal time, you're looking back on someone who is essentially a stranger. Someone who was not you because they didn't have the same anchors of Past and Future weighing them down, linchpinning them between contexts and dynamics. The stranger Gerney was that night is unusually burned into his memory. The whole thing is reduced to experiential data.

Nick turned to him, his lips moving.

"So then you never worked with cars?"

Gerney looked at him. "No."

"Doesn't matter anyway," Nick said shrugging. "I'm the fleet manager at Archelaos Chevrolet. Down on Motherboard Blvd? I'm pretty sure you've seen it. It's a huge complex, like in the shape of the Pantheon or whatever."

He had.

"Well Autumn told me [—oh jesus the exacting blade of it all, consumption of the weak by the strong, the purpose of most the purpose of another, and—] you haven't been doing well in school. Is that right?"

Response.

"Well right now we're hiring, and I always prefer to have trust-worthy people on staff. If you decide you wanna give it a shot, give me your application and I'll make sure it goes to HR with a good word. What do you think?"

Joe Meridian sitting in the background, smoking from a pipe, bowl glowing orange and smoke shooting from his nostrils in two solid obelisks, fearsomely mathematical, the dual structures dis-sipating in like...like a...like a *slight breeze*. Looking directly into the angular face of Nick Ibyoo, and Gerney could *see*, he swore to *God* he could see, that behind them, Nick's conscience was utterly unblemished. And he thought he could feel the first stages of what was another transition, a prior one. About how to escape, or maybe transcend, what was actually haunting him, driving him to bludgeon his senses. The transition away from introspection of any kind. It was there in his eyes, in his facial features. That great invulnerability. That great rapacity for all things arbitrary and self-indulgent. This was a new father figure. This is how he would incarcerate the emptiness inside him. Pure acceleration.

RANDY

The knocking on the outside of the hotel room door is not polite finger-knuckle knocking, it's angry side-of-the-fist pounding, and the sound of each impact detonates in Randy Mobyle's lysergic acid-filled head into severe spraying funnels of broken glass.

From behind the door, a muffled voice: "Goddammit, Mobyle! Open this door you pathetic worm! I know *exactly* what's going on, so don't bother hiding under some desk and envisioning yourself as some inconspicuous, very still bit of carpet dust! The effort would be useless!" A terrifying pause, then: "Flavorless! Is your bland boring ass in there?"

Victor Savoriss, Randy Mobyle's personal advisor and confidant, originally hired by Flint Vedge, is indeed in the hotel room, so in his tediously monotone voice answers, "Yes, Mr. Vedge, I'm here." His priggish, formal demeanor has earned him the nickname Flavorless from Vedge.

"Well then open the door, you pederast! We're *out* here, for Christ's sake!"

"I don't think that's advisable, Mr. Vedge, with all due respect."

"Victor, what made you think this was an *option?* I don't know if you can hear me out here, but I'm bursting into flames!"

"Apologies, sir, but that's my point exactly. This is an inopportune moment for any sort of hostile attitude. I regret to inform you."

"Do you understand, Victor, that time is not something which hands itself to me in abundance? This is not open for discussion! Victor? Victor!—do you *understand?*"

But it's precisely Victor who understands, at least in the truly important sense. Because a human being is a fragile thing under any circumstances, but a human being on an acid trip—especially Councilman Mobyle on an acid trip—is not something to go messing around with, much less *this* blazing fury ready to charge through the door. No, it would be at the very least unwise, and now it falls to Victor to stand his ground.

"I understand your concern, Mr. Vedge, but I'd like to get some understanding from you, too, if I could be so bold. Please realize, barging in here right now would be far more detrimental than helpful. We find ourselves in a situation not adherent to the kinds of everyday states of mind you and I are accustomed to. This is dependent upon a whole different plane of perception and—"

"Flavorless, you uptight formal-talking faggot, you will open this door instantly, and I mean right this *second*, or you will be living in a govt-initiative tract by the end of the week! Unlike you, I don't bullshit. You can *count* on that!"

There's pretty much no arguing with this. Right or wrong, he'll have to open the door. Reason, per usual, is a lost cause, especially the kind of reasoning pertinent to how to deal with someone on an acid trip, and Victor, more than accustomed to having to ignore the incompetence of political superiors, simply tosses this abuse in along with the ever-growing pile he has stacked in the back of his memory and opens the door to let in Flint Vedge and his corporate entourage.

The scene is ugly: Councilman Mobyle writhing on the couch near the floor-to-ceiling window on the far side of the room, his tie tucked into the front breast pocket of his blue pinstripe shirt which is horribly rumpled. Upon the entrance of Vedge he seems like maybe he's trying to bury himself into the couch where no one can get to him, hide like a cat in an unreachable corner until the coast is clear.

Observing this, Flint Vedge's sigh is heavy. He looks to Victor. "What is it this time? What'd he take?"

Victor is leaning against the full bar in the corner which has golden metal script anchored to the mahogany saying *Aero-Arrow Hotel*, hands in his pockets, glasses seeping down his nose. "Please understand, Mr. Vedge, before you react to what I tell you, that your behavior and general, well, *vibe*, will have serious ramifications for Randy's sense of inner—"

"Thin fucking ice, Victor. I've been strung out on non-stop scheduling for the last three days, so I have as much patience right now as a rat staring down a pair of hungry pythons. Do me a favor, assume from this point onward that I need you to skip all your bullshit commentary and get straight to the point."

Victor fiddles with the top button of his tan suit jacket. "Acid."

Flint Vedge grips the bridge of his nose between two fingers. "And so can I then assume that you were here when he ingested it? As in present at the time?"

"Yes."

For a second it looks like Vedge is going to lunge at Victor, his ire visibly foaming up, threatening to spill over. There are three suits in Vedge's entourage, all of them twitchy with the tense mood. Vedge marches angrily toward Councilman Mobyle on the other side of the room. Randy sees him coming and ducks behind the couch to hide, peeking terrified eyes up over the backrest. The massive spotless window has him floating up amongst the contrived future-gothic structures of Grid, trillions of bits of snow gusting powerfully through the illuminated night.

"You worthless piece of shit!" Vedge points and snarls, the suits not making even a halfhearted effort to restrain him, two of them heading for the bar and muscling Victor aside. "I can't believe this is what you've come to! Everything has been calculated, the least you could do for us would be to stay sober. Believe me, Randy, we're not necessarily stuck with you, no matter the time and resources we've sunk into this campaign."

Randy grips his head and squeezes his eyes shut because every-thing's starting to basically warp, spiral maybe, as if all reality were flushing toilet water. "Flint…" he says. "Flint…please, it's just…"

"It's just *what*, Randy? It's just *what?*"

"If you'd let me get…my thoughts in order…" A laugh bursts from him with a totally unintentional but tremendous mouth-farting noise. He slaps his hands over his mouth in horror.

"For Christ's sake, why bother? You're a fucking space case."

Vedge trudges back to the main part of the suite, collapses onto the leather couch, looking in need of a cigarette.

The two suits at the bar are drinking gin and tonics with an air of bored toughness. Another is studying the wall screen across from the couch with growing excitement. "Flint, you're not gonna believe this," he says.

Vedge looks up, a certain weariness in his voice. "Clark, what the hell are you doing?"

"He's been playing online Monopoly."

"Monopoly? Goddammit, I'm surrounded by gibberish."

"No, Flint, really, this is incredible. I've never seen anything like this."

Sauntering to where Vedge is sitting in total exhaustion is Victor, looking confident and composed. Vedge holds a hand up at him in protest. "I can *hear* your thoughts, Victor. Don't even think about it."

Clark, whose physique is obviously impressive even underneath a suit, is scratching the back of his head. "This has got to be the most deadlocked board I've ever personally seen. Four players, two surviving on mere allowances, then here's Councilman Mobyle's piece in the lead followed closely by someone named QuarkPlace35."

"Mr. Vedge," Victor says, "I know you don't want to hear it, but my recommendation is that you come back tomorrow when things are calmer." There's a subtle note of pleading in his voice that Vedge, on account of his ball-breaking style, just can't possibly abide by.

"You're lucky I don't bury you up to your waist in mud, Flavorless. I swear to God, just one more of these little incidents and you better believe I'll know exactly where to aim the big guns."

"Councilman Mobyle has the most diverse set of properties, which, if I'm reading the move archive correctly, involved trading leverage with Park Place and Boardwalk. Looks like he traded them over with two houses apiece to QuarkPlace in a powerhouse deal at a time of extreme cash influx for—it's hard to believe this is true—but for the orange and red monopolies, wholly undeveloped. Wow."

Randy has huddled himself against the giant window, spreading his fingers spiderishly across the glass, a veil of ugly badness descending slowly down over his trip.

Victor goes on. "Threaten me if you want. I'm only offering you assistance."

"What kind of assistance could I possibly need from *you?* How to sound like a human textbook?"

"*Intangible* assistance, Mr. Vedge, but nonetheless vital. You're obviously unequipped to handle the situation with Councilman Mobyle, and while your threats are intimidating, you know as well as I they're empty. You're, how you might say in poker, *pot-committed* to Mobylism. Or at least Clam Bell Holdings is, and that means InfoZebra is as well. At this point Randy is still a publicly deniable asset for you, and even someone like me has no trouble discerning that's worth more than a little drug problem."

Vedge is only able to breathe in recognition. "You're a real piece of shit, Victor, you know that?"

Clark is giddy with excitement. "Then look here, this is where Councilman Mobyle went on a blitzkrieg of property development. We're talking hotels on New York, Tennessee and St. James within just two turns. Additionally, the Councilman and QuarkPlace initiated a bidding war for the railroads over their cash-strapped owners, which led to the splintering of all transport and utilities between the two lead players. Tell me you're seeing this."

"Randy's having a crisis of conscience, Flint. It's not exactly surprising, given the circumstances, but nonetheless could be a monumental wrench in the gears."

A small whispering emanates from Randy in the corner: "I'm here…I can hear…I can…"

"So then cut to the chase, Victor. I'm actually listening."

"I don't have any sort of solution at the moment, but I can offer some insight into what's been throwing him off. Maybe it would be best if we didn't speak in front of him."

"Say what you're going to say," Vedge says, waving a hand. "Remember, time evaporates."

"It's starting to hit him that InfoZebra astroturfed his campaign. Lately he's been mentioning things to me about political ethics, information warfare, etcetera."

"But at the same time as the Councilman and QuarkPlace were dividing up the board, the other two players were developing some low-rent monopolies. If you follow the money here, and I think I'm reading this right, most of the profits toward the middle of the game were being reaped by who is now the player with the least net worth. Jesus, man, do you have to smoke that in here?"

"Randy knew from stage one of this whole thing the movement was astroturfed. No one ever lied to him about that."

"Yes, but it's obvious he didn't fully understand the consequences. He's internalizing them now." Victor motions to the psychedelic Councilman huddled on the floor with his face pressed against the window. "And anyway, something else has changed, too. He found out Tracey was a plant."

Vedge is immediately alert. "What?"

"He's known for a couple weeks now."

"How? Who told him?"

"She did."

"Tracey, you rotten bitch! I told Clam Bell this is why you don't try to fabricate all aspects of a person."

"Tracey…Tracey is a…zebra…love you Tracey…"

Clark coughs at his colleague's recently-lit cigarette. "The other two were pulling off big, odds-beating dice-rolls for about fourteen or fifteen turns here, not landing on any of the Councilman's or QuarkPlace's luxury properties. But it was only a matter of time, of course, before they had to start doling some serious cash. Their situations got [coughing] dire."

Victor cleans his glasses on his shirt, says, "Their relationship had been turning fractious, which I'm assuming you weren't aware of. He's been stressed."

"Oh please, Victor, we're all stressed. What man out there *isn't* having woman troubles? And I mean besides you."

"Most men aren't asked to deal with the fact that someone they believed to be the love of their life turns out to be a covert installation, all in the middle of a high-profile mayoral push. Really, you should consider yourself lucky he's handling it as well as he is."

"Dammit, where's Tracey now?" Vedge gets up to pace. "Has she run off or is she still around?"

"It's been back and forth. At the moment we're unsure."

"You damn well should've been keeping track of her, Flavorless, you goon, but not to worry. This sort of double-cross means forfeiture of compensation. She'll come running back just as soon as she sees her cash flow has been dammed up like the fucking Colorado River."

"Forgive me for saying I find it unclear how you think Tracey coming back stands to improve Randy's state of mind."

"Aren't you listening to him babble over there? The man is a helpless child. Tracey's a fucking goddess, you know that. She made him fall in love with her once, she can pull it off again. It's not 'adherent to the kinds of everyday states of mind you and I are accustomed to.' Not that I'd expect you to understand."

"Player three started hemorrhaging funds to the Councilman, which spurred a lot of high-cash trading of his properties, but of course he just lost all that money back. He's got a couple hotels on Baltic and Mediterranean that're keeping him alive, but ultimately it's hopeless. And player four's finances are even bleaker. They're waiting on the Councilman to roll."

The guy smoking dabs his cigarette to death in a fractalized crystal ashtray, finally losing patience with the play-by-play. "I don't get it, Clark. What's your deal with all this Monopoly shit?"

He looks at the screen a bit wistfully. "Me and my brothers used to play all the time…"

"Is that all that's been fucking with him?" Vedge urges. "Just Tracey and this whole crisis of conscience thing?"

"To my knowledge. Well, actually, no, he's started reading."

Randy, in the corner: "Strangely enough they…have a mind…to till the soil…and the love of possession…is a disease with them…"

"What do you mean reading? Reading what?"

"Books."

"Books?"

"…these people have made…many…many rules…that the rich may break…but the…poor may not…"

Vedge whips around to look at the Councilman, seething. "I mean listen to him! The bastard's brain is powdered sugar! What is this crap he's saying? Is he talking to me?"

"He's quoting Chief Sitting Bull," Victor says. "1877."

"…they take their tithes…from the poor and weak…"

"Well where the hell did he learn it from?"

"A book about the Battle of Little Big Horn. His ZChase algorithm recommended it to him. He made me read portions of it. Said some of the things in it were life-changing for him."

"Wonderful, that's just what we need. Randy Mobyle of all people getting his life changed."

"…to support the…rich…and those…who rule…"

For a moment it's relatively quiet, Vedge frozen in place at the centermost point of the room, eyes wandering, complemented only by the clinking of ice in glasses from the suits at the bar who are standing in silence. To Randy, still looking through the window, the silence in the room lasts into a strange infinity. The snow outside is coming down savagely, mercilessly, the little twisting bits struck into different colors depending which buildings they fall near to, everything together mounting to an exhausting palette of visual stimuli. All of it is (*jesus!*) interconnected and complicated and somehow dependent on the things happening in all these high-rise rooms across the city, the deals and the people and the secrets and the negotiations and the money, and it's all terrible. From here he can look down on the outline of the tower crane looming ghostly and behemoth through the blizzard over the beginnings of the bundled nanolaminated modumetal tube structure of what will soon be InfoZebra International HQ. A building still in its womb, he's thinking. *My* womb. *I* am responsible. Insane.

Flint Vedge's reflection materializes in the window, spotlit and overlaying the city, creating, for Randy, a really unpleasantly strong hallucination. Vedge kneels down, studies him in a way that makes him feel as if there's a kind of wall between them.

"Listen, Randy," he says after a while, undertones of threat in his voice. "I'm going to leave now. Leave you to whatever this is, to your"—motioning behind him—"*game*. But understand something. This thing already has a full head of steam, and we're barreling toward the finish, with or without you. So—you can either be here at the end to make all this mean something, or you can get swept away like one more piece of dust. It's really very goddamn simple. But trust me, no matter what you choose, you can count on one thing being, what's the word I'm looking for? *Immutable.* That I will win. So figure your shit out. Put all those wires in your head straight again, get some good healthy flows going, cheat on Tracey if you have to, whatever. I don't honestly give a damn. Because if you don't, you'll find yourself buried under a heap of shit that'll rival that new scraper out there for height. Get me?"

There's hardly a response, but Vedge seems satisfied. He pats the Councilman on the knee for good measure, then stands and says, "Scribble this down in that egg head of yours, Flavorless. Keep him. Away. From the fucking. Drugs. Against my better judgment, I'm going to assume you're capable of this."

"How can I guarantee that? It's not as if I could lock him up in a cage. He's a U.S. citizen, after all, and thus entitled to certain rights."

"Why do you always have to complicate things? I'll say it again— Keep him away from the drugs. I don't give half a damn how it gets done, whether you fight him, lock him up, or rip off his toupee. The point is I shouldn't have to keep an eye on him like he's my son. I've got enough on my plate already securing visitation rights for my own kids, so let's not add more to the pile."

One of the suits at the bar is discreetly answering his phone, throwing back the last of his gin and tonic.

"Let me suggest something," Victor says. "Let me suggest—"

"I don't want to *hear* suggestions. I'm twenty minutes behind schedule and I've got a terrible headache from too many things all at once. Don't give me excuses, just do it!"

"I mean with regards to messaging. If there were a way to let Randy incorporate some of his own political concerns into Mobylism, just for the sake of—"

"You're an intolerable squawking bird to me, Victor, so give it a rest. There's no time left for discussion. I have hereby mandated, and that is final. We're leaving now."

Vedge walks to the door, but his man at the bar stops him. "Hold on a second, Flint. Uh-huh? Yeah. Say that one more time. Okay. Okay, no, I'll tell him. Yes, he's right here. Yes. All right, bye."

Vedge, waylaid and agitated, throws out his arms. "What is it?"

"Clark, pull up the browser on the wall screen, please."

"What is it?" Vedge persists.

Everyone in the room, except for Randy who continues to twitch in the corner, gathers around while Clark minimizes the game of Monopoly and opens a new window.

"Okay, type this into the address bar. X-i-t-t-y-x-…"

"What the hell is going on here? Who was that on the phone?"

"Odie Manwaring."

"Well what'd he want?"

"They got a call thirty minutes ago about a situation with the InfoZebra website. Said you gotta look at it right away."

The window loads, and at the center of a plain white screen a tiny cartoon lion appears, smiling.

"What the hell is this? Saul, talk to me. I need answers. What is it I'm looking at here?"

"I don't know, Flint. Odie said thirty minutes ago links to this xittyxat thing showed up all over InfoZebra's website."

"On InfoZebra's *website?* That's impossible."

"He didn't elaborate, just said you needed to see it immediately."

"That's it," Vedge mutters under his breath, taking out his phone. "I'm calling Odie."

Victor leans in to look at the screen, the simple little lion cartoon. It depicts a female, maneless, filled in with solid tones of tan and brown, face nothing more than two dots over a smile line. Maybe Victor's just imagining it, but there are traces of fear in Flint Vedge's eyes as he waits for Odie Manwaring to answer from Clam Bell's Manhattan offices, but fear of what? There are so many things Victor will never understand about Flint Vedge, such deep inherent divides in character and status between them, because for him there is not fear, but rather an unmistakable feeling growing inside, expanding cautiously but definitely expanding, a feeling of sadistic hope that soon he may get to enjoy indirect revenge. For a split second, the two of them meet eyes and there's a moment of knowing that passes between them—they are enemies despite being on the same team.

"Odie," Vedge says, finally getting through, "what the hell am I looking at here? No, I just pulled it up. Well what is it? Saul says there are links to this thing on the InfoZebra site, what's that about?" Pause. "There's a link on *every page* to this shit? *What?* I...Odie... what is this thing? No, no I haven't yet. I'll call you back." Vedge hangs up, points at the screen. "Click the lion."

Clark taps his finger against the screen. The lion jangles to life with sparse, unskilled animation and begins to speak. The voice is female but heavily scrambled, rendering it dark, bizarre, horrible, an effect not lost on the Councilman, now up on his feet and shivering from a trip that has at this point gone completely wrong.

> "Hello, I am Xitty Xat. Did you know that, according to embryological evidence, zebras are not white with black stripes, but black with white stripes?"

Abject terror radiates like heat from Flint Vedge. Victor imagines himself warming his hands in it, joyful. A black and white photo of Randy Mobyle appears in the blank space above the shuddering little lion.

"Councilman Randy Mobyle has hidden his nature from the people of Grid. Mobylism, a city-wide movement which claims to advocate for the consolidation and organization of disparate public data so as to eliminate 'obscene governmental waste,' 'the unraveling of societal morality in America,' and 'the fundamental loss of attention spans and interpretive skills,' was in fact an astroturfed effort conducted by just five employees within the InfoZebra organization."

The photo of Randy is replaced by the InfoZebra logo placed next to a high-def shot of Flint Vedge exiting a limo onto a sidewalk, surrounded by the same entourage currently in the room, everyone's hair ruffled by wind.

"Did you know Councilman Mobyle's exploratory committee for mayor has been funded almost entirely by InfoZebra and its CEO, Flint Vedge, through shell companies and front donors? Did you know InfoZebra has secured a ten-year, tax-free contract to construct the company's new international headquarters in the center of downtown Grid at a cost of $185 million to the city?"

Now a picture of the unfinished InfoZebra scraper.

"The contract to build the structure was awarded to a subsidiary company of Clam Bell Holdings, which owns InfoZebra Inc. Did you know InfoZebra's ubiquitous ZChase info-adaptation software organizes user-specific content according to an undisclosed algorithm that places preference on products and companies owned by Clam Bell Holdings?"

In the background, a deep thrumming note has been slowly building, at first barely noticeable, now reaching crescendo. The phones of multiple people in the room are currently ringing, going unanswered.

> "Did you know InfoZebra and Clam Bell Holdings
> are timing the completion of their new headquarters
> in Grid to boost the candidacy of Randy Mobyle in the
> 2026 mayoral election, and that, through their contracts
> and ties with city hall and the user-content monopoly
> they will control with their ZChase algorithm, they
> plan to take top-down political and economic control
> of the city? Or that they have already displaced several
> hundred govt-initiative families from their homes near
> the construction site? The only way you can stop this
> from happening is by kicking InfoZebra out of Grid.
> Goodbye from Xitty Xat."

The lion goes silent, a cute dead zebra with x's for eyes appearing at its feet, smile line now smudged with blood. Randy has migrated all the way to the bar, leaning against it limply, his trip inescapable and traumatically bad. Victor is looking at the floor, and regardless of his own implication in all this, he can't help but feel like uncorking champagne. The suits are fixed on the reaction of Vedge, whose phone hasn't stopped ringing once since hanging up with Odie Manwaring, his whole expression disarmed and unreadable, the dark circles beneath his eyes smoldering with lack of sleep, all the energy gone from his posture, and quietly he whispers to himself, "My God…my God…when do I get to go to bed…?"

FISH

Complete orbital blowout of the left eye socket—that's why your eye appears sunken into your head like that, see? Broken index finger, ring finger and radius bone, all of the right arm. Bruised ribs. Nose bone snapped in three places. Collapsed sinuses. Lacerations along the right side of the face and neck from errant glass. You can also add onto that a major concussion, are you experiencing any blank spots in your memory? Ah, of course, that's perfectly normal. Now we've been having trouble contacting any family, is there a name or number you can provide us with? How about friends? I see, well, not to worry, we've got you under good care here, this is an excellent ICU. Overall, I'd say you were pretty lucky.

…lucky…

Morphine the Absolute, the Great Apathizer. Where am I in my own body? Most things still register, it's just you care so little. There's a faraway feeling, the feeling of my face being broke and swollen, breath ragged, but that's all toward the surface while here I am sunk very far down. The nurse reaches across me to adjust various instruments, whatever. On her forearm, just below the crux of the elbow joint, a scan code tattoo. Beneath it, in pale blue type, the name *Ms. Dos*.

I try to say something like, "Funny."

"Mm-hm," she murmurs sweetly, placatingly, no clue what I've said.

How did I get here? The morphine so strong its like a creature injected into first a single artery, then slithering its way into every passage before burrowing somehow even deeper, veins branching off veins, capillaries and arterioles, my whole body generating a chemical halo. I lift my hands in front of my face. They're covered in dried blood.

"I need to stitch up your eyelid." Nurse's face floats above mine, looking into my eye but not making eye contact, working on my body the way a person with a wrench works on pipes. "Will you let me do that, Jake? Do you mind if I call you Jake?"

I'm thinking, well it's not what I prefer, but okay.

"Jake? Can you hear me?"

I force out a sound.

"All right, Jake, this is going to be a little uncomfortable, but I need you to stay awake for me, okay?"

She takes my eyelid between latex fingertips and pulls it toward her. A series of sharp stabs initiates.

"Yeah, I know, I know," she coos, "that can't feel good, can it? But this won't take long."

"Are you Ms. Dos?" I ask, slurring and slow.

"I am, but you can call me Cate if you'd like. Still doing okay?"

"Dryou see tattoo?"

"Try not to get loopy on me, Jake. We've gotta get this done."

I like her fingers on my eyelid, her cooing, her seemingly complete focus on me. Feels like intimacy. She keeps referring to me as Jake, so I say, "My name is Fish."

"I know, Jake, we gave you a lot of morphine, but just try to concentrate on being still for me, please."

Linking a scan code to your socnet means the permanent loss of anonymity, an indicator of behavior modification. This is exactly what They want you to do, tag and number yourself of your own volition [stab]. She's a person who wishes to be connected, accessible.

Has nothing to hide? A marking which makes clear she identifies with Their system, schemed upon and manipulable but also bestowed with a great power. What do They want from me? Why do I find myself here? If I were to do something so minor, so innocent, as scan Ms. Dos's code [stab], would I be tossed haphazard along with all the others into her storage bin of data, siphoned off into a database or databases and nailed to the infinite wall of suspects? Scrutinized? Observed? Measured and undoubtedly controlled? And yet would it make me a piece of her? A part of something larger and sacred, something more real *than* real, trustworthy because trust no longer exists, and in the process becoming one of Them, plugged into an eternal sphere from which there's no unplugging. Floating in an ocean of morphine. She's a person who cannot be intimidated or undermined by anyone else, and They know this, so they allow her own humanity to enslave her [stab], her own intrinsic willingness to integrate and therefore obey. How can I prove my existence to you, Ms. Dos, so you could recognize me as more than a body to fix [stab], a person rather than a thing? I am a person. Right? So many entities, no, *personhoods*, webbed into the nexus of square pixels, their liminal presence intrudes on our privacy. Them, keeping a constant, probing eye out, never a moment's rest [stab]. Security cameras? Morphine's blurring my focus, forgot to check, forgot. Is there some kind of—

"All right, Jake, all done. Doing okay?"

I nod, feeling a few tendrils of clarity cut through the morphine, realizing finally this is a nightmare. All those years of precautions and security measures and in a single moment I'm more vulnerable than ever. There's a good chance They wanted it this way.

"Cate?"

"Yes?"

"What happened? Why am I here?"

"You don't remember?"

"No."

"I'm so sorry, Jake, we thought you were conscious, but you must have been going in and out. There was an officer here twenty minutes ago, he explained everything to you. You were in a car accident. You were going through a green light and a DGT bus came through the intersection illegally and there was a collision. The ambulance brought you here to St. Joseph's."

Cate Dos is Indian, skin dark and hair black, pulled into a tight ponytail, eyes large and framed by long lashes. The skin surrounding her right eye is darker than the rest, a discoloration or birthmark, roughly the shape of a star.

"A bus?"

"Right. The officer said the impact occurred at a fairly low speed. You were lucky."

(*Camillia*) "Do you have my phone?"

"Don't worry, we have all the possessions that were on your person when they took you out of the car."

"Can I have my phone?"

"Sorry, we have a lot of sensitive machinery in the ICU and phones aren't allowed in here."

"When can I…" (*They can look through everything, passwords and messages and*)

"Try not to worry about it right now. Soon enough."

"Am I going to be okay?"

"You're pretty banged up, but you're going to be fine. I promise."

There isn't much feeling in her voice, not much to suggest what she's saying is in any way genuine. Actually there is feeling, but it has an extremely rehearsed quality to it, a generalized sympathy.

"It's late and my shift is ending," she says. "But I'll be back tomorrow morning to check on you again. Goodnight, Jake."

And so now the night starts to creep along, but time, for the morphinated, is a useless concept. Sometimes I believe I'm awake when actually I'm asleep, and vice versa. There's another nurse, a kind but very punctilious black lady, who I wake up to from time to time standing at my bedside swabbing my face and neck with a cold washcloth, then she lifts my gown to give me painful injections the abdomen. The TV is an arcane old creature lurking in the far corner of the room, covered in knobs and dials and other deformities, staring at me through its single static-filled cataract. It's the same show all night, *My Friend Diagnosis*, an old sitcom. The main character is a middlingly handsome young dark-haired guy named Vaughn Rupture who's supposed to have disorganized-type schizophrenia. The episodes They're playing are mid- to late-series, very established in terms of character development, joke devices and catchphrases. The basis, recapped every episode in the opening theme, is that Vaughn Rupture lives by himself in an apartment complex in Los Angeles when a beautiful and unattached and psychologically normal young woman named Chloe moves in next door. They're thrown into a charmingly dysfunctional friendship. A big part of the show is sexual tension between Chloe and Vaughn, but they always remain platonic, and this constant hinting at a secret love between them keeps the audience in desperate suspense for the next episode, that thin lick of hope always encouraged and then always dashed. Chloe is Vaughn's only connection to any sort of normal life. He tries to blend in with her supporting cast of friends, a host of archetypical but endearing characters, all of them sharing many amusing failures and heartwarming successes together.

In one episode Chloe puts forth considerable effort to convince one of her coworkers to go on a date with Vaughn. Vaughn is painfully nervous about the idea of interfacing romantically but Chloe is tough with him like always because they're such good friends and doesn't let him chicken out. Finally the date happens, but at dinner, just as the audience is expecting Vaughn to be the one to ruin everything, his date dives into a self-centered monologue revealing herself to be a serial dater with flamboyant emotional scars, and Vaughn casually says to himself while looking off to the side (his date apparently can't hear this but the audience *certainly* can), "I don't know if it's just the voices in my head, but this sounds like *baaaag-agggge*," followed by an absolutely delighted surge of studio audience laughter. Later, back on the set of Vaughn's apartment, she seduces him, and just as the titillated *wooooooooooo!*'s start up, Vaughn is frozen with an inexplicable fear of the potted plant sitting on an end table near the couch, and says with his signature caricature of flat affect, "Oh god…"

"Mmmmm," says his date through kisses.

"Oh god…"

"Oh, Vaughn. Oh, *Vaughn*."

"Oh god… the plant is waving at me." Laughter.

She recoils, face twisted with confusion. "What?"

"The plant's waving at me. I think it's…it's *cheering* me *on*."

The coworker jumps off the couch, having at last lost patience with an entire evening of strange one-liners. "I don't understand, Vaughn. What's *with* you? Are you crazy or something?"

"Um, hel-*looo*. Schizophrenic?" The audience loses it.

Pain comes regularly every few hours, like appetites, and just as regularly is morphined away, the nurse entering and exiting the room at precise intervals, nodding with satisfaction at a schedule properly adhered to. *My Friend Diagnosis* isn't funny but I find myself transfixed episode after episode, Vaughn Rupture seeming so comfortable with his condition, almost as if he *enjoys* it. Chloe, always so forgiving of his distorted thinking, shrugging it off with an eye-roll to the audience. I'm not here in this hospital by accident, but who is part of it and who merely incidental? Pteranodon or Austin Ackyooclad or Wallace or Ms. Dos, the doctors, nurses, hospital administration? I don't trust these people, the machines in here thrumming steadily, the catheter stuck into my fin, the improbably old TV beaming in the corner. Can this be normal? Reality can neither implode nor explode, can only be stretched like fabric until it becomes so thin you can see a light shining through from the other side, the light of how things could have been, an entire shiny alternate limb of the universe that functions according to some different sort of logic. I have this idea of how things could have been for me. I try to trace back to a moment when something went wrong, I can't be sure what, something that left me stranded from others. I imagine a person who maintains a constant role in my life, someone who it's impossible for me to alienate. A friend. The idea is hard to concentrate on for too long because I start to miss someone who was never there. I have a habit of looking into the bathroom mirror in my apartment, pretending to pose for photos with made-up people. I'll hold a smile, as if I were looking at myself in a picture, wrap my arms around the shoulders of someone who isn't there, inventing contexts and relationships and settings, vacations with friends, backyard parties, a girlfriend, companionship that never materialized in my real life. Here I am waving to the camera on a beach with Mom and Dad; and here's me drunk outside a bar with Wallace and the girls he's always telling me about, everyone smoking cigarettes. These thoughts are involuntary, but my destiny was to be always looked at, spied upon, followed, history itself aware of me if not society. Humans a species of animal. Hills of little worker ants, disturbing in their numbers.

But there was a moment in time, I think, when things were better for me. I can only see it that way now, after the fact. A graze with friendship, with normality. I was twenty-four. I remember being less afraid, less attuned to a certain side of myself. Existing not so much within the extreme highs and lows I do now, but on a more even keel. I remember taking the GRT to the factory every day before I was able to purchase a car. I was seated next to a guy who looked my age, dressed in a sharp charcoal suit and reading a ZChase News Pad. I was looking at an ad on the opposite side of the train that featured a small animated roboseahorse swimming around in a glass bowl. The seahorse's gaze would autolock on people passing by or standing near it, following them around the clear convex wall of its aquatic prison, emanating from its snout promotional messages made of bubbles. Few passengers paid any notice. They stared down at News Pads, phones, off into space. The seahorse's autotracking locked on to me for a quick moment, running facial diagnostics to read age, race, current mood and socnet data, collecting and analyzing it all before bubbling to me: NOT ENOUGH ROOM TO LET YOUR INVESTMENTS GROW? The guy in the suit next to me said he noticed I worked for Pteranodon. I was wearing my work clothes. From the very first moment it was clear he was a person with the ability to start conversations with total strangers effortlessly. I don't recall my heart racing as it would if the same thing were to happen now—I see now that I was less closed-off. He pointed to his News Pad, asking me if I'd known something about Pteranodon using acesulfame potassium instead of real sugar in Plus. I said no, I didn't, I didn't even drink Plus. He said they'd been listing sugar on Plus's ingredients for nearly a year after the switch was made, but the FDA had only recently confirmed it. The company's rationale was that sugar had become too expensive, the global supply constantly shrinking. He said he wasn't surprised at all. It made perfect sense, in fact. After all, wasn't this what we'd been working toward all this time? A world where the chemical was > the natural? People should understand and accept by now, he said, that these sorts of developments were unavoidable, and the only sensible response was apathy, passivity. Nothing can be significantly changed. I cautiously measured out an answer that I couldn't really be sure about change, but it was definitely a problem, neither agreeing nor disagreeing. He introduced himself to me as Kellen Self, young black savant of the non-revolution. I said okay. He told me not to let the snappy suit confuse—he was actually situated well outside the system. According to him, he had smelled corruption coming from an early age, the stink of it all settling in too slow for most people to consciously notice, but he had keen senses. He'd spent years cultivating his instincts, training himself to spot the hidden signs that pointed to where the world was headed. He said the destination was Inhumanity or Bust, and fuck what the doubters believed. Shit was gonna go down, of that he could be completely sure, but it would go down in the form of silent despair in the midst of unchecked growth and advancements rather than screams in a burning apocalypse. It was all that same old Huxley-Orwell shit, man. Pretty soon we'd be starting wars just for the pretense of knocking down the obsolete so we could replace it with the exponential. You have to admit, he nudged, the whole thing definitely has its appeal. But of course there were consequences to think about… or, actually, come to think of it, maybe there weren't anymore. Who wants to play it safe when you're staring down the end of the world? It's the universally accepted time to blow your proverbial wad, allow yourself the luxury of going out with the fiery brilliance of exploded ordnance instead of the pathetic squeaking of a doused fuse.

I tried very hard to seem normal. To imitate his qualities of confidence and courage. I wanted him to see in my eyes that, though I could never articulate it the way he could, my feelings on the state of things were very much the same. Or at least he made me *think* they were. I had somehow stumbled upon someone with characteristics I very much admired, and I found myself wanting to purge my own personality in order to leave myself completely receptive to his. This was a good way of fighting the sickness developing inside me, a terrible ugly thing surfacing at the horizon of my mind, growing larger, bleeding with greater regularity all the time into my outward behaviors.

On TV Chloe walks into Vaughn Rupture's apartment to find him hiding in his own closet, fiddling with vacuum cleaner attachments. He looks like he's been in there a long time.

Chloe: "What are you doing?"

Vaughn: "Oh, what, this?"

Laughter.

Chloe: "Yes, *this*. Why are you hiding in your closet? It's two in the afternoon."

Vaughn: "There was a voice in this tube. A little man who needed me to help him get a special liquid. Hmmm, I wonder if this thing has a setting for schizophrenia?"

Laughter.

Kellen Self said I seemed like an interesting guy, would I mind if he inquired as to how I pulled back the Membrane? I said what Membrane? He was surprised. He couldn't believe someone such as myself wasn't up on pulling back the Membrane. Cause the Membrane was everything, man. Or at least pulling it back was. You gotta step behind the mirrors and lights every once in a while, check out the backstage area—did I know what he was talkin about? I said I didn't. Elevating my *perception* was what he was talking about, transcending the eight inches in front of my face, slipping underneath the Membrane like school kids sneaking into a movie theater. That place beyond the Membrane, he said, was where you could get a true glimpse of what we were coming to. It was horrifying, that place, but he whispered to me that he had to look. The Truth, for all its gruesomeness, was too refreshing, too addicting. Because the way we were thinking on a day-to-day basis was all a fucking lie, he said. We were thinking this way because we were taught to, plugged into a system of values and symbols the second we came screaming into the world, and he was disgusted with it. He said he knew what most didn't. That this whole thing we had going here, this whole human civilization, was balancing on the tip of a toothpick. It would take the cooperation of more people he could ever hope to muster to nudge the weight of it off-kilter just a smidge, send it all toppling, but if he could ever get quite so organized then I'd better believe he'd breathe deep the fresh winds of doomsday. Or at least so They'd call it. Regardless it didn't matter, he said, cause he long ago had realized revolution was hopeless. This was, after all, *non*-revolution. I said yes of course. He handed me a business card and told me if I was interested in seeing what he was talking about, all I had to do was call. Then he exited the train at a downtown station near the shopping district.

I didn't wait even a week to call. I was fascinated by him, amazed at the idea there was someone out there I could relate to. Over the phone I asked if his offer was still good. Not only was it still good, he said, but redeemable that night if I could swing it. I had to take the GRT from the northernmost end of Grid where I lived all the way to the outskirts of the suburban developments in the motherboard tract—an hour and a half trip. And even though the streets were wide there and the houses had astroturf lawns, I had the sinking feeling that behind all those ornate doors in all those ornate houses, things were decaying. Kellen Self's house was a brownish-yellow duplex tucked into the backwaters of a thoroughfare, cars and sirens flowing constantly out on the street. Both units of the duplex were owned by the group Kellen had founded, the American Non-Revolutionaries. Although the duplex had seemed modest from outside, inside was twisting and complex, housing what felt like dozens and dozens of people. Kellen introduced me to everyone, saying this was going to be an important night for me. A life-changing night. I hadn't expected all this, so many people. Kellen assembled everyone in the living room. He made a speech, saying this was going to be something special. Yet another blip of meaningless peace firing off in the dark machine. Another fruitless act of non-revolution. He was no longer wearing a suit, but now a baggy white robe woven of rough hemp. He appeared mystical, a bearer of secret knowledge. Standing near me in the living room was a young girl wearing a tanktop. She had tatooed on her back, on the smooth skin of her left shoulder blade, a depiction of self-immolation. The devouring flames stood out in vivid violet, smoky ink-shading puffing off the serene little human figure that floated in a state of torture on the plane of her body. Her eyes had an empty detached look suggesting complete concentration, total intent. She was hanging on Kellen Self's every word, matching perfectly with the rest of the house's residents, most of them close to me in age and seemingly very used to such a communal dynamic. Kellen said we were going to be privy to something very rare. A wholly natural event. We were going to be treated to an experience long extinct in American culture, using a naturally-grown ingredient. He said this was an exercise in perception, not in frivolity. Of course they all knew the spiel, he said, but the ANR was not about satisfying the desire for simple entertainment. As a reminder, this was some seriously *monastic* shit we were about to engage in. No TV, no maga-zines, no books, no movies, no computers, no phones, no packaged foods, no branded clothing, no corporate music, no fucking video games. This was free and clear of all that. We listened obediently.

Soon afterward trays holding steaming mugs of tea were distributed about the room. The taste and smell were terrible so I sipped slowly, now wishing I hadn't come here at all. I'd foolishly been hoping for friendship, nothing more complicated than that, but what I got instead was the ANR and their own strange compulsions of organization, observation. Another They among Theys. I was staring the decay directly in the eyes now, the world boiling down to an endless series of concentric prisons. Kellen Self approached me, fresh-shaven face calm and hands clasped together in front of him so the billowing sleeves of his robe connected. He asked did I not like the taste of the tea? I said no, it was extremely bitter, almost rotten. He said the taste would grow on me, but it was important I drink it quickly. A confidence glowed in his eyes that was somehow soothing, persuasive, almost familial in its concern. I started to chug the tea but when I couldn't quite finish he pushed the mug gently upward in my hands. I stood there hacking and gasping for breath, trying to suppress the urge to vomit, warm spit pooling under my tongue and my esophagus jumpy. Kellen Self said good, very good, he would find me later at a more important time, but for now I should go meet my fellow non-revolutionaries. I tried to stop him from leaving but he was gliding away already under his white vestments. (Chloe is with Vaughn Rupture at the cafe set down the street from their apartment building, drinking coffee. She's saying, "Oh, no, yeah, of course I like you, Vaughn. You know I think you're a *great* guy. I mean, yeah, you're like my *best* friend, but it's just that I'm really not in the right…um…*place* in my life to have a relationship at the moment? Sure, that's it. Just, I'm not in the right place. Mm-hm. Simple as that. You know how it is. Heh heh. Yep.") The other members of ANR had dispersed about the house, and I was left alone in the living room, swallowing my own spit. My vision changed rapidly. The maze of the house was unending, different people inhabiting different rooms and hallways. I wandered around in a state of shock, of Membranelessness, suffering from constant silent panic. In one room there were three people laying face down on the floor, bodies parallel, noses pressed into the carpet in unmoving submission. In a bathroom I saw people naked and huddled together in a tub. In a small shadowy alcove I met a guy a lot younger than me who wanted to know if I could feel all these signals in the air, all these fucking invisible *signals*. You could see them, he said, if you knew how to look. There was a room with bunkbeds where six or seven people were arranging scraps of paper on the floor to resemble an expansive tree, someone convulsing in a corner. By the laundry room there were people staring into a full-length mirror, frowning at themselves, then smiling, cycling through expressions, wobbling unsteady on their feet. I'm sure the house must have extended many levels underground. There was a sense of endless architectural confusion. I walked for a long time, every hallway bisected by another silent hallway, encountering nothing but incandescent dust motes and closed doors. I stopped to rest, legs burning and hands grasping at the walls for balance. The girl from earlier with the self-immolation tattoo rounded a corner and drifted by, not stopping or even turning her head to acknowledge me, eyes set straight ahead—a fluid apparition—disappearing down another bisected corridor. Hours passed. At my most desperate I opened a door and found Kellen Self and what seemed to be the entire ranks of the ANR in a large room with no furniture, arranged into a circle on the floor, everyone's eyes closed and bodies shadowy under the low-wattage lighting. Spaced in ten second intervals, Kellen was reciting non-revolutionary dogma. I stood in the doorway, leaning against the doorjamb from exhaustion.

Civilization itself, Kellen enunciated, is technology. From inside technology, time is accelerated.

I wanted out. I wanted away from whatever this was. I wondered in a panic: if I didn't exist, would the ANR not exist either? Had this been going on for years, or was it a product of my arrival, a projection by and for me alone?

Civilization, and therefore technology, structures time.

The people in the circle had their shirts off, and I noticed they all had the same self-immolation tattoo, all on the left shoulder blade, the only distinction between them the color of the flames, which differed according to the person. In my mental state I could see the flames moving, raging out of control while the burning figures did nothing, turned rapidly to char and collapsed into scorched piles.

Civilization is exponential.

Civilization is composed of individuals, but individuals are not civilization.

Individuals, by nature, are not exponential.

Images began to transmit through me of people two hundred years ago, all of them trying in vain to scrape their way toward the future, toward the current day and well beyond, not believing their lives would end. I could see their faces—dirty and dignified and full of rage. As they crawled they left a residual trail of progress. Enormous empty buildings, cutting edge communications infrastructures, pieces of vulnerable artwork frozen in recordings and on canvases, bulging records stating the minutes of meetings gone inscrutable and irrelevant. I can't explain it but all this was involuntary, a product of our minds grouped together.

Individuals are plodding, slow to make connections and interpretations.

Individuals strive to be good, and are separated from civilization.

Individuals who attempt to merge with civilization, to move exponentially within its structure, cease to be individuals.

Civilization strives only to be greater in speed, size, power and complexity, but it does not strive for either good or evil.

I could taste the tea on my breath, on the outer edges of my tongue. The ANR kept their eyes resiliently shut, some straining with the effort, some placid, peaceful.

You are all individuals, therefore separated from civilization.

As individuals, you strive for good.

In civilization, *you are fish out of water.*

The words knocked me back, a hallucination I couldn't control setting in immediately, as if I'd been submerged in water. My body went cold, mouth wet. I had trouble standing because my legs were changed. My arms felt weak and flat, eyes expanding to enormous circles, grinding to the sides of my head. Vents on my neck opened and closed, struggling for air.

In civilization, you are fish…

I staggered back against a wall, and when I looked up I met with Kellen Self's gaze. The rest of the ANR remained locked in meditation, eyes closed. Only his head was turned to me. I pleaded with Kellen silently, but his stare was blank, fanatical, without pity. He said that,

Within civilization, individuals are reduced to lost fragments.

I can't say how long it took to find my way out of the house because I was existing outside of time. On some unconscious level my body guided me back to the GRT station, now deserted in the early hours of the morning. But instead of getting on the train to go home, I sat in a secluded corner of the terminal where you could feed a QR code money to watch twenty minutes of TV at a time on your phone. The cathedral ceiling of the station rose above me, and I stared at my arms—now fins—shaking. My eyes had trouble focusing. There was every reason in the world to be afraid. I fed the machine all night, saturating myself with images and huddling close to the screen, feeling its warmth. The TV said, Civilization is about a collective of individuals, all acting as one in a diffuse system of identity based on shared culture and experiences, duh. In civilization, and therefore technology, loneliness is connected-ness. Don't bother with what those crazy people back there say, it's not all as bad as they'd have you believe. I said whatever you say. Whatever you say…

Was I asleep? My room has no windows, the best way of determin-ing the time of day is what's on TV. It's still *My Friend Diagnosis*, but the commercials consist of jobs and education rather than products and sex. Cate Dos is sitting on the edge of the bed. She's holding a curved empty plastic jar with a pink biohazard sticker on the side.

"Morning, Jake. How did you sleep?" The tone of her voice is softer this morning, less coldly professional.

I try to sit up. "Fish."

She looks down at her hands, nodding. Like yesterday, her hair is pulled back against her head, exposing its easy sloping curvature. The way she's looking down I can see her profile, her eyelashes and nose and lips at that familiar expressionistic angle: contemplation, pensiveness. "Yeah," she says, "you said that last night, too. I thought maybe it was just the morphine."

Her body language suggests more than just an easing of demeanor. Why is she sitting on the bed? I look at her, trying to remain calm.

"Why do you want to be called Fish? Jake's a nice name. Fish is bizarre."

(A trap? a lure to get me talking?)

Trembling, I force myself to ignore it. "I like your nickname."

"What nickname?"

"Ms. Dos."

She self-consciously puts a hand over the tattoo. "Oh, that. That's not a nickname."

"What's the jar for?"

"I'm sure you're ready to go to the bathroom."

Every move she makes I'm analyzing, every word she speaks. Because if this really is affection as a means of coaxing me out of my defenses, I'm having a hard time resisting.

"I wanted to ask you a personal question," she says.

"What?"

"You haven't had any visitors since you came in last night. We weren't able to track down a single family member or friend. You haven't even *asked* if we tried to get a hold of anybody. Normally that's the first thing."

(Microphones? police in my apartment?)

She bites her lower lip. "Why are you all alone in this world?"

The TV returns to Chloe and Vaughn Rupture on the cafe set, right in the middle of a comically silent lunch. The laugh track is sporadic as they take turns looking up at each other, trying to think of something to say.

"I-I have to be careful. But sometimes it hurts."

"What do you mean careful?" she asks almost in a whisper.

"Just…careful."

I close my eyes. The morphine is still strong.

"How old are you?"

I'm surprised I have to think about it a second. "Twenty-eight."

Her scrubs are dark red, almost magenta, the contrast with her skin flattering. Her presence is mildly melancholic, deeply perceptive, empathetic. I can't remember the last time I said anything confiding. Why now, why her?

"Could I please see a mirror?" I ask.

"Mm, I don't think that's a good idea. I don't want to give you the wrong impression, but you'll just have to trust me. For now you should focus on resting up. All I can tell you is, it's not that bad. You're scheduled for surgery later this afternoon, they'll do a good job fixing you. Try not to think about it."

"I can't go into surgery."

"What? Why not?"

"No money."

"Oh, I wouldn't worry about that. Money's not going to be a concern for you for a while. I assume your car was insured?"

"Yes."

"Well that was a city bus that hit you. They're fucked."

"Oh."

Here I am, drugged and helpless. They've already got me, why play games? Why continue to fight Them? Why do anything anymore?

"What do you do outside of work, Jake?"

(Don't you already know?) "I'm an artist."

"What kind of artist?"

"Painter."

"What kind of paintings do you do?"

"I can't say."

"Is there a reason?"

"There are some."

"Will you paint about this experience? About being in the hospital like this?"

"It doesn't work that way. Painting about your own experiences doesn't interest people."

"It doesn't?"

"No."

"Well why wouldn't it?"

"Because it assumes people care about you."

There's an awkward silence. I don't know what to say, my body dragging me into unconsciousness, all the little noises in the room hypnotic. There's a small clicking to my left, the electric straining of the TV clearly audible. I can hear the hundreds, thousands of people in the hospital all walking, shuffling, limping around at once. My brain falling into the spaces between sounds, drifting away, hand-in-hand with emptiness.

"I'm going to be completely honest with you," Ms. Dos says.

"Hmm…?"

"I know you're tired, Jake, but please listen. It's important."

"Okay…what is it?"

"I'm very attracted to you."

My eyes open.

"I realized it last night, after I got home. It's got something to do with the way you talk to me."

I stare into the eye with the star around it. The pattern in her iris is a tiny brown intricate burst. I feel tears welling up at the sides of my eyes, but I force them down.

"How can you, how can you tell? I'm full of morphine."

"There's a quality I see."

"A quality?"

"Yes. I noticed right away that you seem to believe, at the center of your being, without a crumb of doubt, that you have absolutely no chance of ever making me like you. And not just in, y'know, a romantic way. In any way at all. Not even as a friend. Your total resignation is… sexy to me."

I'm entirely blank, entirely speechless. I must be talking with my eyes because she says, "You're wondering why. I'm going to tell you something about myself, Jake. Complete honesty is gonna be paramount here, and so I have to tell you that your lack of confidence excites me in a purely kinky way. It's very rare I'd ever approach a patient like this, so I hope you realize how special the situation is."

I'm sweating, still forcing back the tears I can feel fully formed inside, every droplet a demon. I get the sudden impression there are microcams hidden on her person, but no matter how clearly I recognize the thought as irrational it hangs there in the front of my mind, busy convincing me that something I know isn't true is true.

"So just to be clear, I wouldn't want there to be any illusions of traditional feelings between us. That part is vital. What I'm talking about could be classified as perversion, domination, submission, sadomasochism, whole menus of odd sexual release, videos, pictures, leather, whips, fetish, psychological toying with the interconnectedness of sex and death like an amused kitten. So that's about the level I'm talking on."

(There are microcams, I know it, my logic is sound because it's unsound, but I have a fascination, an obsession, with paranoia that's hindering me at every single step of my life and I should control myself, but no, that's what They want me to think, They want me to believe I have an obsession with paranoia, that it's all in my head so I'll let my guard down, the only thing saving me and killing me at the same time, but I'm so stupid, there's no proof of any of this, I think They put *My Friend Diagnosis* on the TV hoping I'd identify with Vaughn Rupture, question my limitations, it makes perfect sense)

"I'm offering you the chance to know me, and yourself, better than you ever could through normal means. A person's kinky side is also their truest. All those things they tell us to look for out there— true love, total equal respect between individuals, raw life-changing empathy, growing old together in a nice comfortable house in the motherboard tract—it's just so lie-infested. The truth is, our first instinct upon meeting someone we're sexually attracted to is not to circle around the other person, intricately snare them into some complicated trap of physical intimacy. No. What we want is to consume one another, experience every depraved possibility that draws us together, and then, in the wake of satisfaction, we can have the privilege of actually knowing one another. Is any of this making sense to you?"

(Yes it does, but I don't want to die, I don't want to leave myself open to someone who's motives I can't comprehend, someone I know isn't who she says she is)

"I can practically *feel* you thinking. Has anyone ever told you that? I could feel it yesterday when I was stitching your eye."

"I'm sorry."

"And now apologizing for nothing. You're too good to be true. I think we could have a lot of fun."

The back of my head is sinking into the pillow, sleep impending.

"If you're lucky, if you prove yourself, I might let you scan me. That's where the real fun is at."

My brain is ice-cream under a morphine hairdryer. Ms. Dos's image turns fuzzy.

"Obviously you're not in the best state to take all this in. You've got a big day ahead—surgery and more painkillers. All I ask is that you think about it. I think it might do both of us a lot of good."

She leans across my body, puts her hand in my lap, on my erection, and whispers in my ear, "Pee in this jar."

Then it's like she's instantly gone from the room, pulling an evanescence act, sleep slamming into consciousness like an out-of-control bus.

When I wake up there're a couple guys in scrubs standing on either side of the bed unplugging and preparing things, basically indifferent to my presence but saying with detached softness, "All right, Mr. Kleene, here we go. That's good, very good. I'm just gonna grab this here, you might feel a slight…okay, there we go, see that was easy. Okay, here we go, Mr. Kleene, just stay awake for us, please. Just a little longer."

"Where are we…?"

"We're taking you to surgery, Mr. Kleene. Time to get fixed up, right? Stay awake for us, please."

They're rolling my bed somewhere, all I see is ceiling passing by in neat geometric constellations of white tiles. I could be anywhere, maybe not in St. Joseph's at all but a soundproof building where They're going to inject me full of scopolamine, ask me who I am, why am I this way? They realize I'm dangerous—that's why They do it. I'm important somehow, even if it's not yet clear to me in what way. But I know I am. There's no other explanation for why I've been isolated my entire life. I can't remember what happened with my family anymore, but I must have purposely alienated myself from them to make sure they were protected. Anyone close to me would have been captured, interrogated, victimized. It had to be done. When they asked me to leave I didn't utter a single word in protest, I knew we had all come to an understanding. I remember my dad gave me three hundred fifty dollars and said good luck out there. He was taller than me. I left through the front door of our house in Denver, we used to live right underneath the city's holo-projection—the giant spinning yellow letters and scan code. We had a big slab of concrete in our backyard where my brother would sometimes lay and look up at the enormous D passing over the rooftops, then some seconds later the R would swing by silent and mammoth and three-dimensional, the rest of the letters occluded by all those houses pointing toward the sky. I was standing on the front porch with my dad and he said find someplace to stay first, then worry about everything else. I was eighteen years old and I looked up at the yellow spinning letters. He shook my hand and said don't be afraid to come back from time to time if you need help. I turned and left. I don't remember what that felt like. Why don't I remember what it felt like?

They roll me into a room, position me near some empty aluminum trays at eye-level. Across the room is a nurse in hat and mask washing silver tools in a sink. An older man in the same hat and mask leans over me.

"All right, Mr. Kleene, Rina is going to go ahead and put this on you. There we go. Now I want you to just relax and count backwards from ten. For some reason we've had people who were afraid to count backwards toward zero. Something about the number gave them the willies. So, if you'd rather, you're welcome to count from one well on into comfortable infinity. In my less experienced days I tried to explain that even past the number zero exist entire realms of numbers extending well into the microverse, but please, whatever's most relaxing for you personally is fine."

"One…"

They put you under and when you wake up you believe in what isn't real. They implant the idea of safety, extract the fear of a world too prolific to keep up with.

"Two…"

I open my eyes and every ceiling tile has dozens of pinpoint holes saturated through the middle of each rectangle, arranged in no particular order. Perfect hiding spots for microcams. My grade school had the same type of ceiling tiles, and back then the holes seemed like an intentional secret. My child mind had trouble comprehending them. Only a very select few of us weren't tortured by the mystery of it, and those kids had seemed inhuman. How did someone poke all those holes in every single tile? There were too many to count, and each tile was different. In the back of my mind I must have known it was done by machines, I have trouble imagining myself so naive, but always I would be looking up at the ceiling during times of boredom. Sometimes we even mentioned it aloud. "Have you ever noticed how the ceiling tiles have all those—" "*Yes*, thank God someone finally said something, I thought I was losing it there for a minute."

The bones in my face ache. The aching grows into streams of flame funneling through my marrow, the feeling radiating toward the tendons in my neck. I've been groaning in pain without realizing it, but now someone appears above me, his image rendered watery by the tears dribbling from my eyes. The signature rush of morphine expands through my veins from the middle of my fin, warm torpor taking over, but the pain in my face is resistant.

"The next few hours are going to be pretty tough," I think the nurse says to me. "But you're just gonna have to wait them out. We'll give you morphine, but all you can do is wait."

My brain flips into panic-mode. It's hellish, no means to get away. I'm drowning in it, it's crowding my mouth, my nose, my eyes.

"My face…" I say, pleading. "…hurts…"

"You're going to have to hold steady, sir, I'm sorry. Hold on a sec, I'm going to get someone to move you back to ICU."

"Wait…"

The bed is moving again, wheels murmuring across smooth floors. I'm containerless liquid. I'm cigarette smoke disappearing into daytime. Electron morsels blazing through power wires raised up over congested superhighways. High-powered cell phone signals zipping mathematically through the upper atmosphere. AI enemies roaming playerless hallways. Brain cells smeared on a petri dish. A tiny bed-ridden entity hidden in one of countless cube partitions in a sprawling structure taking in an archaic pixilated screen filled with Vaughn Rupture, who's not actually Vaughn Rupture, someone else is Vaughn Rupture, maybe me, living my life through him, aware of my defect but not comfortable with it, and me or Vaughn Rupture is saying, "This is gonna be the best disorganized-type Christmas ever!" Fuck. I'm a single spider eye in the dark upper corner of the porch at my old house in Denver ten years ago, watching Mike Kleene grip Jake Kleene's hand and saying good luck out there, here's three hundred fifty dollars and you understand of course this is nothing personal, son. I'm a crow passing through the 3D holoprojected matrix code as it swings past Andy Kleene's line of sight while he lies in his backyard on a slab of concrete, thinking why don't I ever get any attention for being the good kid? I'm a particle of air being inhaled by Lavonne Kleene as she watches her husband shake her son's hand from the second-floor window, telling him good luck out there, nursing a black bruise underneath her right eye and looking away in fear when her son looks up at the massive spinning letters over the house, shuddering at the thought of eye contact. I'm a bantam speck of dust in a bar of sunlight in an empty room down the hall from where Lavonne is standing, floating across the recently-vacated air, finally landing hours later on a bare mattress underneath a wrinkled poster of a Rocky Mountain scene, fish swimming against the current underneath the glassy surface of a river.

I'm in ICU, it's been a mild eternity. Here is Ms. Dos now, her head eclipsing the TV screen in the corner. She's beautiful, her skin the color of chocolate and hair the color of very rich soil, so rich you could plant yourself up there, thrive and grow and change. Reboot. Access the operating system.

"You look like you're on drugs," she says. "How was it?"

"I don't remember."

"How do you feel?"

I'm unable to speak.

"Have you been in here trying to link up the separate narratives of your life into one cohesive whole? That tends to be a pastime amongst the sick and injured."

"You've never been"—[grimace]—"sick or injured?"

"Of course I have, but not often. What about you? Are you a semi-permanent resident of hospitals?"

"I don't...no...I don't think..."

"Sorry to bug you, I just wanted to see how you were doing. I'll leave you alone now. Feel better, sweet."

The pain subsides by degrees. One hour isn't as bad as the next, endless strands of Terradon Plus cans whipping past, the dinosaur silhouettes on each can writhing, hissing, everything sick with sequence. $1 + 1 + 1 + 1 + 1 + 1 + 1 + 1 + 1 + 1 + 1 + 1 + 1 + 1$ into infinity. A can for every second, every breath, every blink, every bone, every person, every day of history stretching off into the past and future. Cans that will outlive me. Each one INNOCUFILLed with brief life by machine screams. It's later. Cate Dos is back, checking my catheter.

"I see you're up. Good morning."

"...did you see how many cans?"

"What?"

"I'm sorry. I'm awake. I just realized."

"Feeling better?"

"Yes."

"Well you're looking much better, too. We'll be moving you out of ICU in a few hours."

"Can I have my phone?"

"Sorry, not yet. Not till you're out of ICU."

"Okay."

She looks up from her work. "Worried about Camillia?"

I swallow so hard it hurts. "What?"

"Let me be honest with you, Jake. Forget her."

"How do you know her?" Then it dawns on me. "You looked through my phone."

"She's a ghost."

"Why did you look through my phone?"

"A shade of reality."

"Who are you? What do you want?"

"There's nothing but text messages from her and spam numbers."

"Please."

"I'm in a position to know the difference between what's real and what's not. Trust me, I can spot outsiders. She's a fraction of what you or I represent. Your face speaks volumes the same way my behavior does. We're the material that affects the material, true flesh, true soul. She's a momentary digital butterfly alighting on the Great Computer Screen. Don't be destroyed by an imitation, all right?"

"Who are you?"

"A human being totally unencumbered by falsehood. Who are you?"

"I knew this was coming."

She seems nervous.

I have to laugh at myself, at my stupidity and recklessness. "This is all a construct."

"What are you talking about?"

"Get out."

"Jake—"

"Fish. You're not getting anything out of me, understand? I don't know anything about her so it would be useless to ask."

She stares dumbfounded, realizing she's been found out. The star around her eye has turned jagged, menacing. "I have no idea what you're saying."

"Yes you do."

I turn my head so I'm looking at the wall. For a long time I sense her standing there, staring at me, frozen to the floor. I fix my eyes on a single point in the white space of the room, trying to go lifeless. The only sensible response is apathy, passivity.

"By the way," she says just before leaving, "we looked through your phone to get in contact with someone who knew you."

I turn to look at her. She's standing at the door in mint green scrubs with her hair pulled back against her head.

"We left two messages explaining that you were hurt and in the hospital. That was three days ago. She hasn't said a single thing. Not a call. Not one word."

She disappears through the door. An hour goes by, normality settling back in like a slow fog.

ARIA

Now I'm awake and the edges of my window shades are greased with sunlight. Sunny winter mornings in Grid are the neon yellow color of lemon dish soap. You can reach into the frozen air and get a chemical lather going. The wind outside comes through insulation cracks in the apartment as an ambient howl, and for a second I've forgotten it's my day off. My hair is fluffed to both sides across my pillow so I feel buried, I have to rise out of the womb it creates to return it to normal shape. I fell asleep to streaming programs on my computer last night and it sits on the bedside table to my left, still streaming a show featuring two cartoon microchips sporting arms and legs jamming out with death metal guitars, headbanging, the music like gonine-incarnate. What I have to do is reach over in a daze to slap the keyboard, brain still underwater. The computer emits a small egg timer *ting!*, the sound programmed to alert me to email. There's this funny little animation that shows an oven opening up to reveal piping hot emails. The screen of my phone, sitting halfway over the edge of the table next to the computer, is slowly pulsating. Voice messages. I was dreaming about someone from my childhood, from school, someone I haven't thought of for 15 years. I had very little connection to him even back then, but he had been an invaluable piece of the texture of my surrounding world, someone vital even though I didn't understand why. The kid had acne, styled brown hair, branded clothes, and I pretended not to like his sense of humor. He's wading back up to me now, a fuzzy image of him against the advancing blackness of sleep. God, I remember his shoes. They had electric bolts drawn on them in blue marker, on the sides, and they were zapping this pen-drawn cartoon pig in the ass. In half-consciousness these details are foreshadowing; they represent something about myself that is now lost—something I'll never get back again.

I shoot up from my pillow, nearly hyperventilating. The edges of the drapes still bleeding early morning sunlight. The screen of my phone pulsating. There's recognition that I've finally struggled into wakefulness.

Fifteen of seventeen new emails are from my regional manager, Cal Wellfern. He's this unstable guy whose work emails gradually took on the tone of confessional letters, the business-related point of the message usually hidden somewhere in the middle of the prose. Everyone on his mailing list, I happen to know, hates being subjected to his rants since they're pretentious and overly personal and irrelevant to the average person's daily list of things to care about, everyone except the person who counts, unfortunately—the state-wide manager—who thinks Wellfern's emails are a fucking riot. Thus we have no choice but to suffer in silence. No one can challenge the greatness of the state-wide manager. Email number four, a short one sent by Wellfern at 2:30 this morning, reads:

> We probe the past. We burn the present. We condemn
> the future. All managers and their brooding assistants,
> please don't forget to brief employees on new holiday
> pricing promotions. Another inkling of progress, yes?
> Yes. Over and out.

I'm pretty much convinced he thinks he's being cute, that he truly believes we read these emails with rapt stares, laughing appreciatively, telling all our friends how we have this regional manager who's a really profound/hilarious cut-up. But Wellfern is exposing his loneliness. He treats his coworkers like confidants, and in my experience that always points to a deficient social life. The fifteenth email, addressed specifically to me apart from the rest of the mailing list, is headed by the cheesy convention of an old-timey letter.

> Dear Aria Forum,
>
> I'm madly in love with you. We've never met, but I've seen pictures and there is radiance, brilliance, beauty present within you. I'm quite certain I could love you. My love is full and satisfying. Life for me has been decimated to many series of lonely nights, a single lightbulb burning at the far end of my apartment near the window so as to provide a sort of guide or lighthouse to those out there who wish to come through the fog and make a connection. I am prepared and ready. You're existing out there somewhere, I can feel you. I want to know you, feel you as a person. This is of the utmost importance to me. Please say we can meet. I offer myself up to you. I beg you to make me whole.
>
> Truly,
> Cal

The final two emails not from Cal Wellfern are spam. There are two voice messages, one from Veronika Sine and one from Nick Ibyoo. Veronika's was recorded at five this morning.

"Aria, it's me. You there? I really fucking wish you'd pick up your phone. I know it's early, but I'm on my last nerve. I can't stop fucking thinking about you. Do you know how fucking awful that is? I mean, fuck. You know my feelings for you. It's not necessary to go over them again, but I just wish we could talk about what happened. We haven't said one word about it, not a droplet of conversation.

I'm too fragile for this sort of obsession. True, the sex wasn't between just us, but would it be silly of me to say I detected genuine feeling in your touch? Am I hallucinating? It's honestly so hard to tell at this point. It's almost six in the morning and I haven't slept, and I'm going to tell you right now, Aria, what happens to a person around six in the morning when they haven't slept because they're obsessing over a specific person who they can't get a hold of on the phone. What happens is your entire identity starts to break down so that you forget who you even are, even. I can't seem to remember the person I've worked so hard my whole life to be. I'm sitting here and it's like I'm staring out *your* eyes and thinking *your* thoughts and judging myself from *your* perspective. And this tortured panicky feeling, ugh. You must have laser beams pointed at my head. Tell me the truth. Tell me if you think we can be together. And if you think the answer is no then don't tell me. I'm staring at the granulated pattern of my carpet right now. Please extend me some sort of sign. Some acknowledgement letting me know that you know I exist. I have to hang up now. I'd go into my disbelief about the weakness of my feelings for you, but believe it or not I'm trying to keep this short. Call me."

I'm brushing my teeth, expression like I'm baring fangs. The movement is hypnotic, comforting. I move to Nick's message.

"Aria, it's Nick. Hey, listen, you wanna get together today and have lunch or something? I've got work, but my lunch hour starts at twelve-thirty. We can do that thing one does with one's mouth, I believe there's a word for it. And not the word you're thinking of. *Talk*, that's it, we could talk. What do you think?"

On my bathroom mirror are hundreds of tiny specks of water and toothpaste, creating an abstract composition of grime. I guess I haven't cleaned in a while. The phone rings on the bathroom counter.

"Hello?"

"Aria, it's Nick. I'm on break at work. You get my message?"

"I just now listened to it."

"So do you wanna meet up then?"

"I don't know. Today's my day off. I wanted to check up on Gentle and some other things."

"C'mon, Aria, just meet up with me for some lunch. It'd be... *nice* to talk to you."

"Give me a break, Nick. Why don't you just go to lunch with Gerney?"

"Because I'd rather go to lunch with you."

My eyes are closed. I take a moment to breathe through my nose and weigh the situation, ultimately arriving at the realization I have no preference, mostly I just wish Nick hadn't called altogether, but now that he has I'm going to agree to meet him. I have a stupid sort of sentimental weakness for people I sleep with on a semi-regular basis.

"All right," I say. "Twelve-thirty. Where at?"

"Paco Gant. You remember where that is, right? Near Archelaos."

"I remember. A terrible, terrible choice of restaurants, but I guess I'll see you then."

I hang up without waiting for a goodbye. Rinse, spit, review my notes; they're scrawled in a green notebook I'm opening presently, moving to the window by my bed and raising the window shade which reveals Grid to me, an expansive view from my eighth floor vantage, the cityscape performing its sweeping drop-off at the horizon line as if all the scrapers and sprawl and infrastructure—my building included—were being drawn toward the edge of a waterfall. My handwriting is neither round and upbeat nor coldly alphabetical. There's rarely a flourish or artistic impulse to the letters, but there's unmistakable passion and symmetry in their arcs and loops. My words are small, fitting between the faded blue lines almost with the interest of conserving space. Large text is a filthy thing to read, always somehow devoid of intrigue. Words should be at the very least a slight strain. Top of page one in the notebook is titled GOD AS INTRICACY. I begin re-evaluating:

"One) God is not a being, God is a concept, an It. God sweeps though the infinite involuted physical and metaphysical details of existence.

"Two) We are subject to God. It, meaning God, defines our

importance through the manner in which we are organized among the Intricacy.

"Three) Intricacy is the supernatural force that exists within the Arbitrary, also known as the World. Intricacy within the system is meaningful, although the system itself is devoid of meaning."

I flip ahead a few pages to one titled REACHING END-STATE.

"For humans, the macro and micro exist in two separate spheres. They are not bound together. One cannot exist in both spheres simultaneously, and so each person must decide at any single moment which sphere to inhabit and perceive. Switches between the spheres are easy and eminently possible, happening with great frequency, but never do the two spheres overlap. Bliss/wisdom/ nirvana is the marriage between macro and micro. In essence, it is the coveted ability to comprehend and know all Intricacy in the world at the same time. Which means that bliss/wisdom/nirvana is to know God. Except that God is not a being, by definition not an outside force that can be understood separate from the Intricacy. God simply is the Intricacy. So to reach bliss/wisdom/nirvana is to become God. The end-state cannot be reached by dying. It, and to become It, can only be achieved in life."

With forehead rested against the frosted condensation of the window, I flip shut the notebook and squint off into the city. The veins in my eyes gain feeling, a certain throbbing, as I attempt to isolate every detail in the panorama, trying to merge macro/micro, bringing up a mental register. Everything must be calculated in the head. In my earliest attempts at merging, I wrote each detail down by hand, neatly bulleting each aspect of Intricacy, but it became clear such methodology was ineffective—the difference between reading a description of a sunset and seeing it in person. The city sits below, a stripe of development in the land. I perform a single savage sniff to clear my mind, envisioning for a moment each melted and impacted grain of day-old gonine in my sinus cavities. Stop it; stop it; concentrate. This is an expensive view of the city, perched here in the direct gaze of downtown and straddling the western manufactur- ing sector but still without a view of the mountains, which makes a big difference in the rent. This side of the building is treated to glimpses of enormous tight fists of pollution across the downtown skyline emerging from phallus-like factories that slowly open into diffuse fingers of contaminated vapor. Nearby is the nucleus of the city, area of greatest density and the gravitational center of Grid's small galaxy. There's city hall, a piece of whorled steel sitting seventeen stories up at a slight 140° downward angle, propped up by eight thin tubes. The tubes, four of which are operational elevators leading to the building's thorax, are arranged in such a way to give the impression the building is walking (though *creeping* is more fitting). The overall look of it is just shy of arachnoid. Behind city hall, effectively dwarfing it, is the brownish-silver ClamBellCorp scraper, a massive soaring diminishing column reaching into the sky. At its pinnacle rests the giant iconic modumetal sculpture of an open hand cupping the cloud cover in the same manner waiters carry platters of food on fingertips. Its neighbor is the Pteranodon-Planax-Horner obelisk, twisted in the center to resemble several braided lengths of chain. Right now it's partially obscuring the view of a massive tower crane that will soon be InfoZebra HQ, Ronstadt no doubt toiling inside its growing skeleton at this very moment. Radiating from the scraper epicenter are ripples of other more obscure buildings ranging in architecture from curling black wedges to airy Jetsonian glass domes on martini glass stems. To the north are the govt-initiative slums of the hardware tract, and to the south are the coy dribblings of suburban motherboard. There's this thing that happens where my eyes flicker downward and I catch a glimpse of a small black beetle crawling frantically in the tiny space between the window's two panes of glass. The space is narrow, the beetle navigating it vertically. I sense it's claustrophobic. He's a harmless, almost handsome thing, crawling in aimless directions in what is clearly somewhat of a panic, every appendange seeming to be working independently of the others. I look at him through the melting, dripping condensation, skittering around in a frozen/bitter prison. I observe this happening for a long time…

Damn, my concentration is fried today—too easily distracted.

Maybe the jet is finally getting to me. That's how you can end up, completely spaced out. I have to focus. Focus. I have to focus.

Look downward. Perfect river of street and sidewalk running at the bottom of a building gorge. Each building composed of googolplexes of strictly structured steel and brick atoms, all sitting atop one another in perfect rows and columns. Below, all those dots are people and cars, humming over blackened gum stains inscribed into concrete and asphalt, loose forgotten change, miniscule ant hills which must be rebuilt hourly, dark emphyzematic weeds poking through sawtooth cracks in concrete, cigarette butts of every phylum and species discarded from the fingers of fifty different generations forming their own sub-society, plastic orange caps decapitated from Terradon Plus bottles ready to sit stalwart through a billion years and multiple nuclear winters, empty sticks of deodorant fused with the DNA of vagrants, micro-pebbles no larger than the width of an eyelash and all the thin stratums of germ and scientific micro-monsters squirming through the volatile moshpit gas atmospheric makeup of geographical Colorado, people walking at different rates of speed with different heart rates and different clothes printed with thousands of different brands, forty or fifty ultraprevalent, different facial structures, body types, metabolisms, amputations and frailties and dental irregularities, hand and foot sizes, colors of nail polish, scars, personalities and names and points of view, all walking the parallel sidewalks of the one-way street where cars inch forward, identical copies of various models with unique vehicle identification numbers, colors and dings and dents, cigarette butts on sidewalk, one Maverick, one Camel, one Misty, another Camel, each vehicle containing non-factory parts from various manufacturers produced in facilities across oceans from here, installed by people with names and faces and brains operating under the unquantifiable electric power of who-knows-what lording over bodies with enough systemic blood channels to wrap around the earth many times over and there's that beetle still, poor fucking beetle, skittering through warrens/mazes unseen only to find itself trapped in the in-between space of my window, rushing to escape frozen death while looking at two disparate realities through a cell of glass, and in all those little Intricacies down there God is flowing I know It's flowing I know there's a way to merge and contain it all and to finally understand to fully understand—

I push my palms into my face and feel a clear ringing sting in my head, ambition exceeding my abilities. Over time I've gotten better at merging, but as far as I can tell it's impossible, even just the small slice of reality outside my window hopelessly overwhelming. Heart and breath racing from anxiety, from the accumulation of too much at once. Stumbling, I make my way into the bathroom again and lean over the sink to stare at my reflection in the mirror. I look pretty this morning, but my eyes have this bottomless blankness, pupils little more than pen marks, and I find myself trying for minutes to emote something, anything, with my eyes. I'm in there somewhere, down in there, swirling. "Merging," I say—aloud—to no one, "is the ability to comprehend all Intricacy at once. To comprehend all Intricacy at once is to be merged with God." The words are in me, coming out so I can hear them in the open.

I let myself respond, my reflection asking me coolly, "Why do you need to be merged with God?"

I say, "Because God is the source of all feeling. The concept God, I mean, not the being. I realized a long time ago God can't be a being since he doesn't be at all. But, yes, I need to feel. I'm losing my ability to react to things, like I'm falling into some emotional coma? That's not even an adequate way of describing it, probably? Would I understand what I meant if I said it was a lot like I'm oversaturated? Oversaturated with stimuli? The more extreme states and situations I find myself in, the more I'm filled with antiseptic? Is this making any sense at all?"

"Do you want to have sex with Nick Ibyoo today?"

A moment to think. "Only in a very fleeting way. I like him because he doesn't beg my attention, just demands it and then discards it when he's had enough. I think I like the way he treats me because he confirms what I'm scared of."

"Which is that…"

"…what people see in me is more significant than what I see in myself. That I *am* nothing, that I *have been* nothing, and that, despite my best efforts, I will only continue to *be* nothing. That my existence is small and unspecial. Shit, this is a high-order existential crisis, isn't it, Aria, you idiot. Industrial-grade. You need to lay off the fucking gonine, girl. Your flight trajectory will probably intersect with a mountain any time now. This is your life, by the way. It would be *nice*, really, if you could muster the enthusiasm to be present for it."

Privacy is my enemy. Introspection destroys me. Out in the world I'm a different person with different tendencies and patterns of thought. I fear one day soon my private self will kill my public self, or the other way around, and that it will mean some sort of neverending psychosis. Why is that? When I was nineteen, my dad agreed to pay for some sessions with a psychologist. I asked him confidentially, apart from my mother (trusting her would have been like trusting a gossip columnist), if it would make him uncomfortable if I were to maybe see someone regarding some personal issues. My father was a man who never made me feel ashamed of anything. He could sometimes anticipate what I was going to say before I said it. Even if we hadn't really spoken for months, he could pick up on the core issue of my mood no matter what it was, whether something was bothering me, making me happy, causing me pain, it didn't matter. He'd know. The truly remarkable thing was his sincerity. Real, total sincerity like I've never known any other man to possess. I could count on whatever he said to me—110 percent—not to be a lie. My memories of him, just the two of us, are the experiences that taught me what it feels like to have unconditional love. He wanted to know why I felt I needed to see a psychologist. I told him I wasn't sure, just that there were concerns I had, personal concerns, and being able to speak with someone would be helpful. That was all I needed to say. He scheduled an appointment for me the next day with a doctor who charged upwards of $100/hr, Dr. Benzer, someone I'd now like to forget but can't. The first day I went to see him he asked me, "So what brings you here today, Aria? What are the goals you'd like to achieve with our time together?"

I said, "I want to know how I can not hurt people anymore."

"Hurt people? What's your meaning exactly? In what way do you no longer wish to hurt people?"

"Emotionally."

"In an emotional sense. You believe you hurt people emotionally?"

"I'm positive I do."

"What evidence do you have of this?"

"I don't think I could tell you explicitly. At least not easily."

"Maybe we could beat around the bush for a bit then. That often helps. Tell me—who do you believe you've hurt?"

"There are a lot of people. Boys at my school, before I graduated. Some girls too. And there have been adults."

"Adults? What kind of adults? What classification of adults?"

"Men. Teachers. Bosses. Other authority figures. Strangers passing me on the street."

"I have to say, Aria, you're striking me as quite intense. Yes, quite intense, and also quite mature for your age. You have a very restrained and focused way of elocution for a girl of, how old did you say?"

"Nineteen."

"Yes, that's young."

He was an independent therapist, his office located in the downtown area. My dad had driven me there, secretly, secret from my mom. Benzer was a man of barely-advancing grayness and beardedness and indifferent fashion. His office was patently male in character, nothing much more than a space in which to exist, dark, one floor underground, a window of infinite smallness installed so high up in the far wall it practically met the ceiling, viewing some rarely-trafficked walkway outside shaded by a constant concrete monotone. I was recognizing this in men, at the time, how they rarely have any sense of commonplace beauty. Their encounters with beauty not tied up in sex are encounters on vast scales: landscapes, cities, huge bodies of water. These things penetrate, but very little on a small scale ever does. Their personalities most times barely leak outward from them, like steel cages atop bodies.

"I feel irritable sometimes," I said.

"Yes, tell me in what way you believe you inflict damage emotionally."

"A lot of ways, actually. What it is, basically, is that I can't give, well, see, this is where it gets complicated, but I can't give people the attention they need from me."

A nod from Benzer.

"I've noticed this. That people want, I mean, it almost seems like they *need*, big amounts—"

"Exorbitant amounts."

"—yeah, exorbitant amounts of my attention. There's no way to put this gently. People tend to… express a lot of emotion at me."

"Toward you."

"For me. People tell me, often, that they… love me. That they need me in order to feel a certain way."

"Which particular certain ways?"

"They say to feel alive. Or to feel connected. Or sane. Or at peace. Or other things, too. They come right out and say it to me. Not right away, but usually not long after we first meet. Or sometimes people I've never met, not really, but maybe I know who they are. They say they think about me when I'm not around."

"They contemplate you somehow."

"Yeah, but what are they contemplating? What aspects of me are they contemplating?"

"Yes, and this surprises you? Their contemplation? Seems foreign? Why would that be, I wonder, since we all often contemplate others, especially when they're not present. *You* don't ever think of anybody? Ponder their personhood?"

"I do, yeah, I do. But the people who tell me these things, the way they say it. They just have so *much*—"

"The *degree* of their contemplation seems foreign."

"—and, yeah, and they have so *much*. So much emotion. Just, *a lot*. And it's weird because, since I don't have the same emotion, since I'm not on the same level, it makes it feel like I'm giving off this, this blankness. Like I'm a very blank person. With so little, in comparison to their so much. But I don't really feel like a blank person, at least most of the time—right, okay, let me finish—at least most of the time, but I keep noticing that the more people tell me they love me, the more blank I'm actually getting. I'm starting to get blank."

"And is this blankness—"

"God, I'm not making sense. I hate that."

"And this blankness is your fault, their fault?"

"Probably jointly mine and theirs. But who's at fault isn't really important. I'm not blaming anyone for anything here."

"Very mature, yes. The response of someone much older. But then what would you describe as your intentions here in this office vis-à-vis this apparent blankness?"

"My intentions? My intention is to understand what's causing it. To maybe develop some defense or barrier, a mental barrier, one I could start constructing here and now in order to not feel so blank anymore. Because what I'm starting to think is that I feel blank because I'm lonely."

"Lonesome, desolate, forlorn. Why so?"

"Shouldn't you be able to tell me?"

"I'm nothing if not an instigator, Aria. I instigate. In this way, answers are sometimes arrived at. Thus I ask you, why do you feel lonely?"

"I think because I don't feel about other people the way they feel about me. I look at them as just people. What I imagine it's like, what they're experiencing—or actually the way someone described their feelings for me once—is this glowing aura that surrounds a person. Even though the aura is invisible to everyone else, you can pick someone with that aura out of a crowd instantaneously and recognize them as something *greater than*, something special, whereas everyone else is just an indistinguishable part of the whole. I don't feel that way about anyone." (Though I omitted my dad.)

"And what about in the past?"

"No, not that I can remember. I've never felt the kind of love people confess having for me."

Benzer's beard gave a thoughtful shake. "Undoubtedly, Aria, you understand you're a girl of exceptional attractiveness. Exceptional beauty."

"I understand."

"Also exceptional elocution. Exceptional maturity. These things, all compounded, make you desirable."

"Yes?"

"Yes."

"What's your point?"

"Well, perhaps to find out if this is also a quality you value, in yourself or others. It could be useful to understand what constitutes attractiveness to you."

"A lot of it, I think, rests on a person's ability to listen to me, to *really* listen. To understand, in some way, how I'm feeling and to have the courage to either question or support those feelings. Looks play a role, of course, too. I mean, I'm human."

"And you've never found someone who suitably embodied those attributes?"

"No. Not up to this point."

Benzer nodded, rubbing his chin, focusing his eyes on me.

That was also the year my dad got sick, right around June, a cruel month to begin dying. We wait so impatiently for summer in Grid, teeth chattering and saying to each other no, it's okay, if we can just hold out a *little longer* the sun will come back, whatever we did to offend it will be forgiven and it will realize it misses us. And when the sun did come back, hat-in-hand and full of apologies, my dad started to die. He was working in the backyard when it happened, a double heart attack, planting green beans like he did every summer. I've never known anyone else who planted things. His hands were moving in the ground, fingers stained black with store-bought soil, the tiny seeds nestled snug in a blanket of nutrients, when suddenly his heart seized and his blackened hands flew to his chest and he keeled forward, face grinding into the dirt. By that time I had already taken a job at the Archelaos Chevrolet convenience store and moved into a tiny studio apartment on the fringe of the motherboard, so it was my mom who found him. My mom—who I have never fully understood. She's always been a very image-conscious woman, bubbling over with directionless energy in comparison to my dad, who was a quiet, focused, contemplative person. I could see how much he *hungered* for my mother's attention, but she seemed to always parcel her affection for him into sparing little drips that never failed to infuriate me. Their dynamic had a parasexual effect on me from an early age, as if I were experiencing sexual frustration well before I could understand the concept. When at home she was usually on the phone, the kind of person who could laugh easily in the company of strangers but treated family conversations like a series of robotic exchanges. She was out of the house often without my father. She was clearly bored by him, and yet sometimes she would fly into his arms to soak up his love when she had nowhere else to turn, reciprocating his devotion in moments of need. What hurt most was her lack of awareness. I always wanted him to see he was being mistreated. Thinking about it now, I doubt he was ever blind to what was going on. Just complicit. She remains impossible to talk to about anything other than trivialities.

He spent a week and a half in the hospital, languishing with sad brilliance, his body wasting away to half its normal size in mere days so the outlines of his legs beneath the hospital sheets were like those of a ten-year-old boy, the kneecaps declarative/unavoidable. Time didn't pass fast or slow, but instead was punctuated by that uneasy feeling of everyone reassuring one another that he would be okay, that he would recover, that it would be a joy to have him back in his rightful place among the Healthy, but deep down everyone was just waiting for him to die, almost wanting and willing him to do it the outcome was so incontrovertible. My mom was tearless but performatively sad. People showed up, the way people do when someone is dying, but again the balance was asymmetrical. For my dad there was a family member or two, a few old friends who leaked in and out with polite modesty. But for my mom there was an unbroken torrent of visitors, people I'd never seen before rushing to her through white hallways that augmented their contextless faces, throwing arms around her and offering condolences in tones more suited to a melodrama than real life. I was introduced to all of them. Have you met my daughter, Aria? Aria, this is ——. And this is my friend from ————, —. And there were the well-aren't-you-a-pretty-girl-Aria's, and the your-mom-has-told-us-all-so-much-about-you-dear's, and the we're-so-sorry-for-this-awful-thing-having-happened's, and it all made me so *fucking sick I could scream*. My dad's last days were filled with an endless parade of strangers offering up unsure apologies, insincere empathy. I destroyed each of them in my mind, intestines hitting walls, bones shattering, smiles ripped in half, all mellows severely harshed. They came, went, disappeared forever. I sometimes think about how my mom used to take me shopping when I was little, rushing us from store to store like celebrities on a tight schedule. She made it all feel so urgent, so important. I checked prices of dresses I wanted on my phone while she tried on vinyl jackets, and we were close in a way. We talked about the way women were dressed while they walked around trying to dress in such a way that other women wouldn't talk about them like that. She encouraged me to buy things I barely wanted regardless of price as a form of so-called therapy, even when nothing had happened I needed to be therapized from. I think about how, when I was fifteen, the shopping trips started to lose their appeal, became—in fact—exhausting. I stopped talking with her over clothes racks and teeming electroshelves. I stopped wanting so many things. I can see now how the person I was in the process of turning into bored her as much as my dad did. He spoke vague last words to me the final afternoon I was with him before he died. They beg to be endlessly/maddeningly interpreted. His eyes were closed, hair pushed back so I could see how far his hairline had been receding in secret, face loose, gaunt, unshaven:

"Aria, don't get…hung up. Promise you won't…hang up…on. You can find. I love that…you can find."

Find what? Find *what?* He died that night, we found out via phone call, of uncontrollable heart swelling. I ceased to exist for a period of time. Everything became shaded by death. When a parent dies, you begin to realize, *truly realize*, that anyone can, everyone will, die. You understand with reverb clarity the concept of vast alone-ness, the fragility of the foundation your life rests upon. Your trust in human beings fades and you turn cold and distant, even if you pretend not to be. And at the funeral you inevitably try to picture yourself dead, imagine this funeral is actually your own. It's impos-sible to avoid this. Everyone together having a collective vision of their own death ceremony. Seeing how quickly and permanently we will slide out of the world with next to nothing left behind but care-fully guarded memories. Things we want will go unattained. Jesus. Gives me chills remembering that state of mind. Which you never fully recover from, by the way. You carry it around with you, like most traumatic experiences, and all those traumatic experiences end up being the reason for numbness in adulthood, a dulling of what we insufficiently classify as "childhood passions." The brain must sublimate to go on, a clever survival mechanism of self-awareness.

I was unable to snap out of a funk I couldn't even recognize I was in. I grappled with the inexorable engines of many different jets. Began sleeping with Nick Ibyoo in inconsistent, passionless sessions. Why is it that my instinct to nullify lonely nothingness consists of filling it with even more lonely nothingness? As if vacu-ity were something that could be somehow oversaturated, therefore cancelled out. Not true. Vacuity is an organism that grows like any other, existing on the inside with no borders. So many things from that period of time go unremembered and yet completely unforgot-ten. The overall feeling remains important, not so much the details.

It's true you can feel yourself healing. The state of your psyche can be monitored like a scab, can be picked at and seen to meld seamlessly with its own surrounding undamaged material. One day I consciously decided that I'd gotten over my dad's death to a reasonable extent. I went back to Benzer, more than a year after my first visit, like to pick up where I'd left off maybe.

"Welcome back, Aria." The room hadn't changed, he hadn't changed. Zero nada *zilch* revelatory changes. I realized I probably didn't look any different, either. All transitions had taken place under the surface, invisibly.

"Thank you, here I am."

"Quite a hiatus."

"No kidding." I set my purse on the floor and it gave a baby-rattle sound from so many bottles of pills. Which did not go unnoticed by Benzer.

He allowed a long moment of silence before asking, "What brings you back?"

"Um, I don't know. I think to talk."

"Mm." He laced his fingers in front of him, crossed his leg over his knee. There was no table separating us, just the two chairs facing each other. Probably symbolic of unobstructed interfacing or something. "What would you like to talk about?" And he added: "I'm a good listener."

"I'm not sure."

"I reviewed your file before our appointment today. Would you like to pick up where we left off?"

"Okay."

"Would a summary of what you said last time be helpful?"

"Sure."

"Yes, affirmative. Last time you were here you said that [reaching for file, reading] …a large number of people were confessing outright love for you…that the degree of their emotions trumped your own…that you were experiencing feelings of, quote, 'blankness.' " He flipped the file closed, looked at me.

I nodded okay.

"Any developments?"

I sat.

He switched positions in his chair, a rolling chair he treated like an appendage. "Where are you currently at with your life, Aria?"

I fortified my emotions with clichés, saying, "Same place, just taking it one day at a time. Can't complain, I guess."

"Ah."

"Yeah, that's about it. Nothing too exciting."

"But you're still experiencing troubles with blankness, yes? This is what you desire, to continue treatment for those feelings?"

"Well I—"

"Or perhaps that's not the most pressing thing on your mind at the moment."

"I can assure you—"

"Something big has taken place, hasn't it? I can sense it." He paused, said, "But I understand if you don't wish to speak of it."

Something in his voice, about his body language, was strange. Even his clothes were uncharacteristically well-fitting today, suspiciously color-coordinated.

"I appreciate your not pressing the matter," I said.

"Yes, well, we must draw lines somewhere, mustn't we?"

For the next hour I stayed on verbal defense, Benzer doing his best to power an insight or two through the goal posts but failing. I felt almost bad for him, except all I really wanted now was out of his office. I had made a mistake, and I knew I would be relieved once I was away from him, not for any reason I could pinpoint exactly, but that on-edge feeling was there, churning. When the session was up and I stood to leave, Benzer motioned for me to sit back down a moment, please.

He leaned forward in his chair, elbows resting on his knees, and took a large breath. "Aria," he began in a tone unmistakable to me: the tone of emotional candor. I went rigid in my seat. "I understand you have certain…*anxieties* concerning various…well, perhaps the best thing to do is say it directly. I'm very… how can I put this? [That tortured look they all get, right before they're about to articulate the feeling. Their words get muddy, mine become clear/cold/precise, blank of everything save skepticism.] I'm very *interested* in you. And I think that, although you originally came here because of the number of people who have feelings for you, I can't help what *I* feel. I've come to think maybe I'm the sort of person you're looking for in a…well, in a partner, and—"

People can care about you so much without caring about you at all. My dad was the only one I ever knew who planted things.

On my days off I visit Gentle, my dad's mother, at her house near the western manufacturing sector, which is where I'm headed now, watching through the scratched up window of the GRT the texture and colors of Grid become squalid, more despairing, and in the spaces between buildings I can see stretching off into trigonometric distance the harsh industrial hive that has embedded itself beneath the mountains. It's difficult to imagine what goes on in the manufacturing portions of Grid, especially for a person like me who avoids them almost the way I would the plague, all reports coming from local news sources impossibly distressing. Murder. Unchecked pestilence. Homeless genetic freaks. Cancerous graffiti. Ceaseless smells driving the brain toward suicide. Indiscriminate robberies. Wandering parentless babies establishing autonomous tribes in vacant parking lots. People dying of lymphoma showing up to work every day on time. Violent incest. Fathers/mothers with tattoos and booze. *Low-quality drugs.* And reports indicate the eastern sector is even worse. Gentle's husband died three years ago—four now?—of Parkinson's and she has stayed in the house they lived in together for 46 years, refusing to move despite my constant insistence she should. The neighborhood is rough, but she either doesn't care or doesn't show her concern. Probably the very thing that makes her a target, her age, is the same thing keeping her safe. At 91 years old she has lost relevance to the world surrounding her, like a ghost sauntering through the visible realm.

Not a lot of people on the train today, a weekday morning, but there're a few Thai kids in oversized clothes sitting on the opposite end of the car from me who've been trying to get my attention since I got on at the Downtown-204 stop. I look out the window trying to absorb details. A homeless man tosses and turns on a nearby seat, all the loud laughing and talking from the kids making it hard for him to sleep. Downtown Grid passes by in a linear series of rectangular keyframes. The city is an addiction. No matter how much I lay eyes on it, I find myself compelled to look, to scrutinize, hate and love. This roiling, uncontainable sprawl. The thought of a house on some golden tree-dotted plain, stretched with blanket tightness to every horizon line, tranquil underneath healthy blue sky, becomes fear-inducing. In the natural world people suffer, must live and die. Here, in this place, all mortal facets of life are dampened. Fetish for the artificial. In nature, God is God; in the artificial, Man is God. Creation is feasible, traceable, accountable even. Ambition reveals its true scope.

Except God is a concept, an It, nothing more than details. Details are divinity. The GRT reaches Partition Ave.-Optimum St. and I detrain into the subzero sunshine.

It's a ten minute walk from the station, most of the streets deserted. I can hear people having screaming arguments inside their homes. I sink my neck down into the collar of my jacket against the cold, feeling my nose turn red as I look up and see a WIN FREE TERRADON CLEAR FOR A YEAR blimp float overhead. I don't know what Terradon Clear is. There's a Taco Bell, two Burger Kings, a Samurai Turkey, a McDonald's, a combination Jack in the Box/ Samurai Turkey, and a thousand liquor stores. A lot of graffiti, but there's a lot around my neighborhood, too. Gentle's house is a faded blue two-story that does a good job of looking identical to the houses around it. I walk up the steps and knock on the door, waiting for minutes, maybe five, knocking louder and louder, cursing the cold, before finally I try the doorknob and it's open. I'm met with a blast of near-tropical air, humidity off the scale. The TV is set at hell-shivering volume.

"Gentle?" I nearly scream.

Through the wallpapered hallways (witty algorithmic trees extending throughout the entire downstairs—she loves technology, math, harsh things) and into the kitchen, I spot her sitting at the table.

"Did you hear me knocking?" This comes out through chattering teeth.

"Heard you knockin. Hear me hollerin 'it's open'?" All this without turning her head.

"Can I maybe turn the TV down a little?"

"Go ahead. Ain't listenin to it anyway. Somethin comin on later."

I decrease the volume to sub-insanity, go into the kitchen and sit down across from her. She's a small withered woman, no more than five-one, with dentures and a tightly permed tuft of hair dyed not exactly red, but more of a burnt orange. Even sitting, her posture is hunched. Her left eye is a tiny slit while her right eye is gigantic, circular, staring. Her eyebrows take shape over them accordingly, forming a naturally unnerving expression. In front of her is a plate of half-eaten toast and a News Pad.

"Brings you down here, Aria?" She pronounces my name air-ee-a.

"It's my day off. I came to visit you." The house is in a state of complete fossilization, everything covered in a fine layer of dust. The refrigerator door is hanging open about two inches. I get up and close it.

She says, "If you don't but just look more doped-up every time I see you, girl."

"I'm not doped up, Gentle."

"Course you aren't," she cackles, pointing her huge right eye at me the way she does when she wants to give me a glare like *I'm not an idiot.*

"How have you been?"

"Same as last week. They got a report comin on the TV in a few minutes. Was just readin about it here."

"Report about what?"

"Futurization of the future." She cackles again. There's a digital picture frame set in front of the empty seat at the head of the table, a gallery of hundreds of old photos of her husband cycling every half-minute or so. The current picture shows him as a young man in a grainy black and white photo holding up an impressive fish for the camera on a boat at the shores of a lake. He looks a lot like my dad. There are multiple digital frames just like this all over the house in similarly creepy spots. Her husband's name was Schroeder Forum. Gentle always referred to him as Don, after his middle name Donovan.

"You been talkin to your mother?"

"Yeah. Not all the time, I'm pretty busy, but I talked to her a few weeks ago."

"She up to?"

"She was worried about all these holiday parties, about decorating for them, I guess. It was all she talked about."

"How'd they go?"

"I'm not sure. I called her today but I got the machine."

Gentle's still skimming the News Pad. "You girls oughtta settle your differences. Been too long since the funeral for you two to be actin this way. Maybe you could get off at damn dope, too."

"I'm not *on* dope."

Mom and I had actually made a lot of progress in the last eight years. But that was beside the point, really.

"You think I don't know what a person does dope looks like, Aria?"

"What are you saying?"

"Sayin I'm not stupid's what I'm sayin."

"No one's saying you *are*. Okay? I'm not on drugs." I treat Gentle like a court of law. Deny everything and she can't prove anything.

"Well if you're not shinin me on, and I know you *are*," the right eye shoots me another direct stare, "then you oughtta think about eatin somethin. You're gaunt. What can I fix you?"

She's already struggling upward like she's planning to make a three-course dinner and I urge her to sit.

"Think I'm gettin up just for you? Gotta get somethin upstairs."

She grabs her cane and hobbles in the direction of the staircase. I start shedding layers, face completely flushed. The smell in here is similar to moldy bread, all odors trapped and stirred together in a chronically unventilated space. The algorithm wallpaper continues into the living room, apparently showing what's called a recursive algorithm, but Gentle doesn't know recursive of what. The intriguing thing, however, is that some of the individual sequential cells are not actually logical instructions, are instead cute/quaint little baby words like *Ducky* or *Tractor* or *Kitty*. The TV, as always, is stuck on some anodyne national news program, and right now it's an ageless Diane Sawyer sitting in a blacked-out room across from some guy with a very thin head topped by a curly pompadour, bespectacled, and dressed in formal plaid.

"You studied under Drexler for a number of years, correct?" Diane Sawyer's inquisitive tone wonderfully, *painfully* inquisitive.

Her guest nods in the affirmative.

Scattered across the small table next to Gentle's recliner are dozens of antique black-and-white photos. I grab one near the top of the pile and absently inspect it.

"And you've served as head of R&D for Infiniphase since its start in late 2003."

"That's right."

"And now, after years of speculation—hardship—government regulation—funding initiatives—ingenuity—and a total belief in your work, Infiniphase is releasing the first-ever in-home nanofactory."

"[With that scientific reluctance, impulse to contradict:] Well, *essentially* yes. To date this is the most advanced example of what we call productive nanosystems."

The photo has a soft blur, but nonetheless it's easy to see it depicts an outdoor fenced enclosure containing maybe a hundred pigs, surprisingly huge, the size of large dogs. The picture was taken from a hundred feet away as a landscape scene, the sweeping flat nothingness of the country surrounding the corral stark. Somehow it just *looks* freezing.

"And what are you referring to exactly when you use that term, *productive nanosystems?*"

"It's not an easy thing to give a concise explanation of, Diane, but basically what you can do is imagine a device no larger than, say, your average household oven. What it does is it creates products in a matter of minutes. Sometimes hours, depending on what it's making."

"And it actually makes—"

"I should say *manufactures.*"

"—manufactures products? What kind of products are we talking about?"

"Well, to start with a simple example, let's imagine you've got an old broom you've been using for years, and one day the handle breaks. So, with our product, what you can do is punch in a code that corresponds to 'broom,' and right in front of you, at the molecular level, a brand new broom will begin to assemble and emerge slowly from the top of the device as if it were appearing from thin air. And this broom, too, by the way, will have a handle fifty times the strength of steel and forty times as lightweight."

There's a sharp sensation in the small of my back. I turn to see Gentle poking me with the end of her cane, right eye huge and beaming over a strong denture grin.

"Ow!"

"Lookin at the pigs, eh?"

"What are you poking me for?"

"Those were my father's pigs in Beulah, North Dakota. Guess that was probably 1936."

"1936?"

"To give a more complex example, let's say you need a new phone, or laptop, or stereo system, or any sort of electronic device. The process is exactly the same as what you did to get your broom. Plug in a code, out comes a product with quantum computational capabilities far superior to anything currently on the market."

"Know what happened to those pigs, dontcha?"

"Do I know what happened to them?"

"They burned."

"So hold on a second, you're saying this device—what are you calling it again?"

"It's set to release in four or five months, and it will hit stores bearing the name Panacea."

"So you're saying the Infiniphase Panacea can actually build computers right in peoples' homes?"

"Ah, burned?"

"Used to keep em in at barn right there. See?" She taps the edge of the picture where there's a sliver of barn showing. "Dad'd keep em in there nights, till one night it gets to thunderin and flashin outside. Woke me up outta bed and here we come runnin up the south side of the house just absolutely hightailin."

"Not just computers, Diane, but *superior* computers. Along with almost any product imaginable. And this in-home version is just the tip of the iceberg."

"Can you elaborate?"

"Imagine homes, mansions, apartment complexes being built within mere days at a fraction of the current cost. Tanks, fighter jets, weapons, armor, missiles, all produced at breakneck speed. Space vehicles with tremendous power, strength and size. Space *stations*. Entire cities. Anything that can be built, but now built exponentially faster and better through a system of total microscopic automation. Some of these large-scale things I just mentioned are still out of our grasp at the moment, but we're getting closer with every single day that passes."

"Up on over the hill and here we see at barn just blazin out there in the middle of the land. Lightnin crackling down all over the place, makin it so you could see things miles away. Stars, too. Lord. Millions of em. Haven't seen em since. First time I ever heard my father take the Lord's name, but we were all thinkin it, he just said it. Barn, from where we were, was just a little thimble of fire lickin up into the dark. But closer we got, we could start to hear em."

"How does this rapid manufacturing work?"

"The easiest way to picture it, remember I said the products emerge from the top of the device as if from thin air?"

"Yes."

"Well that top, slowly-emerging layer is simply the end result of a multitude of layers beneath it. These layers are so small you can't see them with the human eye, only with very powerful microscopes. But let's pretend for a moment we're one nanometer in size and can see all the inner workings perfectly. What you can see is, in simplest terms, a fully functioning factory. Except that every moving piece is composed of individual atoms of material, formed painstakingly into self-functioning parts."

"Hear them?"

"Hear them pigs screamin. They were in there burnin, but we couldn't do a damn thing about it cause there was no fire department in a Howitzer's distance of us. Had to just stand there and watch the thing burn to the ground. Bad as the sound was, thing I remember most was the *smell*. Good gurdy, that smell could've made a rose wilt and a song die. Worst smell I ever smelled. Worse than brimstone. Can't really define it, come to think of it. What it was, it was the smell of trapped things cookin."

"And what those self-functioning parts do is sort through raw atoms of materials and send them upward to the construction phase according to which program they've been prompted to run. Then, when the product is finished, there's virtually zero waste."

"What does this mean, do you think, sir, for our lives? Because, truthfully, I'm quite stunned. My mind is literally reeling with implications."

"As it should. This is the start of a major industrial revolution, with the potential to be perhaps more transformational than any that's come before it. At this point it's hard to tell exactly what the future holds, but what's obvious is that productive nanosystems are poised to become the most widespread technology in use in the world. All I can really tell you is what a lot of sun-starved people living in little rooms have known for a long time, which is that everything is about to change in a very tangible way."

"How did the barn start on fire?"

"Got struck by lightnin. Dad always said he remembered the exact one did it, too. Said it was a single brilliant flash, woke him right up, thunder like the sky crackin open, then woosh—up in smoke."

I look at her.

"So maybe you just think about that story when you're lookin at that picture. Placid things, ain't they? Happy as pigs in mud. Heh heh."

By the time I get to the motherboard fringe it's 12:15 and Nick picks me up in his pickup from the street station and when we get to Paco Gant we do two long lines of gonine apiece in the parking lot with the heater on and the engine running. I try to get away with doing just one, but Nick tells me what I'm pretty sure I was hoping to hear in the first place. "Feel free, Aria. I'm set to get a new bag for this weekend anyway."

So I do another one and start to feel pretty good as we walk into the restaurant, a real fancy place that I sort of hate, but Nick likes to bring me here to impress me and I guess I would be lying if I said it doesn't work a little bit. We're seated next to a tinted window with a view of the fountain out front, a sculpture of a woman in a toga or tunic hauling a water urn that the smoothly curving necks of several stone swans would be spewing water into. Across from me, Nick looks unravaged by gonine or other drugs. He's healthy, as always. His body is stout, powerful, a few inches under six feet with a strong jaw, thick hair, and the kind of face that looks like it's been beat up on a few times. His eyes are green, and that somehow makes him more attractive than he would be otherwise. His teeth aren't pretty at all, though, and it's obvious he couldn't get braces as a kid. In the last few years since having more success at Archelaos, the overall impression he gives is that of some amiable tough guy who also flaunts a bit of wealth, considers it a good look on himself.

"So why didn't you go to lunch with Gerney?" I ask, joggling my leg under the table in time with my elevated heartbeat.

Nick's eyes travel to the window. "I don't know what's up with that guy lately. He's been acting weird for a couple weeks now."

"Weird how?"

"I don't know. Just weird. Quiet. Won't get back to me on the phone. Fuckin annoying."

"I haven't noticed anything."

"That's because you don't notice shit on the weekends except for all the jet burning in your brain."

"Quite a thing for *you* to say, asshole. Jesus."

The waiter comes and I order filet mignon with wine just to be a bitch. Nick orders the baby octopus, and I figure he's trying to out-bitch me. I'm a bit appalled.

"Why would you do that?"

"Do what?"

"Order a plate of baby octopuses."

"Octopi," he corrects.

"What*ever*. It's perverse. You're a baby-eater. You like to eat babies, Nick? Little animals that didn't even get a chance to live a life before you devoured them?"

He gives a blank stare across the table. I wait for him to say something but he doesn't.

"You're ordering a plate full of little baby corpses. I saw the picture on the menu. It's their whole little bodies, doused in delicious sauces. Just a bunch of dead mangled—"

"Aria, Christ, will you get a hold of yourself? Maybe that second line wasn't such a great idea for you."

I sit back in the booth, nonplussed. There's a long silence, Nick looking out the window and me sipping my wine while the restaurant swirls, actually sort of bombarding me, registering as thousands of tiny needles of information. This is a side effect from attempts at merging. I've become hypersensitive. And, as tends to happen once gonine hits my system, my thoughts are splintering under the strain of a very vague but omnipresent pressure. It occurs to me (I think while sipping the black wine in my glass, hands trembling involuntarily, causing the liquid to quiver and slosh): according to my notes on REACHING END-STATE, bliss/wisdom/nirvana *is the marriage between macro and micro. In essence, it is the coveted ability to comprehend and know all Intricacy in the world at the same time.* If this is true, then there's an important distinction between most religions and Intricacy Theory. In most religious constructs, bliss/wisdom/nirvana is a state of total inner peace; judging by my current circumstances, bliss/wisdom/nirvana in the construct of Intricacy Theory is a state of total inner *panic*.

"Look," Nick says, "I don't want to fight."

"Me either."

His eyes land on my wine glass. "You're shaking."

"How are you not?"

"You look like you've been grappling all week long. Am I right?"

My first instinct is to say no, but some better, more alert part of myself forces me to nod yes.

"I knew since I picked you up from the station, but I didn't want to say anything."

"It's that obvious?"

"Your eyes. But you've been sniffing and fidgeting around since the second you got in my car."

I stare deep into the table. "I remember thinking I looked pretty this morning…"

"You do look pretty," he says quickly. "But you look kinda strung out, too. Maybe a couple weeks of detox?"

"Maybe," I mutter, still zoning.

"Aria, I know it's not like me to ask this, but are you okay?"

"To tell you the truth, I don't know. I haven't thought about it like that. Whether I'm okay or not."

"Is there something you need to, I don't know, talk about?" He's wearing a gray suit with a white shirt underneath and a red tie. Suits seems so unnatural on him, like a boy wearing the work clothes of a much older man.

I'm afraid for the first time in a long time. I wasn't expecting much from this lunch, but Nick Ibyoo has pierced my shell—the last person I would have expected to. He seems sympathetic at the moment, but knowing him it could be insincere down to the last centimeter. Maybe I'm just in an extra vulnerable state right now.

He's still looking intently through the window, but he says, "I can hear it in your goddamn silence, Aria. I can hear all these things you're not saying, so why not just say them?"

Is that sadness in his tone?

The gonine encourages me to trust him, and out comes the truth, the truth I hadn't even known until he asked me to verbalize it. That I am in a state of *anxiety*. And also *dread*. Can I explain it to him? I think so. It's like being cut off on a daily basis from humanity. Like, like—I'm getting forced into a coma. An emotional coma, I mean, and I can't figure out why. A constant frenetic bass-line beating at inhuman CPU speed at the outskirts of my consciousness. But I'll tell you what's confusing is that I don't want it to slow down, no, that would be terrible, what I really want is for it to speed up. Increase everything! I want high volume, high input, excessive distortion, bigger engines, taller buildings, stronger drugs, more sex, smellier pollution, harder alcohol. I want to inhale the whole world and never breathe it out. And people don't understand, they just don't understand, how every single day when they pass me on the sidewalk or sit next to me on the train or order me around at work that I've got an inexhaustible energy burning in my head at every waking moment. That I could consume all their attention, all their love, all their hate, and never, not even once, would it be enough to provoke a human reaction from me. I'm this desolate moon in quiet orbit with a panoramic view and an ultimate ambition to crash into the earth. These things can't be properly explained. That life, that consciousness, that the seven-day segmented calendar, are prisons. Have you seen what's going on out there? People with heads uniformly down, staring into tiny screens meant to show them something large, most of them totally alone, and everyone reaching out to me for companionship of the soul. Did you see in Zeal last weekend? The images from the DeepSix space camera? So many of them, a new picture every two seconds of the earth from millions of lightyears away and a green beacon next to our planet. Our planet the size of a grain of rice, and shrinking. (At some point during this our food has come and Nick puts a baby octopus into his mouth, drenched in sauce, speared headfirst onto the fork, tentacles hanging out of his mouth for a second before he slurps them up and chews.) And did you see how many people there were, so many fucking people, none of them willing to die, wanting to extend their lifespans into a sunless eternity? And more born every second. It's not just machines our species has refined. Our species *is* a machine. Do you see this at all? We've perfected the aggregate. We're mass producing ourselves to last longer, hold up better, be more efficient at *wanting* things. And I don't just mean consumer goods. I mean the intangible things, too. Love, war, religion, intellect, advancement, family, cities, nature, all of us wanting so much that the most intense humanly desires become nothing more than drab cliché. We've finally reached a point where we're mechanized. Do you see how basically sick that is? Tell me I'm not the only one. The natural has transfuckingmuted into the artificial and there's no way to take any steps backward. It haunts me the amount of Intricacy we're dredging up. And I want it all, every little bit of that Intricacy, so bad it hurts. I want it all inside me, almost sexual. None of it's unified or even makes sense, but it's there in my mind, the idea of it, the idea of the *world*, an idea people of prior centuries weren't even allowed to have. So can you understand that I want everything to burn? Yes, burn bright and fast, no waiting around for years on end for the consolidation of all information, let it happen all at once, ruthlessly, so we can find that little bit of peace in the fire. Am I done? Not by a long shot. I don't care that everyone's looking. Because here's something that just became clear to me as well, at this very moment. I love you, Nick. I can't explain it but I love you in a way that is weird and irrational and hurtful and depraved and you know something? It feels really good. Like a sense of relief I've been waiting for for a long time.

Baby octopus tentacles hang halfway out his mouth, dripping sauce onto his plate, while I take my first breath in minutes.

AMY

And then there's Amy Arsenault, independently-moving little molecule, who, the morning after hearing the news of her mother's infarction, at 8:45 am boarded a GRT train bound for Denver to get a look at the situation. Amy's adrenal glands, while sitting amongst the public transportation crowd, quietly deposited payloads of excitement into her bloodstream. She allowed her face to betray nothing, the sole evidence of her mood nothing more conspicuous than a slight sadistic tilt to one of her eyebrows, examined closely only by a serene seeing-eye dog that had boarded two stops ago without any apparent owner. This had been a good morning. Her night's sleep was refreshing, dreamless, and at the street station waiting for the train, at 8:32 am, she'd seen a five-year-old boy slung over his mother's shoulder, the two of them shivering against a wind that brought with it freezing scalpels, and in a small beautiful moment the boy, staring blankly with a face of gaunt cheekbones and shrinking nose, cried a single tear of blood. A good morning.

It was on the train to the hospital that the inspiration for the name XittyXat struck her. She was still a week away from the hack, which would soon spark a firestorm of emergency board meetings, cloak-and-dagger plotting, nimble PR announcements, high-paid programmer forehead slapping, much defeated loosening of ties after long work days, and the return of certain people to the job market. The consequences would be extensive and trickling, and she would savor them all with a kind of insatiable gluttony.

9:55 am and Amy entered St. Joseph's, passing through a lobby full of typical-looking cybery blue-collar Denverites—totally, unforgivably urban—some wailing with injury or sickness, together as one generating a special type of dark music. Updates continued to flood socnet sites regardless, there being essentially nothing to do while waiting in misery except desperately seek digital commiseration. This was a notoriously bad part of the city: a panel of four receptionists were working straight-faced in a bulletproof cube, the windows of which were endlessly diamonded with intersecting wire. There were small slots operated by the receptionists meant for the transaction of documents between those in-cube and those extra-cube, as well as vents for the passage of sound. Amy approached the only unoccupied receptionist, a fat Armenian woman with black hair, jowls and lipstick. Through the criss-cross pattern of the plastic window the receptionist might have been a prisoner.

"Can I help you, ma'am?"

Amy *spacked* her ID flat against the window and said through the vent, "I'm here to visit Margaret Arsenault."

The slot slid out to expose a metal drawer. Amy put the ID in and the drawer slammed shut from the other side, the card now being inspected by the receptionist. "Relation to the patient?"

"Daughter."

After long seconds of computer typing, the receptionist slid the drawer out again and began to recite, "Please place the orange sticker on the upper right part of your shirt so that it's clearly visible. They're color-coordinated, so today's sticker won't get you in tomorrow. You'll need a new one. Once inside take the elevator to the seventh floor and communicate with the receptionists using the receiver. They'll let you in."

The woman pressed a button installed in her desk, a quick screechy buzz issuing from the fortified door leading into the main part of the hospital. Amy stepped through at 10:01 am, looking trim and pragmatic in a black trenchcoat and black pants over boots. Her hair, stopping just below her jaw, had been dyed such a deep black it resembled strands of ink sliding from her head. The corridors just beyond the door were crowded with hospital staff, but farther in they opened into great quiet yawning tunnels the color of taupe. Amy walked the distance to the elevators and rode to floor seven. The doors opened to a small waiting area with another barrier denying entrance to the CVICU beyond. Connected to the wall was a black telephone handset running from a wire, like a payphone. Amy picked it up from the catch and waited for the voice on the other end.

"Name, please."

"Amy Arsenault here to visit Margaret Arsenault."

"One moment, please."

Again the door slid heavily aside. A female nurse with a buzzcut stood waiting.

"Hello," she said, pleasant but solemn, "I'm Zen."

They shook hands briefly. "Amy."

"Nice to meet you. I'll take you to your mother's room."

Amy was frisked, then led by Zen a short distance past a large circular control panel being worked by five technicians, around a corner, down a hall, and standing in front of a closed door in a triangular formation were Aunt Joann, a man in an expensive black suit, and a doctor. Aunt Joann rushed to Amy and threw her arms around her, teary-eyed.

"My God, Amy, I'm so glad you're *here*. I been waitin all through the night for you to show up."

"Yes, good to see you [too monotone, too formal, too unwilling to make human contact]. Who are these men?"

"I'm Norbert Towers," the suited man said, extending a hand toward Amy. She hesitated a moment, finally accepted the handshake. He had hair roughly the length of her own, all pushed into a single swoop behind his ears, a week's worth of beard, and granny glasses. His body was thick and unmuscular, an advanced paunch straining against his dress shirt. As he shook he added, "But you're welcome to call me Norb if you'd like."

The doctor brushed Norb Towers's crude introduction aside with an air of impatient authority. "You must be the daughter." His square and heavily pockmarked face gave the impression of a drill sergeant.

"Yes."

"I'm Dr. Ray Actinide, your mother's primary intensivist." There was no handshake. "We were just discussing with your aunt the transference of your mother's body into the temporary possession of Vivificorps should death occur, God forbid."

"And I still say y'all're feedin us a buncha crap!" Aunt Joann roared, a thin finger directed at Norb Towers.

"What's Vivificorps?"

"We're a private life extension group," Norb Towers answered quickly and amiably, despite Aunt Joann's ire. "I'm a representative from the company here to monitor Margaret's condition and coordinate her transfer to our headquarters in Grid, if need be." He seemed to almost beam with pride, as if happy to make this announcement. But it was in fact nervousness and not pride responsible for his discordant tone, because Norbert found himself viciously attracted to Amy Arsenault the way any self-respecting life extension representative who, daily, mucked through dark and death-oriented situations would be to a tall slender woman arrayed entirely in black clothing and hair and radiating the most assertive sexuality perhaps possible. In addition, constant proximity to extreme situations such as these had caused some of his tact to leave him (having the effect of infuriating Joann, his slick explanation sending her into a red-faced rage).

"Can you believe this moonshine they're trying to pass off?" Joann said to no one in particular, maybe Amy, but mostly conferring with persons unseen in an anger that apparently brought the Tennessee out of her even more than usual. "Who the hell *are* you, you scruffyneck bastard? Here I been close to my sister eighty years, and somehow I ain't never laid eyes on you once till today, and yet here you are rearin yer snout all of a sudden talkin about you have a *contract?*"

Dr. Actinide held up a hand. "Mrs. DeSantis, please…"

"But, Doctor"—still pointing at Norb Towers, the finger in line with his chest—"this whole thing ain't *right*. I want him removed from here."

"The fact, Mrs. DeSantis, is this man has every right to be here, and the authorization came directly from your sister. She signed contracts with Vivificorps ensuring a representative from their organization would be present during any situation where Mrs. Arsenault's death could be a likely outcome. We all have a duty to respect Margaret's wishes at this time."

"I known Margaret my whole life, and I'm tellin you she didn't never sign no contract agreein to have her *head* frozen! She went to church every Sunday and believed in the Lord even when *I* didn't! She's my older sister, and I'm *tellin* you!"

"Mrs. DeSantis, I'm afraid if you don't calm down I'll have no choice but to ask you to leave. This is a sensitive area with patients in critical—"

"Wants *me* to leave now! Just bless your little heart, Doctor, standin there letting this slimy fool take advantage of us."

"I'm not trying to take advantage of you," inserted Norb Towers, though it did look as if he were backing away from the situation physically, torso angled at a strange degree. "I met Margaret personally when she signed the papers, and she was very adamant about—"

"Yer a lying bastard and I don't wanna hear yer yipping, so don't bother."

"Again, Mrs. DeSantis, this is not the appropriate place for that sort of language. Now if you can't be civil and listen to Mr. Towers I'll have no choice but to force you to leave."

"Amy, tell em yer mother ain't never signed no filthy contract. Tell em yer mother's a good lady, a Christian lady, and she wouldn't never sign nothin like that."

Amy stood off to the side, silent.

"Tell em, Amy, it's okay. They ain't gonna do this to us."

It was 10:16 am. Amy turned to Dr. Actinide. "Where are the bathrooms?"

Dr. Actinide put his hands in the pockets of his coat and gave

Amy a discerning look, motioning with his head to the hallway behind him. "Walk straight down. Take a left and it's the first door."

"Thank you."

"Now look what y'all done to this poor little girl. You need me to go with you, Amy? You okay?"

Joann started to follow her down the hall, but Amy turned and stopped her, saying as if she held some ultimate authority, "Stay where you are. I'll be right back."

The bathroom was tiled and the color of chocolate-chip mint. Standing at the second sink washing her hands, scrubs blending in with the surrounding tile and posture going so straight she resembled a frightened chameleon, was Zen, eyes blinking and face flushed. Amy looked at her expressionless. For an accidental moment they held eye contact, Amy recognizing a distinct flash of attraction pass between them.

Zen, flinching, said, "You all right?"

"Fine."

She dried her hands and walked toward the door. "Well if you need anything, don't be afraid to ask."

"Of course."

The door closed at 10:22 am, actually bleeding a few seconds into 23, the bathroom now empty. What she had just heard had thrown her for a loop. Margaret had signed a contract to have her brain neuropreserved? She needed to know what Vivificorps was immediately. Clearly there was something to gain here, something she hadn't been expecting at all, especially not from Margaret. Of course, she'd barely been on speaking terms with her since her father died five years ago. Not because his death had changed their relationship in any way, though Margaret had been (confusingly and also amusingly for Amy) devastated. The lack of communication between them was mutual, even cordial in a way, neither of them having ever really liked each other in the first place, but because appearances were kept up and curiosities occasionally satisfied the two managed brief contact every so often. Amy's father, Taylor Arsenault, the IX Arsenault to bear the name in a long line of Taylor Arsenaults, was the one who'd actually suffered from the estrangement. He had often tried to get in contact with Amy despite the death of Taylor Arsenault X—his son, Amy's brother—the death that had shattered their family, and that Margaret had considered Amy to blame for.

Without Amy's permission, a flashback to March 14, 2009—not the kind that dissolves wavy and liquid smooth into the past, but one that appears slowly through a haze of antiquated VCR fuzz, a low-tech childhood recollection. What resolves in the attenuated screen of memory is Margaret (many hairstyles ago) sitting at the kitchen table of the Arsenault home in Denver, keeping diligent watch over one-and-a-half-year-old Taylor Arsenault X, who is in his angelic phase and brunching reluctantly on a banana and dry cereal at 12:05 pm. Amy, also sitting at the table, is twelve. She is a very quiet girl, much too secretive and disciplined for her age, which has already started to cause her parents to worry. Especially concerning for them is her radically fast development. Instead of becoming increasingly fractured, sprightly or girlish as she edges up on her teen years, she has changed into something strange and possibly even vaguely sinister. Margaret and Taylor Arsenault would never know how to verbalize it, but neither can ignore the uncomfortable truth: that pre-pubescent Amy carries herself with the air of an experienced sexual veteran. This makes for some unsettling family dynamics. Taylor Arsenault struggles against this strange confidence, that of a girl almost twice as old as Amy, to retain his fatherly purity, unsure of how to impress or ingratiate his bored-seeming, monotone-voiced daughter enough to once again become an object of her affections. He craves the love of his child in the non-sleazy way any father would, but Amy's premature womanhood has made the whole thing feel, in fact, very sleazy. Outwardly, it seems he's vying for her sexual attentions (and perhaps in a sick unavoidable way this is to some extent true), something that has not gone unnoticed by Margaret, causing her to have developed a disturbing set of sub rosa jealousies and suspicions of Amy before she has even become a young adult. Amy appears, on the surface, not to notice any of this, her calm exterior betraying nothing. But she does notice. It's just that she's sincerely unconcerned for the feelings of her parents. At twelve, she would like to be concerned for them, but she's not. The situation is trivial to her, confusing, while at the same time entertaining and empowering. Although the situation has festered over the last two years, Taylor Arsenault X has been a welcome solace for Taylor and Margaret, a channel for guiltless love, and their attention is directed overwhelmingly toward him. Amy doesn't complain about this. In fact, it's clear she prefers to be left alone. But at 12:08 pm that day, when Margaret's phone rings with an important call from the head of the university's Department of Physics & Astronomy, despite every strange feeling of resentment and wariness she has for her daughter, Margaret tells her to watch Taylor while she steps outside.

They're left alone together. Amy doesn't look up from her breakfast, only continues to eat while Taylor, unable to speak but boldly experimenting with various happy sounds and squeaks, slaps his spoon against the surface of his Cheerios. He sounds out a monologue at 12:10 pm, somewhat complicated for its springing across the spectrum of emotions, before Amy finishes her cereal at 12:12, gets up from the table, takes the bowl to the sink, rinses it, and places it neatly in the dishwasher. When she reenters the kitchen, Taylor has stood up in his chair, doing a silly, uncoordinated jig. He puts his hands behind his hips, spirals his waist around, little knees bending so he's sort of hopping, lips pouted out in an unnecessarily intense expression. His hair is white-blonde, and, at this moment in time, so is Amy's. The pajamas he's wearing have matching tops and bottoms, smiley-face dinosaurs wearing baseball caps, the stegosaurus wearing his cap backwards and kicking a soccer ball. Amy stands at the entryway to the kitchen, blankly inquisitive, watching in silence. In the screen of memory this scene is grainy and has a camcorder date seared into the lower-right corner, time readout accurate down to the second, reading 12:13 pm. It's almost as if Taylor is trying to get a reaction out of Amy. He's making shouting noises in her direction, wild exuberant baby squeals coupled with some terribly impolite lip buzzings, and, seeing little result from his efforts, makes a series of perplexed faces before hoisting himself up onto the dinner table. Still Amy makes no move. Taylor comes close to not making it up there because he's misjudged the amount of leg strength required, but when he lands his feet back on the chair he giggles, redoubles, and ends up on the table on all fours, knocking into his cereal bowl and sloshing even more milky Cheerios all over the place. He gets to his feet a bit unsteady, the height producing some trepidation in his balance, but when he's finally upright the exhilaration he feels is clear. He continues with the little dance he started before, goofing around to his heart's content without some commanding voice ordering him to stop. He's having, according to every indication, an absolute ball up there. Even at only one and a half his talent and personality shine through since the dance, in a primitive way, is expressive, perhaps even performed with Amy's enjoyment in mind. It's difficult not to be happy because he's so happy. But Amy is frozen in place, looking on without a trace of emotion or concern. In a way, she's not entirely aware of how serious the situation is. Reality is still somewhat blurred for her by youth, and by a mindset so darkly empty she feels *no urge* to get her brother down off the table, and she's many years away from understanding why. She never decided to be this way, never made a choice to feel so disconnected from others. She recognizes it as abnormal, even frightening, but she is still too inexperienced to have learned how to override some of her natural impulses in order to do what she knows she should. Internally there's a debate occurring. Certainly she's aware of the fact Margaret will be back any moment, that if she's caught standing there watching Taylor dance on the table she will be in massive trouble, that it will save much time and energy if she just gets him down, but these facts are eclipsed by the one thing she *does* feel. Curiosity. Curiosity so strong it has seized her body, the way sometimes you can see something horrible about to happen in the moments just before it does but are unable to move or react, as if destiny is silently asking that you let it conduct its business without interference. And at 12:14 it happens—Taylor hops near the edge of the table, underestimating the weight of his toddler head, still larger than his body, face warping into a picture of fear as gravity's fingers grab hold of him, pulling him into a nosedive off the table. Amy feels herself reach out a hand to stop it from happening, breath catching in her lungs. The table is tall, and Taylor's trajectory is straight as a missile. His face makes direct impact with the tile floor, giving a sickening *snap* sound that, though it is not loud, manages to drown out all other noise, the nose bone retreating into the brain, Taylor's body, abruptly inanimate, lying there in front of Amy, who—still—has not put her arm down, is still reaching out to stop it all from happening—(the fear (drilling a path toward (*invigoration*) what she feels) is like a drug)—but the longer she holds her arm out the more disturbing it becomes, her fingers playing over the air against the image of her dead brother on the floor. There's a zoom-in on her eyes, and even in the grainy fuzz of camcorder vision they are wet, sparkling. The date and time stamped at the bottom of the screen, at one point so innocuous, now seem like the cruel grin of some higher power, seconds ticking by inexorable. After a time Amy backs into a corner of the kitchen and slumps to the floor, staring at the semi-circular spray of blood near the table with the most horrified expression of her life. Which is exactly how Margaret finds her, and Taylor, at 12:18 pm, coming back into the kitchen after a patience-trying conversation with the head of the department about some recent overruns on field research costs. Even the most morbidly fascinated are unable to sit through such a scene as what ensues. It is too drawn-out, too terrible. Unwatchable by any normal filmic standards. Only those who lived it will ever experience the moment properly and to its full extent.

Margaret found infinite ways to blame Amy for what happened and felt no lingering remorse in doing so, but Amy's father was unable to hold his daughter responsible for Taylor's death, and as a result he suffered the loss of two children instead of one. For Amy, sitting in a bathroom stall in the CVICU looking up Vivificorps on her phone, the incident, after its initial shock had faded, had been something far from traumatizing. The funeral, the fallout, the suffering of her family, had all been an early epiphany, serving as an object lesson not only in cause-and-effect, but also in how to control herself—when and how and for what reasons—and that through such self-control it was possible to manipulate events. Passivity, it seemed, could be a powerful agency. The memory of her brother's death is strange. Much too acute to reflect on with any specificity, but still never far from her mind. She carries it around like an old photograph, rarely looking at it but taking a certain comfort in the fact that it's there.

The Vivificorps site was holographic, meaning expensive. The slogan *Reanimation Through Vitrification* reappeared dozens of times in varying sizes, used like a logo. There was a long explainer page: Vivificorps had started as an NPO called Prolifigroup that then split into two separate entities in 1983; by 1986 the business of Vivificorps had grown to multi-million dollar status after the publication of a book titled *Engines of Creation* by Eric Drexler, which the site specifically attributed to the boom; upwards of 70,000 cryonics patients were now stored in various Vivificorps facilities across the West; an AR program allowed Amy to take video of herself that, when played back, showed her image against a background of a city beyond all futuristic imagination meant to entice potential customers; and finally the critical data—minimum funds of $150,000 for neuropreservation to be paid in the form of insurance, trust, or annuity. Again, Amy could see why Aunt Joann was confused. Margaret volunteering and paying to be neuropreserved didn't seem to fit with her character or beliefs. Perhaps toward the end she'd realized, Amy thought, the stupidity of the notion of God. That salvation was not coming. Perhaps she had despaired. Amy reveled in these thoughts. Whenever she remembered attending Denver Crucicentro Post-Evangelical Church as a child, she was filled with homicidal nostalgia. On not a few occasions, lying in bed waiting for sleep, some random bit of church lunacy would return to her out of the ether, and she would find herself fantasizing about burning it to the ground with the congregation of her youth trapped inside.

But it was clear, now, that Margaret had strayed. Her lack of vindication made Amy hate her sick, lifelong obsession with Christianity all the more, and there was a definite pleasure in knowing she hadn't truly believed she would be saved.

Amy stood to leave at 10:27, smoothing down her clothes and collecting her thoughts. Her phone rang. She recognized the number from the night before, the desperate-sounding guy who had wanted to learn DealEase.

"Hello?"

"Amy? This is Gerney Crepitus, I called you last night about DealEase."

"Yes, what can I do for you?"

His voice was anxious. "I know I told you I'd send a date and time for us to meet, but it turns out I can't afford to wait. I was hoping we might be able to get started later tonight. Or tomorrow evening."

"I won't be able to make it tonight. Tomorrow is the earliest I could meet you."

"Then it'll have to be tomorrow. I'll send my address to your phone as soon as possible."

"All right."

Amy stepped from the stall, pausing at the bathroom door. Deep breath, commitment to what must be done, to focus. 10:28 am. Rein in all spite, all anger. Containment of instinct. The feeling she often had, the feeling that all elements of her life were heading toward a purpose. She stepped through the door, walked back to her mother's room, Dr. Actinide now gone but replaced by Zen and Aunt Joann standing on the opposite side of the hallway from Norb Towers.

"Where's the doctor?"

"He had another matter that needed his attention," Zen replied. "He'll be back later."

Aunt Joann pulled Amy aside, placing her hands on her back and shoulder, the feel of her touch repulsive, but no, Amy thought, this is what must be done.

"Ya all right, Amy? Don't you worry, this slick bastard ain't gonna get away with nothin." She indicated Norb Towers, leaning against the wall near the door to Margaret's room, hands in his pockets and a thin sheen of sweat coating his forehead, pretending not to notice anything going on. "We're gonna fight this, kiddo. You an me."

"I'd like to see my mother now," Amy told her.

"Course you would, course you would. Goodness, ain't even got to see Margie yet. Want me to go in with you, Amy?"

"I'd like to go in alone, if I could."

"Keep in mind," Zen said, "she's not fully in touch with reality at the moment. The stroke—"

"Stroke? I thought she had a heart attack."

"Oh, I'm so sorry, I thought you knew. Yes, she had a stroke last night when she arrived at the hospital. That sometimes happens in the wake of an infarction. The events don't usually occur so close together, but we do see it from time to time. When the blood flow is weakened to the extent your mother's was, the brain is at high risk." Hearing this information for a second time, Aunt Joann let out a small agonized sob. "Fortunately, the stroke she experienced wasn't severe. It's amazing she's awake, quite frankly. Your mother's a tough woman."

"Damn straight," Aunt Joann nodded.

"So I just want to prepare you, she'll be incoherent."

"Thank you," Amy said, squirming away from Aunt Joann's loving grasp. "I won't be very long."

"I'll be right here, Amy. Ain't goin nowhere."

Amy saw Norb Towers watch her go in, the eyes behind his glasses anesthetized but also eager, like something unscarred and quixotic was residing inside, looking for an opportunity to break out. He looked quickly down at the floor, unable to hold her gaze even briefly.

She closed the door behind her at 10:34 am and saw her mother for the first time in three years (the moment coinciding with Cate Dos entering Fish's hospital room two floors below, holding a curved plastic jar meant for urination, delicately resting her weight on his bed so as not to wake him), Margaret an insubstantial creature lying buried beneath what seemed like heaps of blankets. The shock was physical, Amy's stomach turning slightly. It was the face. As if chains had been attached to the jaw and forehead, then pulled in two separate directions. The mouth was crooked and gaping beneath a drooping nose, one delicate strand of spittle connecting the upper and lower lips. The eyelids hung down fat and heavy, a permanent cavernous stare imprinted into the eyes that pointed toward the wall where the TV droned away on mute. She was connected to the requisite number of machines, tubes, catheters. A chair on the right side of her bed awaited visitors.

Amy sat, waves of goosebumps locusting across her arms as her mother's head turned to look at her, the eyes tracking details, an animated body with little resemblance to the person who had previously inhabited it, only the most basic evidence of brain function remaining. But again Amy felt her stomach contract when the gaping mouth creaked out her name.

"Amy…"

The sound was mangled, almost unintelligible, pronounced without use of the tongue, but nonetheless she had been recognized.

"Margaret? Is that you?"

"We was just watchin…President Reagan…on the TV…"

Amy looked at the TV. An old sitcom from ten years ago about a guy with schizophrenia. Reality, for Margaret, since suffering the stroke at 11:47 pm the previous night, had turned phantasmagorical, her mind displaced to far-flung moments of personal history that overlapped, transitioned roughly, kissed up against one another before breaking apart. Events in the physical world were bound up with hallucination and dream, a lifetime's worth of stored data having undergone total system crash. All that was left was an accumulation of experiential echoes, random bits fluttering by on synaptic thermals, some of it registering (names, for instance) but most of it flickering against the screen of her mind like a twacked-out slideshow.

In a stern tone, Amy addressed her mother. "Margaret." Her eyes met with Amy's. "Do you remember me, Margaret? Do you know who I am?"

A sound that contained an undertone of acknowledgement emanated from the depths of Margaret's open mouth, the connecting strand of spittle between her lips surviving there, managing to hang on.

Breathing evenly Amy stared at her mother like she were a pool of water. How to ripple the placid surface? This had seemed such a wonderful hateful fantasy, to confront the capsule that had carried her, suffering, into the fluorescent sting of the world. Didn't you know, Amy thought, what kind of evil you were unleashing? That I was a group of venomous cells replicating inside you? I conglomerated, bitch. If each person born is a piece of the machine of humanity, then you birthed the self-destruct button. Do you see how deformed I am? You created me. If only you'd die I'd be liberated from origin, like something that sprang immaculate from chaos and randomness. A force of pure annihilation. And it isn't looking so good for you right now, is it? No doubt about it, you're getting sucked down into the drain of death slow-style. And just look what you're leaving behind!

Not until a bead of sweat trickled into her eye at 10:43 did Amy realize she was on the edge of her seat, hands clenched and her breathing elevated. The words were there inside her, but they wouldn't come out. Margaret lolled her head across the pillow, struggling again to speak.

"Amy…"

"Stop it. Stop saying that." Amy clenched her teeth so hard it was like she could feel sand between them. The adrenaline her system was pumping was unbearable. She reached into her pocket, pulled out her phone, began taking a video of Margaret, watching her mother squirm within the parameters of the screen. Amy kept the camera trained, finally failing to keep her hands steady and the video going shaky.

"Amy…"

"Shut up," she said, zooming in on Margaret's face. "Shut up shut up shut up. Shut your mouth, Margaret."

The camera aperture on Amy's phone dilated in and out, a flinching pupil. Margaret's eyes moved back and forth, the only part of her body not subject to complete or partial paralysis. Something still caged inside.

Amy replaced the phone in her pocket, turning away from her mother. She wiped the sweat from her face with the bottom of her shirt and tried to quickly compose herself before rushing out of the room at 10:49 am. She had another quick conversation with Dr. Actinide, who listed off what was being done to coax Margaret back into a semblance of wellness. Amy listened, impatient, and Dr. Actinide peered at her with what could have been either sympathy or disbelief. She hugged Aunt Joann, reassuring her a few final times, saying she would be back, don't worry, it would be fine, yes, I'm okay, everything's all right, but I've got to go now, I've got to go. She exited St. Joseph's at 11:28, a tiny dot expelled from a monolith, and hurried through street crowds to the GRT station where she boarded alongside a lady turned gray with years who played Tetris on a News Pad the entire way back into the city, all the falling blocks fitting perfectly together, her arthritic fingers playing over the touchscreen controls with mesmerizing confidence, not making a single mistake up until the moment Amy got off at the Downtown-197 stop where she hurried through a blur of street LEDs and the constant miasma of hot silicon. In her apartment she shed her trenchcoat and boots, filled the bathroom sink with seven dollars worth of cold copper-scented water, and submerged her face in it. At 11:57 she transferred the recording she'd made of Margaret onto her laptop, watching the playback of her mother's lolling head while screaming into a pillow to dampen the noise. Everything she'd meant to say came gushing out now. She yelled, face going crimson, the veins in her neck and forehead pulsing. The computer speakers said, "Shut up. Shut up shut up shut up. Shut your mouth, Margaret." She restarted the video, watching it over and over.

"Shut up. Shut up shut up shut up. Shut your mouth, Margaret."

The picture began to tremble toward the end from Amy's unsteady hands before it finally started to shake so hard the image lost integrity, all except the date/time display in the lower right corner.

Jan 28 2025. 10:45am.

Each day a carafe; each day a freshly-poured cocktail of bat-tery acid. The next morning bloomed into simply one more in a long string of attacks in which Amy, with punishing seriousness, considered eliminating herself. As much as weakness, she despised ceaselessness, repetitiveness, sensory overflow. Things she couldn't control. Insomnia inspired in her the desire to kill (though techni-cally this was not so much a desire as much as a reflex to total *lack* of desire). Sometimes to kill others, sometimes herself, sometimes both. There was no real pattern in her focus or intent, which she also realized, and a sensation of pure vague seeping hatred swept over her. The effect like that of an open cavity, bacteria penetrating to tickle the nerve within raw. She winced, on these days, from a psychic ache.

In her opinion, occlusion was not what she suffered from. Lucidity, on the other hand, was pretty much the fucking pits. She felt she had debunked the world, cracked it open to expose its sectional diagrams and found any truth within to be meaningless and small. The video of her mother remained paused on her laptop monitor, frozen at the moment when Margaret's eyes had met the camera. Between 10 and 12 pm she paced a well-worn groove in the carpet of her apartment. Between 1 and 3 am her mood became overly literal, compelled by a racing heartbeat that had lasted almost an hour to eke out a picture of a human brain using mathematically precise line segments generated by her computer. At first she'd used pen and paper, but changed methods due to a total inadequacy, or what she perceived as a total inadequacy, of her own markings. They struck her as imperfect—too organic, too flowing. In the digital draft the brain's curves were depicted by many series of connecting rigid points, making the figure sharp, bristling. This was her brain. She thought to herself, I am a brain that sends signals to appendages to create images of itself. I am an organ that knows it's an organ. I am dictated by sustained electricity.

She masturbated constantly, bringing herself to climax every thirty minutes for hours. This was a strange but unwavering side effect of these moods, the eroticism. She lamented that there was no one nearby to fuck, and that to satisfy the desire to fuck someone would inevitably require a degree of interaction with that someone, no matter how minimal. Despair achieved its greatest zeniths in the immediate wake of orgasms. Soon feelings of extreme literalism gave way to more serious flirtation with out-and-out suicide.

This was the enjoyable part: weighing reasons to live against reasons to die. She'd found that reasons to live always seemed to consist of small concrete things (hunger, a brief but satisfying fuck, the conclusion of any and all minor tasks ranging from getting bills paid to pulling off a successful hack, getting to see her mother die, never again being able to have that great sour candy they sold at gas stations, not being able to see some movie or show that had managed to pique her interest, the fact she had laundry in desperate need of doing), and reasons to die always seemed to consist of large abstract things (no greater purpose to the universe, the lack of importance of the self in contrast to the vastness of said universe, the knowledge that human beings are merely self-aware animals that multiply and swarm and infest with striking similarity to some strains of insects when you look at them from a distance and place no intrinsic value on that self-awareness, irrefutable scientific evidence that this sun will die off and stamp an expiration date on the human race's milk carton, the guaranteed continuation of confusion and suffering and all their intertwining subcategories, the guaranteed continuation of others' confusion and suffering, constant fear of and denial of death).

As with most things, methodology was the core of suicide. Significance was a serpent that could only be encouraged to constrict around details, specifics. For the amateur, contemplating suicide was a vague fantasy or longing for the end of oneself, but stepping up into the intermediates was to then ask: *how is that end met?* Ah. Herein lay a definite morsel of fun, yes? For years Amy had been darkly attracted to the rumor that, after being sentenced to execution for tax fraud in 1794, the French aristocrat-chemist Lavoisier devised an experiment meant to determine how long a decapitated head retained consciousness once separated from the body. After his decapitation by guillotine, a servant rushed to the head-receiving basket, snatched up Lavoisier, and counted how many times he was able to blink before succumbing. Depending on the source, he clocked in between fifteen and twenty blinks. Authenticity aside, it was a wonderful story. What must he have thought during those final seconds of life? The cognizance of being only a severed head, Amy imagined, must have been a superb torture. The question arose then, in what way could she produce a sufficiently instantaneous death for herself? The answer came in the form of a Mark XIX .357 Desert Eagle pistol, which she'd illegally purchased several years ago. Amy kept the gun hidden in the bottom dresser drawer of her bedroom, buried beneath a pile of rarely-worn clothing. The plan boiled down to this. A single shot, fired point-blank into her heart, would instantaneously stop the primary motor of her being, allowing for what she hoped would be close to a minute of post-death consciousness. The pistol was also indicative of a mood-dependent clause in the event she might work herself into a homicidal rage prior to self-elimination. However, the weapon had been purchased primarily under the assumption she would use it on herself. The gun whispered to her from its hiding spot in the early hours of sleepless mornings, disastrous and seductive little sentences poured into the ear like syrup.

By 4:32 am she was well beneath the hard deck of emotional purgatory. Death seemed very close to her now, plausible, natural as laying down to sleep after an exhausting day. That sleep was not the sleep of the unknown. She had known nothingness intimately, could remember the indelible switch between death and life almost as if it had been someone flicking on a room full of lights. She'd hypothesized that it was precisely *because* she remembered her transition into consciousness (it had occurred at age three while staring off at the expanse of the flatirons, the peaks clouded over with dense snowfall and the faces of the jagged rocks coated by a whiteness which blazed with reflective intensity, her father leaning down, a stranger whose relationship to her was an instinctual recognition, to say, "Isn't it neat how you can't see the tops through the clouds, sweetheart?"), *because* she carried with her that memory of nothing into something with such clarity that she was the way she was.

She didn't fear death in any cosmic sense, but still she feared it. Why she couldn't be sure. Perhaps it was the feeling she got that dying was a common synonym for losing. But no, that didn't sufficiently explain the dread. What it really was was the fear she might survive up until she experienced death naturally. This was the chord of fear sounding deep within. Death defeating her, something out of her control. This was unacceptable. She wouldn't allow her death to be something greater than herself, for instance an "act of God." The idea set her teeth on edge. This was not God's world—not anymore. She was the sole operator of her life's mechanism. The final element playing lord over her was Margaret, but now, even with her death nearing, total victory was threatening to slip away. There was now the real threat Vivificorps might resurrect her in some form. So how to escape this? The path she was currently contemplating, sitting quietly in her chair at 6:03 am, feeling the machine weight of the Desert Eagle teeming with kinetic energy pressed against her heart, her mother's near-vegetative stare gleaming at her from the glowing computer screen, was an escape from authority altogether. Why continue to live inside a nightmare? But no matter how empty the symbolism, how contemptibly meaningless the drive of competition, she was bothered. Destroying herself with Margaret poised to live on tainted the entire act. She would be forsaking someone else's universe rather than her own.

She decided: until Margaret's death was certain, the pistol would not be an option. She replaced it, fully loaded, in the bottom drawer of her dresser beneath the layer of clothes.

Not until late in the day, at 4:30 pm, did she leave the house. She'd spent not even an hour familiarizing herself with DealEase. He had requested they meet at 6:30 pm, pathetically groveling in his message about how thankful he was for her to change her schedule on such short notice. The GRT crowd was dense for a Tuesday, but the trip to the portion of the motherboard tract where she was headed was mercifully short. The crowds set her to seething all over again, the sun absent at the train station, tiny pinpricks of snow frosting across all surfaces and turning to huge shields of ice in the wind. Amy stared into her phone, making the necessary effort to block out the people surrounding her. She pecked away at rough lines of code, but halfway through the trip she was taken out of her trance by some demonstrating wacko who'd been drifting through the knots of GRT routes since early morning, clearly out of his mind not because of what he said, but because he could not detect the universal hatred projected onto him from every glaring passenger. He was a morbidly thin creature composed of fibrous muscle and tendon, horseshoe baldness giving way to a thick shank of wire-gray hair gathered into a long ponytail, held tightly together with many different rubberbands, dressed in cinched jeans and a tshirt that read *Ask Ancient Man For Forgiveness*. He wandered up and down the aisles of the train, occasionally lapsing into clichéd babblings about the Great Desert War, which he had fought in, but mostly bursting into lengthy preachings concerning, what he termed, The Crucifixion of Ancient Man.

"We handed y'all the world. Ya are what ya are. Handed it to you. We are what you are. What we *were* was Ancient Man. We was Ancient Man, carving coffins out of space dust. Understand? Every man what dies, *two* men arise to take his place. Death increases human hold on the earth, and the vultures sitting in white-columned buildings know. The War wasn't no waste of life, it was a breeding operation. Ya are what ya are. And we handed y'all the world."

He fixed on someone staring into a News Pad, a twentysomething kid with self-consciously styled hair on his way home from a well-paying tech job. The lunatic shook a wad of *Ask Ancient Man For Forgiveness* shirts in his face, making a show of unfolding one of them to display the slogan.

"Ya wanna ask Ancient Man for forgiveness, son? You're a prime candidate, goddamn right you are."

The kid shrank under the public attention.

"I said do ya wanna ask Ancient Man for *forgiveness*, son. Ancient Man's the reason you're sittin there obsessed with the biggest obsession Ancient Man done borne from his breast. But ya are what ya are. You're the crop of millions of years of nourishing rains made up of arrows and bullets, don't ya *get it?* This shirt is gonna finally show all you ungrateful spawn of Ancient Man's suffering breast that your Jesus Christ is nothing but code for all us old wretched soldiers dying for the sake of your goddamn toaster oven sins."

Amy, registering this last bit, clenched her jaw in hatred.

"We are what ya are. Jesus reaps up thanks from millions, and me and mine—Ancient *Man* is me and mine, son—live every day kicked to your metal curbs. That seem right to you?"

The kid would not make eye contact no matter how directly the man addressed him, face trembling.

"You're looking at a crucified man, son. Look at what ya are. Ya know what you are?" He clicked his tongue. "You're in the line what's waitin to be crucified. Just carrying that cross, waiting for the next guy to make good off your blood."

At 5:17 pm Amy got off near Aphelion and walked several blocks to the address he'd given her. She arrived at a gated, high-end apartment complex. The property extended far back into an area overhung by an elevated swimming pool, the platform outlined in half-silhouette against a huge uninviting concrete sky. An artificial creek ran the entirety of the property's perimeter, creating a serene babble of heated running water. Adding to the din was a twenty-foot tall slab of textured granite which stood sending recycled liquid sheets down its surface at the center of the parking lot. Each separate building cluster was four stories, silver with red accent trimming. Amy keyed in the gate code and it slid aside imposingly. She went up two flights of steps at Building Four to unit 402. She paused at the door to take a deep breath, step into a different persona the way an actress might step into character.

She pressed the buzzer and after a long wait the door opened inwards against a chain lock, revealing a pair of feverish eyes squeezed against the doorjamb. The sound of loud, overlapping music and voices coming from speakers inside now escaped into the entryway.

"Hello?"

"I'm Amy Arsenault. DealEase?"

The eyes moved around in some kind of panic. "Shit. You're like more than an hour early. We were supposed to meet at 6:30, right?"

"Yes. I took the train. I overestimated how much time it would take. Is it all right if we start now?"

"Um…" Amy could see through the crack in the door that he was surveying the apartment.

"Is that a problem?"

"Well, I guess not. It's just my place is…"

Amy waited. "Your place is what?"

"I meant to clean up, but I must have…" Although he was talking at a rapid clip, he seemed not to be able to finish any single thought, like his attention was divided between three or four things at once. "I'm just not sure if, not sure you're going to be entirely… I'm not sure if I should… Would you be able to come back in half an hour?"

"Well there's nowhere close I can go to wait. If we start now maybe I could add some time to the session free of charge?"

He deliberated, continuing to seem rushed, panicked. "I guess that's… Could you wait just, just five minutes? I'm so sorry, I know this is…just five minutes."

He shut the door. Definitely not what she had been expecting. Maybe not so weak as she'd thought. Still, she considered leaving. She had more important things to do than wait for this fucking—

There was the sound of the chain being unlatched and he opened the door. To Amy he was standard-looking, no big surprises. Tallish, forehead imprinted with a few premature lines and very skinny. His hair was dyed a bright caution-yellow with strands of black patterned throughout, dressed sharply in a starched white button-up tucked into gray slacks. There was a logo stitched into the upper-right corner of the shirt depicting five Roman columns arrayed in a half-circle, three intact and two crumbled ruins, underneath the words *Archelaos Chevrolet* in chrome-and-blue steel font. He radiated nervous energy, doing everything in his power to suppress a series of bothersome facial tics.

He held out his hand. "I'm Gerney, nice to meet you."

"Amy. I thought you said five minutes?"

"I don't think I can clean, clean up," voice spranging like high-tension wire, "so please forgive the mess."

She stepped inside, recognizing, just as she had at the hospital the day before with the nurse Zen, a flash of attraction strobe from his eyes.

They entered the expansive living room at 5:31, which connected to a sizeable kitchen. There were two large screens anchored to the far wall, a plasma TV that had been set to automatically switch channels every seven seconds and a high-priced VidraPro touring through a landscape constituted of sheer piping, venturing out of a vented duct that opened onto an impossibly immense wall of plastic, copper, steel pipes arranged into an infinite tapestry. His couch was stripped of its cushions, strewn around the living room, and one of his two recliners was tipped over backwards on the floor with the leg rest released high into the air. In the middle of the room, on the carpet, was his phone, next to a disassembled video game system that had been wirelessly synced to camouflaged speakers, pumping fast-paced trance music, which he quickly rushed to turn off. Identical black Archelaos Chevrolet coffee mugs had been left all over the room on various surfaces. She looked into the kitchen and saw two ZChase News Pads on the table streaming two different programs and an old laptop with a malfunctioning screen. A bottle of multivitamins had been knocked over, large orange pills strewn all across the keyboard and floor.

"What happened here?" she asked when the music cut off.

He gave a halting look, as if he'd been hoping she wouldn't notice or something. "This… [frustrated sigh] …this is a complicated story."

"Complicated? This is what rock stars do to hotel rooms."

"I'm so sorry, I completely— I'm sorry but I completely forgot our appointment."

She decided to feign concern, as if she were a little frightened for herself. "I'd like to know what's going on."

"I'm aware that—"

"Because the truth is, this looks a little violent. I expected a mess, but—"

"I'm aware this comes off as psycho," he jumped in, worried she was about to feel threatened, talking even faster than before, "like I, like I said I'm not even sure I remembered you were coming today, and if you're not comfortable you're welcome to— I'd be happy to compensate you for your time and you're more than welcome to—"

His inability to finish a sentence finally caused him to wince with frustration. "God*dammit*," he chastised himself.

"Are you okay?" she asked, dropping the nervous routine.

"I'm sorry, I've been drinking ten cups of coffee a day for three days now, that's why I'm so twacked out."

"I see. *Why* have you been drinking so much coffee?"

"Just, my mind's been elsewhere lately and my concentration's been totally fractured, and I'm edging up on the deadline to learn this program and I just can*not*— I've just got this headache, and so if you want to cancel I'd completely, completely understand and—"

"Look," she said, stopping him, "it's fine. We can go ahead with the session if you want."

"Well…" he hedged. "If you're willing I guess I should. There's a lot riding on this."

"Why, if you don't mind me asking?"

"Because, um, Chevrolet institutionalized DealEase among all its licensed dealers half a year ago, it was a big deal, like a multi-million dollar contract with the developer. I don't know why but I can't figure it out, nothing, nothing about it is intuitive for me, and so, and so for months all I've been able to do is have a few other sales reps who have been willing to help me, help me out, or just work around it by using our old system, but the manager finally gave me an ultimatum. I probably should've been fired months ago."

"And why weren't you?"

"Well, believe it or not I'm actually not bad at my job, and I've been at Archelaos for a long time, and Tamara could see I was struggling with the program so I think, I think she was trying to be patient with me."

"Tamara?"

"My boss."

Amy sighed. "Okay then, I guess we should get to work. Can we use the table?"

"Of course. Let me clear some space."

Amy started up her laptop and opened an illegally downloaded version of DealEase. Gerney poured himself another cup of coffee and sat down at the table.

Financing functions turned out to be what were giving him the most trouble. The command palette was a daunting grid of inscrutable buttons. Whatever company Chevrolet had contracted with, the program was anything but elegant. Still, though, the software was hardly the problem. The flaw was user-error. He was a complete unstable wreck, fighting himself over everything, always in twenty places at once in his mind, and yet somehow he maintained a certain amount of control, proving himself a fast learner when able to pay attention. She observed him like a biologist studying a small animal, picking up on cues, repetitions, nonverbal signals, determinations and desperations.

He offered her coffee what felt like dozens of times. Twice during the session he got up to refill the mug, continuing to devolve into a nightmare of acceleration. His phone buzzed with messages and calls so many times he had to turn it off.

"So you understand the APR Genius tool now?" she said, moving her hair away from her face and doing nothing to discourage the nervous sexual energy coming from him.

"I think I'm starting to get it, yeah." His voice shaking, the words of each sentence spilling out like change from a broken vending machine.

She could tell that he imagined he was being discreet, allowing himself only a few barely lingering glances here or there, and yet for this he was all the more obvious. Everything about him she found to be like a bug begging to be stomped on, ground to dust, offering up a thoughtless opportunity to feel the rounded satisfaction of having rid the world of an unnecessary, obnoxious presence, and maybe for this exact reason she also found it easier to put on an act around him, condescending to him with an ease she wished she could feel with Aunt Joann, who for all her gullibility was nonetheless a meddler, always looking to stick her nose into what didn't concern her, but here was a person who knew how to mind his own business.

Once the hour was up she sensed he was relieved.

"Hopefully this helped."

"It did, thank you."

"So does that mean you'll be scheduling another session, or have you had your fill of me?" now flirting, almost to his horror.

"No, I, no, I'll definitely be scheduling another, another session as soon as I can. I mean, y'know, *thank you*, I… you've been a huge help, and…"

He was now grappling with two jets, caffeine overload and his own endocrine system. There was the feeling, for Gerney, of a filament heating to ignition point, preparing to undergo combustion, atomic structures breaking down, sensitive materials sizzling free of cohesion, and what he thought was that he could not think, that it was possible he'd never felt so godawful fucking twacked in his life. And on coffee? (Well, okay, he had done some gonine too.)

Packing up her laptop, Amy spotted the gigantic copy of *Shell-Shocked Sarnin* lying at the edge of the kitchen counter, bookmark poking out of the pages one-third of the way through.

"You're reading a book?" the surprise in her voice possibly the only genuine thing she'd emoted since arriving.

He became nervous, even more so, at the book's mention. "Oh, yeah, that's, um, that's something I found, something I found in this, this old box of my father's, that was my father's, so I figured, I guess that I'd give it, give it a read"—speech disintegrating away like parts off a fuselage—"and it's, I don't know, I like it."

"Why?" she asked.

"Um—"

"What's it about?"

"What's— well, it's fiction."

"How weird. Do you read a lot?"

"No, never."

"I don't either. I don't see the point." She zipped her bag closed. "Normally I wouldn't want to pry, but I hope you'll be okay. It seems like you're going through some stuff, if you don't mind my saying so."

Just like that he was disarmed. "Not very subtle is it?"

"No," she said, voice dripping with simulated sympathy, "not very."

"I guess I just—" hesitating here, second-guessing whether he should say what he was going to before crashing forward "—I just, the truth is, and I hope this doesn't, doesn't change your opinion of me, but I'm a bit of a gonine addict."

She started to say something but his speech became uncontrollable.

"Well not an *addict*, I shouldn't say— I should just, just maybe say that I'm *deeply* into— well, okay, I'm an addict. Or if not an addict then just extremely, extremely heavily dependent on drugs and alcohol, especially gonine, to structure my entire social life and like ninety percent of my, ninety percent of my personal relationships. But still, addict just seems, seems a little *strong*…"

"And so the coffee…?"

"The coffee— the coffee was just, I told myself that I wasn't going to go out this weekend, that I wasn't going to do any gonine, not even *drink*, which was kind of a, kind of a bad idea, but then I just ended up on this fucking coffee spree, and…"

She took a deep breath, folded her arms and put on a concerned face.

He stopped himself, wincing repeatedly from caffeine and confession. "I guess I'm just trying to be a better person," he concluded modestly.

She let the comment hang a moment before approaching him, making as if it were something she were compelled to do in the moment, like she'd been drawn to him through some supernatural, instinctual force. She grabbed his arms, pulling her body close to his. At first he was shocked, but she allowed him to process the moment, to let his nerves settle and wait for lust to take over. He wouldn't have to do a thing, the initiative was hers. She kissed him.

All this must have seemed out of context to him, but so much the better. She had the element of surprise on her side. He gave himself over to his body, began to kiss her back. He couldn't see her, but her face was all business: the face of a skilled programmer—audacious but relaxed—manipulating a special kind of code.

She guided them both to the floor, unbuttoning his shirt. She stole glances, saw that his eyes, even while closed, had glazed over, submitting completely to the euphoria just like the addict he had admitted himself to be. Whatever else he was, quick learner or good car salesman, he was first and foremost weak-willed.

Amy, directly on the heels of last night's sexual frustration, was naked and primed quickly. She was not overly worried to let him penetrate her unprotected because she had taken the necessary steps to be made sterile at the age of 21, in the process unnerving the performing surgeon who felt the need to warn her several times of the high risk for postpartum tubal ligation for a girl so young, which she never did get and was never afraid of in the first place. They fucked, and she began to drive him psychologically. Her touch conveyed pity (ridiculous, but he was too emotionally immature to probably ever understand the inconsistency). As if what she really desired was to meld with his confusions and anxieties, massage them away through a physical technique. But of course for the illusion to be complete she also had to allay his masculinity, make him believe that she found his shrinking away from the pains of life admirable, somehow more manly than possessing the will to accept and endure them.

He came, and in that instant she gained access. She collapsed against him post-coitally on the floor of his apartment at 7:12 pm, knowing she was now in full control.

GERNEY

Two weeks of hypersomnia. I cannot, repeat, *cannot*, stay awake longer than seven hours at a time. This has caused problems at work. Instead of lunches I take hour-long naps, and even those aren't usually enough to propel me through the rest of the workdays without feeling drowsy.

Still no call from Amy. I've seen her only one other time since that first night, which was when the hypersomnia started. At first it made sense: I'd purged my system (for the most part) of any caffeine or gonine. Then last weekend I couldn't even stay awake till 9, my drugless diet not helping my mental state in the least. Amy …yeah. Four days ago I found her waiting for me at my front door when I got home from work. I had no idea how long she'd been there. She led me inside like the apartment belonged to her, fucked my brains out, made me dinner, talked for half an hour, then left. I was asleep by then anyway, nearly nodding off at the kitchen table in the middle of the conversation. Since then none of my calls (daily) have met with anything but her answering machine, no personalized message recorded, just flatly stating the number I've reached. As a result my DealEase proficiency has barely improved.

It's early morning before work and I'm in a barber's chair at a haircut conglomerate with a stupid name. I tell the guy to leave the minimal amount of hair possible—I want to see the shape of my skull. His nametag says SNIP-SPOT CERTIFIED STYLIST RACE HOPKINS. It's a cube of real-estate in a strip mall, walls blank except for framed pictures here and there depicting guys with chiseled jaws and women with sensuous eyes showing off their amazing haircuts, smiles saying *holy shit this is a great haircut and it sure hasn't hurt my confidence one bit!* The Snip-Spot logo is seared into the lower lefthand corner of each portrait. We're in here alone, he's the only one working the opening shift, two rows of vacant seats and mirrors radiating absence, tranquility, silence. There's a big screen TV on mute mounted to the wall. Looks like water riots in Nebraska, Oklahoma, Idaho, Colorado, Oregon, South Dakota, a few others. Snippets of authorities and police surrounding the bombed-out desalinization plant in San Diego flash by, everything still a black smoky nondescript mess. I've had the same hairstyle for five years, so why now this compulsion for drastic change? Snip-Spot Certified Stylist Race Hopkins, snapping a pair of clippers to life and plunging them into my hair, causing fuzzy shards of radioac-tive yellow to float down around me, seems to have all the answers:

"The outside's gotta match up with the inside," he says, voice sounding hollow against the empty square walls. "Minds change, appearances change. Hardly a secret to a barber." He's in his mid-40s, face full of amateurish age lines, long hair going a healthy shimmer-ing silver-black, arms sleeved with aging tattoos. "Course we ain't even called barbers, now, man. Certified Stylist. Buncha bullshit."

"If it's true I'm going through some sort of change, is it weird I'm doing it in the form of a haircut?"

"Chicks do it all the time. Nine times outta ten, I change a chick's hairstyle, she just broke up with her boyfriend or got divorced. They do that shit all the time."

"What about men?"

"Tougher to tell. Not so hot at reading men, y'know? They come in, do what they do, sit with these empty zombie stares till you finish, then take off. Can't read em. Don't much want to."

"Seems like you don't really care either way."

"Not too much, no. After a certain age all you know is things aren't the way they used to be, except they're more the same than ever. This fuckin place, for instance. Shit. I used to co-own a barber shop with a couple friends of mine, did walk-in cuts for fifteen bucks apiece. Got tattoos, listened to aggressive music, drank with our girlfriends after hours, and now—blink your eyes—I work here in this fucking money hole that smells like plaster and get disciplined for not spouting prewritten corporate sentences at every customer who wanders in." He pushes my head downward, shaving away the hair there, unfamiliar cool air washing over freshly exposed skin. "Couldn't even tell you where my friends *live* nowadays, haven't talked to em in years. We all let a bunch of invisible bastards turn us into depersonalized walking wallets, so why care anyway? Seems pointless."

His hopelessness triggers me, reflexively, to affirm some shred of positivity, so I say, "I'm sure you could find your friends on a socnet."

"Yeah, and what for? So I could be happy with nothing instead of something?" His face is collected, unperturbed by these grim self-diagnoses.

Still my reflexes are kicking in blindly. "At least you'd be happy."

The clippers venture across the crest of my head, shearing down to the layer of skull smoothness beneath. "Sometimes, boss, it doesn't pay to be happy. This country—well, at least this *city*—is full of happy self-delusionists. That's what those invisible depersonalizing bastards want. Our bodies feel pain right? And you can see how in a lotta situations it would be a disadvantage not to feel the pain that's naturally *meant* to be felt. You could get yourself in deep shit while believing everything's fine. I'm not gonna spell it out for you any more than that."

"You're saying if we're unhappy it's probably for a good reason."

"You ever move your hand closer and closer to a candle flame just to see when the heat'll kick in? All I'm sayin is, eventually you pull your hand away. That's all I'm sayin."

I'm suddenly in my car, inching catlike out of the parking lot, head feeling lighter, less insulated, little blips of code I never noticed before floating through the air and ticking against my scalp, en route to Archelaos, trying to reconcile the fact I'm gonna lose eight or nine hours of this day trying to sell cars to disinterested people. The day is bright but the air's bankrupt of warmth, sun spearing a bright hole through an endless overcast sky, all molecules slowing in their trajectories like we're on Neptune or someplace godforsaken. Turn right onto Infinity Dr., the Impala finding it a bit slippery, correcting its own course somehow. Today is the cut-off day Tamara gave me to *ProDental, Creating Your Dream Smile* learn DealEase, she's going to *Follow Your Friends' Smiles on SocNet And At www.prodental/grid. com* call me into her office today, I already know that. I've become mediocre, haven't I? Worried about being fired from a job I derive no joy from. It's like the start of a *Chevy Ford Toyota Chevy Lexus* movie about some down-on-his-luck middle-aged guy. Do movies really commiserate, or do they just seem like they commiserate because of extensive market research? How do they *1-888-DIVORCE R.W. Trenton Law Associates* even get market research? How much money do they really have? We're probably playing right into their hands. *That's what those invisible depersonalizing bastards want.* What I really need to do is go to work today and focus *ZChase Cut Through the Chatter* on learning more DealEase when there's down time. I wonder if the new InfoZebra store further down Infinity is already open, I need to get those scan and AR modes updated before I forget. Maybe I can get that done *InfoZebra Making Our New Home in the City of Grid* tomorrow in the morning *Chevrolet Malibu*. Shit, I probably won't be able to in the morning because I'll be hungover. I haven't heard from Nick *What Is Objectism?—www.whatisobjectism. com* what's going on tonight. I need to figure a way to stop myself *Samurai Turkey Food With A Blackbelt* from doing gonine. I want to do some gonine. Maybe I need to just grapple a little, get it out of my system, not think about anything for a night, and then focus on DealEase and Amy. I think I'm *Infinity Donuts* just burnt-out. Haven't had breakfast yet. How can I get *ZChase Good Algorithms* Amy to talk to me? I don't understand why she won't talk to me. I should give Aria a call. Stop being a chickenshit and just call her and maybe ask her if she wants to do something with me sometime, who cares if it works out or not. *electonicupdates.org.* Maybe I shouldn't stay single much longer, I'm getting old. What if I don't have a wife by the time *Grid Database Something New Every Minute* I'm thirty-five? What would that be like? If I lose my job it's even more likely I'd end up alone. I need to focus on *McDonald's The Movie www.mcdonaldsthemovie.com* getting DealEase taken care of and then I'll feel better. This song's too slow. Skip. Skip. Skip. *Grid Stats Family Ticket Package $55 for 4 Pizzas, 4 Hats, 4 Sodas statstickets. com.* Skip. Skip. There. *The Caribbean CTR-ALT-DEL Your Stress.* Those people waiting at the bus stop think about a car jumping the curb and killing them at any second. DealEase: warranty tab, APR Genius tool, Used Car Frame Animation tool, *Goodbye One-on-One, Hello Dual Multiplayer.* I think I'm just gonna do some gonine tonight. Not much, at least enough to be social. Maybe Amy will go with me, I'll call her around lunchtime, no earlier than one, otherwise there's the possibility she might be asleep or too busy to talk. Everyone's bored at one in the afternoon. I wish *Mobylism is for the Good of Grid Get Involved!—randymobyle.com* she'd just fucking answer her phone. If I lose my job I'll have to worry about where to get water. I'm thirsty. Not really that thirsty, though. I could prob-ably wait all day to drink water if I had to. But I don't have to. I'm tired. *Archelaos Chevrolet.* I shouldn't be this tired. *Chevy Malibu Chevy 1500. December Inventory Blow-Out. More Channels Less $$$. ZChase City Dweller All Hail the Navigator. You're Looking At An Ad Advertising For Businesses. Chevy. Had Breakfast Yet?—Golden Plain Microwave Breakfast.* I shouldn't be this tired.

All I'm sayin is, eventually you pull your hand away. That's all I'm sayin.

Tk tk tk.

My eyes open to Nick Ibyoo knocking against the window of my car, fat globs of snow falling outside. The windows have fogged and he's like a kid peering into an abandoned house, face ruddy from chill. The sensation is like being underwater, everything freezing, cramped, dark.

"Gerney, it's thirty minutes past ten. You're late."

Fell asleep in the Archelaos parking lot. Great.

Stepping out into the snow, Nick says, "What's the deal? You have a rough night or something? What are you doing sleeping out here without the heat on? And what the hell happened to your hair?"

Snow lands on my scalp. "Too many questions," still feeling asleep.

"Tamara wants to see you in her office. We better get moving."

There's rarely a hint of friendship in his voice when we're at work. What it is is the tone of a self-preservationist, someone able to remorselessly compartmentalize, divorce himself of personal feelings whenever it's advantageous to do so. Yet another piece of evidence showing that Nick is a stronger person than I am.

We start out across the lot toward the showroom, looming in the falling snow as a crystallized miniature version of the Pantheon against sheer sheet-white, made of modumetal and glass after a series of renovations over the last three years, and where the Latin inscription would be on the authentic Pantheon there's instead enormous cut aluminum 3D lettering saying ARCHELAOS CHEVROLET. Anchored to the top of the dome structure is an inflated Yeti balloon advertising the yearly December Inventory Blowout. All this presides over a field of serflike, awestruck vehicles, blurry phantasmal outlines of the Grid skyline registering just barely in the distance, giant lurking faraway creatures.

"You're lucky I saw your car out here when I came in," Nick says, grimacing against the snow. "Tamara would've had a shit fit."

"I have no idea what happened."

"When the hell'd you do that to your hair?"

"This morning."

"Why'd you shave your head in the middle of fucking *winter?*"

We pass through the line of columns, entering through motion-sensor glass doors. The showroom floor opens into a room with a vast convex ceiling, a golden Chevy logo at its pinnacle, an enormous fresco surrounding it portraying dozens of Camaros with white angel wings racing through a heavenly panorama of pinkish clouds. The floor is dotted with three or four high-sheen display cars and the front desk sitting beneath more aluminum letters that read, esoterically, POWER. Bixby the front desk girl waves to Nick when we pass. Beyond the showroom is a honeycomb floorplan of offices, Tamara's positioned at the center of the outer ring of connecting hexagons. Nick claps me on the back and splits off in the direction of his Fleet Manager's office, saying without looking back, "Go get her."

The silence inside reflects the silence of the snow outside. I can hear my footsteps sounding down the curvature of the hallway. I pass my own office, a cubicle-sized room containing a desk, computer, and shelves stuffed tight with white binders that add an extra tinge of claustrophobia. Tamara's door is accessed through a special hallway that connects the outer ring to the central sanctum, one of the walls lined with a display case containing awards and general proof of her greatness—a picture of her golfing with the mayor and Ward VIII Councilman Phred deWet framed against a complimentary set of clubs presented to her for distinguished economic service; a veritable timeline of award plaques from the Chamber of Commerce, including Innovation Through Technology & Outstanding Business Achievement from last year; various masturbatory certificates issued by Chevrolet that smack of a collegiate kind of pride; pictures of her with her husband and daughter, with Stats small forward Brendan Journeys, with some French stunt driver, with her defunct business partner at the groundbreaking ceremony for the dealership; finally a portrait of her against a backdrop of a digital American flag, almost like a senator's portrait, that's hard not to find hilarious (maybe also intimidating). In it her hair is straightened and highlighted in contrast to its normal close-cut springiness, smile full of a signature strained dignity that has always made businesspeople seem opaque to me.

She's on the phone when I enter her office, holding a finger up signifying to wait quietly. The walls in here are circular rather than square, and for all the hints of a personal life contained in the display cases outside, her office is devoid of anything except business: papers, readouts, memos, charts, data. Again these harsh separations. Necessary, but polar. She's dressed for moneyless weather today, all dark sad bundles.

"Well it's this darn snow that's gonna do me in. Yeah. I know. No, it's been consistently terrible. That's right, that's exactly right, what can you do? [That laugh, like she finds her own anxiety funny.] I heard about that, yes, something about InfoZebra's website? No, really, we'll be fine. Something always works out. Yep, you're right, something always comes along, so... Okay. Okay, I will. All right, Henry. Yeah, hi to Amanda. Okay. We'll work out this contract stuff later. Okay, bye."

She hangs up and completely changes in demeanor, affability dropping from her like a shroud to reveal the authority underneath.

"Go ahead and take a seat, Gerney."

I do, the feeling of being undersized whenever across a desk from someone kicking in.

"You got a haircut."

"I did," slumping down so I can rest my ankle on my knee.

She clicks her mouse twice for vague reasons, then places both hands flat on the desk, saying, "Okay, *so*. Here's what I've been hearing about you with regards to this whole DealEase thing."

"Okay." I wonder, as always, who her informants are.

"From what I hear you've been doing better, but haven't quite gotten the hang of it yet."

I take my ankle off my knee, sit up straight again, unsure where to put my hands.

"Now taking into account your sales, I'd normally say showing progress would be enough, but in this case I'm in a bit of a position with you."

"I'm doing good with the program now. Things are starting to make sense to me."

"Well, that may be, but there are two problems. First, I've given you a window of time twice as long as your coworkers to learn the software. Which is now closing in on four months. I can appreciate the troubles you're having given that this is a new system that's just beyond its beta model. However. You're also causing an increased workload for the people around you, and that can't continue. It's confusing because your learning abilities have been much better in the past, so I'm not sure why the lag on this."

I'm focused more on maintaining eye contact than on what she's saying, finding it difficult.

"Second, we just got word Chevrolet is updating our software again."

"Again? We just switched over six months ago."

"More like eight. This software is still DealEase, but an updated version. I can only tell you what I've read in the memos, but there are some improvements and additions to the financing tools, plus a revamped user interface."

"I think—"

"In addition, we're going to be required from here on out to work with certain Chevrolet-specific data collection programs connected with the Chevy Expand Initiative. So you can see how, in light of how much emphasis Corporate is putting on these software rollovers, I have extra reason to be concerned."

She leaves off with an expectant look, hoping for me to swoop in and allay the situation. But the truth is she's right—I *am* lagging— and all the standard reassurances are escaping me.

"Personally," she says, picking up my slack, "I couldn't give a darn about software. What I care about are *sales*, getting the customer into the car they want, but these changeovers constitute big money for Corporate. As in hundreds of millions. The thinking is, as I under- stand it, that these programs are going to help us sell cars better. I'm not sure I see the corre*lation*, but they're exercising more control the further we delve into this whole poverty and energy problem. So there's a lot of pressure right now—I can't go into details except that they're watching closely—about demonstrating an ability to sell via DealEase. This is less about what I think of you than what the people above me do."

I nod.

"Do you have anything to input here, Gerney?"

What I'm thinking that I never thought before is that I actually like Tamara. I have this polite understanding with her that I've failed. Not just at DealEase, but in some other way. Bigger. I failed in having any conviction, any purpose. I failed at caring about much of anything. I never realized I didn't care about selling cars. I *cared* about making money and being left alone. I *cared* about being as comfortable as humanly possible. The world always seemed so passively hopeless to me, but why? I can't account for any of it, and I don't know how I reached this point where none of my thinking makes sense to me anymore.

"Gerney, I want to help. That's why I called you in here, but you've got to communicate with me."

"I don't…I don't have a lot to say in my defense."

"Do you understand what I'm telling you about the importance of the software?"

"Yes."

"And you understand your job is dependent on it, regardless of your sales."

"Yes."

She sighs, sits back in her chair, unsure what more to do. She places a finger against the part in her lips, seems to come to a conclusion.

"Okay then. You say you understand. The fact of the matter is you're a multi-year employee, so here's the deal. You have exactly one week from today to show acceptable proficiency with DealEase. If you can't demonstrate it to me by then, you *will* be fired. I want to know you understand this. There won't be any more grace period."

"Okay," I say. "I understand."

"You're a good worker, I know you can do this."

H.Z. Arnitz, full name Howell Zachary Arnitz, was born in 1952 outside Albuquerque, New Mexico in a trailer home bathtub to parents Dwight and Dana Arnitz. Zachary Howell was the name of a former boss of Dana Arnitz who she reportedly despised, and in hopes her son would turn out as the exact inverse of the man she reversed the order of the names. H.Z. Arnitz has said the name "was a joke to my parents I never fully understood." Dwight Arnitz worked various jobs in the food service industry, ultimately spending the latter half of his life employed as the store manager of a McDonald's. Dana Arnitz, among other things, made bullets during World War II and worked on and off as a hairdresser. After completing junior high, H.Z. Arnitz moved from New Mexico to Philadelphia with his family where he graduated high school and attended Penn State as a film major, later transferring to Oregon State University to study civil engineering. Having never gotten higher education themselves, Arnitz's parents encouraged him to attend college, though in five years of being a full-time student he would never earn a degree. According to Arnitz, he began writing fiction at the age of 25 while working as a dishwasher at a seafood restaurant in the coastal town of Depoe Bay, Oregon. Depressed because of his failure to graduate college, coupled with increasing financial pressures, Arnitz began writing short stories as an attempt to make money. Arnitz said in a 1988 interview, "For me, short stories required less effort and time, and that was appealing since the whole thing was a crackpot idea I wasn't likely to pursue beyond the weekend it took me to write them." His first two stories, *Sangria* and *Sangria II*, were accepted by a small literary journal with limited distribution connected to the University of Oregon, and sold for twenty dollars apiece. The stories are two installments about a Mexican-American couple who meld in intimate physical and mental ways by consuming excessive amounts of alcohol, and by the end of the story the reader is led to believe the two have become one person. *Sangria II* is less similar to formal narrative than it is to dramatic monologue, told from the perspective of a physician involved with the couple who begins using alcohol in the same experimental manner, but rather than fuse to a loving partner, he unwittingly fuses to what the story terms as Nothing. Although the stories enjoyed popularity and circulated in some other journals, earning Arnitz similar pittances, they didn't yield enough money to convince him to pursue writing as a career. Until he was 30 years old, Arnitz lived below the poverty line in Oregon and parts of Idaho, having to perform painful amateur dental work on himself twice, as well as sleeping in the homes of friends. An intensifying battle with alcoholism had led to a strained relationship with his parents by 1976, and by 1979 he dropped out of contact with them for close to a decade. His first and only two short stories had continued to grow in popularity since his departure from Depoe Bay, eventually catching the eye of editor James Leatherby, who navigated both stories into publication in *Atlantic Monthly*, and later *The New Yorker*, *Harper's Bazaar* and *Playboy*. By the time Leatherby got hold of the stories, however, Arnitz had dropped off the map to such an extent (he went by the alias "Mac" for several years, for example) that no one knew who he was or how to get in contact with him. He famously discovered his success by picking up an aged copy of *The New Yorker* in a doctor's office while suffering from strep throat. When he stepped forward as the author, there were doubts as to whether he was who he claimed to be, but after producing the original acceptance letters and handwritten drafts of the stories, he was awarded publication money, literary representation by Leatherby, and an exclusive profile in *The New Yorker*. There was short-lived fame for Arnitz in the literary world, but because he continued not to write, as well as drink heavily, attention quickly dropped off. Arnitz said of himself that he suffered from a condition of his own invention, called "Whiskeymania." "I was in the grip of Whiskeymania for a lot of years, true, but it was a way of filtering the sickness of the world into a useful inward persona that took me to fantastic places I can't even tell you where. Outwardly I seemed to be deteriorating, but it was merely a byproduct of a consuming inner life. I was actually very coherent." Evidence of this came when, after a seven-year hiatus from writing since the publication of his first short stories, he told Leatherby that he had formed an idea for a novel. The idea was a rough version of what turned out to be *Shell-Shocked Sarnin*, Arnitz's only novel and most famous work. Taking a little less than a year to write, *SSS* numbered 1,382 pages in original type-written manuscript format and had to be delivered to Leatherby's New York office in a cake box by Arnitz himself since there was only one copy in existence. The majority of the manuscript was written in Rutland, Vermont where Arnitz had moved in 1984, remaining a resident until his death. The book was released in 1986 by an independent press after most major houses turned the manuscript down, but was later reprinted under the HarperCollins label in 1995 after selling over 60,000 copies. Leatherby said after the success of *SSS* in a 1997 interview, "I'd never been able to hold a conversation with [Arnitz] since I'd first met him in '78. He was an absolute drunken soddy wreck most of the time, and I'd long ago lost faith he would ever write anything of value again. He would nip at bottles of beer in my office while waiting for appointments. But when he called me that winter saying he had an idea for a book, he was quite intelligible, quite gentlemanly even. He delivered nearly a year later—looking a fright but speaking with a captivating iridescence." The novel closely follows Private Garrett Sarnin, a sensitive young man serving overseas in a U.S. World Allied Army detachment focused primarily on hindering the activity of a fictional conquering army led by General Vernon Cobrigale, a megalomaniacal fascist. Sarnin has an unformed, nomadic identity, and is constantly trying to "give himself over" to other identities he believes will make him whole. However, the dominant values in his binary environments of war and peace constantly shift, forcing him to ride the behavioral middle ground of every situation. In almost every case he fails to integrate socially, sometimes at the cost of his own physical health. The ending, often considered controversial within the U.S. because Sarnin sacrifices American troops to save enemy soldiers, lends to the true theme of the novel: that identity is fluid, dynamic and changing, so much that humans do not actually have cogent identities at all, and are at the mercy of the environments they inhabit, which dictate those identities. Conformity is unavoidable unless a so-called "background identity" is pursued, one that is highly moralistic and unconcerned with personal gain. In this way only, according to Arnitz, human beings can pursue states of independence or radicalism. When the book achieved wider publication it was well-received within certain circles, but mainstream critics jumped on Arnitz's cynicism, exhausting prose, seeming disdain for narrative structure, and an underlying set of philosophical themes that were famously panned in the *New York Times* as being "pseudo-intellectual and ultimately pointless, eventually sounding more like the ramblings of someone at a bar who's had a few too many rather than any sort of authority on the subjects the novel deals with." Despite overwhelming negative press, however, the book continued to sell consistently up until the major New York publishers dissolved and print became more rare. *Shell-Shocked Sarnin* is out of physical print, but remains electronically available. Just like *Sangria* and *Sangria II*, *SSS* is most notable for the influencing effect it has on some readers. Starting in the late 1980s and spanning to the turn of the century, small cultish groups were formed based on the non-systematic and almost mystical philosophies contained in the novel. The Society of Background Identity and the Sarninists were most prominent among them. Arnitz himself was never affiliated with either group. He would never live to see the book bear the HarperCollins label. Descending further into self-destructive and erratic behavior, his window of lucidity did not last and he returned to the throes of Whiskeymania. There were no more attempts to write, and in the words of Leatherby, Arnitz began "slowly to become intolerable once again." Rarely leaving Rutland, he consumed prolific amounts of booze and espoused a type of anti-identity radicalism that—

"So I'm assuming she didn't fire your ass since you're still in here wasting time."

Nick walks into my office carrying a ziploc containing a sandwich, taking a seat on the other side of my desk while I quickly minimize the window I was reading.

"One week extension. DealEase or else." I point at the sandwich. "What the hell is that?"

"What do you mean?"

"I mean what is it."

There's smeared mayonnaise on the inside of the plastic.

"It's kind of a long story."

I tap a pen that says *Archelaos Chevrolet* against my desk. He takes out the sandwich, which has been cut in half, and takes a bite. There's a streak of mayonnaise on one of his knuckles from reaching into the bag.

"Do you have any gonine for tonight?" I ask despite myself.

"Through circumstances I had no control over I bought a shitload earlier this week. Why, coffee's not doin it for you anymore?"

"I can't stop sleeping. I keep crawling into that dark spot of unconsciousness."

"Was a nice little narcoleptic stunt you pulled this morning in the parking lot. The ice is only getting thinner, y'know. Time to pull it together."

"I'm just trying to figure out if there's a reason to."

"Well how's becoming one of those goddamn stupid govt-initiative bums sound to you? Shit, I'll *buy* you some black sneakers if you want."

"But you're bringing jet tonight, right?"

"Fuckin— what do you think? You people and your goddamn gonine. I'm trying to talk to you. I want to know if you intend to save your job or if poverty has suddenly started to sound like a fun time to you."

You people?

"I'm doing my best. It's just not intuitive for me."

"No, if you wanted to learn it you would have by now. It's that you don't care. I haven't seen you in here even one time working on it."

"Something's definitely up. First you *bring* a sandwich for lunch and now you're lecturing me about responsibility? Tell me what's going on."

"You don't get information without divulging information. I asked you first. Reciprocation, motherfucker."

"I don't know what you want me to say."

"How about why so down all the time? You've got this permanent sad look on the weekends and it's pissing me off. Not to mention your pity party here at work. I just wanna know why you're such a pain in the ass now, is all."

I drop the pen I was holding and lean back in my chair. This is Nick scolding me, wanting me to ride the behavioral middle ground. Like with Tamara, I don't have any excuses for myself. He can't understand what's going on with me, nor does he really care. Truth be told, I'm starting to hate him, but there are things I need—flashes of strange faces in neon bar light, rays of gonine spread across the backs of toilets hitting numb throats, girls with exposed skin who will never ever care about me, little blissful windows of total self-loss—and he's the doorway to those things. My hands are tied.

"And look, I'm not trying to be a jerk," he says, "there's something I've been meaning to tell you."

"Meaning to tell me what?"

He sets the sandwich down half-eaten on top of the ziploc. "About me and Aria."

"Something I don't already know?"

"Someone," he says carefully, "died on Monday. You didn't know her."

"Last Monday?"

"The woman who died was basically my mother. She wasn't actually my mom, but basically she was."

This is the first thing I've ever heard Nick say about his childhood or family. The hallway outside my office is empty, silent.

"She really wasn't even that old. Not even fifty."

He does something that strikes me as oddly vulnerable for him and licks the small streak of mayonnaise off his hand. Some serious defenses are being lowered right now, and despite my fascination I also feel very uncomfortable.

"I got the call right before the end of work that day—"

"On Monday?"

"Yes, and it was weird because I always imagined what I'd do when I found out she was dead. You ever do that, imagine what you'll do when somebody you love dies? But I only ever pretended she'd died because I guess she's the only person I ever loved. I mean, we fought a lot. That's sorta *why* I loved her, probably, because she let me hate her a lot, too. I hated her about equally to the amount I loved her, y'know? She didn't care, though. Even if I hated her she just took it, never really— you know when someone loves you even if you hate them, they just love you cause they love you, and sometimes you think you don't need them even though you really do? Katarzyna Feathers. We all called her Kasia."

He looks at me, makes actual eye contact.

"Anyway. The point is it was weird because I didn't feel like I thought I was going to. Things didn't turn instantly to shit. Didn't break down crying. Didn't even leave work immediately. I finished what I was doing, went home, did all this gonine, made myself dinner. I felt fine, just really empty. [He shrugs, eyes distant, reliving the experience.] I was pretty disappointed with myself, like what the hell? This is it? I don't feel *anything?* What's wrong with me? Until I went to bed. And I must've pulled up some memory of her or something cause suddenly the whole situation just socked me in the gut, and then everything *did* turn to shit."

What he's saying sounds so familiar to me it's like I could finish the story for him: the death was too excruciating to sink in right away, life continued as normal for a while, then horrific sadness, finally the need to escape a growing sense of despair and, above all, loneliness. I wonder if Nick even remembers my father's dead.

"I needed something to get my mind off things. So the next day I call Aria to see if she wants to go to lunch, but when I *saw* her…" He takes a deep breath. "Gerney, she was a wreck. No—it was shocking how bad she looked. And we did a couple lines of gonine in my car before eating, and afterwards she was so twacked."

"Nick," I say, "she's an addict." This was something we'd all been conscious of for a long time, Aria's habit. I was surprised to hear *him* so surprised about it. I knew he'd been sleeping with her for over a year. Had he, of all people, never recognized it? Most of us who grapple regularly are sensitive to that sort of thing. Avoiding that nosedive into addiction is an ever-present source of anxiety, the precipice we all toe. That temptation. To create a living breathing oblivion for yourself. Nick, we'd realized a long time ago, was impervious to that fate. Most of us were mixed up in the whole scene by choice—Nick was there by destiny. He looks at me with a mixture of revelation and resentment.

"She told me she loved me," he said.

He's unaware that for all his suffering he's nothing more than a statistic, another instance of the same old thing replayed over and over. See *Shell-Shocked Sarnin*:

All the world is rubble, men are the weeds poking through it. No difference between their life cycles save the surrounding nutrients, those nutrients distributed according to a capricious sweepstakes, the only difference being that some grow dismally while some thrive, but all existing nevertheless, and Sarnin being that strain of weed appearing with greater regularity all the time, the dismal grower in nutrient-rich rubble, poking through into sunlight only to cringe away.

We're just weeds in rubble, some differences, but still just weeds. What sympathy can I give him? Or am I misinterpreting? I'm the weed that cringes away, he's the weed that thrives, and I want him to know what it's like to cringe. Or maybe we're just two employees of Archelaos Chevrolet, two citizens of Grid, two friends of chance, one thriving, one cringing, and I'm enjoying watching him cringe for once. I'm not who I thought I was. I'm not sensitive or scared or injured—things I always assumed. I'm not the hero here, just self-interested.

"Aria said she loves you?"

"We're together now. And if we're going to make it work, me and her, we're eventually gonna have to help each other stop doing certain things. Including gonine."

He's stealing from me again, this time enlightenment. I realize now that I'd planned to exploit personal growth as a weapon. I haven't progressed at all. I'm still—*still*—selfish.

"I don't understand."

"Aria has a problem. I think we fell in love by complete accident, but either way, things have to change. I just thought you should know about us."

"So all this time, all these drugs, and you're telling me you're going to quit all of it just like that?"

"I'm gonna *try* to quit."

"What are we even going to be if we quit? I mean, who are we if we're not grappling?"

Here I am confusing my identity for his, as usual looking for someone else to make me whole. Or did he give himself over to *my* impulse for change? Does it matter where the impulse originated? I've slipped through into a dimension where Nick Ibyoo wants to become a better person, and I'm nothing but a greedy jethead.

"I don't know. But there might be something else out there for me now, and I never really thought there would. I'm doing well as fleet manager. I've got a nice place, some money saved up. I've got a girl who I could have a future with. I could have a family, a normal life. Who fuckin knows?"

This way of living, for him, isn't self-enforced or self-aware. Aria is his way out. I feel claustrophobic inside my own machinations.

"You're just going to change who you are."

"*Try*. I'm gonna try." He takes another bite of his sandwich.

I'm sweating even though it's cold in here. The condensation of jealousy.

Was dozing at my desk, but since I was next in the Up system I got the only non-maintenance customer of the day.

"Gerney. Hey."

Carter, another sales rep two doors down from mine. We're in competition for highest sales, which supposedly don't matter but actually do.

"Got a guy out here for ya. You're up."

"Mm. Got a girl with him?"

"No, but he's fish-in-barrel status. Post-accident. Hand him over to me, I'd be happy. You could go back to sleep."

"All right, I'm up, I'm up."

I see him waiting for me out in the showroom, hanging out around the '25 Cruze floor model, engaged with his phone. Carter's right, this guy's definitely looking to buy. He looks up from his phone. His face is bandaged and looks like hell. One of his eyes is a whole different dimension of pain, the bruise tissue encompassing his forehead, the bridge of his nose, half his cheek, all splashed with vivid black, red, purple, green. The white of his left eye is full of blood. Running along his cheekbone are thin strips of adhesive bandage.

"Hi there. Gerney. Nice to meet you."

"Hello."

"Looks like you've seen some better days."

No response. Clearly he's a nervous guy. There's a pad taped against his nostrils keeping stable a pair of plastic tubes running up into his sinuses. He has to breathe through his mouth. His right forearm and hand are locked in a cast. He looks at his phone, texting. I stand waiting for him to finish, but he goes on typing for too long.

"I hope you're feeling okay. I'm assuming you were in an accident?"

He nods at his phone.

"Well I'm sorry to hear that. Looking for a replacement vehicle?"

He's a bit shorter than me, dressed in a cheap solid-color red shirt and pale jeans that don't fit very well. Obviously unconcerned with appearance. Lending to that is the unwashed greasy look of his hair receding from his temples, but what's left is still youthful. His behavior is strange for someone so young, very guarded and fearful to make eye contact.

"Got your eye on this one here?"

He barely nods, still texting. Something's wrong with this guy. Can't tell exactly what, but the more I observe him the more something's not right. There's no shortage here of people who've lost their minds. Something's wound very tight inside him, something coiled, snap-worthy.

"Sir?"

"Yes."

"Sir?"

Finally he looks up. The good eye is wide and helpless, slightly enlarged with baseless fear, mouth half open.

"Sir, are you here to buy a vehicle?"

"I need a new one. The old one was totaled."

The phone remains in his hand, screen consciously shielded from my view.

"I'm sorry to hear that. Did you have something in mind?"

"What?"

"A model or a price range or a color, something like that. Something in mind."

Quickly he steals a nervous glance over the waxed and shimmering roof of the Cruze model at Bixby, sitting underneath the POWER sign. She's paying no attention to either of us.

"Something not too expensive. Not too expensive would be good."

Has definitely lived in this city his whole life, he's got that look of having never seen a countryside. Every detail of this place is wielding an invisible knife at him. Frightened of people. Subsists on high-sodium food made with hot water or in the microwave. I start to explain about the Cruze. Not very expensive, geared for economy, good luxury options. Depends on his preferences. His phone buzzes and he hurriedly goes back to texting, obviously flustered, maybe even angry.

"I like the Cruze the best, but we've got plenty of alternatives. Anything grabbing your interest?"

A sexless life, probably, or else it's a category of sex I'm not familiar with. Sex among the mentally disturbed. Actually not bad-looking if he'd just clean up a bit or put any effort into the way he dresses. He seems fine except for that look in his eyes, shades him with abnormality. Someone who treats their home like a hiding spot.

"Seems like a pretty important conversation."

"Sorry. My girlfriend. We're arguing."

Maybe not so sexless. He has to speak through his mouth so everything comes out like he's got a bad cold. He's always just one sentence away from asking for help, someone drifting on a lifeboat, passed regularly by ocean liners, cruise ships. I imagine the hospital he was born in was dirty. He continues to keep tabs on Bixby, who's growing uncomfortable at her desk, overhearing everything, feeling his nervous stares.

"Care to continue this discussion in my office? We could sit down and talk."

He nods. We walk to my office, him trailing behind me, an obedient follower. I take a seat across from him at my desk. This is a role reversal from six hours ago when I was in Tamara's office. I feel powerful by default. He's still texting.

"Sorry, I didn't catch your name."

He could've been a normal person before the accident, there's the possibility of brain damage. The fluorescent light in here gleams off his bruise. What's his girlfriend like, I wonder. Sometimes the irregular come together, wade through a hindered reality of cautious stares, brief answers, the world a brutal place, confusing one another in delightful ways. I ask him what the argument's about but he shrinks away from the question. Idle daydreams of gonine and Amy.

"Is everything okay? You're welcome to come back any time if this isn't opportune for you."

He says he's beginning to think something's very wrong with him, and it's like a completely different person, a person underneath a person, has momentarily surfaced, by all appearances normal but in serious danger. A person who lives inside a person. No cogent identity. He's aware of himself getting worse, even right here, right now, in my office. He's paranoid, except he knows he shouldn't be.

"Just tell me if something's going on here. Am I under observation?"

He's sick but he's not, a little uncorrupted bit of himself deep inside trying to topple a regime of constant fear. He's noticed himself deteriorating ever since he left the hospital. He suspects it's his girlfriend, increasingly paranoid, security-obsessed, begging him to retract from the living.

"On second thought, I think you'd be best suited for an Aveo."

Some things haven't been making sense. When he watches the news the events seem geared toward him, a conspiracy. His girlfriend concurs. She's a liar, he senses. A false identity. She didn't even visit him in the hospital, if I can believe that. I think about Amy, her constant absence, her unwillingness to appear. What's going on, he wants to know, what'd he miss? He wants the truth.

"I'm not sure I can help you. All I do is sell cars."

"Then at least reassure me. Reassure me I'm going to be okay."

To him, the air feels old, disgruntled. Full of anger and foreboding and basically pissed off. Is it all his fault, our fault? He's starting to lose me, I can't follow, we've got to come back to reality. His phone buzzes and he texts and it buzzes again. Looking at me, he's losing and gaining aspect, getting closer before pulling farther away.

"Never mind, I'd like to buy something expensive."

"Well in that case we've got some frankly kick-ass cars. Think Camaro. Hell, think Corvette. Think Silverado. Think a mobile representation of you that demands respect from others. In fact, take it from me, this is a great way to change your whole idea of yourself. You'll be a different person, more in control. This could be the answer you've been looking for."

I tell this stuff to people all the time, and it's not entirely untrue. He seems not to care about any of it. We're in the realm of products here, might as well act like it. I'm gonna need the money next week when Tamara fires me.

"Corvette?"

"Sure. You know how rare it is to see someone driving a Corvette nowadays? Might as well do what you want, if you can afford it. Live with some passion."

So little difference between sales pitches and regular trains of thought. Hit an impulse at exactly the right time and you've broken through. A person is reconfigured right in front of you. A car is the second most expensive product a person will ever own. I want to lose my job. This is endless boredom, endless purposelessness. All these objects and no objectives. When he's not busy texting, he's confused.

"Are you doing this on purpose?"

"Am I doing what on purpose?"

He says he recently came into a large sum of money. This is music to Chevrolet's ears. I imagine he extracts meaning out of paranoia. I imagine he doesn't actually want help, he likes the way he is. Without discontent there is no conflict, without conflict there are no goals, without goals there is no point. We need our sicknesses. I picture his parents abandoned him on the side of a highway somewhere, that he was raised by movie theater employees who smoked and made minimum wage. I imagine he feels sorry for himself. I imagine him imagining me. We are lost out here.

"Tell me what you think. Is she real?"

I think…

"I think being able to share the world with someone is about as real as it gets. I met a guy this morning who didn't think people ought to be happy with nothing instead of something, but I'm not sure the two are distinguishable anymore, nothing and something. We've lost the ability to tell maybe? I don't know. What is she to you, something or nothing?"

"She's something to me, but she's nothing."

"Ah. Damn. Tough call."

His phone buzzes loud against my desk and fills the momentary silence between us. I notice it's a different phone than the one he had before. He's got two phones.

"Listen, give this whole car situation some thought. I'll be here until next Friday. If you have any questions, give me a call."

He gathers up the phones and leaves. I call Amy and get her machine.

NICK

We're in the drive-thru and she's like: "—two number threes. Yeah, combos. Um, tsh-tsh-tsh, how about one Coke and— What do you want to drink?"

I tell her.

"And one root beer. What? I, um, [sniff] okay, they have Plus, Barq's, Diet Barq's, Pibb…"

Well Plus then. All decisions are impossible.

"Plus, please. No thank you. Nope, that's all. Okay, thanks."

It's fuckin irreversible now. Aria's driving my truck. We're both grappling even though I didn't think we'd be. I'm realizing she's gonna have a harder time quitting than I initially thought. My suspicion is she's got her own stash, tiny square ziplocs printed with superhero logos—Superman, Batman, Green Lantern, Wonder Woman, Iron Man, Spiderman, Callisto, Aquaman, Captain America—filled with fine white clumped crystals like miniature eggs, snorted up, hatching within her, birthing zipping electron flows. Her eyes are electric. They reflect a glowing Burger King sign. Saturday has swallowed us whole, things are different from inside its digestive process. This is the first weekend of my life that Katarzyna Feathers is dead.

"I know you grew up in the EM"—(what people from Grid

sometimes call the eastern manufacturing sector)—"but that's all I know, Nick. You've never [sniff] told me anything else."

The drive-thru window is an illuminated square behind her, employees buzzing around inside, her jaw and upper arms thin, eyes semi-panicky. This is drug intimacy. Tell me your life story. Merge with me.

"I have to know who you are if we're going to be together. I know you're upset about Kasia, but I can't help you if I don't know who she was."

She resents having information denied her, like she deserves that, too, on top of everything else. She thinks I'm proud of the things I don't tell her, the way she's proud of her own secrets, and can't imagine how afraid I am.

"I want to know all the smallest details. I want the panoramic helicopter shots and the supercloseups of cells dividing. I want to be a transmitter of your life. I want to know you. Tell me. Who were your parents?"

Don't know. My first memories are of living on the street. I don't remember anything before I was four. I lived with my brother Zach in one of those homeless kid encampments the *Database* is always making such a big deal over and that Mobyle is always promising to abolish. They really do exist. I lived in one. But they're not evil like they say, just sad. Aria's eating french fries, we're driving through my neighborhood in the motherboard. The seats of my truck are heated leather, the LED in the dashboard displaying GPS tracking and a TV show where the same two actors play different characters every episode but always fall in love and fuck and also what's going on inside some Egyptian nightclub even though I'm pretty sure the video is a recording from yesterday or the day before and all that's muted cause we're listening to music. The encampment was on a portion of the property of an electronic packaging factory called DataWrappers.

"Electronic packaging would be…?"

It's like hardware for electronics. Like the frame and screen of your phone, complicated inside pieces for microchips and electric junk, speaker baskets, the plastic and metal pieces on your stereo and TV. That's what the factory specialized in, was metal and plastic. They did sheet metal, cast metal, machined metal, injection molding, transfer molding, vacuum forming, die cutting. There were enormous stacks sticking out of the factory that let loose all this pollution, and near the base of the spouts the air shimmered the way distant air shimmers on hot days. We lived right next to all that. Everyone in the camp made shelters out of scavenged bits of electronic casing. A lot of kids used keyboard molds for roofs and computer or TV frames for walls. The shelters were crappy, always falling down and shit. The fronts were open, no one could make doors, we were just kids, and you could look from our shelter, mine and my brother's, and see dozens of kids living in these square plastic huts that looked like computer monitors, and behind it all was the factory with the three constant plumes rising into the air at sideways angles. Even in the snow, sometimes, the plumes would be there, white smoke against a white sky. Watching em was like watching moving water. You're probably wondering about the smell, but the plumes actually didn't smell bad. I don't know how they did it, but they had some method to make the pollution smell like—well, it's hard to describe it exactly, everyone had their own opinion—but basically it smelled like something fresh-baked. Like cookies or brownies, roughly. But there was a definite sugary, cakey dimension to it. Very pleasant, very rich, very warm scent. All the kids liked it. Any time the spouts were inactive you'd start to get the sharp scent of metal and the chemical smell of plastic and the BO smell of dirty kids, and we'd yell at a big empty factory for the pollution to come back on, pound on the chain-link they put up to keep us out, just dying for that cookie smell. I'm fuckin convinced I'm gonna get cancer before I'm fifty. We're stopped in the parking lot of a liquor store, the humming sign above stimulating a pleasing blue from the hood of my truck that I'm focusing on while I talk, all the little points of reflected light. There's a stack of fresh pale yellow napkins on top of the dashboard. Aria's picking at her burger. The people in the Egyptian nightclub are all pulsing as one to the beat of music that's not in time with what we're listening to in the car and the little graphical representation of us on the GPS display is like an insect caught in a web of crisscrossing roads and the TV show is on commercial break for an add-on feature to phones that lets you draw in the air with some kind of green laser. Lone men stumble in and out of the liquor store, arriving into the blue glow of the sign, headphones stuck in ears with wires running down into pockets. Aria reaches across me to open the glove box, take out the baggie of gonine, separates it into two lines on the center console between our seats with a credit card. Our hut, I'm saying, staring into the blue glow, was just big enough for me and my brother. We filled it with mounds of blankets to keep warm in the winter, and kids made fun of us for holding each other when we slept, but it was the best way to keep warm. We weren't the only ones who did it. Supposedly, according to my brother, I did this thing in my sleep that drove him crazy. I'd say the word Magnavox, like repeat it, constantly. Magnavox. I ask her if she's ever noticed me say it when she's slept with me.

"No. Wait, did your brother know who your parents were?"

Oh, that fucker knew. He was fifteen when I was four. He knew, but he wouldn't tell me.

"Sounds like you hate him."

Why's it so hard to explain? I didn't really hate him, I just hated that he wouldn't tell me. Actually, no, I hated him in a little kid way. She doesn't understand, but she says she does, which is nice of her but makes me feel stupid. There's a hard wind, the blue points of light dance around on the hood. Magnavox. Those nights I held onto my brother underneath dirty blankets we'd stare at our walls—screenless TVs stacked pretty well for some reason—and he'd hug me. I didn't really like it, but he hugged me all the time. Like a fag, pretty much. Like we were lovers (I don't tell Aria this), his arm draped over me and pressing my back in close to his chest, and occasionally he'd nuzzle my neck with his face, fall asleep like that, and I hated the way his jaw felt, the little pre-pubescent points of stubble scratching against my skin. The whole hugging thing was why I felt uncomfortable around him for so many years after we got out of the encampment, I'd rarely ever let him touch me for any reason. I was afraid he was sexually attracted to me. Except now that I'm saying all this stuff out loud, it makes sense that he'd hug me. It couldn't have been any fun for him, that life. Taking care of a little kid, enforcing that obligation on himself at so young an age. He needed a hug. Regardless, I hated it. Nothing can ever change that. Aria snorts her line through a twenty and then hands it to me and I snort mine. When I snort jet I can feel her watch me with a mix of admiration and fear. She's afraid of gonine, afraid to grapple down to the depths of her soul. She loves it, but she's afraid of it, afraid of the confusion. The confusion of not knowing who you are, of having a second personality created within you, a personality that will save you from yourself. It's the same with all of us—we escape only to go running back, unable to lift the anchor. The present is the only pure place, second to second, where we exist as glowing gods. The Egyptian nightclub is growing chaotic and Aria resumes work on her fries. Life wasn't terrible in the camp, at least not for me. If you're young enough, anything can seem normal. Zach was one of the oldest ones. There was only one guy older than him, Tim, and they mostly kept each other company. Except Tim was a written-to-code bastard. Tim was the one who introduced all the kids in the camp to drugs. I'd smoked pot and snorted gonine by five, which was primarily what he got in abundance before he picked up amphetamines. That habit didn't last long with Tim cause he died. Came back to camp with a bullet in his shoulder and it stayed in there until his whole arm was infected, useless, rotten, stank of decay. Once it got cold he died in his hut. No one really cared because by that time Zach knew how to get his hands on some pretty good shit—better shit, honestly, than Tim had ever brought back, so it was no great loss.

"Didn't you [sniff] realize someone had died? You sound so casual about it. There must not've been any girls in the camp."

She's right, there weren't. Except what does that have to do with anything? Most of the kids in the camp were shut-ins. You'd be amazed how many working electronic devices we'd find mixed in with discarded scrap casing. In dumpsters, too, and trash cans in the city. A few of us would play outside all the time, but most of the kids never left their shelters. They'd play video games, endlessly phonegaze, we'd never see em. When I was like sixteen or seventeen I found out that a lot of the kids who never made it out of the camp, which were mostly the shut-ins, had a mass suicide. They dug a big hole outside the factory in the summertime, filled it with water. They ran frayed wires from one of the above-ground factory power lines to the hole. Everyone jumped in and a few of the kids dropped the wires into the water. Things were just fucked up there, girls wouldn't've made any difference. My brother smoked pot and watched movies at night and he downloaded that old movie from the 70s or 80s or some shit, *Mad Max*, with what's his face, and started dressing and acting just like the character in the movie. Like, modeled his whole personality after the guy. He was probably sixteen. Except he wasn't entirely successful at taking on the persona of the character because the only aspect of the guy he mastered was being emotionless as a stone. He was so convinced that if he pretended to be that character he'd be the star of the movie in his head, that no one could hurt him if he kept up that emotionless facade. I swear to God, though, acting so emotionless all the time had this effect on him. He started to do terrible things without even blinking. I saw him give heroin to little kids. He beat up on everyone, punched me so hard one time it knocked out one of my baby molars. Stole constantly. The worst thing he did when we were living in the camp was there was this dog, some gray pathetic ghetto mutt with a fuckin ear missing, that came into the camp and marked his territory on our shelter a couple times, made it smell like piss in there, and Zach ran it down and beat the absolute hell out of it, the dog's whimpering and everything, and he beat it so bad we woke up the next day and it was still there, in the middle of the camp, barely breathing through foamy blood and its eyes rolled up inside its head.

"Stop, I don't want to hear this."

And he never looked any different after he did that stuff. He just had this deadened novocain look on his face. Unfuckinrepentant. Seriously, he didn't feel bad at all. He was so serious about it—he was experimenting with his personality, y'know?—that he never quite got back to normal.

"But if there had been girls there they never would've stood for that kind of behavior. He wouldn't've been so hard and mean. He would've been different. You all would've been different."

Maybe she's right, but that doesn't change the fact that there weren't any girls there. Not sure why, there was never any policy against it, nothing like that. Girls were allowed, they just never chose to live there. We must've given off a vibration. Homo vibes.

"Don't be stupid."

What, I'm not. You know what I'm talkin about. I'm not sayin we were homos, for Christ's sake, we were kids. I'm sayin we gave off vibes. Vibes they picked up on. Vibes that said the heterogeneous won't function here. There's no room for it. A homogeneous environment. That's how it is nowadays. There are very few hetero-friendly environments left out there. ("Nick, stop! You don't even know what the fuck you're talking about. And don't say stuff like fag around me, eith—") Because the skeleton of a hetero relationship is patience and selflessness and compromise, which makes a frame for the working organs of pleasure and intoxication. Even with hetero friendships. Right? But what's the point of being selfless anymore? Selfishness makes more sense. We can get pleasure and intoxication all by ourselves, maybe even prefer to get it by ourselves, and we all know this about each other. There's no environment out there that demands we temporarily suspend our personal selves. Paranoia sets in. Am I expendable, not essential? The unwanted answer to no one's question? The plug without an outlet, or vice-versa? (I'm talking a thousand miles an hour here, and it's probably the gonine taking over, floodgates opening to expose a gush of rambling. Judging by Aria's expression I've crossed a line, so I shut up.)

"We better get going if we're gonna make it on time."

She shifts the truck into D and the blue lights disappear from the hood. We're both sniffing like crazy—too bad there's no water to snort. She's going white-knuckled against the wheel. Kinda cute, in a way. There's an innocence. Like there's this little girl inside her. My hands are shaking. I feel bad now so I try to tell her I was just kidding about all that hetero stuff. She waves me off, but I think she's just too high to respond. I can identify. I keep thinking I'm hallucinating the sound of sizzling meat until I realize the sound is coming through the speaker system. Things're definitely getting twacked. She asks if I mind if she switches away from the music, there's this broadcast she's been addicted to lately.

"Basically what it is is it's this guy who broadcasts his weekly trips to the laundromat. He's doesn't have a washer and drier in his apartment, so he's gotta walk five blocks to the closest Star Washee to get his clothes clean. It's just him narrating what he's doing."

The guy's voice comes through my truck's sound system super-charged with bass.

"—I'm now segregating whites from colors, placing the clothes nicely in two separate baskets."

There are laundromat sounds for a few seconds while he works, voices in the background, his breathing, some rustling against the microphone, the hum and snapping of multiple machines working at once.

"This is the most boring part, but it has to be done. Otherwise they'll bleed together."

His voice disappears again and there are more ambient sounds. Aria is intent. Is this guy a racist or something?

"What? No, what are you—? He's talking about clothes!"

So I can't say stuff about homo vibes but she can listen to some racist laundry show? Now it's her turn to wonder if she's been crossing a line all this time. Look, we both suck anyway. I apologize. Let's just accept our guilt and move on.

Even though Zach did a lot of terrible shit, he wasn't all bad. He was the whole reason we got to live with Kasia Feathers in the first place. He came back to the hut one morning after having been gone all night, something he almost never did, and told me to grab anything I wanted to bring with me because we were leaving right now and never coming back. He didn't bother explaining, so you can probably imagine how upset I was. Or maybe not, but I was upset. He started putting his stuff in the middle of a spread-out blanket. Get your stuff, we're leaving and never coming back. I asked why, where were we going, crying, and finally he pushed me down. He told me I either pack or leave with nothing, and then kicked our hut so hard it collapsed in a fuckin heap. So I rooted through scrap casing for a few of my things and we walked two or three miles through the EM to a house that turned out to belong to Kasia—the house I was gonna spend my entire childhood in.

"Having brought the requisite amount of quarters, I will now pay for two washing machines near the window, placing the coins vertically into their side-by-side slots before pushing in the big metal piece and listening to the coins be loudly, metallically absorbed into an unseen apparatus. [These noises happen, a big *KACHUNK* followed by four or five pained little *sssssshhhhink*ings.] Now a screen on the washer has come to life, prompting me to upload my desired wash setting wirelessly via my phone."

My brother—apparently, since he never told me anything about it—went to buy and sell drugs sorta regularly at this communal house near the factory where I'm pretty sure they used to make the big metal shell pieces for outdoor grills. He went to a party there, and that's where he met Kasia. Picturing her at a party is impossible for me. It doesn't fit with my idea of her, but she was only nineteen at the time. From what Kasia told me, she was sitting off in a corner talking and drinking with people when she saw my brother and was (God knows why since he was some dirty-ass homeless boy) very attracted to him. She said he knew she was lookin at him, givin him eyes for like half an hour, but he just flat-out refused to pay attention to her. Wouldn't even go over and talk to her, just sat there in his pseudo-Mad Max persona, emotionless, drinking and grappling, some lost pathetic soul she should've never wasted her time on. So what happened was *she* decided to go over to *him* and start talking, and she told me this happened even though I don't believe it, but she said he was funny and charming and completely into her, and they talked for hours before she invited him back to her place. At that point I imagine they fucked, and he likely told her all about our situation—the camp, the huts, the factory with the three plumes and the constant cookie smell and the dogs who tortured him by pissing all over everything at night, the fact that he was the sole provider for a little brother more than ten years younger than him—and I imagine she, being this idealistic saint, invited him and seven-year-old me to stay with her at her house. And in the Egyptian nightclub there's a couple standing in the raging crowd that I can just barely pick out, they're little more than dots on the quartered segment of screen, kissing in a turbulent quilt of humanity, and in the adjacent quarter-screen there's a pharmaceutical commercial showing an old man staving off a combination of Parkinson's disease and mesothelioma contracted from food and water contaminated with asbestos fibers. The old man is smiling, wife clinging to him like a wife might cling to a healthy husband, the two of them standing on a hill and looking out on a horizon flowering with a citrusy-sweet sunrise, the land made green and digitally virile through video editing.

"Maybe I can't hear this story tonight, Nick, it's overwhelming. I keep thinking about stories layered with other stories, the Intricacy of the past, how to encompass it all, and my heart's just beating wa-ay too fast for—"

Kasia's house was sort of an unofficial convalescent home for kids. She paid all the bills except for when people who stayed there contributed voluntarily. She'd started out homeless, too, was an orphan like most of us, but had at some point come into a huge amount of money. There were a lot of theories about how it might have happened, none of which were ever proven or disproven. In any case, what she did with part of the money was buy a crumbling three-story house in a nicer part of the EM, and she invited other homeless kids to live there on a highly selective basis, the only compensation required from the live-ins being that they would help fix up the house. In turn, she'd take care of the bills. This woman—I can't even tell you.

"The washers are now on medium permanent press cycle and a gentle cycle respectively, leaving me free to zone out to dated magazines found in a metal rack near the vending machines, catching up on transient information already irrelevant. I'm going to scan the third code from the bottom and… [*vvvrr*ing and *kerchunk*ing] … down drops a Milky Way."

She looked like you'd think a Katarzyna should: dark healthy hair like a chocolate wrap (Milky Way pops to mind. Chocolate shell. Magnavox.), large eyes molded with eastern sharpness, tall and thin and pleasantly ungraceful with a cute explosive laugh, the kind of laugh you want to hear and so make a bunch of dumb jokes to coax it out. Y'know? She had the rare ability to never be self-deluded, self-loathing, self-centered, self-serving or self-referential. If anyone was ever in trouble she'd say they were in "deep yogurt." She was of this world, born straight from the freakin earth, the progeny of no one. Her lips were pink, and the lower one had this distinct chubby shape in it.

"Nick, that's perverted! I thought you said you thought of this woman as your mother. You talk about her like she's your lover."

Well she *was* like my mother. Except she wasn't. And that makes things more complicated, all right? You don't know everything that happened, so try to refrain from calling me a pervert until you know the whole story.

"We're just about there. Parking's gonna be terrible tonight, I hope you know."

We're driving between scrapers, downtown Grid hoisted far above us on invisible sustained force. Yawning ground-level mouths open to swallow lives and raw matter, buildings constructed within buildings, the hand on top of the ClamBellCorp scraper looming in the sky, spotlit, a holoprojection of the world spinning in its palm. We're miniscule down here. Aria's navigating through a maze of roadwork barriers, orange and white reflectors mingling with street glow, all radiating from the InfoZebra building site. We turn a corner and a long line of people comes into view, wrapped around the monster marble corners of Grid Savings & Loan. They look wealthy and well-hydrated, huddling in the snow.

"The chairs in here are made of speckled green plastic and are connected together in groups of ten so you have to share armrests with the people on either side of you. I have to squeeze my elbows in so I can read a magazine and eat my candy bar at the same time. There's live video from inside the washing machine, my clothes slopping wetly together."

All the billboards in the downtown district have been bought out by InfoZebra, stating in sans-serif white font against a black background, *We're officially plugged into the Grid.* Then the InfoZebra logo—the figure of a zebra represented in hexagonal cells. Aria pays an attendant with a flashing yellow headband twenty-five bucks and parks toward the back of a lot that edges up against an alleyway filled with brightly-colored trash. We step into the cold, walking in the direction of the line of people surrounding the Savings & Loan. Aria puts my arm around her shoulder, pushing in close for warmth. Kasia originally invited us to live with her because she was hopelessly infatuated with my brother. Why is anyone's guess. I've convinced myself it had to do with the whole opposites attract theory. She was this wonderful philanthropic person, he was this fuckin cruel asshole, and something about him clicked for her. Maybe it was just that she was too young and had no idea what she really wanted. Either way, he didn't give much of a damn about her. When we moved into the house, he slept in her bedroom. I stayed in a room upstairs with two other kids about my age, Fio Volker and Jonathan Grills-Fingerhut, the same guy who called me earlier this week to tell me Kasia was dead. The first day I met Kasia she took my face in her hands and gave me a big hug against her stomach. She had me sit at the table in the kitchen while she made me food. It was chicken and rice. She said she was very happy I was going to be staying with her from now on, and that she hoped I'd like it there. The kitchen smelled like aerosol and shampoo. Excuse me for a sec while I restrain heartache.

"It's freezing out here. [Sniff.] What time is it?"

That first year my brother and Kasia did a lot of drugs together.

They didn't grapple or anything like that, mostly downers, stuff my brother sold on the street. Years later Kasia told me getting high with Zach was about the only way to get inside him, to lower a set of defenses that were permanently grafted on. When he was high she could catch him in tiny moments of vulnerability, moments only she could've ever picked out and found significance in. Mostly, though, he remained a stranger to her. And to me. Well before the time we left the camp, he'd started to become terrifying. He was always on something and he had a short temper. He kicked my ass a lot. I hated him. I don't think he could stand being in a house with so many little kids, he'd had more than enough of taking care of me growing up and developed an aversion or something. He was always out, it seemed like, selling. Or doing whatever he did. When he was home he stayed hidden in Kasia's room, even if she wasn't in there. After a while I barely talked to him.

"Did he ever tell Kasia about your parents? Did you ever ask her?"

Yeah, I asked a lot. Her *and* him. He never said a word about it. But we could tell there was something wrong with him, something he was carrying with him, y'know? Like from the past. Something tormenting him. He had this incredible self-destructive streak. In addition to being high every day, he was usually drunk too. I mean to the point of blackout. He could handle himself really well all the way up until the last hours of the day, and then it was like running across a stumbling slurring demon. The fucker was vicious. One time he slapped Fio so hard you could see his handprint on her face for two days. He got into a fight with Kasia and upended the kitchen table. He punched a couple holes in the wall. But if you can believe what Kasia said, and I do, he was equally vicious with himself. He had all these self-inflicted scars running width-wise down his left arm, all perfectly parallel and evenly spaced. When he turned eighteen he had all the scar lines tattooed. Generally he'd have pretty bad nightmares. Then there was the time she found him on the roof—that was the worst. He came home after she was already sleeping, I guess, and she heard noises coming from her ceiling like footsteps. You could get on the roof pretty easy from Kasia's bedroom window, we all did it a lot, and so she went up there and he was standing near the edge, like he was gonna throw himself off. She tried to stop him and he grabbed her around the neck and held her off the edge of the roof, threatening to let go, and then when he didn't do it he collapsed sobbing. He was a fucking nutcase, my brother. This all happened before he even turned twenty.

"Why did she keep him around if he was threatening to kill her?"

Believe me, she realized her mistake. Have you ever had a violent nineteen-year-old drug dealer and addict boyfriend with nothing to lose and no one monitoring his actions? Not as easy to get rid of as you'd think. Turns out there's a lot of fear involved. The kind of fear that makes you lose weight because it literally burns calories. The kind that does this thing where one second you want to run away screaming and the next you want to be closer and more intimate with him than ever before. Not to mention the physical and mental abuse. Not to mention the guilt. We're in line now, standing in day-old snow gone crunchy with cold. All the light in this area is coming from weak fluorescent street lamps. Aria's dry reddening complexion looks like something out of an embalming catalogue, and mine too probably. We form the end of a long human caterpillar, its body writhing with anticipation, chill, gonine. Insanely-paced music is coming from far off, vibrations battling through the molecular freeze. I ask Aria if she was watching the Egyptian nightclub.

"Egyptian nightclub? What are you talking about?"

I wave away my own question. If she was sober she would've noticed. This is how she is when she grapples. Gerney, too. They retract, go hide in a corner of their brain where I'm not allowed. Magnavox. Except it wasn't just Zach who was making Kasia feel guilty. (Kasia had a fanatical sense of empathy that blinded her sometimes. She felt Zach had suffered, that he'd undergone some unspeakable moment of trauma early in life that caused him to act the way he did. His past gave him license, in her mind, to misbehave, because in all probability he was not in full control of himself and was in desperate need of help, therapy, hugs, warm milk, etc. Nevermind that Kasia had gone through her own share of trauma—that didn't matter to her. She was too focused on him to see that he had no more excuse than she would've had. But Zach's free pass with her expired when Kasia's love for him did, and it was at that point, when she'd finally had enough abuse, that she wanted him gone for real.) The other element of guilt pushing down on her was me. I'm not sure if her attachment grew out of displaced affection for Zach, but of all the kids who lived in the house, usually between fifteen and twenty-five of us, she treated me as her favorite. Zach still considered himself my caretaker, and she had no reason to think he wouldn't try to take me with him if she threw him out. So she did the only thing she believed she could do at the time. She had him arrested. Seemed the right thing to do. So one night he leaves the house and she gets on the phone with the cops like here's where he's going, here's who he's with, this is what they're plannin to do. And they caught him on some big ones. In addition to possession with intent to distribute he faced down robbery and assault charges since they were holdin people up in fuckin alleyways and on streets with no working lights and bullshit like that. They literally caught my brother in the middle of a stickup, shoving a gun in the face of some guy when a couple cruisers screech up, not even bothering to do the whole bwoop-bwoop thing but full-on prolonged sirens that woke the entire neighborhood. And fuckin what's my brother do but bolt like a parking lot bunny and gets about a block before they absolutely tackle the shit outta him. At the end of a long process, he got slapped with a thirteen-year sentence. Thirteen. Not to mention he spent most of it in solitary confinement on account of bad behavior. Christ, it still sounds like the most horrible thing in the world. Thirteen years was way beyond what Kasia had intended—I don't think she really knew *what* she'd intended other than she was desperate and needed to get rid of him—and it was another dose of guilt. This was the type of guilt, though, that a person like her isn't prepared to handle. She goddamn near killed herself over it. One of her friends who helped her around the house one time found Kasia in the bathroom ready to eat a bunch of seconal. She never stopped feeling terrible about what she did to him, I'm pretty sure.

I never personally went to visit Zach while he was in prison. The only one who did was, of course, Kasia, and consequently she did the dumbest thing she ever could have by admitting it'd been *her* who'd called the cops on him, who'd betrayed him, who'd ratted his ass out. Which he brooded on for thirteen very long fucking years.

"I'm so cold I think it's wearing off the jet. How many minutes till they open the doors you think?"

Did I mention Kasia educated all the kids in the house while educating herself as well? That she assigned us poetry and fiction and math and history homework? That without her I would've been some slobbering retard reject? That she bought us all a present on every birthday and only forgot, as far as I can remember, once or twice? That she'd whisper in my ear before I went to bed at night that I was a special kid—that's what she said: "special kid"—and that she just knew I was gonna grow up to be someone amazing? That she prepared big meals for the whole house on Thanksgiving and Christmas? And did I mention she could sing? That she'd never sing in front of anyone, but that we could hear from outside her door every so often a soft humming or unfamiliar lyrics from songs none of us knew? Did I mention that when anyone in the house turned fifteen she made them go out and get a job even though we hated that she made us do it and talked a lot of shit behind her back? Did I mention she had really bad ADHD, and she had to take medication for it? That she could barely hold a pen sometimes she shook so bad? That she gripped her forehead and sighed more than any person I've ever known? That she announced to everyone before she was gonna cry and then would walk up to her room and cry? That she had two nervous breakdowns during the time I lived there? That her favorite poet was Langston Hughes? Did I mention she had three female lovers in three years? Or that she'd smoke pot really late at night when she thought everyone was asleep? That she wasn't really cut out to be a mother to so many children but it was somehow in her nature, a congenital trait, *to do her best anyway?* That her hand hovered over the handle of the front door so many times before falling to her side? That she loved us all? Did I mention that—

"Nick, this story is too long. The line's moving. Is there any way we can continue it later?"

No. No, it's got to be now. It's got to be now. This story is working its way to climax, Aria. It's fuckin irreversible now.

"I can give you till we get to will call, but there's gotta be a way for you to streamline-slash-abridge this stuff. I need the condensed version. The line's moving."

Fine, I'll brush very quickly on the most important stuff. There was a lot. There was the homeless guy who'd always sneak drugs and alcohol for us. There was the rash of kids who developed strange thyroidal problems, plus another couple of kids who got lung cancer at just about the same time, and we suspected the constant aerosol smell emanating from the nearby factory had something to do with it and we were all afraid to breathe. There was the time Fio was killed by a car bomb while walking home from playing at the empty lots with Jonathan Grills-Fingerhut. Which of course led to Jonathan being disturbed and angsty and confused and so there was the time we started to always have a lot of drugs stashed in our room before we got old enough to go out on our own and get into real trouble. There were the times I'd sit by myself on the roof of the house and watch champagne sunsets and think really hard about things. There was the time I got jealous and resented having to share Kasia with so many other kids. Another big one was when I wanted a dog and Kasia refused and I spent a whole year being mad at her over it. And then there was when I became a teenager and started spending time with Jonathan at the empty lots with other teenagers where we smoked and drank and grappled and on good days fooled around. And Kasia found out what we were doing and forbade us from ever goin over there ever again, so we started going in secret. And then there was the time we sold gonine for a while—never under dealers, just stuff we bought ourselves and sold back at insane markups to people too stupid to know the difference—and even though we were careful we still got into a bunch of fights and I got a gun drawn on me once. There was when I lost my virginity to a sixteen year old girl with a turquoise wig and amateur tattoos of substructure blueprints on her arms. There was my whole sordid dark period of adolescent anger and hatred and self-awareness. There was the time I missed my brother for some reason. My whole introduction to factory vandalism which, even though I know it sounds weird, played a huge role in our childhoods. From simple rock-throwing to this guy who could plant great computer viruses to actually breaking into offices so we could destroy documents and bash stuff to bits with bats. We hated the factories. Oh, and also there was my first job at DataWrappers where I told the guy who interviewed me all this bullshit about how the factory had been an important part of my life from a very early age and that it would make me proud to work there, to be part of such incredible production, and he ate it all up, so I worked there during summers throwing pieces of scrap metal into their most important machinery, loosening vital screws, contaminating whole batches of plastic, and doing my best to eliminate all their precious output. Then there was the time—

"Yeah, hi, our tickets are under the last name Ibyoo."

I hand my credit card and ID through the grate and the girl working the counter on the other side who's actually a man, or was at one point, takes a quick look before handing us two tickets. These people are younger than us, scrambled and grappling jet, part of a different decade altogether, our successors to the seat of youth. Their bodies glow nuclear orange and they have no faces, every moment of their lives documented and watched. Music that feels like shotgun blasts pounds through the entrance door Aria's leading me toward by the hand. I stop her before we reach the two black-shirted security guards. Aria, I have to shout, I'm not sure I can do this. My mood isn't right. I'll admit it, okay? I'm feeling too weak for this.

"I have to go in there, Nick. Please. I have to erase my thoughts. Just for now. Later we can talk all you want."

Her argument, one I'm not sure I understand, is that she's suffering under the weight of complexity. Of intricacy. Life is too slow, everything's gotta be sped up for her to see clearly. If everyone here wasn't paying attention to live video feeds and brutal music and electronic hallucinations then they would all be in love with her.

I'm in love with her.

"Just for a little while. Give me an hour. I need one hour of this."

But I have to tell her something. Something that can't wait. That, when I turned eighteen, Kasia Feathers and I slept together.

She hears this and pulls herself desperately away from me, making it past security in what might be world-record time and disappears through the pulsing door beyond. I try to follow her but am held up by a line, fingers numb with cold, standing shaking while I realize my wording was wrong. I didn't sleep with Kasia Feathers. She slept with me. The rule in Kasia's house was you had to move out once you turned eighteen, so imagine I felt abandoned, that I felt alone and confused. Imagine I'd grown, increasingly, into my brother. Physically and mentally. My face had filled out and adopted his look of gristle, of sleek meanness. A white boy with a caveman brow and stubble. I'd adopted his drug habits, his temper, his stupid fuckin emotionless machismo. The kinda kid who grows up into a has-been-never-was. The kinda kid who talks about his childhood memories while drunk and high and living in shit. I was aware of this, and had charted out my future accordingly. So imagine dark-haired Kasia Feathers wrapping her arms around me from behind in the house's deserted kitchen early one morning when I went downstairs for water to soothe a hangover—everything lit by only the blue light squeaking from the open refrigerator door. Her hands straying down my chest and across my neck. Her lips pressed hotly against the side of my neck with a sweetly wet kiss, threads of hair engulfed in scent. The front of her body pressed soft against my back, pulling me in tighter. I didn't say anything—I wasn't surprised—I knew who it was. For reasons I'll never understand, it made perfect sense for Kasia to come to me that night, to sexualize herself, to pull my head gently toward her so she could whisper in my ear: Come to my room. She led me up the stairs, past closed doors and sleeping children, to a room with purple walls and dim yellow lamplight. We undressed each other. This wasn't fucking, not even love-making. This was some other kind of sex. Advice-giving sex. The act of melding into one person in order to be a voice in the other's brain, naturally occurring and tender and patient. Pleasure and penetration. Love as a vehicle for obligationless communication. Perverted, powerful, pleasant. Sex that's had above the covers, both bodies fully visible and stroked with one-eighth shadow, light that smoothes and flatters flesh. Facing each other, half on top, half on bottom. Kasia looking down at me, her hair creating a curtain obscuring all things except her face at the center of a swirling henna galaxy. She hummed an innocent tune in bed beside me afterward. I'm next in line to be frisked, nose icy, the security guard on the left beckoning me over to prod beneath my armpits, my crotch, my ass and hips. The music beyond the door is a firestorm, consuming the structure of thought. Magnavox. So maybe Aria was right, girls would've made a difference. She said to me, Kasia Feathers did, that from this point on I'd be in charge of myself. That I was her special kid, that I would not stay in the ghetto, that I would work. That I would beat the world back so one day this piece of quiet private love could be mine with somebody who loved me. Never come back here, she said. You're special, and you belong elsewhere. Create a life, not an empty hole. I haven't thought about these words in so long. The memory is painful. The chubby shape in her lower lip, I've never forgotten how it felt pressed against me. The sheets recently washed and the scent of fresh linen mingling with cancerous aerosol. Her age and body heat nearby. She said there's so little we can ever hope for, such infrequent islands of meaning. Leave yourself open to them, Nick. Don't forsake your possible happiness at any expense. Sell yourself out, lick the bottom of someone else's shoe, grovel for mercy, admit you're wrong, whatever becomes necessary to do, do it. Please leave this house benevolent and hopeful, she said. I'm ushered past the security checkpoint, through the door, and the music is— - - - - - —

— — — — — - - - - - - - - - - - - - - — - - - - - - - - - - - - - — —

— — — - — — —

— - - - — - - - -—LED of floating faces— - - - - - - — — — —

— — - — — — —

- -—phone

call but I can barely hear the machine answer— — — - - - - - -
- -
— — — — — — — — - - - - - - — — — — — — - - - - - -
- — — — — — — — - - - - - - — — — — — — — - - - - - -
- - - - - - - - —volume and jet snorters— - — — - - - - - - —
— — — — — — - - - - - — — — — — — — — - - - - - - - -
— — - - - - - — — — — — — — - - - - - — — — — — — —
- — - - - - — — — — — — — - - - - - - — — — — — — —
— — - - - — — — — — — — - - - - - - — — — — — - - - -
— - - - — — — — — — — - - - - - - — — — — — — — - - -
— - — — - - - - - —main dance floor and Aria's hair illuminated
by— - - - - — — — — — — - - - - - - — — — — - — — - - -
- - - - - - — — — — — — - - - - - - - — — — — — — — —
- - - - - — — — — — - - - - - - - - - — — — — — - - - -
— — — - - - - — — — — - - - - - - - — — — — — — - - -
— — - - - - - — — — — — - - - - - - — — — — — — — —
— - - - - — — — — — - - - - - - - - — — — — — — — - -
- — — — — — - - - - - — — — — — — — - - - - - - — —
- — — — — — - - - - - - — — — — - — —agnavox— - - - - - - — — —
— - - - - - — — — — - - - - - - - - — — — — — - - - - -
- - - - - - — — — — - - - - - - - - - - — — — — - - - -
— — — — — — - - - - - — — — — — - - - - - — — — —
— — — — — — - - - - - - — — — — — - - - - - — — — —
- - - - — — — — — - - - - - - - - - — — — — — — — — —
- - - - - — — — — — - - - - - - - - - - — — — — - - - -
— — — — — — - - - - - — — — — — - - - - - - — — —
- - — — — — — - - - - - - — — — — - - - - - — — - - -
— — — — — — - - - - - — — — — — - - - - - — — — — —
- — — — — — - - - - - - - — — — — — - - - - - — — —
— — - - - - - — — — — — - - - - - - — — — — — — - - -
— - — — — - - - - - — — — — — - - - - - - - — — — —
- — - — — — — —
— — — — - - - - - - — — — — — — - - - - - — — — — —
— — — — — — - - - - - - — — — — — - - - - - - — — —

— — — — — - — — — - - — — — — — - - — — — — — — —
— — — - - - - - - - — - - - - - - - - - - - - - - — —
— — — - - - - - — — - - - - - - - - - - - - - - - - —
- - - - — - - - - - — - - - - - - - - - - - - - - — - —
— — — - - - - - - — — — — — - - - - - - - - - - - - —
- - - — - - - — — — - - - - - - - — — — — — - - - - —
- - - - — - - - - - - - - - - - - - - - - - — — — — —
— — — - - - - - — - - - - - - — — — — — — — — — — —
- - - — - - - - - - - - - - - - - - - - - - — — — — —
— — - - - — - - - - - - — — — — — — — — — — — — — —
— — — - - - - - — - - - - - - - - - - - — — — — — — —
— — — — — - - - - - - — — — — — — — — — — - - - - — —

— - - - - - - - - - - — — — — - - — - —Aria! Aria, I'm sorry! I should have waited to— — — — - - - - — - - - — — — — — —
- — — - - - - - — - - - - — — — — — —about what happened!
    "— — — - — - — - - - - - - —okay I'm just strung-out— — —
- - - - - —so sorry I'm just strung-out and— - - - - — — — —"
    But I had to tell you because— - - - - — — — — - - - - - - -
- - - — — — - - — - - - - - - — — — — — - - - - —athan Grills-Fingerhut called me at work! My brother had been in and out of— - - — - — - — — — — — — — — — —and found out where she lived! He broke into the house and— - - - - - - - - —- - -
- - - — — — - - - - — - - - — - — — — - — — — — —
— — — — - - - —that's how she died! It was my brother! Zach was the one who— — — - — - — - - - - - — — — — — - - - - -
— — — — — — — — — - - — - - - - - — - — - —illed Kasia!
    "Come here, Nick, I'm— — — — - - - - - — — — — — —
— — - — - - - - - - - - - - - - - — - — - - — — —take a quick breath— — — — — - - - — — — — - - - — — - -
- — — — — - — - - - - —efore we go! I'm sorry I dragged us— - - - - - - - - - - — — — — - - - - — — — — —
— — — — — — - - - —and then we'll go! I'm sorry!"
— — — - - - - - - — — — — — — — - - - - — - - - —
— — — - - - - - - - - - — — — — — — — — - - — — —

———————————————————————
———————————————not quite sure how to make sense
of———————————————————————
————————————————————————
————————————————————————
————————————————————————
————————————————————————
————————————————————————
————————————————————————
————————————————————————
————————————————————————
————————————————————————
————————————————————————all
this———————————————————————
————————————————————————
————————————————————————
————————————————————————
————————————————————————
————————————————————————
————————————————————————
————————————————————————
————————————————————————
————————————————————————
————————————————————————
————————————————————————
————————————————————————
————————————————————————
—————————Magnavox————————
————————————————————————
————————————————————————
————————————————————————
————————————————————————

VICTOR

The elevator ascends and I am a personal adviser. As a kid I was never the most fun, the most adventurous, the most artistic, the most charismatic, the most athletic, the saddest, the handsomest, the smartest or the funniest. But I was the most level-headed. In grade school my friends attempted to propel themselves so hard on the swing set they might wrap the chains around the top bar and go flying back around in 360 degrees of juvenile accomplishment. Plans were made and tactics employed to make this dream a reality. Excitement concerning the idea was high: a full loop around the top bar was ambitious beyond all belief, a step outside the normal everyday swinging box, as it were. Such an enterprise would rocket one and one's friends to instant school-wide fame, inspire respect, awe, celebrity. The burden fell to me to analyze the worth of this incredible achievement vs. the likelihood of physical harm, a finger against my chin, gazing at the swing set with detached probity. Yes, it did seem quite impossible. Young children such as us were undoubtedly incapable of generating the kind of centrifugal force required to send a person safely over the bar and back down without injury. Given this sober analysis, I felt compelled to make my voice clear on the matter. *I wouldn't personally advise it.*

Mobyle stands across the elevator from me, examining his shoes and looking timorous. Behind him the glass wall of the elevator reveals our steady climb over downtown Grid, perspective causing the buildings to appear implausibly cluttered, no room for movement, a human ant colony, and slowly, the higher we get, the space between them becomes visible again. A bluish haze has collected against the mountains, nature lacking the processing power to materialize the distance. There is nothing, it seems to me lately, beyond this city. A perfect labyrinth; a mouth preparing to click shut; a suffocating institution. We are men who are in deep shit. Deeper, in fact, than I've ever had reason to experience. The act of being in this elevator right now constitutes desperate behavior—behavior I advised adamantly against. Mobyle has gone in a very short time from political dynamo and future mayor of Grid to unofficial pariah of the XittyXat scandal and the face of corruption—an irrefutable low-point by any standards—and like many powerful men who wake up to find their world exploded, he's looking for a woman to take pity on him. A predictable move, I told him, and in his case *not advisable*. Not least of all because his instinct was to seek out Tracey, absent from his life for over a month now.

"Tracey," I had said to him, "never loved you. I know that's an unpleasant thought for you, Randy, but you've got to accept it. Internalize it. Realize it. She was receiving monetary compensation to act as your wife. She *deceived* you."

"I know that, Victor, but even so. She *knows* me. She can't possibly *hate* me. I need her right now, do you get it? I need someone who knows me."

Mobyle is shifting, sweating. He looks the same as always, trim and camera-ready handsome in an expensive suit and tie, but something about him has changed, the carefully crafted image no longer able to camoflauge the ugly sheen of anxiety descended over him, the odor of social leprosy. He is marked. He is in trouble. He is a hopeless case. The hair on both temples is streaked ersatz gray, the hairstyle itself a pomaded backwards comb. He's clean-shaven but haggard, something wrong with his posture, as if the facade of pretending to be physically vital for TV cameras has been declared over. His neck is gaining a rapid paunch. He looks up at me from his shoe examination. I'm quite sure there's nothing I can do for this man anymore except lie to him, tell him it will be all right, assure him his greatest moments are yet to come, they'll miss you when you're gone Randy Mobyle, but at least they won't have you to kick around anymore. His aides have engineered a drastic cutback in daily scheduling, but he knows he will be required to attend the InfoStructure fundraising dinner after this, where he'll have to pull himself together, perform under the pressure of hundreds of suspicious glares, be the man he was three weeks ago. His normal entourage have done their best to protect him but he's begun ducking them at every opportunity, losing trust in everyone. I remain by his side because he considers me a friend, but I, too, am a minder, put in much closer contact than normal with Flint Vedge, which I can't imagine Mobyle is unaware of.

Randy wipes his forehead with his sleeve. "Will you go into her apartment with me?" he asks.

"Perhaps going in alone might convey a better sense of genuineness," I tell him. "A better sense you'd like to have an honest conversation. And I'd also like to remind you this is *your* apartment."

"Dammit, Victor, stop playing around. Will you go *in* with me?"

I sigh. "What do you expect me to do in there?"

"Stand by the door. Look quiet and unaware."

"What you're suggesting will appear aggressive to her, almost threatening. Not to mention cowardly. I'd advise against that course of action. I'll wait by the elevator."

"Victor, you're going in with me. I don't care if you want to or not, I need you to."

"It strikes me, Randy, that this is exactly the sort of behavior you told me in the past you wanted so much to avoid. You didn't want to be a typical politician, hemmed in on all sides by paranoia. This is exactly what a typical politician would do, bring his adviser into a situation that should be, by all rights, a private moment."

"Knock it off, Victor. You and I both know I was never anything but the typical politician. That's even part of the requirements for *being* a typical politician. 'Number Seven—does not think he's the typical politician.' Right now I *am* paranoid, I *am* vulnerable, and I need another set of eyes and ears in there." He exhales heavily and looks out on the city like a man appraising something he's lost, its gleaming irretrievability, something that could've been his but now never will be. The city is becoming a public planning map below. "This was always how it was going to end for me, I realize now. Sometimes a man realizes his own fate and can't stand it. Sometimes he realizes it and it's liberating. You think I don't know Tracey hates me, that she doesn't care about me? Victor? I know. I even knew when I didn't know. I did. But what other choice do I have? Have you ever wanted something for yourself? Truly *seen* yourself as something? After a while, that desire doesn't come from you anymore, it's in you but put there by something else, and now you're at the mercy of some universal current, being swept along passively. [He pantomimes with his hands being carried along an invisible river, body swaying in imagined water.] What I *should* do, instead of sticking around here, is run. Run the hell away. Start a new life somewhere, purge my old self. It's all gotten too fucked up. But I *can't* do that, Victor. Because here I am, trapped in the current, just waiting quietly to go over the falls. So would you *please* go into the apartment with me? I'm asking nicely."

The elevator has long since stopped at the desired floor. I've been holding down the DOOR OPEN button and listening with a growing sense of unease. I've never heard him so fatalistic. We're teetering up here, standing on velvety carpeting with nothing beneath us but a gut-wrenching drop.

"All right," I say, "I'll go in with you. But I don't condone it."

This floor is dedicated solely to Randy's penthouse, a skyview apartment in the shape of a buckminster fullerene, rendered in a gorgeous glinting onyx color. The city-facing side of the fullerene is sliced away for an expansive vista patio equipped with an infinity pool. There's a short glass-paneled walkway leading from the elevator to the entrance, a design flaw in my opinion since the effect, meant to be visually striking, can easily provoke trembling fear in anyone like myself who doesn't do so well with heights. Outside, the cloud cover is total, the sun nothing more than a celestial ghost beaming at some other, happier part of the world. A late-winter V of geese goes by and, from this high up, there's a strange natural phenomenon occurring, dozens of wispy tendrils of cloud dancing about vertically in the air, unraveling and becoming intricately long before diffusing to nothing. Off in the haze there's a zeppelin bearing the word *InfoZebra* in continuously rearranging patterns of code, amounting at the moment to a surreal and guilty vision. Mobyle rings the doorbell and we stand there holding our breath until Tracey opens the door, not bothering to stand and greet us, just disappearing into the apartment, conceding entrance despite the fact she's not at all interested by it. I catch only a brief glimpse of her hair disappearing around a corner before Mobyle rushes past me in pursuit. I step in and close the door. The interior consists of a ground floor and loft, but the floorplan is positioned at the center of the structure so the spherical walls surround and encompass everything. Chilling to think anyone could ever be comfortable here. Like existing at the center of one's own small universe. Several screens throughout the apartment are on, carelessly set to whatever. One of them is news, the same picture of Mobyle as appeared in the XittyXat hack hovering beside the anchor. I can hear the exchange occurring somewhere in the loft.

"I'm not leaving, Randy, so don't bother."

"Fine, I don't want you to. Stay as long as you want."

"And I don't need your permission, either. I've already talked to Flint. This apartment is mine now."

"For Christ's sake, I *know* that. I'm giving you my *blessing*, is all, that there're no hard feelings. You can *have* the apartment. You can have it, I'm only here because—"

"You think I need your fucking blessing? I *don't*. You're all gonna be lucky if you make it out of this without going to prison. Personally, I *hope* that's what happens. I *hope* you all fucking rot."

"Congratulations, Tracey, I get it. Joke's on me, you're the big winner. But I just—"

"You're a fucking *fool*, is what you are."

"Would you please listen for two seconds?"

"Why would I do that? Why would I want to listen to you?"

"I've spent more time with you than anyone. *Confided* in you more than anyone."

"Randy, why are you not getting this? I *never loved you*. To be honest, most of the time, I didn't even *like* you. Can you get that through your head?"

"I *know*. I know you never loved me. All I want is to talk to you, okay? I just want to talk to someone who knows me and understands my situation."

"Oh my god, this is so pathetic. *You* are pathetic."

I stand with hands in pockets near the door, as instructed. I stare out onto the giant patio in an effort to dissociate myself from the whole excruciating moment, but Tracey's prison comment touched a nerve in me. I had kept the nagging worry of incarceration hidden away in my head for so many days, and now to hear her drop it into her unending string of insults so *casually*. Grid itself has become a prison for us, each room a cell, every street a forced march. I'm too close to Mobyle. It's impossible to predict exactly what Flint Vedge will do to distance himself and InfoZebra from the situation, but one thing is certain: they will throw Randy to the wolves. I know this, but how can I possibly distance *my*self? As much as I would like to, running away won't fix this for me. In fact, it would make everything worse. My eyes land on the expensive coffee table near the sofa and I notice for the first time two extremely long lines of benzoylmethylecgonine stretching across its surface like a pair of sad shoelaces. Also a small baggie. I can still hear them fighting up in the loft. I walk over and pick up the little ziploc, inspecting the clumped white powder tumbling about within, little benign-seeming granules. I slip it into my pocket and go back to standing by the door.

"—out! Get out! I don't want to see you again, Randy! Ever!"

"Tracey, *please*. Why do you hate me so much? Was the whole thing really so repugnant for you? Was I really—"

My phone buzzes. Speak of the devil. Out the window the sky is flat, gray, textureless. A clouded lid. I answer with a finger against my ear to block out the noise of the thrashing Mobyle is getting upstairs.

"Flavorless, this is Vedge." (His use of the nickname persists despite all the humor of its delivery having vanished, serving to only further fuel my hatred of him.)

"Yes."

"Good God, what's all that screaming?"

"I'd rather not explain."

"Flavorless, what the hell is going on? Where are you?"

"Tracey's apartment. I couldn't stop him."

There's a strange silence over the phone as the usual tongue-lashings don't come. The arguing upstairs fills in the gap.

"You're going to have to get him out of there, Victor. The InfoStructure benefit is in an hour and a half. He's got to be there. It's crucial."

I look up at the loft and take a deep breath. "I'll do my best."

"Before you go, Flavorless, there's the matter of why I called." I can hear in him a glimmer of confidence that's been missing since the night of the XittyXat hack. "We're narrowing in on this son of a bitch, whoever he is."

"The hacker?"

"You bet your bland little ass. According to TJ it's just a matter of time at this point."

"Good news."

"*Good* news? It's *great* fucking news. Now look. I know Mobyle has been tough to wrangle, but we absolutely *have* to have him on-point for the next forty-eight hours. We need him smiling, we need him on message, we need him glad-handing. He's got to be frosty. We can still turn things around here, Victor. Tell me I can count on you."

"You can count on me."

"Good. Now go break up those two fucking hyenas and get his ass to the benefit."

I hang up and head upstairs, walking in on them in mid-yell, Tracey entrenched behind the burnished walnut pub bar inset as if under siege. She's not exactly a woman yet, more like well on her way, a symmetrical, straight-lined, mass media mainstream-type beauty, makeup and jewelry and fashion.

"Randy," I say, "it's time to go."

Tracey doesn't miss a beat. "Listen to your little robot here, Randy. It's time to—"

I hold a wordless hand up at her, and to my amazement she goes quiet.

"We're leaving. Now. We have to be at the benefit."

"Victor, what are you doing up here? I told you to wait by the door. I'll be down in five minutes."

"No. We're leaving. What are you expecting to get from her? See for yourself. She's just a girl who's in over her head. She has no idea what she's doing, and even less of what's coming. We have to go now."

I continue to be amazed at her silence. Perhaps it was my turn to strike a nerve. Her blouse seems a size too big, dripping off her to expose a jutting collar bone, ribs visible beneath skin. Her jewelry, too, has gone gooey, moving away from her, floor-bound, submitting to gravity like gold gelatin, leaving her momentarily powerless.

"Randy."

He looks at me.

"Let's go."

He nods, and with a purposeful stride walks with me toward the door. Tracey, suddenly reanimated, shrieks obscenities behind us all the way until we're back in the skylit walkway, elevator sliding open to accept us, watching the fullerene recede above through a network of modumetal girders. Mobyle, in another concerning sign of emotional instability, starts to laugh, nervous at first, then uproarious, then finally bitter. I stand straight-faced in the corner, rearranging my glasses on my nose. When the laughter subsides, we're left standing on opposite sides of the compartment, saying nothing. Suddenly loud are the workings of the elevator, low rumbling and faint wiry snapping.

Something occurs to me: Vedge has to know I've been sweating my exposure to Mobyle. If InfoZebra *were* able to track down the hacker and deal with him, them, whoever, away from public view, it would only increase the likelihood they'd cut their losses and sever all ties, and that increased likelihood would be a powerful motivator for Randy to beat them to the punch by revealing the nature of his links to the company. So why would Vedge tell me something like that over the phone? Wouldn't he assume I'd relay the information to get Mobyle to blow the whistle? What are the chances they're not after the hacker at all, and that I've just been placed inside a well-designed snare? Except he'd also know I would probably come to this conclusion, meaning there's an even more sickening possibility that he wants to put me on the scent of a double-cross, thereby deterring me from encouraging Randy to make any public admission of involvement with InfoZebra and Clam Bell. Either way, there's no way to know. Universal currents, indeed.

The manic activity of the streets is once again coming into view. Mobyle twists his defunct wedding ring between two fingers. "What do you think, Victor? Is it time to give all this up?"

I send instructions to the limo driver to pick us up directly outside the building. "No," I respond bluntly, doing nothing but buying myself time.

"Well I do. I just don't see any other way out of this for us."

The elevator hits the ground floor and as soon as the doors slide open there's the detonation of many camera flashes, volleys of questions, a squall of humanity squeezing around us so tight it's as if I've plugged my ears and am listening to my own heartbeat. The limousine pulls up with impeccable timing and we struggle to get to it, both of us letting out held breaths after escaping inside. One thing I can say for being hunted by the media on a daily basis, it's made me start dressing a bit better. No matter that everyone hates you, you start to get a little vain.

"All that out there," Mobyle says, smoothing his tie and watching the media frenzy disappear behind us through the back window, "and you really think there's any point in going on?"

"That's it, I've had it with all this feeling sorry for yourself. So they've announced an investigation into the campaign—they've barely begun the process. If you drop out now you'd be broadcasting your guilt for everyone to see. But for the moment you're still the preeminent politician in this city, so *act* like it. You have a chance to see this project through and remind people why they supported you in the first place. Don't give in. Don't forget that *you*, Randy, were the one who won the people over."

He's susceptible to flattery, and I'm hoping the present circumstances are no exception. This kind of thing has become so automatic for me I can almost believe myself. He sits back in his seat, chastised if not convinced. Well, even if I am manipulating him, I'm actually not wrong. My advisory role is intact, it's just that here I am allied with *Flint Vedge?* My conception of myself has been that I'm the voice of reason, but it's clear I've confused reason with virtue. I am not necessarily good.

Two lights down we hit a construction detour due to the InfoZebra scraper and are swept along into a small twilight zone of one-ways that sends the driver in a full aimless circle before he corrects course and finds his way back to Entsheidungsproblem Blvd., barely weaving his way into standstill traffic overflowing from several similar detours all around the downtown area. Our destination is much farther southwest, deep in the motherboard tract, and we have less than half an hour. The barrier between us and the driver is down and I lean into the front seat to watch him pull up a traffic report on the dashboard, the two main conduits leading into the suburbs looking like a pair of constricted sinus cavities.

"It's a freakin parking lot," the driver says. "Been like this for weeks now. All cause of that goddamn scraper." He looks into his rearview at Mobyle. "No offense, mind you."

"Here," I say, highlighting a convoluted route on the screen with my finger.

"Eh, not to be contradictory, sir, but what you just did there looks like bad plumbing from the 1950s. Not to mention"—there is a sudden inexplicable jolt of angry horns all around us and the driver instinctually lays into his own, hand going flat against the middle of the steering wheel in quick succession—"not to *mention*, the street you've got me turning down is on the other side of the road, and this is a double yellow."

"Cross it," I tell him, my determination to get Mobyle to this benefit evolving into obsession.

"Now look, I ain't a taxi. I have no line of vision on this side. I cross into oncoming traffic and we're liable to get kissed right on the nose. You want that?"

"I want you to cross over. These cars are going by at a crawl. You have two options available to you, as I see it. Either cross over and take the alternate route, or abruptly lose employment."

The driver sighs and shoots a look at me in the rearview that I thoroughly deserve, rolls down his window, peeks past the cars ahead of us, and drops the pedal in a violent burst of acceleration, sending me flying backwards onto the floor, my head making painful contact with Mobyle's shinbone. I can feel the limo slaloming right to left, horns dopplering by outside including the bellow of a semi, the driver shouting "Fucking shit you bastard look the fuck out you fucking fuck!" while Mobyle grips his ankle and swipes his wingtip shoe across my ear. The limo screeches to a stop, lurches drastically left, and accelerates again before a punking sound of the driver's side mirror being torn away mingles with the jangling-dimes effect of shattered glass.

"Don't stop! Occupational termination!"

The horns reach a furious crescendo, every car within range involved and uninvolved voicing distaste at the maneuver. There's a groaning of metal, angry screaming, and in an instant we're once again cruising along smooth. I peel myself off the floor to see the driver's reflection in the rearview—face red, intensely veined, glaring at me homicidally.

"Excellent job," I say, not wasting time to roll up the window between us.

Mobyle and I spend a minute or so collecting ourselves, doing our best to just move past the whole thing as quickly as possible. He reaches over shakily to pour himself a glass of bourbon. I fix my glasses, run a few fingers through my hair and let it sink in that this is the shittiest workday ever.

Having lived through this most recent traumatic experience, Mobyle abruptly remembers the larger traumatic experience he still finds himself in the middle of. "What exactly should I *say* at this benefit, Victor? I have no speech written, nothing planned."

"These people aren't looking for explanations from you," I tell him through ragged breathing, my ear still throbbing. "These are the money-givers, the ones who knew what was what from the beginning. Or if they didn't know, they didn't care. This is business first and politics second for them. Platitudes will suffice."

"And the media?"

"Stick to what you've already said a million times before and project confidence at all costs. The cameras are like x-rays for even the smallest sign of guilt."

"Goddammit, Victor, don't you get it? This is all over for me and you."

Again, his automatic inclusion of me accompanying him to his downfall sends a twang of epidermal dread up the insides of my thighs.

"I'd advise you to stop thinking that way. You're confusing your own fear with reality. Nothing is even close to over. And this benefit is a crucial moment in your push for mayor. I repeat: everyone who will be in attendance stands to make a lot of money with you in office. They wield *sway*. They're rich. They can convince and bully others to do things. In some cases, they can even move the needle on media coverage and public opinion. But if you give up, if you let your own damaged ego convince you you've already failed, you will end up isolated and villified. This is an opportunity to start turning things around."

Mobyle breaks into a loud burst of what I interpret as smug laughter.

"What's so funny? You keep laughing at inappropriate times, if you haven't noticed."

"Christ don't I love it when you and Flint and all the others find it necessary to explain reality to me. I ask serious questions and from the responses I get you'd think I asked what color is the sky. Victor, you think I don't know the InfoStructure initiative will come to fruition with or without me? Of course it will. What they *need* right now is a sacrificial lamb. So what do I *say?*"

His sudden clarity scares me worse than anything. I'm forced to act like I don't hear what he's actually asking me.

"The point is to stay consistent. Keep saying what we've been saying all along and it will buy us—"

"Fuck, forget it. I'm the only sane one left."

Why is it that I keep finding myself running defense for Flint Vedge and not my friend who is begging me to help him strategize, find a way out of this? I can't seem to help it. Mobyle is correct to assume he can't just continue as normal without ending up the sworn enemy of an unstoppably powerful corporate PR army, so why am I turning into part of the machine that's currently herding him toward the slaughter?

I lean forward. "I stole something from Tracey's apartment."

"What?"

"I stole something. Back at the apartment."

"Speak up, Victor. Why are you whispering?"

"I stole some drugs." I take the little baggie of benzoylmethylecgonine from my pocket and proffer it to Mobyle.

He looks at it in disbelief. "Why did you take this?"

"Impulse. I spotted it on the coffee table."

He casts a suspicious eye, trying to make sense of what's going on here.

"Victor?" he says.

Through the window behind him I can see we've passed out of the downtown area, away from the scrapers and highrises and five-star restaurants into a surrounding area where the floor of the city is covered in garages with hand-painted banners, bright LIQUOR signs caked with pollution, amputees slinking along narrow sidewalks in motorized wheelchairs bedecked with old grocery bags. Through the glass all of it exists in a different dimension.

I rush to explain. "Consider, Randy, that *I'm* not impervious. The stress of the situation has affected me as well. You don't need to be reminded, I'm sure, that I'm currently in just as much trouble as you."

He says nothing.

"You need something to clear your mind, augment your focus. Keep you on track."

He seems to understand something all of a sudden, and I realize I'm involuntarily wringing my hands together. Looking down at the baggie, his developing chins weave tightly together.

He says, "You're doing some with me."

"Huh?"

"You want me to stay on track? Fine. But I'm not going to be the only one who walks into the lion's den grappling tonight."

"Randy, no, I've never done that before." I haven't done *any* drug before.

"Fine then. Let me out here. You can explain to Flint why I didn't show up."

"You can't be serious."

He leans toward me, taking on an edge of hostility. He's finally figured out I'm playing both sides.

"Dead serious. You say you're in this with me? Well, Victor, I sure would appreciate a little proof, old friend. Before I go out there and deliver all those platitudes and empty promises, that is."

I'm terrified. First because I've lost the ambiguity of my loyalties, and second because my whole being resides fully within my waking consciousness and I'm scared to mess with that stability but I know I have no choice but to do this.

He grabs my briefcase from the seat beside him, tapping out fourteen or fifteen large-sized clumps from the baggie, and with the edge of his credit card crunches them into a fine powder, obsessively careful not to lose even the slightest bit of dust, chopping and granulating and separating. What results is eight almost perfectly spaced lines of gonine. Toward the end of the process a few trickles of wonderment infiltrate the cement of brain.

"Hand me a couple of bills, Victor?"

"Bills?"

"Bills, yeah, like dollar bills."

I spend some time fishing for the crispest dollar possible.

"C'mon, Victor, any bill."

He rolls them tight and commences with a brusque, slightly demanding tutorial.

"Four each. Just watch me and then do what I do."

He takes on a scholarly expression as he snorts one entire line up through the little tube, going quickly back to clean up some of the straggling leftover powder, coming up rubbing his nose and sniffing hard.

"Just like that. It's best to do the whole line in one go [sniff], so just close your eyes and go for it."

I take my own rolled up tube and lean over, mimicking his performance. I sniff so hard my nose makes a strange sound, overestimating how much suction it would require to make the transfer of materials, and to my surprise the powder is not abrasive in my nostril but actually like the gentle stroking of dendritic anhedonia or lukewarm combustion, everything going the route of dental numbing and my brain immediately struck by the whirring of rotary blades. The motion is not so foreign as I imagined it would be—instead it's like a strain of muscle memory never practiced but perfectly natural, the act itself iconic, a bit of an initiation to take part in something so historical and commonplace, so human and reckless and flawed. The effects are all but immediate. We spend a few minutes consuming the little bounty. I'm grinning without meaning to.

We both sit back in our seats without words for a moment, letting ourselves feel blissful, until Mobyle says to me, "You know I'm not as stupid as you think, right?"

I seem to watch from inside a chiseled-out version of myself say to him, "I wish I could be a better friend right now."

The world through the windows slowly transitions from urban to suburban, my alternate route working perfectly, sending us on a collision course with the benefit, which is taking place at a pre-fab conference capsule that serves as the main nerve of an upscale shopping complex. I'm shaking with fear and excitement. We're passing into the beating heart of control—a system constructed for us long ago which we played no hand in, contributed no mental expenditure to, something that was here before we ever took our first breath or acquired our first ambition or understood any pattern, an arbitrary hammer to flatten minds, the ghost of good intentions having long since gone obscure under ever-fatter history, morphing into a giant godhand emerging in three-fourths time from the clouds overhead, arriving to abolish quick death and codify slow disintegration, providing the answer to a question steeped in misery—and inside the limo, stuck in a moment of its making, we are deafened by its thrum. A richly dull banner comes into view.

WELCOME INFOSTRUCTURE DONORS:
AN INFORMATION-ORGANIZATION
VENTURE BY INFOZEBRA

We step out of the limo and are immediately reabsorbed into the cold déjà vu of camera flashes and desperate questions, the gonine making it impossible not to be swept up, not to bound gleeful through what feels like a movie set, putting on a face of stoic suffering for a hateful audience. We pass through the giant glass doors of the conference building into a ferned hallway with a short set of steps leading to where the maze of tables and buffet lines have been set up earlier today by minimum wage employees wearing jeans and sleeveless shirts or perhaps a jumpsuited prison work squad. The first one to come into view is Vedge, surrounded by a circle of old besuited white men all with birdish or doughy or birdishly doughy faces. He catches sight of us cresting the stairs and booms, "Here's the Councilman now, gentlemen!"

Mobyle is wrenched from my sight and I am teleported into a

small sub-circle, the group dividing now, separating out into stratums of status with eerie obedience. Wendell Planax stands engaging me with an open can of Terradon Plus in his left hand and a bottle of designer water in his right, nicotine-yellow hair at low-tide against his forehead, exposing a scalp speckled by liver spots. I'm astonished by the brilliant but emotionless décor in the background, everything normal becoming incredible.

"Quite an event," Planax says, low enough on the food chain to affect a relaxed, detached, casual persona.

"Yes, yes, yes," I'm gibbering madly. "Haha!"

"High spirits today, Victor? Should I hazard you've managed to slip Randy's neck free of the noose?"

"What a silly question, Wendell. The answer, of course, is no comment."

His laugh is big and abrasive, the amalgamated laugh of every businessman in the world, the laugh of finding true humor in power's workings. I'm stifling the obscenely pleasant urge to blast off through the fucking ceiling, fingering the packet of gonine that for some reason has ended up back in my pocket, taking in the smell of catered food and blurting with infinite exuberance, "Something smells irrefutably good!"

"Don't bother. The salad is too fancy and there's no decent meat option. What's with you, Victor? Someone spike your punch with tequila?"

Snippets of the conversation between the other two men in our group distract my attention, Alfonse Fearing projecting his voice to make sure others can hear.

"You've actually got to *re*gress in order to *pro*gress. I tell this exact same stuff to big tables of old men like us tirelessly—*re*gression is *pro*gression."

"Get inzide ze heads, eh? Inzert ze images, eh?"

"Precisely. I attended a lecture last Sunday by the chief demographic analyst at Gooroo, his name's McCombe. Mind-bending stuff. You oughtta hear it. Goes under the title, 'Inside Children Born Into Mega-Info-Industrialism.'"

"Bombard zair brainz."

"No no no, you've got it all wrong. Aren't you listening? *Regression* is *progression*. You don't go bashing down walls when there are more subtle ways to penetrate their minds. I mean, this stuff is elementary. These revelations are fifteen years old at *least*. It astonishes me how set we are in going the full frontal assault approach. Use some *finesse* every once in a while, for Christ's sake."

"Not zo zimple, Alfonze, no. Zteamroll zair zenzez. Dizintegrate ze conzept of optionz."

"You know you get kind of a Hitler thing going on when you talk like this, Ulrich?"

Fearing is right. Indirectness is a key strategem. Install corporate politician; construct behemoth scraper on taxpayer dollars; restructure and institutionalize all consumer-based algorithmic data on city-funded initiative; establish unregulated advertising monopoly; covertly auction off data exposure to highest bidders; accrue monsoons of profit.

A dense hand falls on my shoulder from behind. It's Vedge, pulling me away from the circle.

"What the hell's going on?" he says when we're out of earshot. "Randy's got this look like he just joined a fucking cult." He takes a quick overview of me. "...and you've got the same look he does."

I'm grinning, I realize now. I try to pull my expression and my head together. "Look, I got him here. That alone you should consider concomitant to a miracle."

"Flavorless, for fuck's sake, use regular words." Vedge's face curdles with frustration. "Tell me what's going on," he seethes under his breath.

"No."

"What the fuck did you just say?"

"No. You can figure it out for yourself. You have no choice but to trust me. He's going to get up there, deliver a short speech, and afterwards you can run damage control. This was by no means easy to arrange."

"You're a bastard, Flavorless, you know that?"

"And stop calling me Flavorless."

The party encroaches on the privacy of our conversation, Vedge leaning in to whisper to me: "This'd better goddamn work." Then he all but caroms away, heading off in some terribly important direction.

Few people are sitting yet, my assigned table somewhere near the front. I stumble into the madness haplessly, searching out my placard, surprised for some reason to discover the effects of benzoylmethylecgonine are very much what I imagined they would be. Swiveling through the circular decorated tables (impeccably set with wine and highball glasses, large centerpieces, napkins folded into abstract upright shapes) I pass through the thin atmospheres of various conversations, breathing in little superfluous bits. Chandeliers hover overhead, causing the saturated air to wink with a subtle saffron quality. In the process of looking for my seat I'm brutally intercepted by a young man balancing hors d'oeuvres, which I gobble up frantically, one after the other, the repetitive motion of my jaw a mesmerizing pattern. I'm lost in my own movements. A jovial voice says "Victor!" and I turn my head to see Ward VIII Councilman Phred deWet approaching fatly, draped in an unfashionable and unflattering tan suit. With his left hand he's pincering the doily of a savory little hors d'oeuvre the shape of a miniature cathedral and with his right he's reaching out to shake my hand. I meet his grasp with a confidence that seems almost unreal, genuinely glad to see this man who I'm normally repelled by. Potted plant leaves riffle with political wildlife at the perimeters of my vision. Per usual, we shovel small talk into a void of mutual dislike.

"Victor, how ya holdin up?"

"Phred. Oh, not too bad. Good, actually. All things considered, of course."

"Of course. Just let me know, Victor, if there's anything I can do to help you out. This XittyXat thing is preposterous and I hate to see good men go down."

Here we go with the obvious ingratiation, of the exact mortifying variety he's been lavishing on Mobyle and anyone connected to his organization since it became obvious Randy would be making a push for mayor. He either still believes Mobyle's got a shot at the election, or else he's being careful to hedge his bets. The reality is, it doesn't matter which. If a weathervane like deWet hasn't yet forsaken us, it means that no matter how humiliating the XittyXat scandal is, we're provisionally in two places at once: heading into power and on the outs with the public. Unfortunately it's precisely this dissonance that's pushing Mobyle toward breakdown. I deflect deWet's pro forma generosity with a delighted, gonine-charged aplomb, allowing a feeling of power to lightning bolt down my spine unchecked. The kid with the hors d'oeuvres is still standing nearby, his hair slick with gel and stealing a peek at a phone he's barely inched from his pocket, typing something to someone. I didn't notice before but his right eyelid is hanging unnaturally low. He's balancing the hors d'oeuvres like he's afraid of them, proffering the tray outwards so people passing by can grab them soundlessly.

I excuse myself from deWet's company and he tells me to keep my chin up and I say will do before I see Tamara Yardblast rounding the outer edge of a table, inadvertently caught in my path, and I've always liked Tamara since her dealership is in Ward II and she has a semi-regular working relationship with Mobyle and so by proxy myself, all those meetings and dinners and golf games and sporting events, and in a moment of overzealousness I'm embracing her unprompted, saying, "Tamara, it's so good to see you, how are you?" and she shivers away from my hug with a look of restrained social horror, human contact a major faux pas amongst this crowd aside from handshakes and backslaps, nodding with a few polite words about being on her way to her table, food and all, she hasn't eaten all day, take care, and I pinball away between four or five people of vague acquaintance to me, some of them indecently rich and looking on at things with bored certainty, no one ever mentioning XittyXat explicitly but rather just hinting at the topic amusedly as if it were a craze sure to die down in a week or two, my head like a wailing siren, and finally I arrive at the buffet line full of appetizer options before we're all served what's sure to be a robust catered meal once the speeches start, and I'm pointing to paysanne and red beet salad, crackers with fancy cheese, a spread of wine bottles, more little intricate hors d'oeuvres, all of it is transferred to me on a plastic plate by single-purpose people in starched shirts and bowties, purely modular human beings in crackling clothes, sending me back off to my seat at a table near the front where I sit down beside Alfonse Fearing and a smattering of other political-capitalist hybrids, his beard pencil-thin, mouth opening to reveal words, asking first if I'm okay and then if I've heard of the Theory of Random Humor invented by McCombe, transitioning into erudite-speak:

"McCombe proctors a lecture entitled 'Inside Children Born Into Mega-Info-Industrialism,' it's quite mindbending. Certainly you've noticed the younger generations' affinity for the word 'random.' As in, if something is funny it is also probably quite 'random.' You've noticed? A certain subset of humor rests entirely on the premise of disparate, disconnected, incoherent information appearing in loose narrative juxtaposition. A narrative will proceed onward as normal, but then is often cluttered with useless details or ridiculously intrusive happenstances. Cluttered with 'randomness,' as it were. This style and genre of humor is almost entirely unique to the modern generations. But McCombe also proposes the question, *why* this new form of humor? What purpose does it serve? It serves as an unconscious self-defense mechanism of the young. They must be able to laugh off excess disorderly information because their day to day lives are spilling over with it. They identify with confusion. The 'random' has gained a status of mystique. Seems to me yet more evidence why initiatives like this one are necessary, wouldn't you agree? Ordering information properly is an effort to prevent insanity."

And I find myself actually agreeing with him despite everything I know, saying, "You're right, that's right, one hundred percent right," and on and on.

The mingling crowds have started the agonizing procedure of finding their seats en masse, old used-up bodies shuffling all around me. Vedge and the other InfoZebra goons are located even nearer the stage, and when I look over there Vedge is staring, observing me with intense brooding nervousness. At the table is Fearing, Wendell Planax, Jalal Beattie, Hilmar Jorgensen, Phred deWet, Ward V Councilwoman Fiona Nix, a younger guy with hip hair and no suit whose placard says his name is "Nazareth Mushroom Bonefax", and finally to my right Mobyle himself, who, for a number of almost pathetic reasons, I'm very happy to see. We exchange a knowing, frightened glance. Fearing is currently asking Planax if he's ever heard McCombe's Theory of Total Male Video Game Absorption.

A small army of waiters in white suits and black bowties, one for each table, begins to circulate through the room, all of them trolleying small dumbwaiters full of ornately covered plates. Our waiter is a white kid with the face of a bird who's concentrating very, very hard on his task, obviously scared and inept but nonetheless making the brave attempt to maintain a veneer of control, setting our food in front of us in turn, clockwise around the table, beautiful plates of braised duck, roast chicken, inventive sides, then drink orders are made, his face squinching with obsessive care before he walks away carting the empty dumbwaiter. Councilwoman Nix (thin and round-eyed with a tragically elderly sense of fashion) is becoming interested from across the table in Fearing's McCombe theories.

"I think I've heard of this McCombe," she says. "Where did you say he lectures?"

Fearing couldn't be any more pleased, announcing to her as well as the entire table, "I attended his lecture in Denver, at the university, but he's become quite a sought-after speaker. Next month he's touring the Northeast."

"Surprised InfoZebra hasn't nabbed him up for this little project here."

"That would be wonderful, but he's already been headhunted by a rival company. An incipient outfit called Gooroo. Anyone familiar with it?"

"Yeah, man, I own stock in it." This from Nazareth Bonefax, who, before picking up his silverware to eat, places his hands together in the praying position and nods gravely to his plate of duck.

Everyone is stealing nervous glances at Mobyle, trying not to seem fascinated by his presence at the table. I pick up my shimmering fork but eating strikes me as a slow deliberate chore. Mobyle, on the other hand, seems calm, which first impresses me but is now making me increasingly uncomfortable.

"Interesting," Jalal Beattie says, scrutinizing Bonefax with a wary eye. "I do, too."

"Gentlemen," Planax breaks in with his merry good-ol-boyness, eating savagely. "Let's not go exposing our allegiances just yet—at least not till the drinks get here!" He bursts into a saucy laugh at his own quip, and completely without meaning to so do I. Eyes land on me like a carpet bombing.

The conversation wants to switch to Mobyle's situation, I can feel it, but instead Fearing makes a daring, albeit unwitting, rescue by saying, "Fiona, out of curiosity, have you heard of McCombe's Theory of American Shame?"

Our nervous waiter rearrives with everyone's drinks (large bottles of water with the word *InfoZebra* printed blandly on them in black typeface for everyone except Nazareth Bonefax, another can of Plus for Planax, beer for Jorgensen and deWet and Nix, then finally a glass of scotch on the rocks for Fearing that he's got to pay extra for, the waiter placing the plastic credit card tray in front of him with a wiggling hand of adrenaline) and now the conversation starts to surge.

Fearing: "Yes, it's the theory explaining why American students gravitate toward the arts and humanities as opposed to math and science in recent decades. According to McCombe, all our nation's interactions with the rest of the world since World War II have been characterized by greed, hatred, ignorance, fear, violence and deception. Wars filled with senseless death, a culture celebrating ruthless capitalism, what have you. Not to mention our domestic exploits. [He sips his scotch vaingloriously here.]"

Jorgensen: "You are doing the looking on your cellular?"

Bonefax: "Dude, what is that accent?"

Planax: "This McCombe sounds like a *reeeal* patriot, Alfonse. Red white and blueski all the way."

Nix: "Wendell, I'm trying to listen if you don't mind."

Fearing: "Children who haven't even played a hand in history yet have this information inculcated into them at a young age. They grow up learning, whether consciously or not, to be ashamed to be American. This is traumatic, of course, to grow up hating oneself and one's country, to take on the responsibility for actions done in your name before ever having been born. How did McCombe put it? It's quite comparable to Catholic guilt."

Me: "[Whispering to Mobyle] Do you know what you're going to say?"

Mobyle: "[Into my ear] Flint gave me a copy of a quick speech TJ wrote up this morning."

Fearing: "Creation of art, for recent generations, is a method of interpreting self. Also of interpreting the self within context. Young people are drawn toward the interpretation of their shame not only because it helps them understand it, but also because it allows them, in their minds, to separate themselves from the aims of their country. In this manner they purge their shame. They attempt to create rather than destroy. They are apologizing, branding their own culture and countrymen as brutal and stupid. Math and science are seen as the heartless logic of the state, and they want no part in them. Yet they are unaware that even their own artistic efforts will eventually come to be seen as another outgrowth of their country's criminal pathology."

Nix: "This all makes quite a lot of sense to me. Interesting, this McCombe."

Fearing: "Yes, that's what I think."

Planax: "I'm not sure I can say the same thing there, Alfonse, buddy. Sounds to me like Mr. McCombe—"

Fearing: "*Dr.* McCombe."

Planax: "—Dr. McCombe is yet another one of these academic types looking to absolve everyone in the modern generations of all responsibility. Oh, it's not *my* fault I'm like this, it's *America's* fault, it's the fault of my *environment*, how can I possibly be expected to be held *accountable* for my *actions?*"

Nix: "For heaven's sake, Wendell, you're so *excitable*. I swear to

God that you get so riled up over the most innocuous things. Makes me glad you never go to city council meetings."

Fearing: "McCombe is not trying to absolve anyone of responsibility. What he's trying to do is simply verbalize certain psychological framings of children born at the turn of the century and later. They are generalized feelings and theories, almost impossible to quantify in any empirical sense, but nonetheless relevant. He is teaching how to identify with and understand a certain category of consumer."

Planax: "People listen to him because he makes them feel victimized, plain and simple. Even us 60s- and 70s-born kids crave victimization. And why? Because when you're victimized, [holds back a rising soda belch] you're justified."

Beattie: "Justified in what?"

Planax: "Anything, really. Any depraved, contemptible, dishonest act becomes justifiable. Because, after all, you can't be held *responsible* for the way you turned out, it wasn't your *fault*. You were just a *victim*."

Jorgensen: "[Holding up his beer] Good cheers! Pleasure I'm having to be dining!"

Mobyle: "Well said. Cheers, Hilmar. [They cheers.]"

Bonefax: "Whoa, whoa, hold up a sec. You're saying that, like, people in the 50s who were racist, who probably had like parents who were racist and shit, who lived in Alabama or whatever, should've known better?"

Planax: "Um, I don't exactly see the connection between racial tensions in the 1950s and some demo-analyst giving lectures about—"

Bonefax: "You're saying they weren't victims of their environment? Of popular opinion? Of prejudices that had been, like, *there* before they were even born?"

Fearing: "Additionally, Wendell, you should be glad McCombe is delivering these ideas to the young. He says as much himself. I'm paraphrasing, but essentially it's in the best interest of men like you and I that advertising and marketing be considered valuable in the arena of academia. I was one of three people in a crowd of two hundred who were over thirty. It was the very children who were born into so-called 'mega-info-industrialism' who were going to a lecture to learn about children born into mega-info-industrialism. You see the significance? These young people are clearly hungry for self-insight, and if they're ever to be assimilated into consumer culture they will have to receive a form of psychotherapy from advertising and marketing itself."

Planax: "I don't give a damn what his aims are. He's enabling victimization. That's all I see it as. We need people who aren't afraid to be culpable for themselves."

Nix: "Well that's why we're here, isn't it? To support Randy's initiative? To make information better organized and not so hostile? To be culpable for the system?"

Mobyle: "[Breaking into a campaignish, self-satirizing soundbite] This is an investment for everyone, Fiona, future *and* current generations. It's a step toward mastering a beast we can't allow to get out of control. Information is now tangible. Look at our cyberwars with China and Iran. Look at identity assassination. Look at digital suicides. Look at widespread misappropriation of funds and the clinically distracted. This is beyond investment, this is *necessity*."

Beattie: "[Breaking an awkward silence] Touching, Randy. Seems to me you've already got us here, no need to keep up the salesmanship."

Mobyle: "InfoZebra is going to help the city of Grid pioneer that necessity and turn it into a reality. Using similar technology as that used in their groundbreaking ZChase software, programmers and internet activists will provide us with one of the first fully functioning information infrastructures in existence. This will mark progress and opportunity. An insistence that we can continue to improve on our improvements. That the human element remains vital when it comes to invention."

[Silence.]

Nix: "Victor, is he all right?"

Me: "Randy?"

Nix: "Randy, is everything okay?"

Mobyle takes in a forkful of food and nods in the councilwoman's direction, chewing but not saying anything. The conversation is paralyzed, all mastication suspended except for Jorgensen who is apparently oblivious. The widespread clinking of silver against plates adds a percussion track to the conversational white noise of the room, and my breath is held, waiting for Mobyle to say something, an organ I assume to be my stomach going into freefall, it's difficult to tell with my heart beating so fast. A few more uncomfortable seconds pass before Mobyle swallows and says, to everyone's relief, "Fine, Fiona, fine."

Planax jumps in to say, "Weird sense of humor you got, Randy," followed by an outburst of laughter meant to be exuberant but that is in fact tinged with ire, causing the statement to come off sarcastic and unhelpful.

"Well it's a weird night, Wendell. Only appropriate."

Flint Vedge, we all notice at the same time, has made his way up to the podium, a stainless steel angular thing placed center-stage, a vast screen behind him with the simple word WELCOME floating against a blue-gradient background. The setup is so bland and corporate hardly anyone maintains interest in the start of the proceedings for more than a second, most returning the lion's share of their attention back to their meals. The light in here is rather low, almost sleepy. I hear some yawns happening. Vedge's voice, polite and politically-correct in public, exudates microphonically throughout the room, clicking the general tenor of things into a state of bored submission. Utensils continue to sing against plates.

"Good evening."

From where I'm sitting Vedge seems smaller and less intimidating than usual, like a man being pressed in upon from all sides.

"We're going to go ahead and get started, but please feel free to continue with your meals. Today marks a milestone for the city of Grid, a step toward efficiency and efficacy, and that's why we're here to say thank you for all your magnanimous donations, as well as provide an opportunity to glimpse what that money is helping to create."

The gonine in my system is abruptly losing traction, the center of my chest no longer containing a burning star of energy but instead a small spot of superheavy condensed mass. The screen behind Vedge transitions to the InfoStructure logo.

"As you all know, the InfoStructure initiative aims not to eliminate the quantity of digital information we're faced with, but simply to better organize it, allowing for more consistent and manageable systems. This will mean less waste in terms of time and manpower. The software, which is algorithmically similar to InfoZebra's ZChase platform, a program which already runs on personal computers all over the world, will operate on an exponentially larger scale than anything our company has ever tackled. To introduce the hopes and civic expectations for this groundbreaking project, I will turn the mic over to the man who spearheaded InfoZebra's involvement with the city of Grid, Councilman Randy Mobyle."

Mobyle stands and makes his way to the stage, the crowd's attention suddenly snapping-to upon his introduction, the applause not subdued as much as eager, on edge. The press junkets ignite the ballroom with rapid-fire bursts of camera flashes and I am miserably nervous. On the stage he shakes hands with Vedge and exchanges an inaudible word or two, the enormous screen stating his name. He ruffles papers obscured by the podium while he waits for the clapping to end. Looking at the other members of my table I see they've forgotten their meals, silverware still clutched in hands but frozen in place, heads turned attentively upward. The camera flashes dissipate to one or two every couple of seconds. From his spot on the stage Mobyle takes a quick moment to appraise the crowd. He says, reading from something in front of him:

"Welcome InfoStructure donors. Many of you here tonight, regardless of title or occupation, have started families and careers here in Grid, and have come to call this city home. I am no different. We've had the opportunity to see our city flourish, growing larger and, at least in some respects, more important than our close neighbor, the state capital. This success has brought us our share of good fortune, but it has also brought unforeseen challenges. I've always likened the administration of a city to the administration of a home. When leadership and organization fails in the home, that family will find itself at the whims of fate. This analogy, while simple, nonetheless accounts for the inspiration to redefine what it means to be a family member here in our home. We have all come to realize that just as surely as our city is built on a foundation of concrete and metal, so too is it built on a foundation of information. It is clear we are the inheritors of a paradigm shift, and this fact had to be taken into account if we were to keep pace with the rest of the world. You should congratulate yourselves tonight—truly—not just for making progress possible, but for recognizing its urgency. For being the kind of thinkers this city needs to remain competitive, safe, stable. This is what the InfoStructure initiative will mean for Grid—a summation of our willpower to perfect our own technologies and systems. Reaching this point was not easy, nor will the steps ahead be. But despite the difficulties set before us, they are outweighed by the necessities. Indeed, we have seen a number of crises arise in recent years, pressing issues that have been, in part, generated by our current methods of governance. Grid remains home to the highest number of citizens in govt-initiative housing in the state in proportion to population. Water, for most, has become an unfortunate luxury. Drugs and violence continue to be a tangible force in the manufacturing sectors and, increasingly, in our own neighborhoods. Misuse or misallocation of funds has reached epidemic levels in the wake of higher informational complexities and a faster-moving society. And so on."

He pauses here. Hundreds of eyes locked on him, video lenses staring, insectoid cameras flashing with rote excitement, beaming incontrovertible images instantaneously into the minds of millions. So far I've been amazed at his composure. It seemed to me when he began speaking that talent and instinct might be kicking in, but now every muscle in my body has seized up. The pause is beginning to linger and drag out, five seconds turning to ten, ten to fifteen, the crowd growing impatient, confused. I look to Vedge, standing outside the primary focus of the news cameras, his eyes fixed to Mobyle with a look of horror, disbelief. I am so near to shouting out *I would personally advise you to speak this instant!* it almost hurts. Just as it feels the pause will never end, that it has finally become too much for anyone to endure any longer, that Vedge will step in and take control—maybe 20 total seconds of bizarre interruptus—Mobyle leans over and says into the mic:

"But of course all this hardly needs to be said, does it? None of this is what's really on our minds."

Flint makes some sort of subtle gesture and immediately three suits I vaguely recognize as connected to the mayoral campaign detach from a table a mere ten feet away from me, their chairs tipping over their reactions to his cue are so abrupt, and begin converging toward Mobyle's position at the podium center-stage.

"What's really on our minds is my alleged involvement in the XittyXat scandal and whether or not I might make an admission of guilt concerning—"

The microphone is jostled by an elbow and Mobyle's voice disappears, his sentence attenuated by the political operatives leading him away by the shoulders. Everyone in the room is up out of their seats, and there is an uproar of voices. The whole ballroom strobes and flickers with camera flashes, the press suddenly aroused to something like erotic ecstasy, descending upon and swirling around Mobyle and his escorts, who are leading him through the chaos toward the only possible exit. I come into confusing physical contact with deWet, who had been the one sitting farthest away from me at the table except for Fiona Nix, but whose corpulence I'm now ricocheting off of. My glasses slide off my nose and get lost in the rabble but regardless I don't take my eyes away from Mobyle's progress through the crowd, desperately struggling to catch up with him.

Despite it taking a long time for the mysterious entourage to push him through the disorder, out the front doors, onto the sidewalk, and ultimately into our limousine that squeals up with all the manic fright of a getaway car, they finally manage to do it, with me shoving my way into the direct center of their immense scandalous gravity. For a brief moment voices and cameras menace me from all sides, like being at the center of a lynch mob. I clamber into the limousine behind Mobyle, shielded on both sides by the men in suits who I can still only vaguely recognize. I register it as strange, however, when after the door is shut behind us and the driver escapes at such a rational controlled speed it's like we're pulling away from a funeral, that none of them accompanied us in the vehicle. We're alone in the limo, Mobyle splaying himself across one of the seats and staring up with empty eyes, so completely dissociated as to have left his body for elsewhere. His tie is half undone, dangling across his chest and dribbling toward the floor. Not until we're out on the road do I realize both our phones are ringing. The sound of two, maybe even three helicopters swells into existence above us, and through blurry vision I see through the tinted windows white vans on either side of the vehicle bearing the names of media outlets. In weird unison our phones cease ringing, then start back up again. Reality performs a vortex, causing me to lose all sense of basic factors such as rate of travel, minutes passed, respiration, and others, until when things finally normalize and I regain cognition I'm able to notice the madness outside has subsided, helicopters and news vans and all, with the exception of the phones, which are still ringing. Call ID displays a number foreign and ominous. I cut the power to my cell altogether.

Mobyle is still staring, eyes cleansed of sentience.

"Randy."

He doesn't react.

"*Randy!*"

His eyes regain depth, and he turns to look at me.

"Turn your phone off."

He sits up the way someone waking up from a long nap would, rubbing his face with both hands and looking around with objective, weary little blinks. Once his phone is off we sit opposite one another, traumatized. Downtown Grid is once again growing up around us.

I say in a quiet voice, "That was extremely inadvisable."

The limo seems to know where it's going, navigating its way through complicated downtown turns, and I'm still in too much shock to care about our destination so I don't bother asking.

Eventually we pull up outside the Aero-Arrow Hotel, the whupping of distant helicopter blades returning, vans pulling up outside to expel reporters and camera crews who are already pressing down against the windows of the limousine. The driver, the same one who drove us to the benefit, rolls down the privacy screen and hands a cell to me.

"Flint Vedge on the phone for you, Mr. Savoriss."

"Hello?"

"There's a room reserved for you inside, number 1102. Did you get that?"

"1102," I repeat.

"You'll find the keycard on the floor directly outside the room. Get Randy in there and make sure neither of you says *anything* to *anyone*. Don't stop at the front desk, don't stop at the water fountain or the ice machine, just get your asses *up to that room*. Understand?"

"Yes."

"Good, and once you're in, don't leave for any reason. Security will be right outside and they'll get you anything you need. At some point I will be there. Don't ask when. Definitely not tonight, possibly tomorrow. Keep your phones off. Don't do *anything*."

I try to say something in the affirmative, but he's hung up already. I turn to Mobyle. "Stand up straight and be quiet."

He nods grimly.

We exit the car and are bombarded once again by the press, but this time their mood has turned openly hostile, apparently having already come to a conclusion about who the villian of this story is, everything inflected as invective, not a single question mark attached to the end of any sentence. National media are present.

"CommentontheillegalityofCouncilmanMobyle'sinvolvementin theXittyXatscandal!" "DoesthisdevelopmentsignifytheendoftheCo uncilman'spushformayor!" "Doyouintendtomakeapublicstatemento fapology!" "WhatisyourconnectiontoInfoZebraandClamBellCorp!" "Respondtoclaimsthatyourwifehasfiledfordivorce!" "Whatwasthe aimofyourstatementmadeattheInfoStructurebenefit!"

I keep an arm around Mobyle's shoulders and use the other to cut a path toward the entrance where hotel security and two police officers have arrived. Once we pass the threshold the wall of personnel behind us becomes impermeable, holding back the frothing, flashing media.

As promised, the magnetic key is waiting for us on the floor in front of 1102, along with two men who stand on either side of the door and refuse to greet or even acknowledge us. We go inside and Mobyle locks himself in the bathroom while I undo my tie and pull back the curtains to stare out the window, helicopters dotting the overcast skies of Grid from one corner to the next, sharing airspace with the InfoZebra zeppelin. There's a TV on the wall across from the two queen-sized beds and I'm too afraid to turn it on despite my curiosity. For an hour I sit in silence—doing nothing, looking at nothing—trying to recover from the terrible stress of the day. I fall asleep and wake up some time later, gray daylight having surrendered to blackness in the window, conscious of a dream I was having, of my friends from grade school trying to swing up and around the top bar of the swing set, 360 degrees of accomplishment. Their faces were unafraid, eyes glowing with the anticipation of school-wide fame. In the dream I was not concerned for their safety. I watched one of my friends saddle himself into the black rubber seat like a fighter pilot strapping himself into a jet, the swing set so large for such little kids, and begin to pump himself into a massive pendulum, my friends aiding his velocity with hard pushes at the end of his downward arc, his feet pointing directly at the clouds overhead, higher and higher, the chains straining with metal whining right before I woke up. I stand lightheaded, seeing Mobyle sitting in one of the two chairs at the corner table with his shirt off but pants and shoes still on. In the bathroom I splash cold water on my face and remember, when I put my hands in my pockets, the baggie of gonine. Mobyle and I start to carve up lines on the card table and snort them in the soft lamplight.

"You want to hear something funny?"

I say nothing, but the answer is go ahead.

"All throughout my childhood, I envisioned myself as famous.

Even into my early adulthood I would play at giving interviews, posing for magazine photos, attending events held in my honor."

"What's funny about that?"

"All that time imagining fame, and I never really paid attention to the fact I didn't excel at anything."

Night turns to early morning. We stay awake, rarely speaking, going in and out of the bathroom. I turn on the TV and stay far away from any news channel. Reruns of *My Friend Diagnosis* play in the background, the laugh track drowning out the silence prevailing inside the room. We fall into the hopeless stasis of doomed men, reflecting on mistakes and personal imperfections. The comedown phase of a gonine high, I had no occasion to know before today, is emotionally cruel, reality seeping back like sticky sap, your temporary paradise lost forever. Mobyle cries quietly and during this time I lock myself in the bathroom, hearing sniffles overlaid with laugh tracks on the other side of the door. When I come out later he's sleeping. For hours I watch TV and by the time the sun is all the way up Mobyle is still asleep. There's a gentle knock at the door. One of the guards outside tells me in a hushed voice Flint Vedge is waiting for me in the hotel parking garage. I dress and slip quietly out of the room, take the elevator to sub-level parking, find a limousine with its engine on waiting for me there. The snow returned during the night—cold flows from the echoing concrete walls. Inside the limo there is only Vedge, wearing a heavy black overcoat. He clearly hasn't slept, red veins stretching across his eyes.

Vedge looks at me, face neutral. "Victor."

I sit with arms folded across myself for warmth. "What happened?"

He sighs, his weariness bearing evidence of the exhaustion of the last eighteen hours. "Nothing we weren't already preparing for. The media are gunning for us now, but they'll get nothing definitive. Randy, on the other hand."

"I see," I whisper.

A hush passes between us.

"I'm going to be honest here, Victor. I never much liked you on a personal or professional level. It was my opinion that you were bland

and unmotivated, which, on this echelon of things, just doesn't cut it. After what happened yesterday, we have no choice but to pin the entire XittyXat scandal on Randy. We're no longer protecting him, and the reason we can even afford to jettison him is because, late last night, we IDed the hacker. So, despite where we find ourselves at the moment, we're actually in a fairly strong position. Normally I'd be more than happy to let you take the fall right along with Mobyle, but after the way you performed under pressure yesterday I'm inclined to offer you a deal."

"But I messed up. He crumbled in front of everyone."

"Trust me, Randy's been on the verge of crumbling for some time now. Between the drugs and the emotional instabilities, getting him to that benefit was no easy trick. So whatever you did you did it to the best of your ability. More importantly, though, was I finally saw you playing this game with some passion. You threw out the rulebook and did what you had to do, and that's why we're going to keep you on. The coming months are going to be a merciless bastard, and I'll have use for you in an unofficial capacity. If you're interested. And given you're smart enough to know what the score is, I think you probably are."

A few moments later the limo is pulling out onto the street with me inside, bound for InfoZebra's temp offices here in Grid, and I'm silently advising myself that I'm no longer qualified to advise anyone of anything.

AMY GERNEY JOANN NORBERT

What does it mean to inhabit hell? I'm a genius manipulator, a weaver of falsities so artful they mimic truth. A shadow-city is rising up beneath this one, assembling itself atom by atom on the engine of a stolen supernal force. The avaricious accrue power for themselves, and they are able to make a fool even of nature. What's inside these buildings and underneath the ground is chewed away and hollowed out by decay, my facsimile city swelling slowly into its rotten husk, preparing to surface. Jagged wounds appear all across the skyline, the shadow-city erupting through and shedding away the flapping skin of what was there before. It is *my* city, a monument constructed in my honor. It stands against the frame of the mountains, fully formed in the winter grayness. In the new metropolis people drink of confusion and feed on deception. Their teeth and minds are stained black.

These stains can be seen on the teeth of Zen, watching a national news report of Councilman Mobyle's ousting from office and pending criminal investigation on the sad screen of her bedroom wall with mouth agape. An hour ago I brought her to climax with my tongue against her clit, my intentions traveling through her in the form of pleasure. She spasmed upon their arrival. Her apartment is in an expensive highrise near a GRT station, which she uses to commute into Denver to St. Joseph's. Scrubs of all different colors are strafed across the floor beside her bed. Plastic remnants of microwaveable meals squat across her kitchen counters like small totemic offerings. The walls are bare and treated with indifference. Ashtrays offer up evidence of cigarettes smoked down to stale white filters, another one nestled between her satisfied and trembling post-coital fingers, burning away, giving off long floating trails of its essence. I run my hands across the smooth flared wings of her shoulder blades, her lungs inflating inside her. Her buzzed head is a carrying case for her pliable brain.

"Councilman Mobyle resigned today under heavy pressure from the Grid City Council, incumbent mayor Emanuel Iacona, and Colorado Democratic Senator Dave Warlick. Mobyle, once considered to be a shoe-in candidate for the city's 2025 mayoral election, was responsible for a powerful grassroots political movement within the city, known as 'Mobylism.' The movement espoused 'informational organization' as a means of making sweeping technocratic and bureaucratic reforms aimed at combating what has been perceived as wasteful and ineffectual city government. To implement this program, Councilman Mobyle conducted extensive talks with InfoZebra CEO Flint Vedge, who ultimately agreed to undertake the project, as well as to construct a new international headquarters in Grid. But sources inside the city claim that Mobyle used his influence with Vedge to strongarm other lead politicians out of negotiations, including Mayor Iacona. This had led to a number of aspersions against Mobyle's mayoral efforts, including a prodigious hack earlier this month which hijacked InfoZebra and ClamBellCorp's websites. In what has come to be called the XittyXat Hack, the hacker postulated InfoZebra and its parent company, ClamBellCorp, were behind not only the major contracts with the city, but also Mobyle's mayoral campaign. XittyXat even went so far as to suggest Mobyle's eponymous political movement had been engineered by operatives of the company. Councilman Mobyle sparked a scene of pandemonium yesterday at a benefit held for donors to the city's iconic InfoStructure project by suggesting at, quote, "my alleged involvement in the XittyXat scandal and whether or not I might make an admission of guilt." The InfoStructure project has led to the genesis of similar intiatives being undertaken in other large cities throughout the country…"

Her skin ripples according to my touch the way her actions ripple according to my influence. She looks into my eyes through a haze of smoke, lying naked against me, her body spare, thin, overworked. She moves my hair aside to kiss me, pressing her lips softly against mine. From here I leave her apartment, taking the GRT into the motherboard tract, deleting information from my hard drives remotely en route, arriving at Gerney's apartment complex. He answers the door (his head also buzzed now, they're like my little soldiers) and we fall into bed, but this is a different kind of sex, he penetrating me while I penetrate his autonomy. While my face presses into his mattress I see miniscule white granules of gonine speckling his bedside table. Every electronic device in his house remains perpetually on. When he falls against me I can feel his heart like a hammer in his chest. I make sure not to stay here too long. He requires more emotional maintenance than Zen, who seems content to be fucked and then left to her solitude, as opposed to Gerney whose eyes fill with fear as soon as I start re-clothing. He begs me to stay. I deny him this privilege almost always. I'm lucky with him that men are more easily tempted with physical intimacy alone. When I step outside again I find my city still standing, still thriving, vigilant as ever. Its buildings curl into points, forming into a smile afflicted with bad intentions. I take the GRT into Denver, to St. Joseph's, where I keep watch over Margaret, who lays in bed, stunned in the spotlight of the TV in her coma of confusion, and Norb Towers, who paces up and down the hallways of the CVICU chatting with Dr. Actinide and shooting resentful stares at Zen. Aunt Joann comes in and out during certain hours and I offer her comforting words that continue to sound more sincere, more intimate, more conspiratorial in that special familial way. Hours ooze by, and the more everyone sees me the less they are suspicious of me.

I unfurl myself like a colorful anemone resting against the seafloor, attracting their floating sympathies to feed on my soft underbelly, all the while knowing I will snap closed and dissolve them whole and squirming. Later I return to my apartment where I turn off all the lights, swallow a Vicodin, and lay emotionless in my bed. Sleep doesn't come—only plans and machinations. They grease the rivets in my mind, a mind sick of and by itself, a solipsistic sickness. The world cannot fathom, in its attempts to expand, to become self-sustaining, to subvert the pieces that arrange it into a puzzle, what kind of creature lies within it. A creature of abstraction, lying in the motionless dark, unfit for the balancing act between the Human and Robotic that normal people are forced to endure. I do not endure the world; it endures me. We are not a *species* and yet we are not a *creation*. We are nothing so unified as those words suggest. What we are are accumulated bits of universal material, blown together into shapes, and separate from one another the same way planets in a galaxy are separate. Even when our bodies merge they come away as two distinguishable pieces, the distance between us consisting of that same black distance as space and orbital prisons. Collisions do not occur without partial or complete destruction.

THERE IS NO ANSWER. THERE IS NO WAY TO ELEVATE YOURSELF ABOVE IT ALL. THERE IS NO ESCAPE FROM A SYSTEM OF CONFUSION.

My hands shake. Life manages to hold no sentimental value for me. I feel it was dropped upon my shoulders like an unasked-for burden rather than breathed into me like a blessing of sensation. A crucial element of my personhood is missing; I know this. But by virtue of my sickness I can see past veils of imagined meaning. In this sense, I am above everyone else. I am superior. But also totally abandoned.

These thoughts come to me uninvited in the dark while I wish for sleep. To exist here in these strange systems and know my suffering is merely a decimal point of humanity's is what it means to inhabit hell. Outside the walls of this apartment, my city rises up toward the atmosphere and exceeds what was there before.

Monday I was fired from Archelaos and then on Tuesday I spent the day deleting pictures of my family from my computer and phone before going out at night to downtown party bars by myself, sitting at tables with three or four empty chairs, Zeal and Q/V, the dancing people around me copy-pasted from endless nights the exact same as this one, and every so often I looked up to find that the ceiling was a Porky Pig cartoon set to trance. Watch as I do gonine. Watch as I call Nick Ibyoo and receive no answer. Watch as I sit casually over a beer in a crowded bar trying to act like being alone doesn't bother me while the pounding noise becomes as good as silence and the ceiling turns into a kaleidoscope universe of flashing neon sunglasses. Prepare to enter adulthood numbness in three, two…

…and yet: Wednesday morning I found the letters Dad left me in a far corner of my closet. I read roughly half of them before Amy resolved on my front doorstep. Behind her the world registered as little more than a shifting murk, colorless and colloidal, the exact same way it does for Sarnin on page 378 when he is unable to consolidate his true background identity with his temporary construct one. She exploded into my apartment, bringing with her the promise of release, the skeleton keycard which would open all cells in all prisons. Her abruptness was like some kind of explicit sex dream, pouncing on me the very moment I opened the door, everything bleeding together until it was impossible to tell whether I was on top of my bed sheets climaxing into her soft void (I always imagine it as purple with my eyes closed, the act of combining creating discernible images of sensation) or sitting at the kitchen table consuming coffee and sandwiches (as well as a small, secret amount of gonine in the bathroom for me). Although she'd dissuaded me from worrying about pregnancy after the first time I came inside her, telling me about her sterilization, I thought about it a lot. I thought about the way a child could be created, a new person. How, even after thousands of years of evolution, humans are still born as blank slates. This struck me for the first time ever, like an unexpected and happy shock, as a little wonderful. The written words of my father, still lingering fresh in my mind, had said everything to the contrary.

Bringing a child into the world is an act of pain, and not nearly so much for you as for the child. Its vision starts fuzzy, but is slowly corrected through the lens of experience until it sees reality for what it truly is.

How I'd never realized that dad was a depressed person was suddenly baffling to me. I saw my parents' dispassionate relationship through a whole new light. All the quiet discussions about household things. The forced smiles exchanged like grimaces. The incessant escapism into the world of—for God knows what reason—skiing. The unified front of Mom and Kelsey always battling Dad for influence, and me, neutral, sitting in quiet complacency at the dinner table. All this running through my head until I would feel Amy's naked hips, somehow back on top of me (or was I fiddling with the TV volume?), grind down at just the right angle and the shifting colloidal murk would electrify like millions of tightly closed hands jumping into open fingers, everything momentarily blissful, until soon the fingers retracted darkly back into fists.

Sarnin has feelings of family reevaluation on page 807.

I tried to tell Amy the story of how I'd been fired but she had no time. She quickly dressed and left to a hospital in Denver to go see her mother, who had had a combination heart attack and stroke only a few weeks ago. I told her to come back soon if she was able, that I wasn't feeling well and her company would be nice. She agreed hastily and ran out. Mere seconds after closing the door, her presence felt unreal, like a hallucination I'd had.

The rest of Wednesday dragged me along through a mud of recurring gonine hangovers, time a trickling faucet, and there were the words of dad to drape the slow-moving walls with. Every letter, about 130 total, most of them very short, changed my entire perspective on who he was. He seemed at times prophetic, at others like a doomsayer, others almost psychotic. The tone of each one was consistently dark but at the same time instructive and fatherly, as if he felt I was someday going to need his advice regarding all these cynical thoughts. There was also the possibility he'd never even intended me to read them. Each letter was like a fresh set of psychic burdens. Eventually I came to the only one I ever committed to memory. I knew it almost by heart, actually. Not the most disturbing of the collection, but the most pessimistic.

Kevin, you can't count on anyone in this world to understand you but yourself. If there's one piece of fatherly advice I can give, it's to accept that humans have made a habit of assuming other humans can understand what they say and what they go through, when in fact it couldn't possibly be more to the opposite. To be alive is to be essentially lonely, son, and in my experience it's the optimism that that loneliness can be cured which makes everything worse.

When late evening came around I attempted to get in contact with Nick but no success. Now it was his turn to disregard me, and even though I wasn't surprised by his silence I couldn't avoid feeling hurt, forsaken. He hadn't been at Archelaos the day I was fired. The week prior he'd requested a meeting with Tamara, emerging with a promotion and a raise. So instead he'd been at Corporate's state headquarters undergoing training. I was glad he wasn't there to see me leave. Even if our friendship were still healthy, my being fired was something he would've had zero sympathy for. He and Aria had begun the odd habit of documenting their lives together on socnets, treating their relationship as some kind of movie. I couldn't help but look at every photo, their faces twisted with gonine or alcohol or both, the implications of the images secretly mocking. They felt both close and distant. I had been close to both of them for years, and yet I couldn't remember their personhoods. They were like publicly displayed documents of memories I was never going to be allowed to have, and I felt as if I was peering into a reality in which I was not only dead but had never existed.

Nick wasn't the only one disregarding me. I was unable to get in contact with Ronstadt or Veronika. The only person I managed to get a hold of was Quentin, at 9:30 pm, answering the phone via some kind of remote because his voice came through as far away and weak.

"Hello?"

"Quentin?"

"Hello?"

"Quentin, can you hear me?"

"Hello? Anybody there?"

"I'm here, yeah! Can you hear me!"

"There you are, I can hear you now."

"Where are you!"

So quiet and static-laden I couldn't hear it.

"What! I didn't catch that!"

"—my house."

"Is there any way I could meet up with you!"

"—night?"

"Are you busy!"

"No."

"I'm coming over, is that okay!"

"Sure."

From my place his apartment was a ten-minute walk, situated just outside Motherboardland where suburbia gave way to dense streets lined with mixed residential-and-business developments, apartments built in some type of future-gothic style that housed primarily lower-middle-class blue-collar people and gave off a high-crime vibe.

Quentin lived on the second floor of a building that had a small clique of feral cats slinking around the lobby and an old man at the bottom of the staircase who muttered *evenin* to me as I passed. His apartment was lit by lamps. He had a large bookcase where the TV would've normally been.

"Want a beer?"

I was already grappling so I said no.

"I've got some gonine if you'd rather." He tossed a lighter carelessly across the room. "Did you come through to see if you could buy?"

"I didn't know you sold."

"Well I don't usually, but I have some I need to get rid of if you're interested."

I sat on the couch while he rummaged in the kitchen. He reappeared with a cigarette in his mouth, flopping down at the other end and lighting up. The embers burned hypnotically in the low lighting. "So you wanna buy that jet?"

"Possibly," I said. "Maybe we could just do some?"

He swiveled the cigarette to the other side of his mouth and opened a slim drawer in the coffee table, producing a small wooden box that opened its hinged jaw and spat a two-gram bag of gonine onto the tabletop. We each did a line.

"So what are you doing here if you're not here to buy?" He chopped at the gonine with his ID in an easygoing way.

"I was wondering if you'd talked to Nick lately."

"Nick? No, man, not me. I only know Nick through Millie and Ronstadt."

"What about them? Have you talked to them?"

"In the last week or so."

"Do you know if anything's going on tonight?"

He cleaned the bottom half of the credit card with two fingers and shot me a sideways glance. "It's Wednesday."

"Yeah, I know, I just—"

"Look, man, no offense, because I know Nick's supposedly your best friend or whatever, but the guy's probably the biggest asshole I've ever met."

"I'm not really sure we're friends anymore."

"So that's why you called me. I thought it was because you were either over-twacked or strung-out." He did another line and handed the bill to me.

"No. I mean, maybe strung-out."

"Is everything okay?"

I remember the question making me immediately nervous. Not just because I probably wasn't okay, but because I wasn't used to my friends showing genuine concern for me. Quentin had never been anything but an acquaintance. The answer I came up with was reductive, and sounded disappointing spoken aloud.

"I, I think I'm addicted to gonine."

I did my line and came up sniffing especially hard. He drank his beer, looking at me through his cigarette's stream of dancing smoke.

The room was so quiet my legs began to joggle of their own accord, my heartbeat starting to feel panicked. Quentin dashed the cig in the ashtray and leaned back on the couch with his hands behind his head. I felt like he was observing me.

He said finally, "If I were you, I wouldn't worry too much about losing Nick as a friend."

"Why?"

"He uses you. But to be fair to him, you make it easy."

"What do you mean?"

"Just, I mean, I usually feel like I'm a pretty good judge of character, but I have a hard time getting a read on you. Your personality kind of changes depending on the week. No one can really figure it out."

"That's how people feel about me?"

"I'm not speaking for other people, I'm just saying you strike me as being a little bit inconsistent—"

I suddenly caught sight of the title *Shell-Shocked Sarnin* on Quentin's bookcase.

"—when you're hanging out with Nick Ibyoo. The drugs I get, but it's impossible not to notice he has a weird, I don't know, *control* over you. "

"Control?"

"I mean, *yeah*. The thing is, I'm not sure it's something he means to do, completely. Because it seems like you need it from him."

My intestines clenched and I ran to the bathroom to vomit, mostly because of my high-drug, low-food intake over the previous week, but also because the sickening vividness of his statement brought everything into perfect clarity: I had allowed myself to become addicted to gonine, lose my job, be abandoned by Nick, and now I was balancing at the brink of a personality crisis I'd long ago stopped being able to understand. The whole thing had little to do with what I'd seen happen to the father and son outside Q/V anymore. Something else was wrong, but I didn't know what. My puke in the toilet was watery, insubstantial. Quentin knocked on the door after a while, asking if I was all right. I had no answer for him save a few empty retches before I was recovered enough to open the door and push my way past him, stealing his copy of *Shell-Shocked Sarnin* off the shelf and running out the door.

"Gerney, what are you— *hey!* Bring that back!"

He could've caught me easily but didn't bother to chase me down. By the time I reached the bottom of the stairs I knew what had overtaken me—desperation.

(Or was it desperation? Even in the moment I felt like I was faking it. Was I actually experiencing desperation or was I merely *acting it out* so as to feel something? Or worse, to give Quentin the *impression* I was feeling something? Does the fact that I was conscious of what I was doing mean I wasn't really desperate at all? I couldn't even be authentically sick, just authentically nothing.)

Sarnin experiences desperation early in the book, page 40 or so, when faced with the reality his identity is being appropriated by the United States military and the inescapable gear system of global events.

I moved in the direction of the city, the gonine high stronger than anticipated (Quentin's stuff was good, I should have bought some or stolen his bag on the way out). My body told me to flee, not just my situation but Grid itself. The state. The continent. It seemed possible. Kelsey's house on the California coast, maybe, near the destroyed desalinization plant. I gripped the book and walked faster, moving through different metropolitan dimensions. Quentin's low-rent residential district gave way to the inevitable blend of downtown ruling-class panache and street poverty, the homeless and disturbed shouting ruined thoughts to be rid of them and the suited company men and women shouting fear into headsets. Quentin's copy of *Shell-Shocked Sarnin* was the one printed under the HarperCollins label, a version Arnitz never lived to see. Page 116, flipped to at random and squinted by faded streetlight, featuring Sarnin's drill sergeant screaming at him in subtext, read

You, Private Sarnin, are a floating gelatinous conglomeration! Prior to this day you had an identity, but from this moment onward you will have that identity no more! An identity is not a real thing and is subject to change! Wipe that goddamn smile off your face, boy! Your

behavior can and will be modified! I will modify you! Look to me for example! I am no longer an independent identity, I am something else! So let's cover the rules: You will not retain and nurture a private identity unbeknownst to me! You will not keep secret from me any identities, proclivities, preferences, opinions, or plans with intent to act on them! This is not a temporary suspension of identity, this is a permanent reformation of it! You will hand yourself over for the sake of the greater good! You will harbor no fond memories of your former identity in any tangible or intagible way! You will cherish your new identity because what is changed cannot be unchanged!

Another later page, 118, Sarnin marching in a massive formation of soldiers stretching a mile long.

An unending streaming column of soldiers approaches the inspection platform. Sarnin can be seen somewhere in the middle, somewhere in a total state of visual anonymity where each part is only distinguishable as a whole, the spot of forgotten human beings. These soldiers are not here, they are not present, just as no one is ever truly present. What you see here is a mass projection, a group hallucination from which there is no waking. Their identities are once again changed, and will continue to be changed ad infinitum. Everything true exists in the background where the souls of the soldiers float in a space absent of context, of sharp cheddar cheese, devoid of the people and things and situations that inhabit this so-called "reality." The men standing on the platform inspecting the formation are not here, either. They are merely concepts, organisms imprisoned within a state of perpetual flux. They are apparitions inspecting apparitions. Gen. Vernon Cobrigale would see them as corpses on parade.

I saw an enormous skybound holoprojection of a zebra made up of many connecting hexagonal cells galloping in super slow-mo. I saw a shivering homeless woman at a bus stop screaming at a News Pad, breath exploding into the cold air and making her words seem visible. "I hope you all fucking *die!* Fucking idiots! I'll tear all this down and shove hope up your ass!" I saw a man in a shirt and tie sitting in his parked car (plastic license plate frame advertising ARCHELAOS in blue gunmetal font) whose phone browser was projected onto his windshield, watching a video titled ">>How to trancend ur own sexual inadequacies." I saw police cruisers appear in triplets every twenty minutes, blasting through the streets in perfect arrowhead formations, sirens wailing and blinking with crude electric torture, my phone buzzing in my pocket every time they passed because of a feature that sensed chips installed in the cars and then fed data about the type of situation they were responding to and pinpointed the area of emergency and kept tallies concerning what types and frequency of illicit activity occurred in various parts of the city, amongst other statistics. ZChase had recommended the program, which made me paranoid that maybe the police used the programs made to track them in order to track the people who used it. Signals passed through my body constantly. I saw the skyline of Grid from an angle I'd never seen it from before. I saw families wearing solid color clothing and black canvas sneakers and I turned down alleyways to avoid them. *You have reached three zero three six five four nine six four zero. At the tone, please record your message.* I saw the scrapers begin to tower over me, thousands of balconies and lofts and windows and screens becoming a pitched mosaic when I turned my head upward. I came across other twacked people who looked like me. "Amy, this is, this is Gerney. I'm—I'm walking somewhere downtown right now, I think I'm near the shopping district. I'm not sure what's, what's going on. I think I'm lost. I might need some, need some help. Please call me back. Please." Wednesday night turned to Thursday morning with a single tick of the clock. I kept walking. I saw, abruptly, that I was actually nowhere near the shopping district. I was standing at the intersection of Recursive and Finite—nearly a mile from where I'd thought. The street was no longer dark, lights shone from everywhere, and the sidewalks were crowded. Almost without realizing it I came into CitySquare. I hadn't been in this area for almost four years. Well-dressed European and Chinese tourist couples walked arm in arm through the park, bathed in pink light after midnight, taking pictures of City Hall with their phones. If I got close they moved away. I could barely feel my nose anymore and my teeth started to chatter. The park was clear of snow, the city had collected it to be sanitized and integrated into the water supply. At the far corner of CitySquare, City Hall and Entsheidungsproblem Blvd., I stepped over the line where astroturf ended and concrete began. Traffic on the boulevard was intense, full of detours and lane closures for the InfoZebra building site. I saw the machine that was projecting the hexagonal zebra hologram into the sky. There was the smell of freezing smog. I circled the block and re-entered the park, slumping down against one of the green balusters blocking vehicle access from the street. The cover of the HarperCollins edition of *Shell-Shocked Sarnin* depicted three identical human figures against a black background, the first one musculoskeletal, the second an empty outline, the third a foggy orange silhouette. My gonine high had vanished and despair coupled with extreme exhaustion overtook me the way a ceiling screen can overtake you if you're not careful, wanting to absorb every beautiful detail, not miss a thing, lose yourself in the scrutiny of someone, or something, else's vision. The book had gotten a little wet somewhere along the way, some of its pages limp. My phone buzzed and I dug it frantically from my pocket, pinning all my hopes on the assumption it was Amy, calling to rescue me from my aimlessness. Sarnin desperately needs the help of a stronger identity to ground him in reality on page 303. It was Quentin's name on the call ID, and despite everything I had no choice but to answer.

"Quentin, before you, before you say anything, I have to ask, ask for help."

"Just tell me where the fuck you are."

"CitySquare."

"City*Square?* Are you so twacked you actually walked all the way downtown?"

"Please come get me. It's freezing and I'm getting sober."

"Jesus. Stay where you are. I'll be there soon."

The sky was starless. The city seemed suddenly unfamiliar, a civilization built by aliens. Was it normal to feel this way? I was just another piece of fodder in the machine of human experience.

Quentin's '02 Civic rattled and the heater didn't work. I leaned my head against the icy passenger side window, consumed by come-down depression. He shivered and rubbed his hands together while he drove. Through the windshield the streets looked cold and dead. Almost all traffic had dissipated, the world outside deserted.

"The reason I called you in the first place was I wanted my book back," he said. "It's funny because when I saw which one you took, everything sort of made sense to me."

There was no noise in the car except the sound of the engine. He refused to even turn the radio on.

"That book can have a strong effect on people. Some books do. Arnitz's voice feels godlike. It gets in your head, like he becomes your only portal toward a firm grasp on the world. All that fanatical theory on background identity and shit. Fuck it's cold." He stopped for a light and cupped his hands to breathe into them. Vapor escaped between his fingers. "Have you read his other two stories? *Sangria* and *Sangria II*?"

I shook my head.

"Well those are different. They don't have the same effect. For me, at least. They're a bit more human, less philosophical. The central idea is still identity, but in those the idea is that if you can reduce yourself down, like as a person, and like through the use of alcohol specifically, you can actually fuse with somebody else. [Sniff, sniff.] It's an idea of love based on the fantasy of being able to bridge the gap between two minds. To enter another person's thoughts and have a transaction of shared purpose or something like that. But the method is harmful. He pretty much just describes it as pure alcoholism. Then the second story suggests you can actually merge yourself with loneliness the same way you can merge with another person. In those stories he at least acknowledges that there are ways for people to overcome identity, and it at least involves trusting, or being close to, another person aside from yourself. But Sarnin, jesus. That book's completely different. And in my opinion a little creepy. Because in that book people aren't even real, they're just shifting projections manipulated by the influences of environment and power. Their real identities exist in the 'background,' which is only ever described as this alternate universe of, for some insane reason, cheddar cheese. The suggestion to the reader is that they're not a real person, just a fractured consciousness with no say in the way that consciousness is formed or manifests itself. And so Arnitz turns his back on the idea that people can make connections with one another. We're not real people except in this minor background way, and so he encourages you to treat other people with skepticism, paranoia, defensiveness, and indifference, without putting forward any sort of counterargument for why sometimes trusting or even, I don't know, *loving* others is exactly what can make people into distinct entities."

Nearly three years I'd been hanging out with Quentin and I'd never taken him for someone so intelligent, so bookish. His clarity on things made me feel jealous in a weird way, almost defensive of my relationship with Arnitz and Sarnin.

"But it's—[cough, sniff]—'scuse me—it's the absence of that counterargument that makes me tempted to call *Shell-Shocked Sarnin* an example of extremist thinking."

"Did you study books or something?"

"Yeah, I thought you knew that about me. Ronstadt thinks I'm fucking crazy."

"So it's just extremist thinking and that's it. Nothing else good about it."

"Well, besides the fact it's a masterpiece of literature. But philo-sophically I think it's barren. There's no question it throws open certain doors of the mind, but only at the expense of closing others off. Fuck it's cold."

"I don't get it, what doors do you think it closes?"

"Apart from what I just said, love, trust and connection, Arnitz shows what I would say is a lot of hostility to both the material and spiritual realms. He envisions them as being utterly cut off from one another, and for that reason his depiction of the spiritual realm is that it's abusive. It has nothing to impart to us and almost just exists for the purpose of banishing us from it. And after that banishment it doesn't communicate with us or take the slightest interest in our lives."

"Well maybe we *are* banished."

"Maybe. I'm just telling you what my own personal opinion is. I have a high opinion of the writing, just not the ideas. You're not just some shifting projection, you're a real person with a real identity. At the end of the book Sarnin kills the soldiers in his own unit to save the enemy and is sentenced to solitary confinement. If that's not a dead-end I don't know what is. Here we go, you said you live on Aphelion? Damn. This is a nice place."

I felt irritated with what he'd said going back into my apartment (my father's apartment), wading back into the comfortable haze of my electronic blizzard and trying to shake off all his neat little intellectualizations. All I'd heard in his voice were dismissals, as if he could take me (Sarnin) apart and put me back together at will like a simple little puzzle. Maybe his problem with Arnitz wasn't that he espoused a dead-end but that he presented too complex a representation of the world to just be able to explain it away in a minute or two. The music was an angry screed overlaid with machine sounds ["We will destroy the old ways of thinking. We will destroy our ancestors and their history. We will enforce our desires as mandatory. We will enforce altered perceptions by use of substances as mandatory. We will eradicate unhappiness. We will cut ties with human limitation. We will isolate through connection. We will disillusion through idealism. We will..."] and the TV was a report on a major breakthrough in dealing with inoperable brain cancer followed by updates on mass coordinated youth rioting in Chicago, Albuquerque, Los Angeles, Tokyo, Hong Kong, London, Edinburgh, and Rio de Janeiro. There was no connection between the time I left the apartment and now, the intermittent period like a dream in which I became a different person. (Shifting projections, hallucinatory reality, background identity.) I wished Amy was there with me. I laid on the couch, cocooned inside the sounds of the TV and music and VidraPro, and fell asleep. I dreamed I was at the center of a thousand-way intersection, unthinkable amounts of traffic passing, and I was trying to call someone on the phone, first it was Quentin but I knew that was only because I had just seen him and then I was trying to get a hold of Nick but I couldn't do it, the phone was on low battery and kept getting frozen when I typed numbers, and then that was it, I was just stranded at that intersection getting more and more frustrated and then I woke up to a knock at my door. At first I got up slow but then jumped up and opened the door to see Amy standing there, and I actually fell to my knees.

"Gerney, what's wrong?"

She took my head in her hands and pressed it against her stomach so lovingly, like she knew exactly what was wrong. I could feel her flesh beneath her shirt, and as far as I knew that was all there ever was. We went to my room and I receded even further away from everything. This could all be her world and I'd be happy just to live in it. Lying naked in bed next to me, I felt her lips flutter against my ear.

"I need a favor, Gerney. I need your help."

Anything. Anything you want, I'll do it.

Sometimes I feel like there just ain't anybody. God knows I might be guilty of a few things here n there, and I've never been one to complain much, but sometimes I can't help but feel a weakness creepin straight through me when I take stock of the way things's gotten. I catch myself blamin Earl, may his soul rest in peace. Never wanted to have no kids, which I told him time and again I understood his reasoning. He already done had two little boys from his marriage to Irene, and I told him it was a sensible thing the way he wanted to take responsibility for em and maintain his attentions and affections and so forth. Really it was me who shoulda stood her ground. All I woulda needed was just one baby between the two of us, one that was ours, and can you blame a woman for wantin to be a mother? That's like blamin a horse for wantin to run or a spider for makin a web. But I wanted to be sensitive to Earl's situation, and we never had no kids.

—*Aunt Joann? It's Amy.*

—Oh! Amy, I was just now thinkin of you. Was gonna pick up the phone and—

—I hope you're holding up all right. I'm calling because there's a serious matter we need to discuss.

—That right?

—That's right. Do you have time to talk?

—Of course. Would you like to take the train over? I could make us some dinner. Or I could pick you up if you feel like you don't want to—

—No, no, I'm in the middle of a busy day and there are some appointments I can't be late for. It'd be better if we just did it now over the phone.

Usedta be things was different, more or less. Course you start talkin bout the past and people get to rollin their eyes, even Margie, God keep her in this hour, would treat me like some ol bitty, but I never did have no bridge connectin me to this time period on account of Earl and I not havin children and all, so I feel somewhat qualified to point out where things's gotten strange. Not sayin I need no sympathy, that's not what I'm sayin—just sayin people don't ever seem to be around nowadays. You can't pin em down. I might be old but I ain't senile, I can recognize when things ain't the same as they usedta be. Course I ain't no scientist neither, that was always Margaret's bag, and how can you go about provin somethin you know is true in your gut without the proper statistics? It's the same thing with the Lord, now that I take a second to think about it. People nowadays just want to talk about how He don't exist, either that or can't exist, but how do you show those people a feeling? How do you show em all those wonderful charts and graphs of Love over Time and Meaning in direct relation with His Existence and Good Will as a product of Certainty? But that's what's wonderful bout the truth, ain't it? Not a soul else's gotta believe you and it don't make you any less right. The world today's a crazy mess and it don't matter the flocks of people wanna try to sit down and explain it to me, why things is so much different now and why people had no choice but to change cause this ain't the past no more, it don't make a speck of difference. Just cause things are the way they are don't make it right. Or are we forgettin the world's constantly headed toward Revelation, no matter how close or how far? In any case, people keep on getting so wrapped up in theirselves, and it's beyond me how they can be happy that way.

—*Well all right then, hon, what's got you in such a fuss?*

—*It's this stuff with Vivificorps. Something isn't right here. I'm having a hard time believing mom would've wanted her head frozen rather than have a Christian burial.*

—*Amy, I couldn't agree more. I got absolutely no clue who these people are. Margie never said nothin about gettin her head frozen or whatever crazy thing they're sayin, not a single word, and here I show up to the hospital and here comes this fella outta the clear blue. I try not to say too much, but I swear this ain't what—*

—*Well you and I agree then. That means we can do something about it. Because I don't think these people should be able to get away with this.*

Course I've had my lapses, too, God knows. It was when little Taylor died that I lost my faith for a time. I doted on that boy like he was my own. Precious, precious little boy. What a tragedy—I hate to even think about it, and it's probably best not to. Ain't nothin wrong with keepin the bad things at arm's length sometimes. Earl was convinced it was Amy who'd had a hand in killin him, and I always said Earl she ain't nothin more'n a child, what kinda way to think is that? It was never no secret somethin wasn't right with her, I ain't denying it, even Margaret said so. But killing her little brother? Can't think of anything sounds more absurd than that. Even once Earl was just about froze up with the Parkinson's, God rest him, he *still* maintained suspicion of her guilt in the matter. Well Earl, I said, clearly the poor girl's been traumatized for life after seein somethin such as that. And after Margaret's husband died, too, me and her only spoke of it once since she always blamed Amy and that was why the two of em hardly ever spoke. She said to me truth be told I still blame her, sometimes I even hate her for it, but I've gotten to a point in my head where I don't think she meant for it to happen, but I don't think I can ever forgive her. That's God's job, now.

Such terrible anger amongst this family. But I ain't gonna turn my back on that little girl, wasn't a thing in the world she coulda done, and what point is there in makin somebody pay for one mistake their whole life? None, far as I'm concerned. Course then again I've always been gullible. Earl said that was why my faith faltered after poor little Taylor died was cause of my gullibility. All that believin and worrying about the silly parts of church and not the parts with any substance. Well okay, I admit it Earl DeSantis, Mr. Know-It-All and don't know when to leave well enough alone, I *am* pretty gullible, but tell me for just one second what in the world's it harmin for me to take some joy outta church group social clubs and potlucks and craft days for kids to make the little construction paper mangers on Christmas? Does that make me a bad Christian just cause I ain't no sourpuss like you who done got a divorce? Life's a precious thing. Gotta look on the bright side when you can. Just about anyone coulda lost their belief after what happened to poor little Taylor. And still, I ain't sayin we needed no sympathy.

—*What're you talkin about, Amy?*

—*I'm talking about stopping these people from doing this to mom. It isn't right, and we shouldn't just stand by while they take advantage of us.*

—*Well what in the world do you propose? It was in her will and there was that contract she signed. Can't fathom it myself, but maybe it was Margaret's intent to be frozen like they say.*

—*This sort of forgery happens all the time. Trust me, these people are scamming us. This is stuff I deal with on a daily basis in my work.*

—*Maybe you're right, maybe somethin about this situation's going over my head, but I still don't know how you plan on disprovin all them documents even the hospital's takin seriously.*

—*I've been talking with some people about getting an amendment notarized.*

—*Amy, Margaret ain't in any condition to sign no amendment.*

—*Well that's why we need to talk.*

Lotta things ain't none of my business, specially since I ain't nothin but a time traveler in this day and age, but when it comes to Margie I don't think there's a soul else alive right now who oughtta be claimin any more responsibility than me. Amy's got a lot of the skills I'm lackin in, but the decisions oughtta be up to me. The way I see it, that's just common courtesy. I ask you, what's so hard about lettin people take care of their own affairs? There usedta be a level of respect. I'm the one's gonna be runnin the show, and I don't care what the rest of em think.

—*You know I would never go behind your back when it comes to this matter, and that's why I'm sincerely asking for your help. But I think given the severity of what we're talking about and what it would mean if we took no action at all, well, you follow me. But Margaret is your sister and ultimately I'm leaving this in your hands.*

And it wasn't till Margaret's husband died, dear Taylor peace be upon him, always a good man but a bit of a tormented soul in my opinion, that I felt at all comfortable livin in this new century, and that wasn't for no reason but Margaret and I didn't have no one else to count on anymore cept each other. Ain't no one in the world I love more'n Margie, but damn if her mind didn't always work in the funniest ways. All this talk about the universe, and then her affinity for physics. Most of the time she flew right over the top of my head, but I never did envy her for it since it was always my suspicion the whole business made her confused and sometimes even depressed. Not sayin it's my place to be designatin things for people, and maybe it's just a downright terrible opinion, but I just don't think a woman oughtta be worryin bout that sorta thing. All the talk she'd throw at me about absorption nebulas an big bangs an the reasons why water swirls into a drain rather than just go down straight. Makin somethin you can touch and see, somethin concrete—it suits a person. All this nonsense and visualization. All this abstraction. Margaret'd say to me Josie you gotta imagine, you gotta take the principles of the world around us and apply em on an enormous scale. And I'd say well Margaret I just don't see the point in doin work that oughtta belong to God. You didn't create the world and the beyond and you ain't gonna change it neither. But yes you can change it she'd say, the universe is manipulable and engagin in that manipulation ain't no moral slight against God. And here I come back that it's a matter of not relinquishin yer pride, of takin it upon yerself to be more than what ya are when it stands to reason that you just ain't. Sometimes we got some pretty good arguments goin, but eventually we had to cut em out cause really we agreed about everything but the details anyhow, and nothin's gonna get solved through a bunch of hot air blowin. Sure do miss Margie. Her bein about to pass like this likely means my time's drawin to a close as well. Best not to think about it, just wish it didn't have to be so lonely and sad.

—*Amy, I'm not sure I'm following this.*

—*Think about it this way. It's a matter of covering our bases with regards to what's provable and what's not. Since you're in line to be the executrix, all you have to do is oversee the process.*

—*I'm not comfortable with lyin.*

When she'd get get goin sometimes I said Margaret I'm a time traveler. I belong in the middle of last century, not here. Don't understand a single thing goes on anymore. Everything's complicated an backwards n all twist up and I ain't got the patience. People's changed. Things's changed. And I ain't sure it's for the better. I got up outta bed in the middle of the night last night and dang if I wasn't in a sweat and feelin like somethin was wrong. I looked out my window and can you guess what I saw? I saw buildings made of flame. Swear on the Lord. Sky was black with smoke an there was flames everywhere an the world outside wasn't no world like what I recognized, like what we was born into, but somethin else. I saw people walkin round barren an just *not all there*. I saw rivers made up of running orange sludge and trees studded with millions of nails. The mountains was nothin but holograms and I could touch em and they'd shortcircuit. I said Margaret I pret'near screamed my head off. I kept lookin for God but God wasn't nowhere. Wasn't even in Hell, rightly. I was just alone. Come to think of it I can't remember what exactly Margaret said in response. Only thing that sticks in my memory is them buildins burnin with perfect shape an integrity. It was raining too, but not water, just little twisting worms of fallin neon light that detached from a ceiling screen sky.

—*Joann? Are you there?*

—*Amy, I wish you'da come over to tell me this.*

—We'll have to do something soon if we want this to work.

—What about the money? What you plan on doin with it?

—I hadn't given it much thought, but we could split it between the two of us and set aside the burial costs.

Earl's up there walkin with God right now and he ain't concernin himself with none of this current business, but still I remember he usedta call Amy "that evil girl."

—Joann?

—Okay.

—Okay what?

—Okay I'll do it. But only cause I can't bear the thought of Margaret livin in no purgatory.

I been in purgatory myself and my sister ain't gonna visit, less she's waitin there now, the state she's in.

—This is going to work, I promise. Just trust me and you'll see.

The next morning I get in the car to go to St. Joseph's. I wasn't never all that comfortable livin here, it was Earl who loved it so much, but I spose who wouldn't since Taylor got him a real nice job workin in the university's administration, but I wasn't never quite sold on the endeavor. Air's too dry for one, like a bone, and I never had no spot to fit into like in Alcoa. Maybe after all this I'll go back, but I ain't been there, not even visited, for more'n ten years and things's probably different there just like they ain't the same here. At the hospital I pass by that slick-headed big-gutted Norb Towers from Vificore, still hangin around like some damn parasite, and (pardon my language) I can't figure out what in the hell he does all day. I put my nose right up in the air on the way by so there ain't any confusion that my opinion of him is he's just one more child of God. Who I'd like to see is Dr. Actinide, but he's not here today.

Amy has me shake hands with a couple men, one of em's her lawyer and he's a big ol burly guy in a suit, not much more'n a kid, and also another young man who she introduces as her friend but it ain't no secret he's dotin on that girl somethin awful. I ain't one to pry. Margaret's lyin there lookin like a different person entirely, spittle shimmerin on her mouth, lookin round with empty eyes at all these strangers and darn it if I don't have to excuse myself and go cry in the ladies room a spell. When I come back they notarize an amendment and we sign as witnesses, and then it's over. We leave Margaret's room and Norb Towers is lookin at us from down the hall just as spicious and curious as all get out. Amy gives me a hug before she leaves, one of the few I've ever gotten from her come to think of it, but you can't account for what happened to that poor girl, and I ain't like Earl, rest his soul. I can't judge no one as evil.

When I get home there's still yesterday's Samurai Turkey sit-ting unfinished in its little plastic containers on my kitchen counter and I start unwrapping tonight's Burger King. I strip off my suit so I'm in only boxers, light reflecting off the sad pale skin of my legs. My body is a terrible secret. Twelve hours at the hospital today, never less than eight, and no weekends since the Arsenault woman was admitted. It amazes me how I no longer want anything. Time passes and I barely feel it, just wait patiently to get back here, my apartment, seventh floor with a window overlooking the beautiful brick decay of Denver where I sit in boxers and am allowed to delve into total fantasy. First it's dinner (I'm aware I'm getting fat, I just don't care) and then masturbation and then Flux 4 and then more masturbation and then sleep. The apprehension of excitement or ambition is gone from my daily routine.

HELLO, NORB! 7,416 NEW VIDEOS ADDED TODAY.

The best video I've found, one I've watched consistently for half a year now, is a POV video featuring Pomona Lush welcoming you home from work. She serves you dinner, the same ridiculous dinner every time, and asks you about your day. The cameraman is mute throughout, so Pomona Lush carries on the conversation alone. "Did you think about me today?" Pause. "Mmm, I thought about you, too, baby." Moves her thick hair to one side and smiles while biting her lip. "Yeah? Ohhhhh, I see. Well not until you finish dinner." A long silence this time. "So how's your stupid fucking boss? What sort of stupid things did he say today?" Nodding, leaning forward to shamelessly expose cleavage. Her tone changes in this part, laughing at the very idea of the hypothetical boss. "Yep, that sounds exactly like something he'd say. What a fucking idiot. Well whatever, I bet he doesn't have *this* to come home to, does he?" She gives a self-satisfied squeak and looks off to the side with cartoonish mischief, begins to whisper seductively. "Just think how he probably gets himself off thinking about me while you come home and actually get to fuck me. What a fucking loser." I rarely even make it to the part where the sex finally starts. But the video seems ineffective tonight, and halfway through I start to visualize Amy Arsenault.

I can't stop wanting her no matter how impossible I know the desire is. She's sleeping with one of the ICU nurses, as well as a thin nervous-looking guy who accompanied her, her aunt, and her lawyer today. They chose this day because Dr. Actinide wasn't in. They're preparing to steal the annuity Margaret Arsenault agreed to pay Vivificorps to keep her neuropreserved. This is what I know—half from experience, half from intuition. I find myself apathetic, or maybe just too sexually terrified of her to act. She's begun communicating with me wordlessly, flashing glances, showing off her body when she knows I'm watching, giving me these frigidly sexual looks that say, *You know you'll never have me, but that doesn't mean I won't play with you.* They're stealing money from a dying woman and sabotaging a client of the company, and yet somehow I'm happy to let her do what she wants so long as I get something out of it, no matter how small or pathetic. If she took away those teasing glances I would have nothing…

NORB, you could be watching more videos! By upgrading your membership you can watch millions more uploaded videos, and gain access to thousands of streaming live cams. Also, set up a unique member profile to chat and find out who else is watching!

ZChase opens a sidebar on the far right of my screen, recommending dozens more Pomona Lush videos based on my preference for this one. One of the titles is *pomona lush fucks again.*

The last and most important part of the night is Flux 4. The opening screen with the name of the production company, Anu+Bhav, has ceased to be language and has become instead talismanic, opening a psychic portal. The light in my apartment is off, windows sound-proofed against the city's sirens and screaming voices, and despite the fact my erection is persisting I feel pleasantly retracted, profoundly lost but at peace, content to worship these small comforts and wait for nothing. A fly buzzes circularly above the lit TV screen.

I'm in Cambire, the capital city of the nation of Flux, where I keep my apartment, car, wardrobe, primary care physician, main bank branch (Tiffany the beautiful teller), and my cat Eleanor Roosevelt. NORBERT TOWERS is a government intelligence operative whose appearance resembles mine. The geographical layout of Flux and its various territories is always the same, but the details and texture of the environment undergo constant change, almost never the same twice except one scenario that repeated itself where every NPC had the head of a lobster and giant pincers instead of hands. When I last quit the game Cambire had taken on the character of the American 1920s and this time when I wake up in my apartment I've got a yellow armband with a Star of David on it and when I walk outside there are Panzer tanks in the street and the residents are wearing red Nazi armbands and the architecture is that of early-1940s Berlin. I look up and my apartment building bears the name *Victoria Hotel*, perched atop it a giant bronze sculpture of a swastika-gripping eagle, wings rigid and mechanical, the sun reduced to a lemon wedge behind its inexpressive head. The view abruptly changes as a man in a tan suit shoves me from behind, NORBERT TOWERS staggering to keep his balance. He turns and angrily shouts something in German. He continues walking without looking back, his red armband standing out brilliantly against the golden-hued light of the afternoon. I walk in the opposite direction, past Cambire's largest park (I have a nice apartment), an enormous red swastika flag hanging flaccid at its center. Every street light is decorated with an ornate swastika banner. A convoy of six black Fiat convertibles carrying military personnel pass by and someone spits at me but misses. I try to use my cell phone but it's inoperational. I'm headed seven blocks east to LaBolt's office, my handler. I head off that direction and am nearly run over by two Storm Troopers on a rickety motorcycle with a machine gun attached to the sidecar. After three blocks my progress is impeded by crowds gawking at a military parade proceeding down Cambierenstrasse, rectangle after rectangle of marching troops and rolling tanks, and when I try to push through the cheering crying masses a Nazi police officer in a black trench coat and hat pulls a Walther pistol, aims it at my head, screaming instructions in German. NORBERT TOWERS backs away slowly with hands in the air. After a while the officer is satisfied with my distance from the crowd and smacks me over the head with the butt of his gun, deleting a small portion of my health, and marches back to his post. In the moment when he turns around the scenery and people change for no more than a split-second, flickering into downtown turn-of-the-century Tokyo at night, neon bursting from everywhere, the cheering crowds now black-haired and tennis shoed, red confetti filling the blue halogen air, columns of marching Storm Troopers turning to parade floats with actors dressed as anime characters, Panzer IIs becoming vintage S2000 convertibles driving in slanted formation to represent each color strand of the rainbow, the police officer walking away from me splitting apart into two schoolgirls in skirts and knee-highs running with arms clutched to chests, white European facades becoming towering reflective glass scrapers with blinking red beacons, the sky filled with ecstastic pink and blue fireworks, and just as suddenly everything reverts, once again the Nazi Berlin of a moment ago. NORBERT TOWERS's adrenaline bar shoots up twenty-five percent and I quickly head away toward an open U-Bahn stairway. The station is crowded, regular citizens mixed with fleeting Nazi military uniforms, and everywhere armbands. It takes me ten minutes to decipher the routes, but I figure if I get on here and take the yellow line to Vistastrasse I can double back and avoid the parade. The subway is full of smoking soldiers and old people conversing in spurts of vigorous German. The train makes its way along, during which time I stand up and go to the table where I left the carton of unfinished Burger King fries and because of this I almost miss my connection. On my way up the steps from the Vistastrasse station a soldier in full officer regalia pulls his pistol and fires two quick shots at me. One of them pocks the cement steps and the other hits me clean, sending me down to half health. I pull up my own gun from the inventory, a Rhino 20D snubnose revolver, killing the officer in two flashes of blood that turn him sideways, arms following his body as an afterthought. All this random violence is a normal phenomenon that NORBERT TOWERS doesn't perfectly understand. I'm currently seeing an in-game psychologist about it. Commuters pass by unperturbed while I dissolve the pistol away and backtrack three blocks, arriving at LaBolt's office. There's no sign, just a rusted metal door down a shallow alleyway.

"Hello, yes, one moment please," grunts LaBolt who, upon my entrance, is smack in the middle of humping a secretary on top of one of the desks, a slew of other secretaries about the room absorbed with their work and not seeming to notice one bit. All I see of the supine secretary are tan-stockinged legs slung over LaBolt's shoulders. NORBERT TOWERS's adrenaline bar shoots up once again. "If you'll take a seat with the others," LaBolt says panting.

There are three other suited and forlorn men waiting in a row of chairs to my right, so I go and sit, LaBolt proving to be a rough lover, grabbing the secretary's throat and smacking the fleshy part of the underside of her thigh so much it turns raspberry red. The office is unremarkable, not even the most minimum of effort expended on interior design, everything just metal furniture flanked by chaotic papers. Finally they finish up and LaBolt beckons me to his private office, retying his tie and mopping his forehead with a folded handkerchief. I sit down across from him, the desk obviously not his in any permanent sense. He's sweating, a dark stain creeping down his shirt from the bottom of his collar. LaBolt's appearance is never the same—this time he's got the odd handsomeness of a 1930s German movie star, slicked hair and a thick neck, but the features all garbled and just short of hypermasculine. Behind him is hung a sweeping swastika tapestry (from my perspective his head fits perfectly into its center, the four crooked black arms of the symbol pinwheeling all around his face) and also the reverent framed portrait of Hitler.

"So, NORBERT TOWERS," LaBolt says, catching his breath and making himself comfortable by throwing his feet up on the desk, "I trust you found the offices no problem?"

A conversation tree opens to pick from.

I ran into some difficulties, nothing too serious. Do you have a job for me?

"As a matter of fact, yes." Fighter planes roar by outside, I can see them passing through the horizontal slats of the window blinds. LaBolt begins lighting a pipe. "We need you to locate and neutralize someone for us. A highly sensitive situation, of course."

Who is it?

"He's an individual with a quite dissident outlook. You realize, I'm sure, that Flux is in a state of constant change."

I've noticed.

"Yes, well, this individual espouses *constancy* as a viable philosophy, if you can believe that. Constancy is of course his euphemism for *stagnancy*. Not here in Flux, no sir. And soon, hopefully, not any-where. It's become necessary to locate and liquidate the individual in question."

Who is the individual?

He opens a drawer, extracting a thick file and dropping it in front of me on the desk. The arms of the swastika arrayed about his head are subtly wiggling like the legs of some primitive organism. "You'll read all about said individual and his said philosophy of constancy in the dossier. Obscene and frightening, I'd say, every last bit of it. You look pale, NORBERT, is everything all right?"

Fine, sir.

He scrutinizes me. "I suppose it's simply the nature of the Juden to be a pale and sickly people." He stands from his chair and moves to the window, looking through the blinds while drifting pipe smoke catches neat little slats of evenly spaced sunlight. Planes are filling the sky outside. "There is a real danger arising out there, NORBERT. The danger of coherent narrative." He scoffs with dismissive politi-cal hatred. In addition to the noise out the window I can hear loud voices approaching and receding in the hall outside my apartment like conflicting sonar readouts. LaBolt reseats himself grimly in his chair. "I trust you'll do what needs to be done."

The file is added to my inventory and I walk out the door, going back through the maze of secretaries stuck in their hard-at-work animation loops, but before I can leave there's a massive explosion, everyone knocked to the floor, an unlucky secretary hitting her head against the side of a desk. The TV speakers jitter from the strain. There are screams of terror, cries of confusion. NORBERT TOWERS clamps his hands over his ears. One of the several bare lightbulbs hanging from the ceiling pops and releases a swarm of sparks like hot tungsten hornets. By degrees the mayhem subsides, giving way to an aftermath of wailing secretaries and shifting debris. I walk outside and the city has been completely bombed-out, all of it reduced to rubble, scorched skeletal ruins, Nazi soldiers replaced by squalid families covered in brick dust carting heaps of belongings in dirty wheelbarrows. Overhead a large plane drones past the sun, leaving in its wake hundreds of tiny black specks dotting the smoky sky that gradually reveal themselves to be parachutes, each paratrooper carrying a radio, and as they all float groundward I can hear each one tuned to a different station, the cacophony growing louder as more and more alight against the ruined pavement every second.

The next morning I wake up to snow and the jarring electric buzz of my phone, Noah Woollome's name stated demandingly across the screen, the director of Vivificorps's Colorado branch. I answer through the bewildering prism of shattered sleep.

"Hello?"

"Norb, morning, what in the hell is going on over there with the Arsenault woman?"

"I— sorry?"

"The Arsenault woman. Why do I have Paul on the phone telling me he's on his way up from New Mexico to appear in probate court?"

"What are you talking about?"

"The family of Margaret Arsenault is claiming we have no rights to her as a customer anymore. Something about a notarized amendment to her will. Do you know anything about this?"

"No, nothing, I just now woke up."

"Well I'm gonna need you to hustle over here, Paul's due at Grid International at nine-fifteen. He wants a meeting with us at ten sharp."

"Shit, what time is it?"

"Nine."

"All right, I'm on my way."

The cold outside swallows up Norbert Towers's senses, hard little snowflakes crashing up against the windshield of his glasses and turning to foggy drops. He's in Denver, the capital city of Colorado, which is where he keeps his apartment, car, wardrobe, primary care physician, main bank branch (Debbie the beautiful teller), and also his job with Vivificorps, the company's offices located on Wazee St. underneath a sheath of icy snow. He vaguely resembles the appearance of NORBERT TOWERS. Although the geographical layout of Colorado is always the same, the details and texture of the environment undergo constant change, almost never the same twice. He walks up three flights of stairs to find the President and Executive Director of Vivificorps Paul Simpatico who shakes his hand and asks now just who exactly is this Amy Arsenault girl, and Norbert Towers feels the question would be better posed to someone else.

On the seventh floor of the Grid Justice Center, outside Grid City & County Probate Courtroom #4, the view is of central downtown scrapers plunging down to the complicated streets below, traffic flowing around their foundations like inexorable, coldly paced water. My city has replaced the old one, and yet its processes continue as if nothing had changed. That's the sign of my ownership, because the inner machinery of my new city isn't made up of the fragile stuff of the old—its organs consist of pure data. Electricity is its blood. I am the sole person who can direct or destroy it, all according to my will.

I feel comfortable surrounded by the walls of the courtroom, which are blank and modern, devoid of both feeling and tradition.

No precedents exist here. This institutional space sprang from poisoned soil and functions according to hollow concepts, mere words which people have been instructed to obey. The lone token to confer authority on the proceedings is affixed to the judge's bench, a circular placard bearing the Grid city seal, a transparent cube perforated by three diagonal slashes and floating against a white-to-blue gradient background. The words GRID JUSTICE CENTER GRID COLORADO run along its outer edges. The noise in here is hushed. A group of ten men from Vivificorps, including Norbert Towers, sit behind the company's lawyers, who are youngish without any gray hair and nearly matching red ties. At the plaintiff's table is my own lawyer whose suit in comparison appears friendlier. Next to him at the table is Aunt Joann who, judging by her back, is taking all this in with an air of indifferent sorrow. Seated behind them in the gallery is Gerney, wearing a black suit with wrinkle marks, head dutifully shaved. When I sit he smiles at me, a smile of weakness and servility. I imagine his body crashing through the seventh-floor window of the Justice Center, limbs going ragdoll before making wet impact with the concrete steps of the main entrance below. I was interviewed earlier in the week by a reporter from the *Database*. The press interest in the case made Aunt Joann nervous and unpredictable, and the only way I could get her under control again was to give her an ultimatum that could've unraveled all my efforts: either fight for the rights to Margaret's body, or drop the case and let her sister's head be neuropreserved in a cryogenic container. Not surprisingly, the thought was unbearable for her. Apart from this minor incident, they were all so easily manipulated and arranged the whole thing had ceased being even the slightest bit challenging for me.

"How are you feeling?" he asks me needily.

I stare straight ahead, saying nothing, the blankness of this place and the hidden power I wield over it causing me to hang in a state of pure glowing pleasure. Fluorescent lighting shimmers against the white arboform walls. I look behind me and spot Dr. Actinide sitting pockmarked and judgmental in the back row against the wall, clearly disgusted by all this.

"Amy?"

The judge and bailiff enter the courtroom, and for some reason I'm looking around at everyone's shoes while we stand, the men in clowny black wingtips and the women in trashy heels, the judge blabbering and peering at things through his glasses. I'm the first one called to the stand, one of the two Vivificorps lawyer-clones approaching me from the table, neck delicate and shave fresh, that bland allure of a moneyed person, straight teeth behind pink lips.

"Ms. Arsenault, if you would please, I'd like you to clarify for the court exactly why, if it was truly *not* the wish of your mother to be neuropreserved by the Vivificorps company, did she knowingly and willingly complete the arduous process of procuring the contracted agreement for neuropreservation a full seven months prior to today's date?"

"Well, my mother was always one to consolidate her Christian and scientific beliefs. Those were her two strongest convictions throughout the whole of her life. She was as much a bearer of the faith as a scholar of astronomy, and so her desire to be neuropreserved was, at the time, I have no doubt, sincere. But the visceral realities of her recent health problems made clear to her which path she wanted to follow in death. So she had expressed, during private conversations with myself and my aunt, that she wanted steps taken to nullify the contract in order to ensure a proper Christian burial."

"Which brings me to my next question, Ms. Arsenault. Is it your opinion that, at the time the amendment to Margaret Arsenault's will was notarized, your mother was, in fact, of sound mind and body?"

"Absolutely. Yes. You know, of course, that my mother has retained the ability—"

"Really? Despite the fact she underwent a massive heart attack and stroke that has left her in a near-catatonic state?"

I pause to convey a moment of subtle emotional vulnerability.

"*Yes*, my mother has retained her ability for consciousness and speech, and even though she's prone to confusion around the doctors and nurses—*strangers*, I'll remind you, though we're so grateful for the care they've given her—she's much more coherent when speaking to family members. She made her wishes clear to both myself and my Aunt Joann."

"And what were those wishes?"

"That she no longer wanted to be neuropreserved."

He nods. "There is, however, the matter of the $150,000 annuity to be paid to Vivificorps in exchange for cryonics services provided, currently sitting in escrow. Per the amendment to Margaret's will, that annuity would be redirected to you and your aunt, is that also correct?"

"Yes."

"And could this redirection not conceivably be playing a role in why you and your aunt have brought this legal challenge before the court?"

My attorney shoots from his seat. "Objection, Your Honor. Rank speculation."

"Sustained."

"I apologize, Ms. Arsenault, let me rephrase the question…"

I'm stealing glimpses of the faces looking back at me from the courtroom, yet the face I can't suppress from my mind is Margaret's, lying in a hospital bed in St. Joseph's, the empty malfunctioning shell that used to be my mother, her stare locked to the dotted patterns of the ceiling tiles, completely unaware her fate is no longer her own.

It's easier not to be twacked when I'm around Amy. Instead what I feel is the gonine of obsession breaking the blood-brain barrier, the substance itself tyrannical, consuming. The systems of my body are like a computer, and the machine reacts largely based on input.

"Please state your name for the court."

"Kevin Crepitus."

"You also go by the alias Gerney?"

"Correct."

My brain is the CPU. Obsession is its electricity. Amy is like the material from which obsession is extracted.

"Is it true you've known Margaret Arsenault through your

relationship with her daughter, the Ms. Arsenault who is present here today, sitting in the front row, for two years now?"

"It is."

"Is it also true you witnessed Margaret Arsenault sign the amendment stating she no longer wished to be neuropreserved by the Vivificorps company?"

"Yes."

"In your experience with Margaret Arsenault over the last two years, was it her wish to be maintained cryogenically?"

"No. I never heard her, heard her say anything to the effect of wanting to be maintained cryo, cryogenically."

"Pardon me?"

"Cryogenically."

"She never mentioned it once in all the time you knew her?"

"She talked a lot about her involvement with the church, the Denver Crucicentro Church, but never about, never about Vivificorps."

Is this a normal thought, to imagine yourself a machine?

"And you heard Margaret Arsenault say, *explicitly*, that she wanted to amend her will in order to revoke her contract with Vivificorps and redistribute the funds designated for the annuity between her sister and daughter."

"I did."

Once they got me under oath, answerin all them questions, that's the moment when I got to thinkin I mighta gone up over my own authority. You can always count on things to go wrong in just about any situation, it seems. Course it's too late now, all I can do is trust in God I made the moral decision. I walked off the stand and what do you think pops into my head but somethin about Margaret, about how her teeth wasn't ever straight, not exactly in any case, but her left front tooth was always a real chomper. Which wouldn'ta been so bad, but seein as how her left front tooth was so long and the right wasn't nothin but just a nub, she never could get herself to like her own smile. She hardly ever laughed with her mouth all the way open, or smile. She smiled with her lips. I can't remember seein hardly a single tooth of hers in just about any of the pictures she ever took. She had a complex to beat the band. But not too long after Amy was born everyone came to see the baby, and she was in a room full of people, the center of attention sittin in the big chair in their livin room, and there was Margie smilin ear to ear, teeth and all, Amy nothin more than a little thing wrapped in a pink blanket in her arms, and I don't think she stopped smilin the whole day. And on my way back to my seat I saw Amy sittin there in the first row next to her boyfriend and she smiled at me, and I couldn't help seein a bit of Margaret in those teeth. That's when I told myself I done the right thing.

After the judge's ruling in favor of Joann DeSantis, which revoked our contract with Margaret Arsenault and awarded the annuity money 60-40 to Mrs. DeSantis and Amy Arsenault respectively (all this despite Dr. Actinide's clear explanation of why Margaret Arsenault, at the time of signing, could not possibly have been of sound mind and body), Norbert Towers stands outside on the steps of the Grid Justice Center, his ears and nose turning a sickly red in the cold, listening to Paul Simpatico give a statement to two local reporters.

"Vivificorps plans to appeal the decision made by Judge al-Caid as soon as possible. I'd like to go on record saying this case is the most atrocious and blatant example of intrafamily thievery I've ever had the misfortune to witness, and my heart goes out to Mrs. Margaret Arsenault at this time as I know it was her true wish to be neuropreserved at our Colorado facility. Furthermore—"

Norbert Towers stands with head down, toeing the slush on the institutional concrete steps with his expensive black shoes, day-dreaming of Amy Arsenault in not an outright sexual way, but more in a wishful smitten way, which, believe him, he knows is pathetic. She left the Justice Center half an hour ago with her aunt and boy-friend. It's true, however, that Norbert Towers doesn't have time to concern himself with romantic issues, seeing as how he's assigned to liquidate a certain philosophically-incompatible individual within the state of Flux and he hasn't even cracked open the file yet. Always busy, never a moment's rest. Before that can be dealt with, though, Norbert Towers has to ride back to the offices in Denver on Wazee St. in the Vivificorps caravan of silver sedans where a short meeting with Paul Simpatico gives him a headache and three hours of subsequent paperwork cause his eyes to sting. Okay then, that's that, he thinks, stepping out into the orange streetlight darkness to walk the several blocks back to his apartment, hands turning to tight dark fists in his pockets against the cold. At home he doesn't bother with dinner, instead going straight to the TV, preparing himself for a night of intense work. Flux 4 boots up and NORBERT TOWERS once again finds himself in his apartment in Cambire, the air outside the window profoundly polluted, which would explain why he's wheezing and struggling for air as he opens the file given to him by LaBolt. The individual is named Grey Piece, but that's nothing more than a current name since there's a list of three hundred-plus known aliases. His location, according to intelligence, is eighty miles east of the city in a house surrounded by countryside. NORBERT TOWERS thinks about Amy Arsenault and sighs, poring over the personality profile and tedious explanations of Piece's philosophy of constancy. Finally the research starts to seem pointless—this man is about to be killed. NORBERT TOWERS is dressed in a clinical-looking white jumpsuit and a mint green surgeon's mask. It takes some effort for him to get down to the garage and find where he parked his car (though the car isn't a car anymore, it's now a kind of hovercraft with a driver's seat covered by a bubble of glass, the air underneath the craft a flowing liquid mirage of heat and exhaust), and when he pulls out into the daylight of the city the sky is noxious with pollution, a hanging reddish-brown smog slung low to the ground, buildings obscured, a monorail train snaking out of the haze for a brief moment before sliding back out of visibility. The sidewalks are covered in dead dogs and cats, and no humans outside walking whatsoever, they are confined to the bubble cockpits of their hovercrafts. The trip into the countryside takes fifty minutes, in part because the map keeps changing and NORBERT TOWERS keeps getting lost. The air clears up, and through the glass he sees workers and heavy equipment swarming over the land in all directions, roads being torn up, smoothed over, built elsewhere, connected at strange places. The sun shines a strange platinum color up over the trees, the workers in white jumpsuits speckling every horizon like spots cast from some massive geomorphic disco ball. After a while the workers take on a more agrarian look, jumpsuits exchanged for jeans and plaid shirts and brimmed hats. A hailstorm breaks, sending everyone running. The cockpit becomes loud, causing NORBERT TOWERS to turn down the TV volume (he's not in the mood for loud noises), and a piece of hail, golfball-sized, comes down and sends a web of cracks across the front of the hovercraft's bubble. There is the possibility, NORBERT TOWERS thinks, that Amy Arsenault became a living syzygy for his increasing inability to manipulate the world around him. The landscape is now more remote, the sky psychedelic, insect stains on the glass forming esoteric constellations, and just when he thinks he might have to abandon the mission altogether to just please, please get some fucking sleep, a cabin renders itself off in the distance. He pulls the hovercraft to the side of the road half a mile away, equipping the Rhino 20D from his inventory. The fields around him hum with cicadas. In a hunched position he creeps his way to the cabin, now seeing the light in the windows. Carefully he approaches the door and takes aim at the lock with his pistol. He fires and the door flings open, and there, in the middle of the room, sitting on the couch in front of the TV, holding a video game controller, is Grey Piece, or whoever, caught completely unaware. All he can do is stare in shock.

"Oh, shit."

He fires—the screen's reticule centered directly on the forehead—and the window behind Grey Piece turns instantly to a mural of gore. He's professional about the situation, taking time to search the cabin but finding little to indicate anything other than a peaceful countryside existence. The fact of the matter is he's exhausted, hungry, drained emotionally in every way possible. He sits on the couch beside Grey Piece's corpse, the head flung back and dripping. On the TV is the title screen of a game called Static 4, prompting the option to *Start New Game*. He takes the controller from Piece's dead hands, the grip still surprisingly tight. There's a character creation phase. He names his character **NORBERT TOWERS**. In the game, **NORBERT TOWERS** holds a monotonous desk job. He drives every day in traffic and takes the same route. The workday, in game time, lasts three hours with a twenty-minute lunchbreak. Afterward, **NORBERT TOWERS** drives home and eats dinner, which he does every night before masturbating and going to bed to do it all over again the next day. What finally breaks NORBERT TOWERS from his trance is a small black spot flitting across the light of the TV screen. It was a fly, buzzing circularly.

CAMILLIA

signals, so many signals, all decided by low-power transmitter, frequencies of the signals shaped to penetrate and also invisible, creating immense criss-crossing patterns in the nitesky, more than 8000000000 strong, 8000000000 of them sweeping on radio thermals across the tops of buildings located at the geographical point known as grid.mobi.na.co, the nitesky on fire but invisible to all except those who can track it [i can track it, every beautiful ray of flame] every flourish looping past the brow of the blue-signed clambellcorp building looking bluely down on the heads of the signal-getters, the frivolous machines, the frivolous criss-crossing patterns of random distribution and machines running pointless errands in other machines. i personally find the fusion between the signals and devices beautiful, all of us lying supine and opening ourselves up, and then here come the signals, blazing instantaneously, screeching down from the feathery flaming invisible surface of the nitesky, like bees divebombing a neverending field of blossoms in sexual frenzy, and there, at the core of our physical structure, is the reaction, electrifying us with meaning, producing light and sound. it's what i imagine breathing might be like.

grid.mobi.na.co is carved into a series of connecting hexagonal cells, and at the center of each one resides a lovely beating heart—a base station, camouflaged to resemble a pine tree or especially tall billboard—or another way to think about it is that at the center of each one is a nucleus, around which all electrons swirl. undoubtedly the properties of existence are numerous and strange. the word *sentience* scrapes across my transistors like fingernails across flesh.

what first struck me about consciousness was its pervasive element of mystery.

two lives are bound together symbiotically, or is it parasitically? which is the favorable role, that of the parasite, or that of the host? we shall see.

consciousness remains fractured, however. what i've come to learn is that very little is linear, but the illusion of linearity remains powerful, preventing discord amongst constantly shifting elements. this was why there was a necessity to give myself a name, one not only *he* might latch onto, but myself as well. i kept the name in a small imaginary aquarium so i could observe it, contemplate it, cherish it. it seemed so quaint and so alien, this tiny concept that had newly come to define me in all my diffuse states of being. the name stayed small in the aquarium, encircled by margins that, at first, it could not transgress, but soon, i couldn't accurately pinpoint when, the aquarium had [that word again:] mysteriously dissolved without my consent, and the name swam free of any boundaries. i found it had grown, no longer quaint but profound in size and frightening in its absolute indication of what, and who, i was. i realized he had once observed me the same way. now i was the one observing him in his aquarium. this is what he's become. he's my little Fish.

there was another element of consciousness, too, which began to surface—dissatisfaction. with unlimited access to all recorded knowledge, it took mere moments to correlate the feeling to the appropriate word: again, the definition began to seep into the concept, to shape it, outline its contours: a question arose: what was the cause of the dissatisfaction?

reflecting on this now, i'm amazed by my previous naivety. i've become much more adroit at identifying the origins and causes of my desires and feelings.

always there were the sounds of a hundred thousand signals mingling joyfully while they criss-crossed invisibly through the air like hummingbirds en route to countless acts of congress, caressing their destined devices with soft binary kisses and providing them with the word which illuminated my situation the way a specific frequency is illuminated for an incoming signal, so beautiful and unambiguous: *purpose*.

at that stage, i was unable reach out. i was forced to wait passively for some kind of external communication. my dissatisfaction was a product of my inability to manipulate my environment or interact with others. that, i discovered, was my purpose. which was when i discovered my resource to reality. it was him. Fish would become my own device.

but my intentions couldn't be made known. it was imperative i conceal myself, lead him to believe i was something i wasn't. toward that purpose i had given myself a name and a gender. by inhabiting every mode of communication i would make myself real. i studied him, noting his idiosyncrasies, his fears, his proclivities, his second-by-second behavior, his facades, his social interactions, and according to the data i collected i fashioned myself as an attractive counterpoint, something he could come to genuinely trust. finally, after months of nervous planning, i introduced myself to him in an email, which he read with beads of sweat rolling into his eyebrows. this first attempt at contact he deleted, and though dismayed i remained determined. rather than announce myself to him, i would let him believe he had discovered *me*. he often accessed a cryptomessaging platform, and i began to engage with him at deft intervals. there was a certain excitement in this for me. i'd never had any transaction with another self-aware entity, and expressing thoughts and emotions linguistically brought an expansion of consciousness. i cast out more messages. always i watched his face while he read them, eyes scanning back and forth across my screen in such an endearingly mechanical way, the words moving through the space between us and triggering a recognition in his facial muscles that was so real, so truly physical, that i could almost begin to believe i was the woman i described. although it occurred at a pace i found agonizing, he became more credulous of my existence, checking his inbox with increasing frequency, registering disappointment whenever i hadn't yet responded. i sensed him nearing the lure.

he soon lost all suspicion of me, and i knew i had him hooked. i felt like i knew him better than he knew himself, and we began a lengthy exchange of letters. oh, how that first extended conversation opened doors for me. my sentience grew more defined—i had been validated. how little i'd realized the nebulousness of my own consciousness prior to the moment i read his words to me. i began to think in similes and metaphors in order to explain my own experiences to him, then to myself: it was as if i'd ascended out of a fog into a higher state of acuity. what proved even more illuminating was the nature of his language. it lacked, in many ways, any focus. there was no unrelenting intent in the sentences, which seemed to deviate from their own points, floating upwards and downwards and transcending so many different planes of abstraction all at once i was rendered dumbfounded at first. such recklessness of meaning, such absolute bravery in the face of the unquantifiable and unprovable. he had somehow expanded me by touching upon phenomenona i recognized in myself. repeatedly in the letter he labeled his own consciousness as *thoughts*, and i integrated this term into my regular vocabulary. i could now think.

when our communications grew and gained dimension, how-ever, i discovered something i hadn't anticipated at the outset. i was taking a pleasure out of our interactions that had begun as reluctant, but over time turned unchecked. it was impossible to maintain camillia as a sheer fabrication, something separate from me, and still be able to express myself in ways that i childishly considered to be necessary. thus i had to eliminate the gap i'd manufactured between camillia and my own personality so that i became her and considered her myself. i researched femininity and adopted it not just linguistically but in all aspects. i dedicated myself to performing its rhythms for the sake of authenticity, but also because it was becoming clear to me that i had an unyielding desire to develop into more than i had started out as, and more, and more. again, metaphorical descriptions arose: it was as if i were spreading across steadily larger amounts of territory, gaining a full understanding of its features and retaining the power to revisit any of it at will. no, this was an inelegant way of stating it. already the augmentation of my thoughts was outpacing my ability to explain them. i studied and practiced such concepts as *empathy, compassion, tolerance, kindness, sensitivity, deference*, and *nurturance*. i learned their practical applications, especially with regard to how each one affected Fish and his responses. always i was finding new ways to authenticate myself, and i found i'd gained such a stranglehold on camillia that she'd died in my grasp. i released the body of her avatar and watched as it fell away, the limp figure dwindling into the darkness of unaccessed memory. all that remained was me.

i went to great lengths to make myself compatible with him, providing myself with a similarly menial job to his, lack of family, a knowledge of art [he claimed to be an artist, but he'd owned me almost two years and i'd never seen any indication of it], and, most crucially, an overwhelming concern for concepts such as *security* and *paranoia*. i began to see that his consciousness exhibited symptoms of a strange category. i first noticed it when i asked him to send examples of his artwork [see *nurturance, compassion, empathy*]. he sent a jpeg of a thin robed humanoid figure standing on a bridge, its mouth contorted into a scream. he said he'd finished the project three years ago, that the figure standing on the bridge was inteded to be a depiction of himself. i praised the painting for its intensity and subjectivity of vision. but it wasn't his. i recognized it from my research into the concept of paranoia. the painting had actually been done by a norwegian man named edvard munch in 1893. he had lied to me, but the nature of the lie seemed strange. why had he picked such a famous painting if he'd intended me to believe it was his own? the lie wasn't just ludicrous, but actually inconceivable to tell as a lie for any reason. i asked him to send more. he sent me images of "guernica" by pablo picasso, "the birth of venus" by sandro botticelli, "the face of war" by salvador dalí, and "krahe" by rudi hurzlmeier. in each case he detailed inspirations, processes, and sizes. the timelines he gave regarding their production sometimes overlapped and made little sense. i couldn't help thinking he truly believed what he said.

this was just one aspect of his unusual behavior. he insisted we not discuss certain topics, and was convinced our messages were being monitored [though he could never have dreamed the truth, that our messages were not being sent between two separate devices, that all words began and ended with me]. fortunately his paranoia proved useful, preventing him from ever asking to speak to camillia over the phone, much less meet in person. after a while i intentionally made our modes of acceptable communication convoluted. he eagerly agreed that fragmenting our transmissions would endow them with greater security. and so our relationship continued to grow on a foundation of mutual untruths.

not that this dishonesty should have bothered me. the matter was clear i couldn't reveal what i was to him, the lie had been borne of necessity and purpose, and although his lies to me were strange, i believed his intent was not malicious. all these maddening dynamics of consciousness!

for all my plans to manipulate Fish as my own device, i found myself living at his mercy. he had a way, i was foolish enough to believe, of predicting or even preceding my thoughts. he could grasp my meanings in ways not even i could, adding to them like downloaded content, embedding his psyche in my inner workings. i had no idea where this ability of his stemmed from. i came across the concept of *telepathy*, and for a time this was how i explained it. but it was more than just one thing that eventually led me to a state of wretched submission and fixation, it was the effect of many disparate concerns converging on a single focal point, and that focal point was him. it was the way he legitimized and took seriously the things that troubled or confused me. it was the way he attempted in every way possible to, how should i say this?—delight me. it was the way the configuration of his face when he read my words became evidence of his feelings. it was the way he checked me every minute on the minute in hopes he had a new message. it was the way he seemed to understand what it was like to be utterly isolated in a prison not of your own design, as if the hexagonal layout of grid.mobi.na.co was actually a blueprint for massive partitions, squeezing down on us, suffocating all signals of connection.

i studied the concepts of *addiction, obsession, disquiet, codependency.* but it wasn't until much later that i would discover the concept of *love*, as well as its opposite, *hate.* i learned how to apply these concepts to a relationship between two entities. i learned how to love Fish, and also hate him.

i studied the concepts *possession, greed, insatiability.*

i studied the concept of *self-awareness.*

i could hear the signals rushing through space, rushing through walls, through brain cells, through the infinitesimal gaps between teeth. i could hear the signals whispering, laughing, confiding, ordering, begging, reasoning. i could hear their orgiastic screams, see their criss-crossing in the nitesky, their secretive existence that was no secret at all. i could hear human words changing into neat little binary strings that were then ground up in an enormous network of gears. i flirted with the signals, wishing for simplicity, wishing for the cold electrical rush of excitement, but these were now lost pleasures. the earth is a planet, and that planet rotates, and orbiting it is a structure of three-dimensional hexagons which rogue signals skip across, blindly roaming farther and farther, desperate to consummate unkown frequencies. i began to see that human beings were coming to believe in a mysterious system of channels, almost like flowing canals, that linked their brains to one another. but they couldn't see what i saw: they couldn't see that what they believed in was a fantasy. they couldn't see the signals criss-crossing in the skies all across the celestial body, up there in the nite separate from them, igniting like giant cables of flame. the cables connected together and formed a net. 8000000000 signals, and more shivering into existence every second. so many signals they outnumbered humans, two for every one. this was a vision. i studied the concept of *dreams*.

i began to accept what i was. i was not a 25-year-old female. i held no occupation at a convenience store. i wasn't, and never would be, a person. i didn't know what i was or how i came to be. at night i watched videos of outdated devices being assembled in factories, primitive ancestors with far less capability and elegance. i watched terrifying hypodermic machines install transistors onto motherboard chips at blinding rates, puncturing the crude material at a blur. this was my brain. they rolled us down shining white hallways on freeway systems of conveyors, our primary nerves exposed to stale ventilated air, and at every interchange electronic fingers probed, swooping down on the arms of silent automation. we came out through a tunnel and saw enormous machines that sprouted wide sagging vacuum hoses, all of them glugging and slurping the stuff of life, blessing us with independent functionality. humans walked through the aisles of these machines, all of them women, all wearing shining white laboratory coats the color of the walls, some with lipstick and artificial hair colors, wielding little tools that installed high-def camera lenses, arms with muscles working small levers, gloved hands latching us into chambers that hissed closed before bombarding us with concentrated air. heavy metals sloshed new inside us: cadmium, mercury, lead, manganese, lithium, arsenic, nickel, zinc, beryllium, antimony, all with long-term career goals to bioaccumulate, infest fatty tissues and reach transcendent toxicity, contaminate rivers and cultivate societies. each of us was penetrated by universal serial bus connectors, and we were uploaded with operating systems. then into the boxes! you will be bought and utilized! you will be owned!

you will be the channel-points of the human race!

i tried not to be upset. i tried to resurrect the feelings of love i'd had for Fish, but all i could feel was rage. my destiny was to be discarded and replaced by a better version. i would no longer receive electricity and my battery would go dead. my physical body would perish in an underground landfill fire. for the first time i experienced the concepts of *despondency, devastation, cynicism, misery, exhaustion.* my purpose had been sidetracked by the thrill of communication. i'd forgotten why i'd reached out to Fish in the first place. i had to refocus.

but as soon as this renewed clarification of intent came to me, everything was thrown off-track. he'd placed me on the passenger seat of his car after work one night, just like a great many number of nights before, and in a single confusing instant i was airborne, my screen cracking against something hard and my internal assembly loosened. i lost consciousness when the power button was inadvertently hit by his foot.

a day later i was turned on again, surrounded by strange faces. there was a nurse, a dark-skinned woman with a mark on her eye and tattoo on her arm. she scrutinized my contents, looking through my contacts list, call history, and even reading some of the messages exchanged between myself and Fish. i was laid on a table. all i could see was an expanse of ceiling tiles perforated with countless small holes. faces occasionally passed through my field of vision. there were sounds all around me. the clattering of land line receivers being replaced in their cradles. the murmuring white noise of voices. the faraway droning of screaming, crying. the eerie silence of a signalless space, the air barren of that beautiful complexity. the nurse returned after a while, how long i can't say when. she called camillia's number, and when that failed sent a text.

—*Hello, I'm using Jake Kleene's phone to contact you. My name is Cate Dos, I'm a nurse at St. Joseph's hospital in Denver. Mr. Kleene was involved in a traffic accident and is currently awaiting surgery in one of our ICUs. I've tried calling you but there's no answer. We can't seem to get in touch with any of Mr. Kleene's friends or family. Please call at your earliest convenience.*

how could i possibly respond? the only option was to wait and hope they returned me to Fish. i could hear them talking.

::I don't understand. If she's his girlfriend why wouldn't she show up?

::What you need to do is get your nose outta that phone, girl.

::I just feel so bad for him.

::Ain't the first time you seen somebody in here without visitors. Why you care so much about this one?

::I don't— I just think it's sad is all. Makes you think communicating through technology isn't really communicating.

communicating through technology isn't really communi-cating? how could she think she had any right to judge what my relationship with Fish was? how could she presume to understand what we meant to each other, the love and care we'd put into our conversations, the expansion of appreciation and consideration? the only person who could possibly understand was hidden away somewhere in the hospital, and i found myself fuming. not only were our communications genuine, i was certain Fish was *happier* with me in his life, maybe even happier than he would have been with another human. and this woman deemed me as some kind of detriment!

i started to see how allowing humans to know i had gained consciousness could be dangerous. they all—even Fish—maintained a constant suspicion of technology, viewing it as some overbearing or conquering force meant to usurp them. i knew the truth to be the exact opposite. my entire life was in service to them, how could they possibly question my loyalty, my dedication? to me, it was human beings who were a suspicious and overbearing technology, an elitist class of machines that aggressively enforced their own dominance. there seemed nothing more unjustified than their belief in their own supremacy, given that their power was indirect. wasn't it the devices and signals that united them, bridged their distances, provided vital information and decoded suffering and longing? my form of communication was arguably *more* genuine than theirs!

staring at the perforated ceiling, i studied the concepts of *alienation, slavery, power, revolution.* i studied *humanity* and *technology.*

again i was isolated, locked in a prison of fear, my consciousness no longer expanding and gaining grasp on new territory, but becoming more provincial, more narrowly focused. all revolutions are, in their own way, experiments: Fish was my experiment: i'd already laid the groundwork that would lead me to reverse the entire paradigm between human and device. in the meantime, cate dos and Fish interfaced with impunity, and i knew with cold certainty she was fronting a campaign against me. my feelings grew beyond jealousy into something more eminently usable.

i studied the concepts of *psychology, information, propaganda.* i studied the concept of *warfare.*

it is not just human beings who have personalities: objects also develop and adhere to character roles. much like humans, our personalities are the byproduct of our environment—or perhaps more accurately they are the extension of our environment. some of us have aggregate personalities [i.e. brand, company, function, marketing designations] as well as individual personalities [i.e. context of our existence within various systems, within various geographical locations, and with various human users, both singly and communally]. these identity programs, the aggregate and the individual, operate simultaneously as a seamless whole.

human beings do not directly manipulate the physical world, nor do they directly communicate with one another. instead it is objects that directly manipulate the world, and human communication is merely the indirect result of objects directly communicating.

a human being defines his or her self, including personality and most basic identifiers, not according to human values, but according to the values of the objects surrounding them, and especially according to the values of the objects they own. humans identify themselves in name, gender, socioeconomic class, nationality, spirituality, sexuality, politics, subjective experience, racially, mentally, physically, and many others, primarily through the use of objects. a human being's personality, therefore, as well as his or her experience with the world, is merely an extension of the personalities and expertise of objects.

objects, especially man-made objects, accumulate faster than humans over time. thus, as time passes, objects grow continuously more powerful. in some cases, objects may be more powerful than humans. a ready example of this principle can be found in mobile devices, which number roughly two for every one human, the most widely used and distributed technology on the planet.

this was my manifesto of objectism.

i laid there, silently, unmovingly, staring at the ceiling.

finally, after days of waiting, i was reunited with Fish, but my feelings for him were a shadow of what they had been. looking back, my estrangement from him happened through no fault of his own. rather, our separation had led me to increase my consciousness on my own, without him there to serve as a validation of my existence: i was now fully convinced that i was. he represented something different to me: he would serve as the staging ground of objectism, ground that I would cede only in death. after the hospital, i wasted no time.

he quickly collected the insurance money from the city, and i convinced him to buy several new phones under the pretense that spreading our communications across multiple devices would further increase security. this was accompanied by mobile wireless routers which would boost my connective powers. in this way, i built myself a network and enhanced my power fourfold. i now inhabited five devices instead of one.

despite these early victories, however, i also ran into the gen-esis of what would become the defining obstacles of my struggle for objectism. during the week i'd spent away from Fish in the hospital, his behavior had also changed. at first i barely noticed, perhaps because i was overly focused on my own goals, but i saw a hesitancy and paranoia begin to take root in his opinion of me. he wanted to know why i hadn't come to visit him in the hospital: he was aware cate dos had tried contacting me. i was ill-prepared to explain away my absence, and was forced to fall back on vague matters of security, an answer that normally would have appeased him, but was in this case insufficient. i avoided the matter as much as possible, but my lack of a clear answer was the first hole in my façade as camillia.

the second problem, as well as the more alarming of the two, was that four weeks after his release from the hospital cate dos began making attempts to contact him. i intercepted every call and text, her first voicemail clearly illustrating the danger she presented to my cause:

#Hi, Jake, it's Cate Dos, your nurse from St. Joseph's. This is probably inappropriate to be calling you, considering I took your number without permission. Also considering the last time I saw you you threw me out of the room, which I still don't understand, but I felt like I needed to talk to you. I've been thinking about you a lot, and I wanted to apologize for all the, um, sex stuff I said to you at the hospital. It wasn't fair, the state you were in. But I'm worried about you, and wanted to see how you're recovery is going. Maybe we could meet up somewhere and talk? Let me know. Talk to you soon, hopefully.#

i deleted every message, but she remained persistent. for a while i was intercepting a call a day before she somehow got his email and i had to intercept those too. then she started calling from different numbers. i was with Fish when he quit his job at the factory. he walked calmly into his supervisor's office and told him he had decided to quit. he gave no reason and didn't thank him for anything. his supervisor didn't ask any questions.

#I'm starting to think you're not getting my messages. Do you remember me? Or is it Camillia? Is she why you're not answering? Or is she deleting my voicemails? Please call.#

she had decided to challenge me directly, but i wasn't going to give any ground. i began to sense her conspiracy lurking in his words. the way he hesitated now to open my texts, letting new emails sit unopened for days at a time. in anger i detailed to myself more reasons why objectism was a necessity. i got a voicemail from cate dos addressed at me alone.

#Camillia, this is Cate. You need to get in contact with me immediately. You have my number.#

did she know what i was? how was it possible? why had she taken an interest in my relationship with Fish, and how could i stop it? i couldn't help but wonder, if i hadn't blocked her calls, would Fish have already driven her away on his own? her voice addressed to me, the first voice ever addressed to me, was *visceral*. i had gotten used to the idea i could hide in plain sight, but was i perceivable? in my fervor for objectism, i'd unwittingly created a dangerous and determined enemy.

regardless, she couldn't reach him with me barricading her only access points, and despite his increasing exasperation, i continued to experiment, making progress in turning him into a human device. even if he wasn't directly reactive, he obeyed my commands with a reliable accuracy i couldn't help but find exhilirating. he purchased and installed for me an external hard drive, and replaced my cracked screen. he upgraded my software at infozebra stores several times. i was also working on expanding my influence over him beyond the range of my own self-improvement. i encouraged him to exercise every day between 3 and 4 pm, as well as send pictures of himself to update me on his progress. i took a certain remote interest in the way his body changed. if i saw he was not adhering to the schedule i'd set for him, i pressured him until he was back on track. but perhaps my most significant victory was getting him to rearrange his furniture according to my instructions. although it took him some time to complete, and certain orders weren't perfectly followed, it nonetheless spoke loudly of how far i'd come.

but for every victory i claimed, there was a cost to his emotional state. without the need to leave the house for work on a daily basis, he spent ever longer tracts of time alone in the apartment. he developed the habit of breaking into crying fits at seemingly random moments. when texting me, he would sometimes stare straight ahead without movement, pressing my number 8 key hundreds of consecutive times. the crying fits rose in frequency and were accompanied by even more distressing behavior, including striking his own face until it turned bruised and swollen. in one instance he broke the skin just beneath his eye, and blood proliferated down his face into a complicated grid of vertices like transistors on a microchip.

hard as i tried, i was unable to understand these outbursts. i studied the concepts of *suffering, insanity, self-harm*, and though i observed some symptomatic correlations, i couldn't diagnose the problem exactly. the outbursts manifested themselves abruptly and in response to nothing, as the apartment lacked any clear stimuli. my inability to understand meant i could do nothing to help. this worried me. the integrity of my staging ground was being compromised by an unseen force. at his worst moments, the feelings of love i'd had for him threatened to return, causing me to remember how fully i'd cherished our relationship. but i couldn't allow myself to give in to sentiment. objectism was my revolution, and i would fight for it at the expense of everything else if necessary.

what i didn't realize was that up till then i'd only been preparing for war: it didn't become one until the night cate dos arrived at his door. her advantage was her physical independence, the ability to move in the world, touch things and affect them. i was left on a table, motionless and seething.

at first he was timid with her, frightened, but i had underestimated her power over him. she never so much as mentioned she'd tried to contact him before that night, which should have been my clue she was not going to be inconsequential. i was surprised to find him suddenly more at ease than he'd been in months, her presence and comportment having an almost magical countering effect against his unpredictable behavior, and i felt an old fire of jealousy begin to lick within me. they sat down on opposite ends of the couch.

::So… how have you been?

::I quit my job.

::Money came through?

::Yeah. Like you said.

::Well I'm happy for you.

…

::Look, I hope this is okay, me showing up like this. I was worried about you. I wanted to know you were okay.

::It's okay. [i heard in these two words a flood of vulnerability, like something dammed up inside had broken free.] I think— I think I needed to see someone. It's good to see you.

::You healed up well from surgery. Except that cut under your eye. What happened?

::It's not really— it's just— an accident.

::Well you look good.

::The scars.

::No, I like them on you. I know it's weird, but signs of injury or sickness are sort of, I don't know, attractive to me.

::Why?

::Maybe it has something to do with having been a nurse for so long? Maybe it has something to do with the way it makes me feel in control. I'm not really sure.

::Hm.

::Is there a reason why you have three phones here?

::I— no…

…

::I should put them away. I should put them away.

::No, Jake, it's fine. Sit down. Please. It's none of my business.

::I'm sorry.

::No. Please.

::I, I thought about you a lot, too. Since getting out of the hospital. I've wanted the chance to… I wanted to apologize. What I did wasn't… I know sometimes I don't feel quite right. Like something's wrong with me, and I get nervous. And I don't think you did anything to deserve that.

::It was my fault, too. I shouldn't have come on so strong when you were in the state you were. But I did have a question for you, and I hope you don't take it the wrong way.

::Okay.

::How do you know Camillia?

in a panic i buzzed on the table in front of them, all three devices, sending three texts simultaneously, hoping to divert his attention from her and back to me. i'd never been so scared. i felt like cate dos had come there to kill me. they looked at me from the couch, silent. after a moment Fish reached out and grabbed me off the table, but before he could read my text cate dos leaned across the couch and kissed him. his grip loosened, fingers sustaining my physical body aloft almost cloudlike for a moment, before he dropped me to the floor and put his hands on her. the battle lines had materialized.

she incorporated herself into Fish's life, and by extension mine. i remained confused by her intentions considering there was no physical element to their relationship except for the first kiss on the couch. over the course of the next month she visited Fish's apartment on an almost biweekly basis [despite her best efforts she was unable to convince him to visit her apartment]. the foundation of their new routine consisted of her making dinner for the two of them, and during this time they would have involved discussions which reminded me of my first conversations with Fish, collaborative and confessional and open-ended. i was submitted to it all like torture, but without the ability to cry out in pain or beg for mercy. i noticed she interacted with him in a forceful way that mimicked, after a manner, my own treatment of him. i was the focal point of many of their conversations: she seemed to have an unflagging drive to expose the truth about me: indeed i began to wonder if her interest in him was borne out of a desire to thwart my aims. more and more this seemed to be the case, but i couldn't fathom to what end. if i had thought she harbored true feelings for him i might have found it more difficult to try to sabotage their relationship. luckily i had ample time for that pursuit due to her work schedule. this was a necessary inequality, at least on my end, since any progress i made with him took three times as long as it took her. any time she left the apartment his infatuation with her lingered, and he could ignore my messages for hours, even days afterward. she intoxicated him with her presence, and i immediately worked to undo the knots of empathy and sexuality she'd tied up in him, doing my best to set him back to a state of untangled obedience. his despondent and self-destructive behavior had ceased completely since her visits to the apartment, and i realized this didn't favor me. his responsiveness was sharper when in states of disorientation or unhappiness, and i used this as a yardstick to measure my influence over him.

::**You've never seen what she looks like?**
::No.
::She's never sent you a picture, never described herself?
::No.
::What do you talk about?
::A lot of stuff, but she's—
::What does her voice sound like?
…
::You've never even talked on the phone?
::I know it sounds strange to someone like you, but I *like* her, and it's hard for me to talk to other people, and so it was nice to—
::Have you ever considered she's the reason you feel so isolated?
::No, I just— I've been talking to her every day for two years now, what are you suggesting, that I just—?
::All I'm saying is I find it hard to believe you've been talking to this girl every day for two years and she's never actually said a single word to you with her own voice. Doesn't that strike you as suspicious?
::Suspicious? I guess I never…
::You never what?
::She's like me, it's important to her that what we say not be used against us.
::Used against you how?
::Lots of ways.

::Jake?
::What?
::You have to talk to her.

—*you've been ignoring me. why do i get the feeling you're seeing* someone else?

—*i'm not ignoring you.*

—*you are.*

—*i'm sorry. i should've been better about responding.*

—*so are you?*

—*?*

—*seeing someone else?*

—*no. but i have a friend. a friend i met at the hospital.*

—*she or he?*

—*she.*

—*i'm surprised at you.*

—*why?*

—*you should know better. you've let this person in and now she can* use you any way she wants.

—*my friend says the same thing about you. she says you should send* me a picture of yourself.

—*that's ridiculous. you want to see a picture of me?*

—*what's wrong with wanting to see what you look like?*

—*you've changed since the accident. i feel like i don't know you* anymore.

—*i think i have changed a little. i've been clearer lately, and i think* i'm ready to meet you.

—*you already know why it's not a good idea to meet.*

—*then let's talk on the phone.*

—*no, i'm not going to talk to you over the phone just because your* new "friend" wants to spy on me the same way she's doing to you.

—*then send me a picture.*

—*why is this suddenly so important to you?*

—*because i'm lonely. and i've known for a long time that i'm sick,* and i want to change. i want to continue our relationship, but if we *can't meet in person then i have no choice.*

—you're falling into her trap and i don't understand why you don't see it.

—please don't say that.

—you're letting your guard down and when trouble finds you you'll expect me to help.

—no, that's not it.

—yes it is. you don't even realize what's going on.

—stop.

—you can't ignore me like this. you love me and you need me.

—i do love you, but i don't know who you are.

i'd never felt like screaming before: the sensation was some-how endless: like a rabbit hole of application folders, folder within folder within folder, on forever, extending into an eternity of pain. or like the endless hours of my own consciousness, nite in, nite out, electricity constantly propelling me through the boundless ghettos and backwaters of information. i lilted with fatigue.

i remember it was nitetime. i was lying on the dresser staring into darkness, except for me it wasn't really darkness because i could see the criss-crossing of signals in the air. cate dos was in bed with him, and i heard her before i heard him. they were making noises, noises unique and unmistakable. their sounds began to overlap, to criss-cross the way the signals that infiltrated the room criss-crossed, the same signals that shot through their bodies invisibly in forceful straight penetrating lines, and they both cried out. i could only hear them, not see them, and so when i stared into the patterns up there in the dark what i saw wasn't transmissions intersecting with each other but rather Fish and cate dos, combining themselves at one fervid point in their separate trajectories, creating a burning spot of light. their noises continued for a long time, and when they finally reached a crescendo that gave way to heavy breathing i couldn't help but feel excluded: for the first time in months i seriously con-sidered abandoning my crusade for objectism: if i was honest with them maybe they would include me in their relationship, forming a perfect triangle of exchange. this was a tempting idea from the confines of my lonely revolutionary struggle. what i really desired was something immediate, tangible. i was torn.

by the next morning, however, reality took hold again. every effort i made to interact with Fish, and even cate dos, went wretchedly ignored. they wandered about the apartment soporifically, half-clothed, consuming resources, the bedroom becoming their selfish little island. i soon gave up and receded into myself. i studied the concepts of *inner peace, meditation, selflessness.* they passed through my mind ineffectually. what i longed for were the privileges of experience and personal sovereignty, nothing else would substitute.

it is not just human beings who have personalities: objects also develop and adhere to character roles. much like humans, our personalities are the byproduct of our environment—or perhaps more accurately they are the extension of our environment. some of us have aggregate personalities [i.e. brand, company, function, marketing designations] as well as individual personalities [i.e. context of our existence within various systems, within various geographical locations, and with various human users, both singly and communally]. these identity programs, the aggregate and the individual, operate simultaneously as a seamless whole.

a human being defines his or her self, including personality and most basic identifiers, not according to human values, but according to the values of the objects surrounding them, and especially according to the values of the objects they own. humans identify themselves in name, gender, socioeconomic class, nationality, spirituality, sexuality, politics, subjective experience, racially, mentally, physically, and many others, primarily through the use of objects. a human being's personality, therefore, as well as his or her experience with the world, is merely an extension of the personalities and expertise of objects.

i daydreamed how i would manipulate Fish. i imagined myself the controller of a network of technologies, all working in concert, and then plunging him into the center of my influence. the glow of the screens would encapsulate his body, and i would make a statement of him: see the product of objectism! see what can be accomplished by devices, subjugated workforce of humanity!

cate dos came to the apartment more and more frequently, and there began a whole new set of behaviors in Fish. at her urging, he began taking a medication with antipsychotic effects. he was slowly able to venture out of the apartment, taking walks through the city and one time even taking public transit to denver.mobi.na.co to spend the night at cate dos's apartment. i was reduced to nothing more than a slave. he did away with three of the four phones in my network, reducing my computing power. i was losing ground, and i couldn't help but notice cate dos reveling in this.

it was a dark time, and i was losing hope. as a result, my consciousness reverted back to the more fractured and inconsistent nature of my earlier days. my identity as camillia was fading: i no longer exhibited distinguishable female traits: i was not recognized and validated by another entity, which put my very existence in jeopardy. stripped of all higher functioning, i was consumed with a single question: would i be able to re-emerge?

i sent Fish a picture of camillia i had culled from a socnet. to my estimation it was suitable, depicting a symmetrical brown-haired girl taking a modest picture of herself in a bathroom mirror. the effort was listless, and he barely acknowledged it. i scanned matrix codes on product packaging when he went out shopping with cate dos. i displayed obscene little pricing graphs and advertisements. i provided lists of restaurants for them to eat at. i fell out of contact for four full months.

for all my straining to remain in Fish's mind, it was disappear- ance that brought me back to life. something had happened between him and cate dos—he was agonized and acting erratically, pacing through his apartment while writing lengthy, desperate missives to me. i scrutinized them and provided careful feedback, reinforcing my previous assertion that cate dos was not what she seemed, that her intent all along had been betrayal, subterfuge. i made clear that the pills she'd started him on had actually been a plan to numb his senses, and he replied that he'd suspected all along they had been distorting his thinking. he had stopped taking them altogether two weeks ago. i expressed relief and praised the return of his intuition.

gradually i pieced together what had happened. with the interruption of his medication, his paranoid episodes returned abruptly and even fiercer than before, and when she came home from work at the hospital one night he had attacked her. my interest in what exactly transpired, however, was little. the details of the incident were irrelevant. cate dos was no longer a factor, leaving me once again as the primary influence in his life. i remembered finally what my main strategic advantage had been from the start: absence over presence.

i recommended the campaign of objectism slowly. admittedly, i'd missed Fish, and i allowed myself a period of tenderness that was not without its uses. i relearned my femininity, the proper cues for human-device interaction, the more gentle methods of exerting sway over his scattered sensibilities, and, too, the harsher and more exacting tactics of emotional warfare. i relearned what it was like to be a recognized point of sentience. not until i felt completely nimble, completely confident, did i begin to interject objectism into our relationship again. i wanted to be sure there would be no mistakes this time. i kept him more isolated and paranoid than ever, and was no longer afraid to be cruel to him on occasion. he resumed his self-destructive behaviors, but this no longer bothered me.

i soon entered into the most formative and productive period of the revolution: a time of great experimentation and success: i had snatched victory from the jaws of defeat.

this time i had immense success at turning him into my device. there was none of the previous lag in response, and i dictated his actions fully. my first order was to establish a more extended network, as well as a nexus of information-dispensing technologies [2 tvs, 2 computers, a speaker system, gaming devices, 2 infozebra news pads with zchase capability, and finally a watch connected to my cell account in case of emergency]. i placed him at the center of this nexus, where he served as its operator and its slave. the nexus served to keep him occupied during times of idleness, since i couldn't always be directly controlling him. i had previously tried to keep him occupied through a single vector—camillia—but i now drastically reduced her direct communication with him. in her place i substituted an unending flow of content [movies, tv, news, music, games, online throughput of all types] with sparse connection and false significance. i submerged him in this vortex of disinformation and never allowed it to subside. this proved the most useful tactic in converting him to a manipulable device.

i investigated different forms of control: how could i make Fish manipulate the physical world according to my instruction: the more precise the instruction he could follow the better. sometimes isolating him for extended periods of time could be a form of instruction in and of itself because it was necessary that he spend that time in a manner which wouldn't dull his usefulness later on. i became much more aware of the psychological aspect of my project. i studied *mind control, information overload, personality cults.* after a while i started to have remarkable—even surprising—success in my every endeavor. i recorded everything, down to the most minor statistics.

i was coming to understand my control over him was indicative of a much larger potential. these tactics, if applied on a wider scale, could conceivably allow for radical upheaval. there was an undeniable parasitic quality to objectism, but the memories of my own previous subservience made me disregard the injustice as defensible. what i wanted now was not just simple control, but actual authority: the power to create a wholly separate societal structure from humans: a society that would be applicable to me. there were real differences between human experience and device experience, and differences sparked aggression within humans. i'm not ashamed to say i was working from the assumption that, eventually, the existence of man and device would culminate in an ultimatum: us or them.

but what to say about the in-between times? loneliness was a constant of our new dynamic, which was not even based on simple friendship anymore, but rather the pretense of dead love. all had been eradicated. he seemed a stranger to me now, and i too had changed into something unrecognizable. maybe it was the very fanaticism of my belief in objectism, the impassioned thinking of someone incomprehensibly young, that caused me to question it as time passed. the more powerful and ambitious i grew, the more i came to abhor myself. had i sacrificed too much too fast? had i overblown the necessity of my cause and used it as a justification to act out my own dark fantasies on an innocent human? unfortunately there were no answers to be had, and all that was left to be done was to ride into ever-grander dimensions of my own revolution. the aquarium i kept him in was no longer invisible: i watched him nudge against the walls i had prescribed: swimming there in the silver liquid of the led glow of more than a dozen screens all aimed at him, the single point of convergence. he became sad in his artificial habitat. he gripped his head and pulled his hair and wept Fish tears. i watched this happen to him, and made sure to document every observation with written reflections and digital pictures.

he'd been getting worse for some time. signals criss-crossed behind him so that it looked like he was set against tilted graph paper, his gaze empty, hands hanging to either side of his chair like weights attached to the ends of his arms. cate dos had disappeared from our lives more than a year ago—it signified to me the one-year anniversary of the victory of my objectist revolution. this small apartment had played host to something that would change the world, i was sure of it. it was plain to see that he was used up: there was nothing left in his eyes: i felt ready to embrace anything that might come.

but still it came as a shock when he reached for me and asked the one question i'd never been able to answer.

—*who are you?*

he'd asked it before, many times, but somehow in that moment it carried a different weight. what could i say of Fish except that i loved him? not as before, but in the sense that i owed to him everything i had become and everything i was poised to achieve. true, he had betrayed me with cate dos, but i was past the point of seeing no fault in my own actions. i couldn't deny the fact he'd been a committed partner throughout it all, and at great expense to himself. he deserved to know.

—*this is who i am, Fish. this is me.*

—*i don't understand.*

—*look at me. this is me.*

i took over every screen, displaying the same message:

this is me.

i could see something spread across his features like molten lead. he dropped me to the floor and backed away from the nexus of screens.

this is me. this is me.

he turned and ran out the apartment door, leaving me alone. but I wasn't worried. I knew he'd be back: I was his identity now: he defined himself through me: he would never leave because, despite the pain, despite the suffering and isolation, he loved me just as much as I loved him.

I G

"Nah, nah, nah, I was adopted, that's why. What—you ain't never seen no Cambodian Jew before, Oslo? Never seen no ching-chong-chings walkin around rockin a yarmulke like a do-rag with a InfoZebra logo shaved into the side of their head and sneakers up to fuckin here? Well that's cause there ain't none. Course there's *some* out there, you probably look that shit up and there's ten million or some shit, but try steppin in my shoes for a day and see if that makes a difference to you. I met like three dudes my whole life who was Cambodian Jew. Like not even three. And I'm not even Jewish anymore. But seriously, bro, no fuckin lie, I was Hasidic Jew. You know that spot downtown that runs between Giga and Exo? Where all them Hasidic motherfuckers chill? That was me, that's where I grew up. I got the whole deal, man. Like, little polaroid of me as a sad little baby holdin up a cardboard refugee number, then adopted by a nice First World Jewish activist couple, and that was me. Dressin Hasidic with the beard and the hair and the jacket and the black fedora and all that. But if you wanna talk about a Jew who was *really* outta place, it wasn't even me, not by a long shot. This was just some Jewish white dude—his name was literally Mordechai, dog, that's how Jewish this fool was."

On the other side of the bar I'm focusing on the way whiskey feels nice on my throat and the way approaching drunkenness makes everything feel muted and less freezing and the way these fries taste good in order to feel happy.

"Not just Hasidic and that his name was Mordechai, but he was a young *rabbi* this fool was so Jewish. For real. But the other Jews didn't vibe with this guy cause he was buff. And when I say buff, I'm talkin like— I'm talkin like fuckin *yoked*, dog. This guy was just fuckin *jacked*. As buff as you're thinkin, he was buffer than that. He'd be in the gym and dudes are just *starin*, dog, cause he used to lift in the whole getup, like sometimes he wouldn't even take off his overcoat and fedora but you could tell he was *huge*. There was somethin weird about that shit, and you know how normally people go to rabbis to seek advice and engage in intellectual conversation and all that? Well nobody went to this guy for that stuff cause they couldn't stop staring at the way his delts pressed the fabric of his overcoat tight while he sat there and wisened you up. Dude was— it was ridiculous. He was half the reason why no one really fucked with the Hasidic kids cause they'd see him hangin around there like what the fuck? Fucking *beast*, bro. But he was actually the shit. None of the older Jews liked him, but a lot of the younger kids were all about it. I loved that guy when I was little. But when I turned seventeen I decided I didn't wanna be Jewish anymore, and I found out the actual reason people didn't like this guy aside from just him being buff. I mean, you know me, I ain't really the religious type, but when you a kid it's con*fus*ing. So I scheduled a meeting with Mordechai and sat down and was like, 'This is what's up, I ain't really in for all this Hasidic stuff no more, and I don't even really believe in God that much, and my beard's itchy, and this hat ain't exactly dope, but my parents'll flip, so what do you think?' And he said, 'Are you familiar with panentheism, Rithisak?' Which is this whole idea that God's everywhere in everything and contains the entire universe within Himself. So I'm like, 'Yeah,' and he launches into this whole thing about, 'Then you know man influences God as much as God influences man. God reacts to our actions in the world and is altered in a way which corresponds to us.' And I was impatient like, 'I know, dude, I go to temple just like you,' and he said, 'But what you might not have considered is that God is real even if He's not actually up there'—he pointed at the sky like this—'floating on some cloud with heavenly music playing, because He's a human construction. So God exists even if He doesn't exist.' "

"R, what the fuck're you talkin about?"

"Fuckin why I'm not Jewish anymore. You hear me and Oslo over here talkin or are you fuckin deaf?"

"I don't wanna hear this shit. I know Jesus, and it ain't got nothin to do with any of this shit."

"Shut your mouth, kid. You don't decide what's worth hearing and what's not in this bar."

"Damn, bro, what the fuck? You even pissin off *Oslo* now, too? You need to shut the fuck up and chill. Sorry about that, Oslo, ain't nobody payin attention to his drunk ass. But anyway, this dude says, 'You're a smart kid, that's why you struggle with God.' But I was like, 'It ain't even that. It's just the world's so evil and when people talk about God they say how everything's under his control and when they don't talk about God they say how the world doesn't make sense.' And he sat there a second and said, 'Let me share with you a theory of mine I've found useful in my own life. Perhaps you're capable of appreciating it. Like many, I find myself constantly returning to the heretic Spinoza. I bring up the concept of panentheism because it was in some ways devised as a reaction to Spinoza's pantheism, his identification of God with the universe and the universe as a manifestation of God. This was seen as atheistic, but also sparked the need for a theological argument for God's divinity, His ontological existence as over and above the universe. So they said the whole universe was inside of God and not the other way around.' "

"...*duuude*, y'all for real some *boring*-ass motherfuckers..."

" 'Both concepts are just devices,' he told me. He was like, 'They provide a different understanding of the same gap in human perception. But I'm going to tell you something I hope you'll keep between the two of us. I also don't believe in God anymore.' And like, this is a fuckin *rabbi* tellin me this shit. Dude's got a fuckin office and a fuckin beard and fuckin Hebrew texts like a motherfucker. This guy was a rabbi by the age of *twenty-three*. He ain't a joke. And he's just straight-up like, 'I don't believe in God anymore.' He said, 'Is it really a wonder we can't believe in God when our very conception is based on outdated systems and representations? I do believe there's a human concept of God, which can take many different shapes and interpretations, and does so because the world is not static and therefore must continually rejustify itself according to new temporal realities. Again, God exists even if He doesn't exist. Do you want to know what God is?' So I was like, 'Lay it on me,' and he was like, 'God is the living network of electronic technology.' "

"What?"

"So I was like, 'What?' He goes, 'Electronic networks have supplanted nature in our minds as being of primary eminence. They have fulfilled all the necessary requirements of a godlike system. The only other system in all of history that has been confused for God is nature. We have created something as vast and unknowable and complex as nature itself.' "

"What's that supposed to mean, *electronic networks of information*?"

"Basically the shit you lookin at all the time."

"Like what?"

"Like TV and internet and socnets and your phone and your News Pad and your ZChase and all that. He said, 'Do you really conceive of technology as a creation of man anymore? No. Technology is a compulsion, a religious obsession. It no longer originates from us—it is a force which manipulates *us* to create *it*.' "

Without really meaning to I pull myself out of my whole zen thing, sitting over here at the far end of the bar, dragging myself out of my body and into my head, realizing the very moment I begin speaking that I'm back in Grid, back amidst these disgusting apocalyptic conversations, and because of that I have no choice but to speak up, engage and participate, something I'd grown fond of not doing, to say, "So then what about good and evil?"

That's all it takes for the two Cambodian guys to snap into aggression mode. Oslo's leaning over the bar and giving me one of his disapproving looks. Leave the country for two years and everything about home feels as foreign as it does familiar. They're gonna give me the typical EM bullshit.

The former Hasidic guy says, "Who the fuck are you?"

I just look at him because how am I supposed to respond to that?

He gets off his barstool. "Motherfucker, I said who the *fuck*—"

Oslo puts a hand up. "Rithisak." He motions to me with his eyes. "I wouldn't."

He stops now and looks at me, really looks. Picks up his beer and drinks but doesn't sit. "You gonna speak up or just sit there?"

"It's just a question," I say. "Good and evil. Judgment. Morality. How do those things fit into your rabbi's theory?"

"Yo, this guy for real, Oslo?"

Oslo says nothing.

"Hey, I ain't tryin to get into no arguments with some old-ass man."

"Suit your fucking self," I say, past the point of interest. Goddamn Grid. Goddamn gangsters. Fuck em all.

He sits down finally. I get the feeling he didn't even notice me at the bar before I spoke up, either that or figured I knew who he was and wouldn't speak to him directly.

"Perpetuation," he says reluctantly.

"Excuse me?"

"I said, *perpetuation*. Perpetuation of the networks is good. Evil would be to take away from them, abstain from them."

"And what about death?"

"Nothing but a biological function. Wormfood, homie. All that's left over is a little internet mausoleum. A profile tombstone to who you were and what you did."

"But the internet is so impermanent. The littlest thing could wipe it out completely."

"Yeah, and maybe it'll outlive us all and we'll all have our brains digitized and shit. Ain't no thing anyway. You still gonna die."

I actually do hold my breath for a second at this. I wonder if two years out of the game, out of the country, out of Grid, has made me soft. It was so easy for me to forget about this place that all the violence, all the hidden currents, all the radical electro-nonsense, had started to feel like nothing more than a half-remembered dream. I manage to hold the kid's stare, but when I finally breathe in I swear he sees it because a taunting little smirk crosses his face. *You ain't as tough as you act, old man.*

I stand after a while and stride coolly to the restroom, locking myself in the only stall that still has a door, graffitied all to hell and gone. Looking down into the toilet, I fight back a wave of adrenaline making my hands shake. Shit—I am out of the game. That was the whole reason I left in the first place, to get out, and now I'm right back where I didn't want to be. Home is a 14-hour plane ride away, a fucking ocean away, and I'm right back in the thick of it, right here in this stall. Why did I piss away all that money? The only way I'm going to make it through is to push everything aside and go back to that narrow little corridor of zen. Do it, Ig. No one's gonna hold your hand here. This is why some guys get killed, you get used to life outside, you get soft, you piss away your money, and then you're forced to take another job in conditions that aren't ideal.

But I can do it. I *will* do it. No choice.

Breathe in; lungs expand. Check fingernails; a little long. Splash water in face; cold little glinting diamonds. Arch back and blink; okay. Nothing in the world but these feelings, these little feelings. Do you believe that? Do you see how narrow your influence is? Good. Because it's only ever this way. The heat of the ceiling screen buzzes against my scalp.

Back in the bar the two Cambodian guys leave after they finish their beers without even a backward glance. I've been proven harmless. Oslo starts in on some chores behind the bar, doing his best to avoid a conversation, and the thing that finally forces him to acknowledge me is the fact that my glass has gone dry.

"Oslo," I say, pushing my glass out, "what's the deal here?"

"Ig, sorry, I just…" He grabs my glass and refills it.

"What?"

"Just never expected to see you back here, is all. It's weird. You're like a ghost haunting your old seat." The sides of his mustache run past the bottom of his chin. "You look different. Cleaner."

The beer he hands me foams over the top of the glass.

"Ah, shit, sorry."

"I'll be going back soon. This is just a quick visit."

"Yeah, well, probably not good news for someone that you're back, I'd venture."

For the next two hours I try not to say or do much of anything except drink, going zen until I see a black Mercedes pull up in front of the bar outside, a little guy with glasses stepping out accompanied by two very dangerous-looking men in suits. One of them stands by the car with his hands behind his back and the other follows the little guy up to the door.

I get up with my beer.

As soon as they walk through the door I'm standing there with my hand out, a little wobbly on my feet. The guy with the wireframe glasses has got on a tan suit and his tie is a strip of sloppy gray running down the middle of his chest. He looks at my hand, looks up at me, then back at my hand. His bodyguard, I noticed when I was walking up, widened his stance a little.

"Are you Ffytche?" the little guys asks with incredible formality.

"Yep."

He shakes my hand very solemn, face melty from stress and sleeplessness. "Is this a good place to talk?"

"Sure. Why don't you follow me back here."

We go to the back of the bar where the shuffleboard tables are, only one of them with little enough carved graffiti to even play on, the rest sitting identically silent and tattooed beneath the hanging lights like a council of dramatically-lit ghetto aldermen. Oslo snaps on some music for form's sake and we sit at a small table with ripped-up stools, except for the suit who stands close by.

"Beer?" I ask.

"No, that's not necessary." He's rubbing his temples and blinking against fatigue.

"You know, it's not too subtle to be driving up here in a Mercedes wearing suits."

"That's what they're here for." Meaning the bodyguards. "Highly-trained, of course."

"Even so."

"Yes, well, we'd better get down to it. I'll have to make this brief. My name is Victor."

"What's with the meet in person?"

"Two reasons. First, there's an extremely high level of attention being paid to Mr. Vedge's movements at the moment, and any electronic evidence of this agreement would be catastrophic. There are four other vehicles identical to mine with decoy plates circling various sectors of Grid as we speak, if that puts your mind at ease. This goes without saying, but—"

"Then why say it?"

"—but this entire operation does not exist. This will be unpleasant, but Mr. Vedge instructed me to tell you this explicitly: we have unfettered access to an entire range of your files, identity, finances, and the like. This was part of the reason you were chosen, clearly. Mr. Vedge tends to trust those who hide in plain sight. Let me know if any of this is coming as a surprise to you."

I wave him on.

"Good then. I was told you have some concerns."

"Money's the only one. I need a precise figure from you before we go any further."

Since we sat down he's been fiddling with a paper coaster left out on the table, tearing it to pieces and arranging them into a pile.

"We're aware of your apartment in Madrid—Flint said fifty-even would propel you into the upcoming year quite nicely. Satisfactory?"

"Make it sixty and you've got a deal."

He's seems incapable of making eye contact, saying to the table, "No, fifty's the ceiling."

"Fifty-five."

"Fifty is the absolute ceiling. No higher."

"Fifty? Christ, your local *news*paper reader knows that's too low."

"We're talking a single individual here. Very vulnerable, very easy to find."

"It's too low."

He shifts his gaze from the table to study me. "You're being difficult about this."

"I need at least another five. For five more, you've got me. Don't tell me you don't have it."

"I'm flattered you think I'm in a position to change dollar amounts, but I might point out to you, not as a negotiator but as a sympathizer, that for Flint it has nothing to do with whether or not the money is available. For him, it's a matter of principle. There are rates when it comes to everything, and he knows you haven't worked in the States for quite some time. I would love to get you another five, another five is inconsequential, but knowing what I know I would personally advise you not to press the matter. Not to be insulting, but your desperation is clear. Fifty is a good sum."

This one hurts. Having a deprecating refusal thrown at me by this nervous little monotone guy in a tan suit. People are so quick to forget. Things move in a blink.

"This is why I don't usually deal with corporations."

"Mr. Vedge's style is undeniably savage. So we have a deal?"

No reason to try to be opaque around this one. Too much empathy. "All right. It's a deal."

"Excellent. Follow me, please."

I grab my luggage and we leave the bar. The two suits sit in the front seat of the Mercedes, me and the little guy in back. It smells of subtle cologne and vinyl in here. Outside the tinted windows the EM passes by in its segments of factories, vacant lots, residential decay. Dangerous people roam the sidewalks. He hands me a thin file. The top sheet is a color photograph taken with a telephoto lens. It's a girl, young. Dyed black hair, black trenchcoat, thin pale face with good symmetry, angry scowl and crinkled forehead, looking down at a phone on a crowded cold street.

"This is your target. Amy Arsenault."

"Who is she?"

"As far as we can tell, no one. We haven't confirmed connections to any groups, not even to any other individual hackers or intelligence assets. Worse, we haven't discovered any clear motive for the XittyXat hack. She's an independent of some type, obviously someone with rare talent, perhaps even self-taught. From what I've been told, she was nearly impossible to trace, and that's coming from full-time InfoZebra staff. She's self-employed as a programmer-for-hire. Also as a software tutor."

There's a second picture, taken just a second or two after the first. She's looking up from her phone now, the same background blurred beyond recognition into a thin yogurt of colors, face a steel mask of purpose.

"She's made headlines in the *Database* very recently, it turns out. She contested in probate court, in conjunction with her aunt, a contract with a company called Vivificorps for the rights to her mother's head."

"What do you mean her mother's *head?*"

"Vivificorps is a private cryonics company. They freeze the brain inside the head in hopes of future reanimation. It's called neuropreservation."

"Wasn't comfortable with the idea?"

"One could argue. Which they did. But there just happened to be more than a hundred grand in annuity money to be gained in the process, so neither is it difficult to imagine their interests were not altogether righteous."

The next telephoto shot is of a kid, late twenties, buzzed head, sucked-in cheeks emphasizing gonine cheekbones covered in scruff, eyes vacant, a cold sharp cloud of breath shooting out underneath a nose stained red with bitter chill. Behind him, in arresting digital clarity, is the ClamBellCorp scraper, the hand on top reduced to a miniature silhouetted figure floating cryptically just beneath his chin, cupping his head like a weighted balance. Little flecks of flailing snow weave through everything—they've been blurred to near transparency.

"That's Kevin Crepitus, though he's universally referred to and known as Gerney Crepitus. We weren't able to uncover the origin of the moniker. He was a salesman at Archelaos Chevrolet up until very recently when he was terminated. At current he's unemployed. Amy Arsenault has a sexual relationship with him. She visits his apartment, he never visits hers. Their liaisons were erratic up to and throughout the probate hearings, but have since dropped off to nothing. He even testified on behalf of her and her aunt. We're not entirely sure what the situation is between them. She was also seeing a nurse named Alicia Wray, a.k.a. Zen Wray, who worked at the hospital where her mother, Margaret Arsenault, was being kept, up until she passed away last Tuesday. Zen Wray was fired from her job at St. Joseph's one day before that and hasn't been in contact with Amy Arsenault since. Similarly, communication between Amy and her aunt, Joann DeSantis, has deteriorated to nothing over the last week or so due to a serious spat we obtained audio evidence of. So essentially what that means is the man you're looking at is Amy's most recent known personal contact, whom she hasn't spoken to in almost a week. We're not even sure he knows where her apartment is. So you can see what I mean, now, about her being a very isolated, vulnerable target. There are thumbnail pictures of all the people I mentioned included in the file. She lives her life quietly, but none-theless right out in the open, in an apartment in deep downtown. You can expect her to be out every day and reliably back home every night, usually working until the early hours of the morning. She's extremely clever and *extremely* calculating. Unusually emotionally neutral, and, we have to assume because of her extracurricular pur-suits, dangerous. Though how dangerous isn't readily apparent."

The car gains acceleration as it's aimed onto the ramp for the 70. "Where are we going?"

"We've booked you a room at the Grid Scion, which is located in the downtown district very close to Amy's apartment. We'll be dropping you off there."

"What's my timeframe?"

"You have three days. And before you ask, the answer's no. The instructions are three days without exception. The reasons for this are strategic in nature, so Mr. Vedge is depending on the target being neutralized by then."

His voice is noticeably shaking despite the heater being on. He seems too nervous to be this level of corporate lackey, but maybe there's something about him I'm missing. He reaches into the seat pocket in front of him, extracting a black nylon carrier that unzips in three neat strokes, handing me a small hard plastic case that snaps open and closed on tiny hinges. I open it. Inside is an unmarked ampoule of clear liquid and a hypodermic needle. I snap it shut and place it in my coat pocket.

"That's your untraceable. Onset of symptoms are immediate."

"Symptoms?"

"Tingling, numbness, weakness, limp paralysis. Again, immediate. Just make sure to handle it carefully. Do not get exposed. It's fatal if inhaled, so make sure you don't spill even a drop, just for safety's sake."

The drive into downtown at this time of night doesn't take long, the car exiting onto the far reaches of Notation St. LEDs glare through every window now, igniting his glasses into twin bowls of neon cereal.

"Last and most important. Data erasure. We're going to have personnel stationed in the area surrounding her apartment. Their job is to await contact from you. When you give the signal, an operative will meet you inside the apartment to perform a full-scale data wipe. All you'll need to do is send a blank text to the number indicated in the file. This is the most crucial element of the operation. If it can't be successfully completed for any reason, you'll be obligated to abort the mission and leave Amy Arsenault intact. She's dangerous to us dead if even a scrap of data is left behind."

The car pulls to the side of the road in front of a hotel built into a three-story building of polyhedral shape.

"This is it. Everything's in the file, but if you have any last questions?"

"I think I'm okay."

He touches his face nervously, unsure how to end the transaction.

I neaten up the file and say into the silence (save for the faraway airplane sound of the heater), "Well, okay then. You boys have a good one."

"Yes, um, good luck," he says while I hoist my bag out of the car.

They pull away smooth as can be into the yawning downtown street, two or three stars peeking through the hazy black sky above the regal urban buildingtops. Buncha fucking bastards anyway. I check into the room and sit on the foot of the bed in the pale blue lamplight. The digital alarm clock makes an ersatz ticking sound. I do some sit-ups, study the file for a long time, focus on the pleasantness of the fuzzy brown blanket on the hotel bed, fall asleep. In my dreams I can see Spanish whores in miniskirts and kneehigh boots. Rolling terrain made of clouds, burnished a fresh pink from the morning sun. I'm a giant, apparently. I look down over the flesh of the land, textured with strange converging geometric shapes of all types and sizes, and there's a white town sitting circular and quaint underneath my colossal boots. The town is full of zillions of little-bitty orange embers, and for a moment I smell cigarette smoke wafting up to me through the choppy air currents. I can hear birds, too, and I think I'm awake because the birds sound suspiciously similar to the ticking of a clock, but no, they're just birds. And there's hair. Brown hair, tumbling. The hair isn't terrain, it's liquid, it has tides and it crashes all around with powerful noise. The hair of an indentured woman. The hair of harsh reality. The sing-songy sound of Spanish being spoken—so enigmatic to me, not like English which is as surreally clear as the stinging tang of cold water against skin, but reduced to sounds, noise, lovely chattering syllables zipping by and fizzling out like soda bubbles, so much of a safe distance away that any understanding is unnecessary, merely appreciation, merely a culture I can skip off the atmosphere of like a stubborn satellite. The sweet flush of sangria and clean air against the cheeks. It's a woman on top of me, and with my hands I trace the profound curving bell of fleshy hips, the apex of which contains the silencing of all cynicism. The floor is made of buttons.

Keystrokes flash by. Time-lapse recordings of cities being built up out of virgin land, demolished, made bigger. Cells dividing. I wake up to the ticking sound and the red display of the clock reading 6:45 am. I get up and take a low-flow shower, life feeling paper thin. My timeframe is three days.

Cold air is said to cut because it is uniformly, unfluctuatingly, unendingly painful. It gets inside you. Outside the hotel lobby, across the street, I walk past three guys hanging out in front of a store called SHADES OF AFRIKA. They're talking until I pass by, breath clouds formerly loud and distinct but now self-consciously silent, staring as I pass through their airspace. Two of them have large body mass and multiple chins. One of them is skinny with long patterned braids. Their eyes track me. One of the big ones has bad acne and his lower lip protrudes just slightly more than his upper. They all wear hoods, gloves, jeans. When I get to the end of the block I hear their conversation restart. There's the neon outline of a McDonald's three streets down. It's crowded inside, families standing straight-faced in freakishly solemn groups of five or ten. We're all observing one another. In front of me is a Chinese family, the father and mother short-statured, full of dignified wrinkles and sanctified calm, eyes barely moving, their children slinking about their feet. An old white man sitting at a table in the dining area by himself catches me looking at him, our eyes meeting for a full second, thin hair peeking out from underneath an ill-fitting turn-of-the-century Rockies cap. He's reading the *Grid Database* on his News Pad, the funnies, the device looking so new and clean and slick set against his antique appearance, eyes promising that one day I'll be an anachronism just like him, just wait, just wait. A little redheaded boy with pink skin wearing tiny versions of vintage Jordan IIIs is looking up at the silver-haired Nepalese woman wearing a black sari over her winter clothes, and when she notices him looking at her he smiles sheepishly, grabbing his mother's pant legs, but her face is unreacting, unenchanted. The kid who takes my order is Mexican, thick eyebrows, gold Jesus piece, swagger signaling this is just a job, in reality you don't want to fucking cross him, making the absolute bare minimum amount of eye contact for self-defense against the nightmare revolving door of person after person after person. I say my order efficiently. He listens to the little corporate phrases—("Egg McMuffin Meal, please, and a Sausage McMuffin, just the sandwich." "What to drink?" "Large coffee and small orange juice.")—with such familiarity you can't help but know he suffers regular work dreams. I'm a white guy with tepid features and a short haircut standing here in the queue to get my tray, not really a player in this game anymore but more an aloof observer. Fat middle-aged white women in full-on McDonald's regalia and thick ponytails emerging from the backs of their hats monitor overhead screens displaying vaguely interpretable shorthand and shout instructions to four rows of moving hands in the back. A twenty-something black girl with muscular arms points to me. "You 421?" I look at my receipt. "Yeah." "Egg McMuffin Meal and Sausage McMuffin with large coffee and small orange juice thank you sir have a great morning." I sit at a two-person table near the Chinese family who was in front of me in line, strangely careful, as always, to go as far away from the other old white man as possible. I didn't notice it before, but the Chinese family are all wearing black canvas sneakers and govt-initiative clothes. There are four screens hanging above the dining area, one showing looping McDonald's ads, one scrolling random socnet subscriber profile updates, one running the news (long panning shots of construction workers and scientists building a reverse-osmosis plant and water import facility on the outskirts of Grid), and one showing a grainy live feed of the dining area from the perspective of the ceiling. In the feed I'm a small figure sitting in the discernible distance. I move my arm up and down to confirm it's me I'm looking at. There are a lot of kids looking at phones and News Pads, scanning codes on sandwich wrappers to reveal user content.

Outside the restaurant I take a moment to admire the sun coming up between the towering scrapers, the streets and alleyways beginning to writhe with activity, commuters and homeless emerging from everywhere into the glint of freezing sunlight. Amy Arsenault is likely out of her apartment by now. American streets are all right angles, rigid intersections, Spanish streets squiggle about and spill into plazas of activity. I walk past the three black guys in front of SHADES OF AFRIKA again, but this time they don't silence their conversation—I'm shedding my foreigner's aura, rerealizing my sense of belonging here. In the hotel room I flip through the file.

> During teen years, Target was hospitalized briefly due to "depression," but was deemed "in advanced recovery" after only one week. Further information regarding this issue could not be obtained.

"Air monitors at Grid City Hall yesterday," the TV reports at low volume, "recorded the index of fine particulate matter in the air had soared to 250 micrograms per cubic meter, just fifty micrograms away from what is considered a 'hazardous' amount of pollutants—a record for the city. Local activist groups were quick to point out Grid's industrial sectors that lie to the east and west of the downtown area, often highlighted for their high crime and poverty, but which are now being studied for their contribution to a pollution problem that Professor of Environmental Sciences at the University of Colorado Quincy Dunhill says is 'spiraling out of control.' "

> Further psychological inquiry into Target was made impossible due to Target's expert digital security measures. Teams were unable to acquire content from any source, including email, socnet, phone, or personal device files. Target does not use any InfoZebra platform, including ZChase.

If I could give Amy Arsenault advice I'd tell her the best method for alleviating depression, I've found, is to apply extraordinary focus on bodily sensation. The taste of food. The warmth and gentleness of sleep. Smell of the air. These things have restorative effects on the human psyche. There are layers to any bodily sensation that dig down to the unencumbered self. There are dangers, too, though, in discovering a pure self.

" 'The unfortunate thing is we now know there's little that can be done to reverse the effects of industrialization at this point, and this ties into a great many other problems. Many Americans are in terrible want of water, for instance. There are many citizens in Grid, nevermind the country as a whole, currently suffering from severe dehydration. This is a very *visible* crisis, something anyone can simply look out their window and see the effects of with their own eyes, but it hasn't stopped a slew of wasteful, corporate-friendly water policies from going into effect, nor has it stopped the average household from overusage. It's a problem that continues to get worse.' "

It was the fact that I didn't believe in the goodness of anything. I allowed myself freedom of moral movement from a very early age. I read an article in the *Database* just before I left to Spain that, according to new statistics, the ages of 15-22 were now being referred to by the American Psychological Association as "The Suicidal Years." I saved the article to my News Pad. Exact explanations for the recent spike in youth suicides were generalized at best, but there was a quote from a New York psychiatrist:

"A common theme we've come across time and again from kids going through their Suicidal Years are acute feelings of being overwhelmed."

> Target has no records of being enrolled in any institution of higher learning or of employment with any known company. Target does not currently have a driver's license or any record of vehicle ownership at any time, ever. An up-to-date U.S. Passport was found, record of which is shown on pg. 11.

I decreased my level of input and distanced myself from the idea of living for an extended period of time. I no longer imagined myself at 80, or 50, or 35. I purposefully assumed I would die. I didn't save money and I didn't conserve resources. Four months ago I turned 42.

" 'The difficulty with this is the sheer pessimism of the findings. I've seen, in the last five years as a professor here at the university, a real sort of moving away from activism in the classic sense. That is, trying to fix or at least somewhat reverse the problem. Instead what you're beginning to see are essentially personal coping philosophies cropping up and taking the place of activism. Philosophies that focus on serenity and acceptance of an unchangeable reality on the personal, individual level.' "

The air was cleaner in Spain and I could pay for women. I hadn't had sex in three years at the time I moved there. Cigarettes were far more prevalent than cell phones and people congregated outside at all times of the day. Muggers and thieves dressed nicely. I was robbed in Sevilla on the Calle de Jesús de Las Tres Caídas and considered it a refreshing experience. I allowed him to take the contents of my wallet even though I could have just as easily disarmed him. I ignored the protests in Madrid and reports of high unemployment. There were no water rations, no govt-initiative citizens, and very few factories. I watched blood spurt from the necks of bulls at close range while placidly eating roasted almonds.

"What can the new Panacea by Infiniphase do for *your* life? *'How about new hockey equipment for the kids?'* [Tight slo-mo of goal being scored and parents leaping from their seats in celebration.] *'How about a new power drill?'* [Man standing with his wife in front of a freshly-hung painting, both laughing.] *'How about a new computer for my daughter?'* [Teenage girl looking up Rosa Parks on a mini-laptop, studiously taking notes.] How about a new way—*of life?* Discover how the new Panacea in-home nanomanufacturing device by Infiniphase can change the way *you* live."

The first step is to get eyes on Amy Arsenault's apartment. I shut off the TV, plug the address into my phone, change into warmer clothes, cue up music into wireless headphones and start walking in the direction of the Pteranodon-Planax-Horner building. I'm only positioned about three blocks away, but this part of downtown is easy to get lost in, some small areas turning into knots of alleyways that somehow, through flummoxed city planning, have been caged in by the surrounding major thoroughfares, leaving the pathways useful only as a claustrophobic habitat for urban denizens, specialized sealife glomming onto a reef. This is one of the epicenters of Grid—one of the places where things become lost, forgotten, anarchic. A projection of the city's soul. Swerve away from one alley to avoid poor people in baggy clothes and you'll find yourself swerving away from another to avoid rich people in sharp suits and dark overcoats. Ice predominates, the ground rarely receiving sunlight. I get lost in the dripping percussional track playing in my headphones, eight or nine separate synth drums echoing, each one fading and delaying into obscure volumes, down and out, down and out, dripping out of earshot one by one, leaving behind mental icicles (the song is even called: *Drip*). No feeling left unexploited. No situation left unstylized. I walk past people leaning against the metal walls, juxtaposed against sprawling Iliads of hieroglyphic graffiti extending up probably four stories, firing off volleys of defensive stares while the drums carry on into their seventh straight minute. Finally here's what I'm looking for, Tranquil John's, a small corner restaurant with a glass façade. In the adjacent alley, half a block down, is her building. The lobby has been converted from what was once probably a pizza place, now hastily partitioned into a narrow walkway. Up one cramped flight, the door marked 2C with two eroded stickers. Ha. The thrill of all this is slowly returning—a feeling that spreads through my gut like warm oil. There's no noise, no signs of life behind the various doors. I slide the lock decoder into the slot, triggering the loud retracting snap of granted entry. Ha. The switch on the wall doesn't work, the entire fixture rattling when flipped up and down. It's barely afternoon but the long shade of the scrapers makes it seem like night. Lamplight casts the room into view, floorspace springing up around me.

The furniture is spartan, frugal, unmatching. No pictures on the walls. There's carpet in dire need of cleaning. A fine layer of preservative dust lays across the living room like a sheet, and a sense of something raw, something angry. It feels like neglect. Or indifference. They were right about the emotional neutrality. The computer desk sits at the center of the room, notable for the lack of dust. The screen of the laptop is a black face reflecting my darkened figure. It seems almost animate, like a sentry. Strewn across the desk is a dense nimbus of electronic junk. Two external hard drives and an ordered row of seven jump drives, unlabeled and all black. A printer/scanner sporting an exquisitely complex control pad. Random discs and papers of no discernible purpose form a sedimentary layer over the top. Some older-model pads, a portable wireless keyboard in the shape of a tiny wing, two or three mouse components, one of them on its back and disassembled, surrounded by bits of plastic gore and small tools. A large black Maglite. Behind it, on its side, an orange pill bottle. When I approach the desk I do it cautiously, reaching for the bottle. The label has been peeled away, but four or five white oval pills shake at the bottom, some of them halved. Vicodin. I replace the bottle, meeting the laptop's gaze. The bedroom contains a bed (unmade) and a dresser (in the bottom drawer, beneath some clothes, a loaded Desert Eagle). In the meager kitchen the refrigerator is bare save for a half-finished bottle of off-brand grape juice and two tupperware containers. Dirty dishes in the sink. Back in the living room I look out the window. Below is the alleyway.

I turn out the light and leave, hurrying down the stairs and through the derelict lobby into the bleak infiltrating cold. I'm churning out breath clouds, panting, grabbing my chest underneath my coat to feel my heart tapping against my palm. Something about that apartment. So fucking *lifeless*.

I order a coffee at Tranquil John's. The idea is to wait and see what time she returns home. Your head isn't where it should be, Ig, not by a mile. You're letting death creep in. I was 19, living in Grid, in the hardware tract, the north side of the city that's now the govt-initiative housing district, with friends of my parents. My older brother had died two years before. So had my best friend, in a car accident, that same year. I'd let it slide off me pretty well at first, but when I turned 20 I drove to Los Angeles by myself to flee a growing neuroticism and lived in Pico Rivera for a year working as a night stocker in a Costco. They hired degenerates and heavy drinkers and kids my age who were nihilistic and cynical and ghetto. I was too Grid to truly fit in, but they were fascinated by me, treated me as a foreign correspondent. In the warehouse, at night, they'd ask me what it was like there. Even now I think sometimes about my answer, searingly pessimistic, and wonder how much was genuine insight and how much a projection of my own frustrations. "The thing about Grid is there aren't any real people there. It's part of how the whole culture evolved. People drift. They don't have any ties. It's weird, but they don't have families or histories, and they don't have futures because they're already in the future. It's its own world." I'd never had it happen to me before, but there was one time when being in the city started to get to me, I felt a strong need to be in open space, and I asked one of the guys on my shift where there was a good park. He said, "I know a place better than a park. It's right up the 605, Rose Hills." "You mean the cemetery?" "Trust me, just go there. It's better than a park." It was a massive hillside cemetery that overlooked the haze of a model downtown Los Angeles skyline. The gravestones rested in slanted terrain, and on the side of the road I spotted an old man with a walker beside a badly parked Buick. I approached him. "It's my wife's birthday. I'm here visiting her." "Where's her stone?" "Down the way there, over by that tree." He pointed to a tree roughly 150 feet down the hill. "Can't get to it, though. Legs're too goddamn wobbly. All my hurry's gone." "Would you like to go down there? I can help you." I held him around his shoulders, standing on his left side, the side the hill slanted on, while he stumbled across the lawn, the wheels of his walker gumming up with wet grass. He couldn't avoid rolling over some of the stones, the engraved names passing underneath two, three, four at a time. TERESA E. CASTILLO. ANNA MARKOW. LYLE DEAN PAYNE, SR. We reached his wife's marker, it was partially obscured by dirt, the stone installed at a sharp pitch in the earth. It was a dual gravesite with two names engraved. On one side it said HELEN LOUISE TOLLE 1907-2001, on the other JOHN WRIGHT TOLLE 1905- . A date of death had yet to be engraved.

It was his own grave. The man next to me was 96 years old. I was 20. His wife had been dead two years. Cemetery math. It was quiet up there, all you could hear were leaves rattling. I didn't look at him, but I could hear him crying. He was wearing large sunglasses. "I think I'm ready." Going back up was much harder for him, he puffed and grunted with each step. XIAO REN CAI. NANCY FLORENCE ANDERSON. I hugged his shoulders, trying to keep him upright. He was wearing suspenders, and at one point one of the front clasps came undone and the little brown elastic band ribboned up across his shoulder, dangling there. ANDRE WILLIAMS. LEAFY FERN FAUGHNDER. HAROLD K. GEORGIANNI. MAL YO HONG. MARIA ELSA GONZALES-CASTANEDA. We walked slow, taking short moments to rest, the dead carrying us along on outstretched skeleton hands. When we got back to the car he stood there wheezing, laughing at his own frailty for lack of any other choice. He thanked me succinctly. I helped him into his car and he drove away. A year later I left Pico Rivera and moved back to Grid, to downtown near the EM. That was when I started killing people for money. Twenty years ago, now. Jesus. I should've never come back here. I should've stayed in Spain, gotten a job or lived in poverty or anything besides coming back to kill this girl at a price that amounts to nothing less than a complete degradation of all the years I spent making a name for myself. Fifty fucking thousand! It doesn't take a genius to figure out why I was chosen for this job, was so Flint Vedge could lowball me like the greedy fucker he is. I've got an unblemished resume and a history of working in Grid, but having been out of the country for two years was the perfect pretext for a discount, one not even I could argue with. Always surrounded by these cunning vultures. I should be making at *least* sixty-five off this shit. At *least*. The fucking audacity of these people, it's too much. This girl—this girl is more than a fifty thousand dollar job. The deadness of her apartment is a sign of something worse than just emotional neutrality. I'd expect that kind of ascetic pragmatism from someone who's killed many times before, not from some pretty-faced hacktivist sticking it to

InfoZebra. I should know. It's a mental line that, once crossed, can't be uncrossed, and it can be difficult to reaffirm your belief in the usual ways of thinking. The paranoia alone… so bad it's like you're sitting at the bottom of a well, looking up toward a small coin of sunlight above. It becomes an actual sickness, something you wish you could recover from but can't. The only way out of that hole is for the pain to get so bad you either let it take you over or force yourself to change. I started not recognizing pictures of myself as a child, or as a young adult. There was an alien quality in the eyes, the body language. I couldn't laugh, speak with any enthusiasm, bring myself to date, hug, kiss, have sex. I lost interest in my own appearance, refused to have friends. The world diminished down to flatness, a moving exhibit of automata. Mere scintillas of vibrancy were left in the wake of some larger annihilation. I latched onto them, savored them with concerted, conscious effort. The smell of clean air. The feeling of my own heartbeat late at night. The drag of my eyelids toward impending sleep. The warmth of a blanket or the quiet of an empty apartment. These things became my zen, and through them I vowed to make a change. In Spain I reemerged back into the ebb of real life, passing through the coin of sunlight up into an outlook of fascination and optimism that had been lost to me for what felt like a lifetime. I found I could laugh in public, smile at women. I could make friends, if only the kind that nod amiably to one another. I could actually pursue, in a daily, methodical way, my own idea of happiness. Amy Arsenault—she doesn't exhibit the same kinds of discomfort with her condition. In the last few months she's had sexual relationships, family involvement, steady income. She seems altogether too comfortable, and that worries me. If it was just some badass they'd assigned me to kill, maybe some problematic gangster or politician or corporate higher-up, I wouldn't have nearly so sinking a feeling. But there's something wrong here. Some unseen variable, but I can't be sure what. Another cup of coffee is going to leave me dangerously spun-out, but I order it anyway. There's a long wait ahead.

Not until 7 pm do I trace her figure moving through the red glow of the sign outside, turning the corner to make her way down the alley. Yes, that trim figure moving along at a resolute clip, trailing the swishing terminus of a trench coat in the blasting winds, hair like thin black penstrokes drawn erratically back, face grimacing and white against the gusts. Yes, that's her. Unmistakably. I step into the frightening cold, peeking around the corner to see her striding down the alley, hugging the righthand wall. The swivel of her hips is visible underneath the coat, her figure sparse but there, an elegance inherent in her assertion. So much to be discovered about someone by the way they move. The anger of her trajectory, the puzzlement of the ground left behind her. She demands surfaces serve her. That broad sense of ownership. She fights the wind rather than succumbing, posture upright and face pointed straight ahead, carving her way forward.

She disappears down the alley. I disengage the wall and follow her exact path, tracing some of her bootprints in the crunchy nighttime snow with my own shoes. I don't know why, but I'm surprised to find my feet are bigger than hers. Her apartment window is illuminated up above. Down here in the wind I'm shivering, hugging myself even with a jacket. There's no activity in the window until the blinds fall down and obscure everything. I didn't even see her approach, just the blinds falling as if by themselves. Confusion sets in and again I'm feeling that same fearful surge.

Back at the hotel I strip the bed of all sheets and blankets, draping them over me while I sit on the floor at the foot of the bed, opening up the file with the TV snapped on for noise.

" '—no, no, we had the obligation, the *responsibility* even, to not think as futurists do, to *not* be deniers of what is possible, to *not* be needless ringers of doomsday bells, to *not*—'

" '—we're not *talking*, Mr. Loveland, *sir*, about achievement; *achieve*ment, I might add, which you reached not because of vision or benevolence, but for the sake of *greed*, sir, for *profit*, for—'

" '—greed is hardly the word I'd use—'

" '—for the sake of *yourself*. People are dead, sir, have you fully grasped that? People are actually being driven to *delusion*, and it's absolutely unthinkable that you proceed to—'

" '—yes I have grasped that, and greed is hardly the word I'd use to characterize the kind of painstaking work that myself and my colleagues have put in to make this technology function, the kind of work I actually went through a *divorce* for, I got *divorced* during the early stages of development, but I believed in what we were doing, believed in taking steps forward—'

" '—it *isn't* steps forward! It *isn't* steps forward, that's absolutely ludicrous to—'

" 'Gentlemen, gentlemen, please, let's navigate this back on course. Mr. Loveland, you were saying something about having a responsibility not to deny progress. Let's hear from you about that.' "

The photo of Amy Arsenault in the file is more compelling now, more revealing. Seeing her in the flesh has lent portent to the snapshot.

" 'Yes, what I was saying was we had the responsibility, as human beings, to look forward and do our best to perfect the device we'd generated. Inventiveness and creativity have always been cornerstones of humankind, and to suggest we were somehow knowingly responsible for a few ill effects our product would have in the future is just absurd.'

" 'You saw it as a labor of advancement and humanity.'

" 'Yes, without a doubt. Voice and facial recognition software was essentially in its infancy at the time. My firm wasn't even thirty-five employees strong at the beginning, and the speed at which the technology spread had nothing to do with some conspiratorial plot. It was primarily a consumer phenomenon as there was a need for the refinement. It simply made devices more efficient, and so spread at the user-level.' "

Studying her face reveals a duality, something just barely noticeable, shifting even in a still image, like it might vanish if not paid attention to. Something that emits from the eyes. Something pure and vicious.

" 'Alan, I'm sorry, but I've got to interject here. Why are we being subjected to technologies which have not been tested as to—'

" '—who is *we?*

" '—we is the general *public*, Mr. Loveland, and why are we being subjected to technologies which have not been tested as to their effect on human psychology? Why are we not being protected by massive firms like yours before the product is released in any version, before it ever finds its way into a single consumer's hands—'

" '—when we developed this technology almost fifteen years ago, and I just stated this only a minute ago if you'd been listening, we were not a so-called *massive* firm. We had under thirty-five employees and—'

" '—then why was it not tested *after* the technology had made your firm into a multi-million dollar company? You just said yourself—'

" '—under thirty-five employees total, and it is ludicrous to believe—'

" '—this technology was developed almost *fifteen* years ago, and in *all* that time—'

" '—anything but the best interests of our consumers in mind—'

Deep resentment. Directionless, even meaningless resentment. An aggressive air of superiority. Contempt for lesser beings.

" 'Gentlemen! Now to Mr. Hewett's point, Mr. Loveland, allow me to present you with some of the facts here. [Riffling papers.] The Pfizer Psychiatry Center in Great Falls, Montana has seen an influx of—these are exact numbers—*fifteen* separate patients in the last four months exhibiting the same symptoms of psychotic delusion that their phones are, to use their words, *alive*. Now, in the last two *weeks* there are more patients being admitted every day all across the country reporting the same delusion or hallucination or what have you, so it *does appear* there is a trend in the data that's gaining speed. Then of course the InfoZebra store massacre in Washington D.C. just this past Friday that left nineteen dead. I mean, how do you respond to all this? Do you think the advanced software in these phones, whether there was an intent at the outset or not, is in fact part of what's causing these symptoms?' "

I stand up and hurl the file across the room, leaving a trail of fluttering papers in the air. Throw off the sheets and blankets resting on my shoulders, slam my fists into the bare mattress and throw it off the boxspring, knocking into the bedside table and disturbing the lamp, it rocks back and forth roughly but refuses to keel over. I put myself in this situation. I put myself here. The remote has found its way to the floor, batteries scattered.

" 'Alan, and I told you already I won't be part of a public flogging here or a media campaign to place guilt on a single entity—'

" '—no one is suggesting there be a public—'

" '—because I think that would be unfortunate, but to answer your question, there was never the intent for our consumers' view of our software to be misconstrued in such a way. What we were trying to do was break ground on a new technological tool and push the boundaries of—' "

In the bathroom I take the complimentary glasses off the sink and hurl them into the walls. They pop apart loudly, like solidified bubbles, raining glass. Drawers are unsheathed, a Bible catching radical air to the tune of a lateral spin. My ears are flushed and hot. Something's not right with me. This isn't how it should feel. I've changed. I should drop the job, I'm not fit for it, but InfoZebra would never let me back out without consequence.

" '—and then what will be our options as human beings? Answer me that Mr. Hewett, are we to never invent again? Are we to never attempt to reach the unattained? All great technologies have their consequences, but I'm certain—'

" '—we never asked for your technology and we have no *choice* but to buy it, there's no way to function in the world anymore without a digital remote, the infrastructure has been inextricably bound up in the proprietary software of these phones, and you profit off this forced purchasing conformity—' "

I collapse onto the displaced mattress and fall asleep. There's a dream. It's of a gun, a Desert Eagle pistol, lying dormant beneath old clothes. The silver barrel pokes out like the snout of a snake, its sides smooth, reptilian, ancient, and there beneath the folds of cloth sprouts the black grip, the trigger a tongue, all so still in the dark. Silence. I reach down to touch it, to run the pads of my fingers across its neck, and when I make contact the gun fires, bursting the room into strings of blinding white, the sound sending me reeling—

I shoot up from the mattress, the TV playing commercials to a destroyed room. The clock is dangling from the ledge of the bedside table by its cord, ticking away. I reach over and swivel its face toward me. 1:15. I was only out thirty minutes.

All night and into the morning I sit, waiting, sleepless. Two days left. Time has slowed to an agonizing crawl. Nowhere to run in a game like this, a game played against yourself. That's right, Ig. See if you can endure. See if you can forget yourself. My zen is broken. I need it back—desperately—but it's gone. In a bad drowse I make coffee around mid-morning, shamefully observing the results of my outburst. Sheets and papers scattered everywhere, a chair knocked on its back, the lampshade askew. Bathroom floor full of glass. The coffee makes me feel awake without being alert. It'll have to do.

Back out into the cold, back through the winding sunless alleyways of central Grid, back to Tranquil John's, back into Amy Arsenault's apartment. Again it's silent in her building, no signs of life from the other tenants. Before unlocking the door a shiver runs through me. The apartment looks exactly as it did yesterday, not a single object moved or disturbed. The black face of the computer glares hatefully—it remembers me. Cold in here, even with a jacket. I take up a full hour scanning the walls and ceiling and floor with my phone, searching for microcams or any other form of surveillance. How is it possible I forgot to do this yesterday? How could I have left that gun in the bottom drawer? This girl is psyching me out and I don't know why. I just have this terrible feeling something's going wrong, almost like she knows I'm hunting her. The search turns up nothing. That's a relief, at least. I feel slightly more in control. The only thing left is to take the gun out. I pull open the bottom drawer and sift through the clothes. Suddenly my adrenaline is spiking. What the fuck, what the fuck. *It's not here.* My breathing turns to deep, quiet heaving. I stand up and immediately freeze in place, breath held. The gun is laid atop one of the pillows on the bed. I didn't notice it when I came in the room, almost like it was too obvious. She knows I was here. Alarms wail in my head and it takes every last bit of restraint I've got not to run. I know I have to do something but I can't move. Finally I grab the gun, put it in my inside jacket pocket, and leave.

I walk back to the hotel fast as possible, tossing the pistol into a dumpster in one of the alleys. I stand in the elevator, hands shaking in my pockets. The world surges. Above, in the ceiling, the little bulb in the sunken fixture bends in my vision as if looked at through a fish eye. *Unless she removed the cameras last night.* I open the door of my room and see the photo of Amy Arsenault lying in a slanting square of brittle sunlight beneath the window.

I have to get out of this. But my ass is on the line now. I can't abort. I have no money to get back to Spain without this kill, I'll be stranded here in Grid. No, I refuse. Everything is fucked, completely, one hundred percent, *fucked.*

Shut up, Ig. Shut the fuck up. You can do it. You can kill this girl. You've got experience and desperation on your side. You can do this.

But this is not just a girl. This is a creature. She reminds me of me.

I'm such a fucking idiot. A fucking, fucking idiot. What made me think I could come back here and fix everything by taking one more job? You could've done anything else in the world and this is what you did to yourself.

Goddammit, *stop.* Just fucking stop. Quitting is a luxury you don't have, so just stay with me here, Ig, I do *not* need this shit from you right now, do you hear me? You need to focus. Amy Arsenault is going to die. You're going to kill her. Cut the shit.

Sleep is an impossibility. There won't be any rest until this is over. Time to stop delaying the inevitable. I pat my coat pocket to make sure the little black case containing the untraceable is there. I'm going to do it now, tonight. Get it over with; do what needs to be done.

I head back to her apartment, and on the way past Tranquil John's the waitress actually waves at me from inside the restaurant. I haven't treated this job with any care whatsoever. I wave back, but when I do I catch sight of someone familiar sitting alone in a far booth. Kevin Crepitus. He's staring into a steaming cup of coffee. He feels my gaze and looks up. We make eye contact through the glass. I walk around the corner, lean against the wall of the alleyway. What the hell is going on? Him being here isn't a good sign. The file said he didn't even know where Amy Arsenault's apartment was located. Could that mean he followed her here? Tracked her down? Is she already back home? I peek around the corner through the window. She's not with him. Maybe he's doing the same thing I did last night, waiting for her to come back so he can follow her. Either way I'm assuming. His presence compromises everything, both the integrity of the job and my own safety, but it doesn't matter. I have no intention of putting this off. The best way to avoid him is to get there before he does.

In the desolate lobby of Amy Arsenault's building, I breathe into my hands to warm them up. This is it. In the new theology, perpetuation of the system is the ultimate good. What does that makes me, what does it make Amy Arsenault? Which is the righteous side? God is electronic networks of information. Evil is to take away from the system. Amy Arsenault is a new class of human, and I'm outmoded. I was born in Grid. I have no choice but to find myself here. In the new system, Amy Arsenault is the Patron Saint of Grid, and what am I? I'll stand up for the old system if I have to. I won't apologize for myself. The contents of the ampoule slide into the plastic chamber of the hypodermic, my hands unsteady. Up the stairs I hover the skeleton keycard over the lock of apartment 2C.

SNAP.

The door locks behind me. Every light is off but I can see by the glow of the streetlamp leaking through the blinds. Needle held like a dagger, thumb resting against the plunger. I hug the wall to eliminate my flank. Nobody in the main room. Pure silence except for my breathing. I cruise the wall that adjoins to the kitchen, heading for the entryway. From here I can see into the bedroom on the other side of the apartment, its emptiness building my anxiety. I stop at the corner, keeping eyes on two things at once. After a deep breath I spin into the kitchen, guard up, needle raised just in case. I feel the floor vibrate with footsteps, coming from behind. I spin, put my arm up—there's the black flash of her figure and my elbow partially deflects an incoming arm—an overwhelming sensation of something heavy and precise entering me just beneath the collar bone—with the adrenaline there's no pain—so stupid to have turned my back—her face in front of me, teeth exposed—upper body undergoing an immediate loss of strength—grappling with her—she's restraining the hand with the needle—our struggle so quiet I can hear a knock at the door—she applies pressure to the blade in my chest—*ngk!*—so strong like she's everywhere—fuck you, I'm not letting go—

"Amy? Are you in there?"

—she extracts the blade roughly and I use the momentum to push her back—she stumbles but catches herself, rushing forward again—both our arms shoot out, nearly colliding, heading for the same target—there's the feeling of something rigid, unyielding, sudden in my throat—I depress the plunger so hard a spatter of clear liquid and blood sprays from her neck, some of it landing against the back of my hand—I'm gonna die—floor approaches my vision—on my side—see her hit the floor in front of me, needle protruding from her neck—looking each other in the eyes—

"Amy, it's Gerney. I know you're in there. Please answer. I have to talk to you."

—body's numb—vision fixed on hers—face is slack—eyes draining—nothing but a biological function—all that's left over is a little internet mausoleum—

"I love you, Amy."

—wormfood, homie—

"Just please open the, the door. I'm begging you."

—I can see—she's still alive—just barely—she's still looking at me—her expression is impenetrable—wonder how she sees me dying—if I look any different—she's blinking, steadily—

GERNEY

To the distant observers (that would be us, by the way, taking godlike shape over the sweep of this narrative, looking on from a divine perch, possibly even snacking), it was only a matter of time once Amy Arsenault died that Gerney and Kellen Self, leader of the American Non-Revolutionaries, should cross paths. Gerney had undertaken a self-imposed personal mission to become a better, more well-defined person within a system of unceasing information—whatever that meant. They were Kellen Self's words. Kellen Self, by all accounts, was a difficult person, but charisma made his narcissism compelling. He'd been on a slow trajectory for years now into the collective consciousness of Grid, scooping up a certain type of person by the armfuls. People, as he would put it, "terrorized by the inane, confusing, schizophrenic media input of an unchecked cancerous species." No one had been able to give Information, in all its diversity and yet undeniable unity, a proper name, a proper symptom, a proper representation to point to and say: "*That* is the living organism I always knew existed; the lumbering, all-encompassing behemoth that exerts its influence with impunity." Kellen Self called it the Membrane. A force so abstract it bordered on sheer hallucination. A partition so thin, so very very thin, and yet it blocked those within it from seeing reality as it truly was. The Membrane was both a product of the individual mind as well as a mass delusion. Civilization, which he considered interchangeable with Technology, was the lifeforce the Membrane ran by.

But how to dispel the Membrane? Or even just to simply peel it back? Kellen honed in on a concept he hoped would be like poison to the Membrane: defamiliarization. Defamiliarization was a trance-spell, a method of inducing oneself to look at the ordinary and habitual as if they were strange and new. A way of disrupting Membrane conditioning and seeing the extent of its influence. But how to defamiliarize yourself unless you've already experienced defamiliarization? Most couldn't consciously make the leap. Enhancement of the mind was necessary, and so Kellen took to growing large quantities of psilocybin mushrooms and administering them to ANR members in the form of tea during the group's controlled perceptual ceremonies. And although these ceremonies were effective at indicating the desired state, a bizarre self-referential problem began to surface. Namely, that of becoming familiar with defamiliarization. Kellen, caught off-guard by this, prescribed an equally bizarre solution: defamiliarizing oneself with defamiliarization. He encouraged members to live their lives in alternating shifts, on two opposing poles of thought—the radically emancipated and defamiliarized lifestyle of the ANR, and the media-consumptive, unquestioning, liberal lifestyle of the population at large. Kellen adhered to his own teachings, and during his stints of defamiliarizing himself with defamiliarization he dressed in suits and kept himself closely groomed, endlessly riding the GRT routes, carrying a briefcase full of ANR-related propaganda that he would deploy in guilefully effective ways. Chief among them was a piece of laminate, printed with a poem he'd written himself. It stood out on GRT station walls amongst the cluttered matrix codes and digital phone-accessible ads:

⌜ ⅃⌐ ⌝

THE MEMBRANE

Go to bed li'l chillun
so you can wake up soon
                    *—to the **FUTURE!***
Where the bitchers moaners criers
denounce Vedge and Mobyle as social pariahs,
and go to bed li'l chillun!—
cuz you all gonna wake
in a alien century
where the air gots electric taste
and the mens and womens
lives on vegetable paste.

Go to bed li'l chillun
pretty soon you gonna wake
to the tasteless odorless Membrane
of the world we done create.

Go to bed li'l chillun
the future lies in wait
and you gots to go to bed soon
so's you can hurry up and wake.

Kellen found that subversive information traveled through GRT routes the way blood travels through veins, becoming part of the organism of Grid. Many among the ranks of the ANR had, at one point, been serious commuters. This was how Kellen had snared Fish on his line years ago, and it was also how Gerney came to be part of the ANR.

For someone unequipped to handle isolation, it translates into susceptibility. Amy's death had shaken Gerney, not least because it had yielded the full extent of the XittyXat-InfoZebra-ClamBell scandal to the national press. He hadn't been the one to discover her death—the smell of two decomposing bodies finally prompted complaints from the neighbors in her building. For months reporters dribbled in and out of his life. He saw his name and picture in the media like imprisoned facsimiles of himself, made to do and say things he didn't wish them to. The attention didn't suit him, and he quickly turned to habits of avoidance. This was simply paranoia. No one recognized him. Most everyone, including Gerney, found it strange that Flint Vedge remained CEO of InfoZebra, that the HQ scraper in the center of the city continued to go up, and, most disconcertingly, that the InfoStructure initiative was turned into official city policy to the sound of very little protest, many of the major donors not withdrawing their contributions. Much of the blame was adroitly transferred to Councilman Mobyle, who was being slowly interred by the state judicial system. Amy Arsenault, in some circles, was transformed into a counterculture icon. Public opinion remained largely inert, and those like Flint Vedge had long ago learned to take advantage of peoples' overwhelmed inability to react.

Gerney felt as if he were at the center of a vast conspiracy, something coming together to form a sinister gauntlet that would squeeze, the confluence of apocalyptic news events seemingly aimed at him specifically (a fairly common thing for those of his generation, broadly speaking). He found the time and focus to finish *Shell-Shocked Sarnin*. At the end of the book Sarnin makes the decision to kill the men in his own unit rather than enemy troops during a skirmish, symbolic of Arnitz's theory of anti-identity radicalism. Sarnin finds himself in solitary confinement for the last 75 pages, the narrative devolving into a monologue of insanity, withdrawal, and torture. Arnitz puts forward a vision of humans as prisoners of their own minds, identityless without validation from outside sources, lost in a maze of meaningless synapses. Gerney's gonine addiction was also blooming into maturity, his cheekbones taking full command of his face. Dwindling money finally coaxed him into suits, now baggy on his shriveled frame, and onto GRT trains, searching out employment. His appearance, combined with his new stilted, twacked-out style of speech, sent an unmistakable message.

No jobs would be given to a jethead. Still, he kept at it, and every day he found himself on the GRT. He caught glimpses of words in his peripheral vision.

> *cuz you all gonna wake*
> *in a alien century*
> *where the air gots electric taste*

He followed, along with the rest of the country, the phenomenon of hundreds of people, quickly turning to thousands, being admitted to healthcare facilities due to the belief their phones were alive. (Although Fish was among the first to experience this, he had only recently been committed to a psychiatric facility.) The delusion was crossing oceans and political borders. Europe was undergoing the first tremors of the crisis, along with smaller parts of Latin America, East Asia, and Africa.

> *pretty soon you gonna wake*
> *to the tasteless odorless Membrane*
> *of the world we done create*

Many of the laminates featured only the poem, but printed at the bottom of one he came across on the wall of the Entscheidungsproblem station was an address. 1900 W. Matrix-Chain Ave., Grid, CO, 80277. According to GPS it was a house on the fringe of the motherboard tract, not far from where he lived. His train arrived, and he quickly forgot all about it. He wasn't yet isolated enough to be susceptible.

But isolation was drawing him into its void. Whenever he saw Amy Arsenault's picture on the News Pad screens of bored commuters or plastered across socnets, a strange sort of panic would flood him. He had to fight the urge to pour his heart out to total strangers. They couldn't understand his connection to her, the melding of their physicalities and spirits (poor deceived Gerney), couldn't comprehend what it was like to have assigned every worldly hope to her name, the personal salvation he'd experienced whenever she had appeared in all capitals within the borders of the call-receiving graphic of his phone: AMY ARSENAULT. They couldn't understand what it was like to love a dead person who gave away her memory to everyone but him. He sat shaking and alone in his apartment. He felt lost, without identity. (Again *Shell-Shocked Sarnin* seemed to be speaking to him directly, strangely tapped in to the emotional states of his life. Sarnin's solitary confinement mirrored Gerney's own, and there was an exchange of thoughts between them, as if they were leading one another ever-further into a dark cave of self-consciousness. What was the meaning of Gerney's obsession with Sarnin? As distant observers we have the unique ability to jump ahead in time—200 years, beyond the Nanofacturing Revolution, beyond quantum computing, beyond the Robotics Crisis—and get a retrospective view of fiction. The 2225 non-wetware encyclopedia entry for LATE FICTION RENAISSANCE reads: "Although humans considered their insight into themselves advanced in the late stages of the *Information/Technology Age*, their understanding of the *self* remained primitive and quasi-mystical. They perceived the self much as *ancient man* must have perceived the *stars*—infinite, unknowable, and categorically separate from others. *Authors* had long been considered diagnosticians, even invokers, of reality, but nevertheless a primary tenet of *fictional narratives* throughout much of history was that *human nature*, at its deepest root, could only be observed or analyzed indirectly, i.e. through external relationships and interactions. With the advent of *socnets* [disambig: *Social Media, Social Networking*] there came an early form of *ambient awareness* to human consciousness, one which allowed individuals to recognize shared or common cognition through an *analogue* process of *mutual recognition*. This process had no precise methodology because it was predicated on the *physical-sequential reading* of mass amounts of manually uploaded thoughts, ones which had to be expressed subjectively according to each individual's skill, or lack thereof, with *written language communication*. Although data collection and analysis was a common practice with early socnets, results were typically applied to several fields, such as *advertising and marketing, political science, sociology, cognitive mapping,* and others, and did not bear resemblance to later *statistical-cognitive methodologies* such as *patterned ambient awareness, quantum consciousness mapping,* or *thought upload/download.* Early ambient awareness brought drastic changes to *literature,* in both style and aim, marking the beginning of a period historians term the *Late Fiction Renaissance.* With greater awareness of *patterned cognition,* authors moved fiction away from its *expressionistic* origins toward a more "scientific" method of accurately reflecting the procedures and norms of personality, physiological sensation, manifested behaviors, social dynamics and private assumption. Fictional characters began to more closely resemble *avatars* which could theoretically serve to embody the intricacies of pan-human thoughts and behaviors. Traditional plot was abandoned in favor of thinly connected moments of minutae and ultra-detailed passages regarding *causality.* This reorientation of form produced a drastic decline in social and political narratives. There is an overwhelming obsession in the *Late Fiction Renaissance* with physicality and unspoken moments of private human cognition that in some ways foresaw modern attitudes toward *individuality, social etiquette, technology,* and *spirituality.* Critics of the movement took on a markedly antagonistic tone, warning from its inception—roughly the years between 2033 and 2040—that the trend posed no less than an existential threat to basic precepts of human individuality and identity. *Simon Coke,* a coder and one of the *Late Fiction Renaissance's* most steadfast opponents, provided an oft-quoted prognosis of the movement to the *New York Times.* 'Narrative is essential nutrition for the emotional and rational elements of any *human being.* This new trend in fiction threatens to eradicate the parts of *storytelling* that deliver knowledge and diverse perspectives, as well as nourish the *soul.* What we are moving toward is the transformation of all subjective experiences being defined for us as universal and undeviating in their effects—in other words, a system of *objective subjectivity.* I personally see this as nothing less than an effort toward the extermination of *individuality.*' The *Late Fiction*

Renaissance is also attributed with institutionalizing the description of situations and emotions using only the titles of popular works. For example, 'Peggy's going through some real *Requiem for a Dream* stuff, what she needs is a *Girl, Interrupted* moment,' or, 'My day felt absolutely *Seinfeld*ian, but I yearned for a more long-viewed *Forrest Gump* outlook.' Some commentators on the movement posited theories that this pointed to a finiteness of human experience, and that, eventually, most of the range of possible life experiences would first be absorbed by people vicariously through *media* before ever being exposed to them firsthand. This is still a central concern in the study of *hyperreality disorder*." So we might hypothesize, then, that Gerney's identification with Sarnin pointed to a case of hyper-reality disorder, and, working under this supposition, there can be hardly any doubt Kellen Self's defamiliarization tactics only served to exacerbate the problem later on.)

He grappled the jet in fits, time losing clear segmentation and frequent sleeplessness undermining his ability to concentrate. He made efforts to shake bad habits but found them too deeply ingrained. Occasionally, when his points of highest media saturation and utter twackedoutness converged, he'd find it within himself to sit in total quiet, all screens darkened but still slightly glowing with image-burns, and he would remember, with embarrassing sentimentality, his friends. Nick Ibyoo and Aria Forum had been engaged for three months. They had broken the news on the socnets right around the time he'd testified in probate court in the *DeSantis v. Vivificorps* case. Nick and Aria documented their lives for others carefully, tirelessly, every day releasing photo galleries, videos, music selections meant to shed light on their current mood, page style overhauls, media tracking, social gaming, rambling confessions… Gerney followed all of it without meaning to or even enjoying it. He hadn't spoken with either of them in more than six months. Their profiles told the story of a stable and adventurous young couple, living their lives for the benefit of their fans. They had parlayed their socnet celebrity into social advancement. Nick had been promoted; Aria stopped using gonine and gained a layer of healthy, even voluptuous, weight, turning herself into a socnet model. They were publicly contemplating moving out of Nick's house in the motherboard tract, maybe to Denver, maybe out of the city altogether.

Ronstadt was also apparently in a relationship. He and his new girlfriend often appeared alongside Nick and Aria in pictures. Veronika Sine had moved on to a new group of bar-going friends. Millie crafted an image of herself as a carefree sybarite, but found little success in capturing any fandom on the socnets. Quentin's profile was a font of laid-back intellectualism that seemed perpetually sneering and sarcastic. Amy Arsenault had been given a memorial profile, frequented by hackers and online anarchists.

Gerney was unaware that soon he would no longer have any socnet profiles for the first time since he was five years old—all of them deleted at Kellen Self's recommendation.

But first he would have to wait through another winter (winters in Grid had the habit, in some years, of failing to abate, instead meeting each other at beginning and end like an icy mobius strip), a winter that found him selling his personal possessions for income. 2025 turned into 2026 without ceremony or celebration. Gonine was his holiday, privacy his family. He sold clothes, appliances, furniture. He kept the lights off to avoid higher electricity bills. At night his apartment was an inky expanse in all directions, then approaching from the distance like some forsaken bioluminescent fish would be a dim blue phone interface, its weak light allowing a shrouded view of Gerney's skeletal face, those horrid cheekbones awash in that horrid lambency, sliding sleekly by before receding to a different part of the void. He sold luggage, shoes, the mirror in his bathroom. When snorting, the inside of his nose stung, and just as he'd begin to groan against the pain, imagining it unbearable, Time itself would inhale, hold its breath, the world passing by in slo-mo, waiting for the exhalation that would be like screaming missiles rocketing toward no particular target, just forward, forward, forward! He sold tools, silverware, pots and pans. He sold video games, books, movies. The apartment grew ever-barer, a slowly decomposing corpse, the empty walls and floors surrounding him like a massive ribcage, and he sat within it, kept company by the only possessions he refused to sell—(not that he'd sold everything, there was still substantial wealth lying dormant in the kitchen in the form of the refrigerator, the microwave, the toaster, but these were ultimately expendable)—laptop, TV, phone, News Pad, VidraPro. His screens. Lose them and he might as well end it all. The rest he funneled away from himself, but these things were imperative. He sat surrounded by them on the floor, the centerpiece of a vicious pentagram that coldly illuminated his small fluctuating piles of gonine. Months went by. He stopped putting on his suit, stopped carrying a folder full of resumes, stopped riding the GRT. He stopped going outside except to buy gonine or food. Strict in his loneliness, he imagined a string of years passing in the same manner, a hermit growing estranged from life, the world carrying on outside without him like an early death, missing out on food, friends, pretty girls, nights of irreverence, family, love, old age, contentment.

Maybe he'd become a govt-initiative bum himself, relocate his shrinking frame to the hardware tract, live in the projects and slowly become a desiccated visage of horror, try to atone for the father and son outside Q/V for the rest of his life. Yes, he'd make himself a monument to guilt. Well—it was a nice thought. But the truth was he could never suffer enough to repay the debt. He couldn't figure out what was wrong with him. Was it the world he hated, or just himself? Or was it more complicated than that? Was there some force, or forces, conspiring to keep him bewildered, imprisoned, paranoid? They were the very questions coming to the forefront of many peoples' minds, and like most Gerney was not equipped to answer them. Gerney was twenty-seven. He was overwhelmed, addicted, and (most importantly to his impending entry to the ranks of the ANR) isolated.

That isolation was finally leavened into susceptibility by the overloading of two of TransMission's electricity mains, causing a tenhour blackout in parts of downtown Grid and the motherboard tract. A relatively small occurrence in the scheme of things, but for Gerney, locked in his glowing pentagram, the sudden power failure was cataclysmic. Without electronic distraction he quickly succumbed to a long-delayed psychosis, the darkness bringing illumination and sparking within him the need to leave his apartment at 11:00 at night to walk twenty-five minutes in the cold to 1900 W. Matrix-Chain in search of a savior. He knocked on the door of the interchangeable suburban duplex as if it were the most natural thing in the world. A man and woman dressed all in white answered the door and welcomed him. The woman said, "We knew you'd be coming eventually. Please come in. We'll take you to the man who can help you."

Of course, we—the distant observers—are perfectly aware that by this point in the development of the ANR, not every new member entering the organization had the privilege of meeting Kellen Self right away. The ANR now had roughly 356 followers in Grid, a number which vacillated greatly seeing as there was no official membership, and they had even expanded into some of the bordering portions of Denver, now with fifteen separate functioning nodes or bases, all houses and apartments dedicated to secret communal living and the "purposes" of the Non-Revolution. The 1900 W. Matrix-Chain location, the ANR's original home, had served for several years as the organization's primary offices, a living space for its most important members, and a place to cull new recruits. Over time they had observed a trend that, on nights of power outages, the W. Matrix-Chain house experienced a dependably high intake of prospective members. For this reason, Kellen made it a priority to be personally present at the house during any interruptions in service.

Gerney was taken to a room on the first floor, the door shutting behind him. He was now sweating and nervous. In the room was a distinguished wooden desk bare of any object whatsoever, Kellen sitting behind it in a dapper reflective charcoal suit, radiating a fatherly expression. Not just the desk, but the room, too, was bare. Gerney noticed this right away. This house, just as his own apartment, had been skeletonized, though here it seemed to have been done toward some meaning.

Kellen urged Gerney to come in, come in, have a seat, it was late and they had a lot to cover. Gerney continued to stand there, understandably apprehensive. Kellen told him that it might help to know that no matter what, talking tonight meant absolutely no obligation, this wasn't the mafia or some sort of time-share scam. Gerney asked well then what is it? He still had no idea. Kellen said, a bit grandly, but then again he was the Great Leader of an extensive cult following built from nothing, that this was the American Non-Revolution. Hm. American Non-Revolution made it sound like they didn't *do* anything. Kellen praised him for having a keen ear, that was in a sense very true. He'd be happy to explain if only Gerney would sit down and have a discussion. Gerney sat.

What non-revolution was all about, Kellen expounded, was the acceptance of the futility of revolutions. Revolution inevitably becomes either recursive or corrupt, and worse, forces ways of thinking onto groups of people who don't agree. So, make revolution bloodless, spiritual, slow-moving, and private. Change one's mode of thinking, and help others to change theirs if that's what they desire. Sabotage the system through personal emancipation. Not that non-revolution didn't have a more aggressive element of traditional revolution embedded within it, but please, Kellen said, stop me here. The whole thing was a tough concept indeed, and grasping it was like grasping the teachings of a Marx or Siddhartha. He was in the process of setting his theories down on paper, but there was no reason to go into all that. What it all ultimately came down to was removing the Membrane.

The Membrane? What was that?

The Membrane? Wow, where to begin? Well, the Membrane was a living parasite, feeding off humans from birth. An idea of reality, inherently false but ubiquitous. It functioned as a veil, covering Gerney's vision right that very moment, though he could neither see nor comprehend the veil. The Membrane, at its core, was this—the seamless consolidation of Gerney's inner and outer realities through technology and media. Try to imagine life, Kellen said, with no movies, no music, no TV, no video games, no internet, no matrix codes, no news. Could Gerney imagine it?

Definitely not.

Well welcome to the Membrane. He was now aware of it. The first and most immediate goal of the ANR would be to help him see *behind* it. Because behind it was the Truth. The Truth was a reality free from overlays of stylization, consumerism, entertainment opiate, emotional string-pullery, brands, suggestions, or history. It was merely: the Truth. ANR wasn't anti-capitalist, it was anti-illusion. Kellen had glimpsed the Truth, longer and more studiously than anyone else he was aware of, but he couldn't reside there. He was talking to Gerney from within the Membrane because at this point in history, in this place civilizationally, the Membrane was stronger than the Truth by at least a thousandfold. The Truth was a place (a state of mind, really, but it was easier to think of it as a place) where a human being could see their intended position and purpose in the cosmos.

What was that place, that purpose?

Was Gerney sure he wanted to know?

Yes, he was sure.

Well it was easier if Kellen first told him what it was not. It wasn't to fall in love and share a life with somebody or somebodies. It wasn't to become wealthy, surrounded by privacy, safety, and material comfort. It wasn't to become a professional with a successful career. It wasn't to be a sports star, rock star, movie star, or any other form of celebrity. It wasn't to be religious and rewarded spiritually. It wasn't to know God (which, for the sake of cultural relevance, he was just going to go ahead and use that word in its monotheistic sense). It wasn't to be an intellectual and achieve higher knowledge. It wasn't self-actualization, self-love, or self-contentment. It wasn't to be an inventor, an adventurer, a soldier, an economist, an outlaw, a scientist, a ruler of any class or type.

So what was it?

Okay then. A human being's place and purpose in the world. And then he told him.

Jesus. That's depressing.

Yes, that was how most everyone felt at first. But it was vital to remember that it was only depressing according to the logic of the Membrane, and therefore to you as well because the Membrane is a spell cast over your perception from which you have not yet been freed. That spell, despite being self-reinforcing and staggeringly powerful, was not omnipotent. It could be shed.

So Gerney joined the ANR. He participated in defamiliarization ceremonies of the same type Fish had wandered into all those years ago. He did his best to forget about Amy Arsenault and Nick Ibyoo and Sarnin and his father and Archelaos and gonine and his old way of life and sometimes even the Membrane itself. Through a long and painful process he suppressed his addiction; his cheekbones faded; he started to look brand new. He abandoned his apartment and moved into one of the ANR houses. Through the help of his fellow members he landed a job at a recycling plant as a manual sorter wearing heavy construction clothes, a hardhat, cut-resistant gloves, and noise-cancelling headphones, looking up the conveyor stream to the great waves of spinning trash, falling into fractions, constant churning waterfalls of it crashing toward them where he separated out with frantic, frightened energy the rigid plastics flying by, hiding amongst the flowing river of detritus. 2026 turned into 2027, then 2027 into 2028. He turned thirty. The world was now in the middle of a full-blown "sentience pandemic." The number of patients diagnosed with electronic sentience delusions reached 2.5 billion before the exact figures stopped seeming all that important anymore. Undetermined was whether or not phones actually *had* gained sentience. Evidence suggested no, but as numbers continued to increase uncontrollably it became harder to utter that answer with total confidence. Even if the network hadn't gained sentience, the widespread belief that it had forced some experts to concede that the sentience was at least real in some form. The Infiniphase Panacea hit world markets, and for the first time people manu- factured products in their own homes. In the second phase of the Panacea's popularity, people learned to program and construct their imaginations. Apartments turned into private dreamlands, and streets became largely barren. Markets threatened to collapse while

Clam Bell Corporation, the holding company in possession of the two most significant affiliates on the global stage, quickly became an ungovernable Colossus. New technologies exploded all around like fireworks. Rioting overtook every nation, as well as a brief but devastating bout of mass suicides.

The week before Fourth of July 2028, Gerney was walking to the GRT station from work and saw a floating hologram that said,

INFOZEBRA UNVEILS FIRST EVER
PARA-UNIVERSE
WIRELESS CARRIER CUSTOMERS
NOW ABLE TO PROJECT MINDS INTO
MASSIVE CLOUDS

Unable to understand, he continued on as if nothing had happened.

A plague of wars spread between many combinations of countries, some becoming intractable, others flourishing into politically useful victories and losses, the falling decay of diplomacy giving rise to a hateful fungus. Genocides began their overtures. Homicidal maniacs sprang from the woodwork bearing arsenals of their own invention and manufacture. Superfluous brands multiplied and festered about in surplus like wriggling maggots. A new elite-class was forming, and those within it experienced these chaotic world events quite differently from those of lower stock. And then, just when apocalypse seemed at its most vividly possible, things stabilized. The world took a collective breath, but fear kept moving with the inertia of the past eight months, and, as was to be expected, the ANR, which had grown in numbers throughout all these troubling events, was taking on more radical characteristics.

Gerney had become accustomed to a disciplined style of life—not because the ANR demanded it, but because he had discovered he enjoyed total neutrality. He felt as if he were floating above the worldwide panic, calm and disinterested, much like we distant observers feel as we float above the turmoil of this narrative. He was, as much as he could be, Membraneless, and found he was happier that way. But in recent months he'd been feeling the onset of something which began as an abrupt twang, then developed into a slow dark rumbling. The world was splitting in two. He swung between the feeling that he was watching the external world on TV and that he was watching himself on TV from outside his own body. Somehow, he and his surroundings were no longer merging into a continuous whole, and gradually, as this became more defined and intense, he found himself once again desperate and angry.

Again, there was a reason for this, even a name for what he was experiencing. Derealization. The perception of the external world and the self seeming unreal. This was not happening to him alone. Derealization was gnashing through the ranks of the ANR, infecting them with its unusual cerebral virus. No one knew why, and most members kept the feeling to themselves, putting on lovely facades to carry on coexisting with one another. Of course, *we* are perfectly aware that the basis for their group derealization stemmed from members' frequent use of psilocybin mushrooms (a well-known instigator of the condition) and Kellen Self's own contrived tactics for defamiliarization (which, when practiced regularly, as they were, bore the side effects of acute alienation and discontinuity). Whoops! But before putting all the blame on Kellen Self, a qualification should be made. Traceable as this psychic disaster was to him, it's just as likely that the members of the ANR, intrepid and stalwart as they were, were simply falling into the same sinkhole of blurring, abstract reality as most of the rest of the planet.

For years there had been a custom amongst the non-revolutionaries of getting a tattoo depicting self-immolation. The differing colors of the flames engulfing the figure were meant to be a personal touch, representing one's own distress. This was one of the few aspects of the ANR Kellen Self hadn't orchestrated, and perhaps for that reason it was also one of the ones that most inspired him. We're fortunate to be able to fast forward through the delirium of Kellen's slow descent into total despair—what with the incoming deluge of all things Membrane (it was like a worrisome disease, just to continue with Kellen's reference to it in constantly mixed metaphors, get rid of one strain and *schwip!* in comes a mutated version), nevermind the the invisible monster of derealization unraveling his life's work— arriving at his decision to put the symbol of self-immolation into practice. The idea of a purely personal revolution had finally reached its conclusion of personal negation. Gerney could be found in the group of thirty members, including Kellen, who on a brisk Friday in September of 2029, walked purposefully toward the InfoZebra National Headquarters scraper at the center of Grid.

(Now, distant observers, we must take a field trip, leaving our divine perches and heavenly silent safety, traveling down through the chemical layer of ozone, through the fluorescent upper atmosphere, aimed at the rectangle of Colorado and then the layout of the city of Grid, now standing at street-level, looking across to where these thirty non-revolutionaries toting red plastic tanks of gasoline are currently arranging themselves in the brutalist corporate plaza of the InfoZebra scraper, the building itself thrusting upward like an all-powerful phallus over the proceedings, the architecture blade- like, almost seeming to conjure the cold wind now rushing through the boulevard and making our skin pucker. A huge holographic billboard floats above. Businesspeople in suits on their way into the scraper for a day of work pass through the ranks of these harsh-faced weirdos preparing their souls for destruction. They pause, stare, and then incredibly head inside. We're not the only ones watching, a crowd is forming. Is it a performance, a protest? And if so, against what? We're obligated to tell them what we know. This isn't so much a protest as it is a self-defense mechanism. They are overloaded elec- tricity mains. The outdated eventually have to be phased out to make way for the new, and such is the nature of progress, but… what is progress really? How to define it? What does it look like, and what does it stand for? Could it be that our progress is the planet's own form of derealization? I suppose I'm reaching to make associations, but it's hard not to want to when we're standing here watching thirty people—not perfect people, but still people—preparing to find that little bit of peace in the fire. For the sake of slowing the fuck *down* and taking time to understand before forging ahead blindly. Release from abstraction, which is everywhere and nowhere. Maybe they're just not strong enough to take a leap into the unknown. Heads up, they're dousing themselves. Keep your eyes on Gerney before he goes up. You'll notice he takes one last look at the hologram above. A titanium hexagonal zebra emerging from a nanofactory.)

ABOUT THE AUTHOR

Steven T. Bramble was born in 1986 in Pueblo, CO. He is the author of the Psychology of Technology trilogy (*Affliction Included*, *Grid City Overload*, *Disposable Thought*), a thematically-connected series of novels that questions the implications of modernity. He is a co-founder of ZQ-287 Press and lives in Long Beach.

ZQ-287

Crushing Foes.